THE BEST OF WORLD SF

LAVIE TIDHAR is the World Fantasy Award-winning author of *Osama*, *The Violent Century*, the Jerwood Fiction Uncovered Prize-winning *A Man Lies Dreaming*, and the Campbell Award-winning *Central Station*, in addition to many other works and several other awards. He works across genres, combining detective and thriller modes with poetry, science fiction and historical and autobiographical material. His work has been compared to that of Philip K. Dick by the *Guardian* and the *Financial Times*, and to Kurt Vonnegut's by *Locus*. His latest novel, *By Force Alone*, was published by Head of Zeus in 2020.

VOLUME 1

THE BEST OF WORLD SF

**EDITED BY
LAVIE TIDHAR**

HEAD
of ZEUS

An Ad Astra Book

First published in the UK in 2021 by Head of Zeus Ltd
An Ad Astra book

9 7 5 3 1 2 4 6 8

A catalogue record for this book is available from the British Library.

ISBN (HB) 9781838937645
ISBN (TPB) 9781800240407
ISBN (E) 9781838937669

Typeset by Adrian McLaughlin

Printed and bound by CPI Group (UK) Ltd, Croydon, CR0 4YY

MIX
Paper from
responsible sources
FSC® C020471
FSC
www.fsc.org

Head of Zeus Ltd
First Floor East
5–8 Hardwick Street
London ECIR 4RG
WWW.HEADOFZEUS.COM

Contents

Introduction

1.

They say the more things change the more they stay the same, but things do change, and science fiction has to change in order to survive. For too long, the future was dominated by one country and one viewpoint: the future was white, male and American, and it was going to stay that way – until it didn't.

I look at *The Best of World SF* with something like awe, because it doesn't feel real. As I write this, it *isn't* yet real. I look to the future and imagine holding the book, reading the introduction. I have read anthologies and I've been published in anthologies but I never thought I would see one like this. The sheer breadth of talent from across the planet gathered here is something no one could imagine twenty years ago. Publishing certainly wasn't interested. And it wasn't just then. I spent ten years trying to get someone, anyone, to publish this book, or one like it. The last time I tried it took the publisher an hour to turn it down.

Less than an hour, if I'm being honest.

If you make yourself enough of a pain, eventually people notice. Or so I tried to tell myself. In 2008, I convinced my friend Jason Sizemore to publish an anthology of international speculative fiction. Jason runs a small press out of Kentucky, of all places, and is a stubborn man, and I told him he will make no money doing this but that it will be good. We put together *The Apex Book of World SF* out of string and sticks and polish and buttons and it came out in 2009. No one had done a book like that before, not in this way, not with an editor who himself didn't belong to the Anglo world. And I was right: we didn't make any money, but the book *was* good.

It was a ridiculous thing to do. And no one was interested. Reviewers didn't even know *how* to talk about the book. It wasn't exotic, it wasn't strange: it was just a collection of stories written by people from places like Malaysia and China, Croatia and the Philippines, and the only thing they did share was that they weren't a part of Anglo-American science fiction. And they were good.

So we did it again. I edited *The Apex Book of World SF 2* in 2012. And then we did it again with *The Apex Book of World SF 3* in 2014. We published writers no one had heard of – then. Aliette de Bodard and Tade Thompson and Lauren Beukes and Silvia Moreno-Garcia. Nnedi Okorafor's in there. So are Hannu Rajaniemi and Amal El-Mohtar. Between them, now, these writers *are* science fiction. They have the awards and the hardcovers in the bookstores and the film and TV deals. It was easy to see this is how it should be, back then, because they were good. But then you'd talk to publishers and they'd say things like, 'Oh, we don't publish books set in Nigeria.' And that would be the end of the discussion. I had never heard a more ridiculous thing. I went and wrote a science fiction novel set in Israel in the sure and liberating knowledge no one would publish it, and it came out from an independent press and won a couple of awards and ten editions in translation, at last count. And I had to face up to the fact that maybe the world really *was* changing.

Mahvesh Murad came on board to edit *The Apex Book of World SF 4*. I think she is the first editor from Pakistan to edit a genre anthology, and she went on to do more, and get nominated for a World Fantasy Award, though not for that book, because still no one cared.

Cristina Jurado came on board to edit *The Apex Book of World SF 5*, and it was great, and there we stopped. And I tried to sell a bigger version of those books to publishers large and small, and kept hearing that familiar 'no' – or, more commonly, not hearing anything at all. I watched those writers I published early on become established, and I watched talented new writers pouring in to the new magazines and the electronic publications, and they were terrific. Some of them are in this volume. And some of the old gang are here too.

Science fiction *has* to change to stay relevant. It deals in futures, after all. And the Internet was a great liberating force for those of us who lived elsewhere, who spoke English in a strange accent, who wrote in it as a second language or not at all. There are more translators now, enthusiasts mostly, but there are more places open to those stories now. They weren't there before. The editors weren't there and the publications weren't there and we had to create them somehow. The future couldn't stay uniform or it would die.

And *we* weren't there. There was a time where every year Aliette de Bodard and me would be placed on the same panel at the same SF convention to talk about the same thing in front of the same people, and one year a guy accused me of taking publication spots from native speakers and why can't we publish in our own countries? And the next year he repeated the question because he said he didn't think I understood him the first time he'd asked.

But I did understand. And I never did that panel again after that. In fact I try not to do panels at all and let other people speak instead, and I refuse to talk about translation. I have my own body of novels now and my own awards, but for some reason I never get asked to talk about *that* – that privilege is still reserved for 'proper' writers. Things change, but slowly...

2.

It's hard to put my finger on the exact moment the idea for a World SF anthology first crystallized, but the seeds for it were sown long before. I grew up on a kibbutz in Israel, and even as a child I was drawn to fantastical works, many translated from Europe: not just Tove Jansson's Moomins, but Janusz Korczak, Michael Ende, Astrid Lindgren, Erich Kästner and many others, alongside the numerous translations from the English.

Even then, I was drawn to seek out homegrown Hebrew fantasy too: my favourite being Eli Sagi's mid-1960s trilogy of science fiction novels, the *Adventures of Captain Yuno*, in which a pair of children, Yuno and Vena, travel throughout a solar system teeming with mysterious alien life (charmingly illustrated by the prolific artist M. Aryeh). When I wanted to write a high school dissertation on Israeli science fiction, I contacted the foremost translator of the genre, who dissuaded me rather bluntly with the words: 'There isn't any.'

It always stuck with me, that line. Even then, I didn't think it was true. Perhaps he had meant that what there was, was not much good. Or perhaps he meant that it simply was not American enough. I changed the topic I was going to write on, but my interest remained.

The first time I went backpacking, at seventeen, through eastern and then western Europe, I sought out obscure works of local SF: I still own the two Nemira anthologies, for instance, published on thin rice paper in 1994 and 1995 in Romania, or strange works of fantasy published by a still-Soviet imprint in Moscow.

But I think one defining moment was a visit to China back in the turn of the millennium: I had been so warmly welcomed by the science fiction community there that I felt almost duty bound to repay the favour in some way, and I could best do that, I thought, by helping Chinese SF be published abroad. This did not happen immediately, of course... and for a long time seemed likely never to happen at all.

In 2005, a single issue of a magazine called *Internova* came out in Germany. It was edited by three German fans, and I became involved relatively early on, also helping bring in several other contributors. It was the first time that a magazine dedicated to international speculative fiction was launched in decades (there had been a short-lived attempt by Fred Pohl in the 1960s) – but more importantly, it was the first time such an endeavour was undertaken by people from outside of the dominant anglophone sphere.

Internova was not without problems. It was a slick paperback production, but it was hard to get hold of. E-books were still not a very common option and distribution made it difficult for anyone to find. In addition, the committee style structure didn't allow for quick decision-making. *Internova* was an inspiration, an eye-opening experience that such things were even possible, but it did not last beyond its first issue (it did re-emerge as a website later on, though).

What *Internova* couldn't do, I thought (with a mixture of naïve optimism and not a little hubris!) a single person might achieve. The idea for a sort of 'Best Of' anthology, selecting stories for reprint from a wide variety of venues, seemed possible – if only anyone could be convinced to do such a strange thing.

Back in 2008, print-only submissions were still a barrier to many international writers. Electronic magazines were still considered lowlier than their print counterparts, though this was rapidly changing. My intention with the series was to focus on the now, to offer a snapshot in real-time, as it were, of core genre from outside the US/UK block. I have the same aim in this volume.

Back in 2009, I had also begun the World SF Blog, initially a promotional outlet that very quickly outgrew its original purpose. In its four years it published hundreds of articles, links, interviews and discussions on every aspect of international SF, and itself began to publish fiction. By the time it had ended, in 2013, it had won a British Science Fiction Association Award for non-fiction. People prominently involved with the blog included Charles Tan, a massive supporter of the entire project, who took on the task of producing much of the original non-fiction content of the site, and fiction editors Debbie Moorhouse and then Sarah Newton. To them, I can only offer my sincere thanks.

Alongside the blog and the anthologies, we also began the World SF Travel Fund, to allow international writers to travel to the World Fantasy Convention on part of full funding. We were able to run this for three years and send several people to the convention.

I watched the number of writers virtually explode; the rise of online publications such as *Clarkesworld*, which made a conscious effort to publish global works, as well as translations; the death, finally, of the dreaded print-only submissions as even the last of the print magazines at last adopted electronic submissions, removing one great big barrier to publication; and the rise of new, specialized anthologies such as the excellent *Afro SF* series.

The world *was*, slowly, changing.

When I look back on it all, I wonder how it ever happened.

But the truth is, we were there all along. The future of science fiction is dependent on its global nature, on its international authors, who each bring their own unique visions and experience, their own background and culture, and their shared love of the fantastic to their work. From Ghana to India, from Mexico to France, from Israel to Cuba, science fiction is alive and kicking, a vibrant new generation of writers changing the face of the genre one story at a time.

I think that's something worth celebrating.

3.

My use of the term 'World SF' is, of course, a joke.

'World SF' came about initially as a rubber-stamp association of writers back in the halcyon disco days of the 1970s as a way for writers from the West (i.e. America and Britain) to meet up with their counterparts in the East (i.e. the Soviet Union). The Soviet writers required an official document of invitation, which the World SF Association gladly provided. Their meetings were, by all accounts, great fun, but in truth did little more than prove an opportunity for socializing over drinks. Which was, of course, the point! There were a couple of associated awards, one for translation, but they didn't last long, and a couple of anthologies like the *Penguin World Omnibus of Science Fiction* back in 1986.

That's over thirty years since an international SF anthology was published, if you're counting.

The first 'World Science Fiction Convention' took place in New York in 1939. It was named not for being a collaborative, international project, but because the 'World's Fair' took place in New York that year, and it seemed fun to give a grand title to a tiny event. The Worldcon immediately split in two between rival factions of fans, one of which banned the other from attending. It has ever been so.

What people tend to forget is that science fiction as we know it was created by a Jewish immigrant from, of all places, Luxembourg. Hugo Gernsbacher (later, Gernsback) arrived in America aged twenty. English wasn't his first language, likely not even his second. He not only gave science fiction its name, founding *Amazing Stories* in 1926, but also created modern fandom, recognizing the power this new kind of literature could have over its readers. The prominent authors of the time called him 'Hugo the Rat'. The anti-Semitism and racism of many of those early practitioners no longer goes unremarked, thankfully. And poor Hugo is still celebrated, at least, in the Hugo Awards.

At some point, I decided to claim back the 'World SF' term for myself. It was my idea of a joke, but it had a serious purpose. The term was only used by and for anglophone writers and editors before. And they were not going to help me. So I took it back, and stamped it on a bunch of books, because the only way international SF was going to flourish was if we did it by ourselves. I watched editors return story after story; I watched publishers make mealy mouthed excuses about not publishing international works. 'Wouldn't it be better if it were set in New York?' I was told once, plaintively. 'Or at least London?' Many of the contributors in this volume have heard the same.

So I called *this* book *The Best of World SF*. It is for everyone who's never been to London or New York, or doesn't much care for those fine cities' peculiarities, or who only knows America from the television screen. The future doesn't belong to London or New York, after all. It belongs to everyone.

•

4.

I feel obliged to offer a very brief snapshot of the genre rock-face as it is at the time of writing, if only for the benefit of any hopeful writers reading this. Perhaps it will remain as merely a historical footnote.

The three main print magazines remain. *Analog, Asimov's* and *The Magazine of Fantasy and Science Fiction (F&SF)* continue, though editorial changes have made them more accessible in recent years, and the last magazine to hold out for print submissions, *F&SF*, finally succumbed with the appointment of a new editor. They publish good works (including my own) but as attention shifted online they have suffered somewhat in the notice of the field when it comes to award recognition. In the UK, the venerable *Interzone* remains the main print publication, publishing good work.

When I began writing, online magazines were little recognized, but were more open to international writers. Many came and went over the years. Now, of course, the online magazines dominate. The largest, corporate-backed online magazine is *Tor. com*. It is not generally open to submissions but uses several independent editors to acquire work instead. Tor.com Publishing, which runs alongside it, has done excellent work in novella length, with a strong focus on diversity and international writers.

Clarkesworld began all the way back in 2006 (I had a story in the first issue). It does remarkable work, including publishing Chinese, and now Korean, short stories in translation on a monthly basis.

Strange Horizons is one of the oldest online magazines in continuous operation. The editorial team has changed several times over the years. It is an excellent publication with a focus on both fiction and non-fiction, and runs themed country and region based issues from time to time. It also hosts the newer *Samovar* publication dedicated exclusively to translated fiction.

Also excellent are *Uncanny* and *Lightspeed,* similarly professional publications who have published very strong work. *The Dark* focuses on dark fantasy and horror, while *Beneath Ceaseless Skies* is dedicated to longer works of secondary world fantasy. *Daily Science Fiction* specializes in short-short stories, while *Escape Pod* focuses on audio in both reprint and original fiction. *Fiyah* is a magazine dedicated to Black SFF. *Apex Magazine* returned after a brief hiatus and remains an excellent publication.

There are various other magazines. Two good resources are ralan.com, the oldest genre market listing site on the web, and the Submissions Grinder at thegrinder.diabolicalplots.com.

5.

In putting together *The Best of World SF,* I have come up with a different anthology to what I thought it would be initially. If my approach before was to include all flavour of speculative fiction, including fantasy and horror, I have tried to narrow *The Best of World SF* more to the science fiction side. You will find plenty of robots ('Prayer' by Taiyo Fujii, 'Fandom For Robots' by Vina Jie Min Prasad) and spaceships ('The Sun From Both Sides' by R.S.A. Garcia, 'The Last Voyage of Skidbladnir' by Karin Tidbeck). One time-travel story too ('Bootblack' by Tade Thompson).

There are plenty of near-future visions of Earth here, from Tlotlo Tsamaase's 'Virtual Snapshots' to Silvia Moreno-Garcia's 'Prime Meridian'. And some award winners, like the openers and closers of this anthology, Aliette de Bodard's 'Immersion' (winner of both the Locus and Nebula awards) and Zen Cho's 'If At First You Don't Succeed', which won the Hugo.

I could not resist including a few weird stories, though, so be warned. These include Ekaterina Sedia's 'The Bank of Burkina Faso', Nir Yaniv's 'Benjamin Schneider's Little Greys' and Kofi Nyameye's 'The Old Man With The Third Hand'.

Hey, it's my anthology, I'm allowed to have fun.

This is mostly a reprint anthology, but I have picked up just a handful of originals. These are Francesco Verso's 'The Green Ship', Cristina Jurado's 'Dump', Gerardo Horacio Porcayo's 'Rue Chair' and Emil H. Petersen's 'The Cryptid'.

There are nine translated stories here, three of which were translated by the authors themselves. The translators have been paid equally to the authors, which I felt was important. Too many times translators are underpaid and go unrecognized (I should know!). My thanks therefore to Blake Stone-Banks, Kamil Spychalski, Michael Colbert, Steve Redwood and Toshiya Kamei for their work. I translated one story myself, and worked on the translation edit of one other.

I am grateful to all the contributors for entrusting their stories to me. Thank you for writing, thank you for pushing through, thank you for continuing to re-imagine the world and looking to the future so we, here in the present, can continue to try and be better than we are.

And my thanks to you, the reader, for picking up this book, for taking a chance. And if I have introduced you to some new works and writers, then I am content.

LAVIE TIDHAR

2021

Immersion

Aliette de Bodard

France

Aliette and I started writing around the same time, and I always saw her as a kindred spirit of sort. Like me, she was writing in English as a second language and breaking into the conservative world of English-language science fiction magazines at a time when the very idea of writers like us seemed absurd. We both went on to sign debut novel deals with the same publisher, and our literary concerns often seemed to mesh, or so it seems to me. We run into each other every now and then (once in Paris, another time in Toronto, and once at an event at a truly terrible Heathrow Airport hotel…). Since our early days, Aliette has fast become one of the most significant writers of the fantastic working today, with a slew of awards to her name, too many to list. When I came to edit *The Apex Book of World SF* back in 2009, Aliette was the first person I approached. I particularly admire her short fiction, which effortlessly moves between modes and genres, from hard space opera to alternate history steampunk to fantasy or noir: she can do it all. My main problem in putting together this anthology was just which of Aliette's stories to ask for! In the end, however, I could think of no better story to open this volume with than 'Immersion', set in Aliette's ambitious, expansive Xuya universe. Aliette draws on her Vietnamese heritage in this story, which won both the Locus and the Nebula awards. I hope you find it as powerful as I do.

I n the morning, you're no longer quite sure who you are.

You stand in front of the mirror – it shifts and trembles, reflecting only what you want to see – eyes that feel too wide, skin that feels too pale, an odd, distant smell wafting from the compartment's ambient system that is neither incense nor garlic, but something else, something elusive that you once knew.

You're dressed, already – not on your skin, but outside, where it matters, your avatar sporting blue and black and gold, the stylish clothes of a well-travelled, well-connected woman. For a moment, as you turn away from the mirror, the glass shimmers out of focus, and another woman in a dull silk gown stares back at you: smaller, squatter and in every way diminished – a stranger, a distant memory that has ceased to have any meaning.

• • •

Quy was on the docks, watching the spaceships arrive. She could, of course, have been anywhere on Longevity Station and requested the feed from the network to be patched to her router – and watched, superimposed on her field of vision, the slow dance of ships slipping into their pod cradles like births watched in reverse. But there was something about standing on the spaceport's concourse – a feeling of closeness that she just couldn't replicate by standing in Golden Carp Gardens or Azure Dragon Temple. Because here – here, separated by only a few measures of sheet metal from the cradle pods, she could feel herself teetering on the edge of the vacuum, submerged in cold and breathing in neither air nor oxygen. She could almost imagine herself rootless, finally returned to the source of everything.

Most ships those days were Galactic – you'd have thought Longevity's ex-masters would have been unhappy about the station's independence, but now that the war was over Longevity was a tidy source of profit. The ships came and disgorged a steady stream of tourists – their eyes too round and straight, their jaws too square, their faces an unhealthy shade of pink, like undercooked meat left too long in the sun. They walked with the easy confidence of people with immersers: pausing to admire the suggested highlights for a second or so before moving on to the transport station where they haggled in schoolbook Rong for a ride to their recommended hotels – a sickeningly familiar ballet Quy had been seeing most of her life, a unison of foreigners descending on the station like a plague of centipedes or leeches.

Still, Quy watched them. They reminded her of her own time on Prime, her heady schooldays filled with raucous bars and wild weekends, and last-minute revision for exams, a carefree time she'd never have again in her life. She both longed for those days back, and hated herself for her weakness. Her education on Prime, which should have been her path into the higher strata of the station's society, had brought her nothing but a sense of disconnection from her family, a growing solitude, and a dissatisfaction, an aimlessness she couldn't put in words.

She might not have moved all day had a sign not blinked, superimposed by her router on the edge of her field of vision. A message from Second Uncle.

'Child.' His face was pale and worn, his eyes underlined by dark circles, as if he hadn't slept. He probably hadn't – the last Quy had seen of him, he had been closeted with Quy's sister Tam, trying to organize a delivery for a wedding: five hundred winter melons, and six barrels of Prosper Station's best fish sauce. 'Come back to the restaurant.'

'I'm on my day of rest,' Quy said; it came out as more peevish and childish than she'd intended.

Second Uncle's face twisted in what might have been a smile, though he had very little sense of humour. The scar he'd got in the Independence War shone white against the grainy background – twisting back and forth, as if it still pained him. 'I know, but I need you. We have an important customer.'

'Galactic,' Quy said. That was the only reason he'd be calling her and not one of her brothers or cousins. Because the family somehow thought that her studies on Prime gave her insight into the Galactics' way of thought – something useful, if not the success they'd hoped for.

'Yes. An important man, head of a local trading company.' Second Uncle did not move on her field of vision. Quy could *see* the ships moving through his face, slowly aligning themselves in front of their pods, the hole in front of them opening like an orchid flower. And she knew everything there was to know about Grandmother's restaurant; she was Tam's sister, after all, and she'd seen the accounts, the slow decline of their clientele as their more genteel clients moved to better areas of the station; the influx of tourists on a budget, with little time for expensive dishes prepared with the best ingredients.

'Fine,' she said. 'I'll come.'

• • •

At breakfast, you stare at the food spread out on the table: bread and jam and some coloured liquid – you come up blank for a moment before your immerser kicks in, reminding you that it's coffee, served strong and black, just as you always take it.

Yes. Coffee.

You raise the cup to your lips – your immerser gently prompts you, reminding you of where to grasp, how to lift, how to be in every possible way graceful and elegant, always an effortless model.

'It's a bit strong,' your husband says, apologetically. He watches you from the other end of the table, an expression you can't interpret on his face – and isn't this odd, because shouldn't you know all there is to know about expressions – shouldn't the immerser have everything about Galactic culture recorded into its database; shouldn't it prompt you? But it's strangely silent, and this scares you, more than anything. Immersers never fail.

'Shall we go?' your husband says – and, for a moment, you come up blank on his name, before you remember – Galen, it's Galen, named after some physician on Old Earth. He's tall, with dark hair and pale skin – his immerser avatar isn't much different from his real self, Galactic avatars seldom are. It's people like you who have to work the hardest to adjust, because so much about you draws attention to itself – the stretched eyes that crinkle in the shape of moths, the darker skin, the smaller, squatter shape more reminiscent of jackfruits than swaying fronds. But no matter: you can be made perfect; you can put on the immerser and become someone else, someone pale-skinned and tall and beautiful.

Though, really, it's been such a long time since you took off the immerser, isn't it? It's just a thought, a suspended moment that is soon erased by the immerser's flow of information, the little arrows drawing your attention to the bread and the kitchen, and the polished metal of the table, giving you context about everything, opening up the universe like a lotus flower.

'Yes,' you say. 'Let's go.' Your tongue trips over the word – there's a structure you should have used, a pronoun you should have said instead of the lapidary Galactic sentence. But nothing will come, and you feel like a field of sugar canes after the harvest – burnt out, all cutting edges with no sweetness left inside.

• • •

Of course, Second Uncle insisted on Quy getting her immerser for the interview – 'Just in case,' he said, soothingly and diplomatically as always. Trouble was, it wasn't where Quy had last left it. After putting out a message to the rest of the family, the best information Quy got was from Cousin Khanh, who thought he'd seen Tam sweep through the living quarters, gathering every piece of Galactic tech she could get her hands on. Third Aunt, who caught Khanh's message on the family's communication channel, tutted disapprovingly. 'Tam. Always with her mind lost in the mountains, that girl. Dreams have never husked rice.'

Quy said nothing. Her own dreams had shrivelled and died after she came back from Prime and failed Longevity's mandarin exams, but it was good to have Tam around, to have someone who saw beyond the restaurant, beyond the narrow circle of family interests. Besides, if she didn't stick with her sister, who would?

Tam wasn't in the communal areas on the upper floors; Quy threw a glance towards the lift to Grandmother's closeted rooms, but she was doubtful Tam would have gathered Galactic tech just so she could pay her respects to Grandmother. Instead, she went straight to the lower floor, the one she and Tam shared with the children of their generation.

It was right next to the kitchen, and the smells of garlic and fish sauce seemed to be everywhere – of course, the youngest generation always got the lower floor, the one with all the smells and the noises of a legion of waitresses bringing food over to the dining room.

Tam was there, sitting in the little compartment that served as the floor's communal area. She'd spread out the tech on the floor – two immersers (Tam and Quy were possibly the only family members who cared so little about immersers they left them lying around), a remote entertainment set that was busy broadcasting some stories of children running on terraformed planets, and something Quy couldn't quite identify, because Tam had taken it apart into small components: it lay on the table like a gutted fish, all metals and optical parts.

But at some point, Tam had obviously got bored with the

entire process, because she was currently finishing her breakfast, slurping noodles from her soup bowl. She must have got it from the kitchen's leftovers, because Quy knew the smell, could taste the spiciness of the broth on her tongue – Mother's cooking, enough to make her stomach growl although she'd had rolled rice cakes for breakfast.

'You're at it again,' Quy said with a sigh. 'Could you not take my immerser for your experiments, please?'

Tam didn't even look surprised. 'You don't seem very keen on using it, big sis.'

'That I don't use it doesn't mean it's yours,' Quy said, though that wasn't a real reason. She didn't mind Tam borrowing her stuff, and actually would have been glad to never put on an immerser again – she hated the feeling they gave her, the vague sensation of the system rooting around in her brain to find the best body cues to give her. But there were times when she was expected to wear an immerser: whenever dealing with customers, whether she was waiting at tables or in preparation meetings for large occasions.

Tam, of course, didn't wait at tables – she'd made herself so good at logistics and anything to do with the station's system that she spent most of her time in front of a screen, or connected to the station's network.

'Lil' sis?' Quy said.

Tam set her chopsticks by the side of the bowl, and made an expansive gesture with her hands. 'Fine. Have it back. I can always use mine.'

Quy stared at the things spread on the table, and asked the inevitable question. 'How's progress?'

Tam's work was network connections and network maintenance within the restaurant; her hobby was tech. Galactic tech. She took things apart to see what made them tick, and rebuilt them.

Her foray into entertainment units had helped the restaurant set up ambient sounds – old-fashioned Rong music for Galactic customers, recitation of the newest poems for locals.

But immersers had her stumped: the things had nasty safeguards to them. You could open them in half, to replace the battery, but you went no further. Tam's previous attempt had almost lost her the use of her hands.

By Tam's face, she didn't feel ready to try again. 'It's got to be the same logic.'

'As what?' Quy couldn't help asking. She picked up her own immerser from the table, briefly checking that it did indeed bear her serial number.

Tam gestured to the splayed components on the table. 'Artificial Literature Writer. Little gadget that composes light entertainment novels.'

'That's not the same—' Quy checked herself, and waited for Tam to explain.

'Takes existing cultural norms and puts them into a cohesive, satisfying narrative. Like people forging their own path and fighting aliens for possession of a planet, that sort of stuff that barely speaks to us on Longevity. I mean, we've never even seen a planet.' Tam exhaled, sharply – her eyes half on the dismembered Artificial Literature Writer, half on some overlay of her vision. 'Just like immersers take a given culture and parcel it out to you in a form you can relate to – language, gestures, customs, the whole package. They've got to have the same architecture.'

'I'm still not sure what you want to do with it.' Quy put on her immerser, adjusting the thin metal mesh around her head until it fitted. She winced as the interface synched with her brain. She moved her hands, adjusting some settings lower than the factory ones – darn thing always reset itself to factory, which she suspected was no accident. A shimmering lattice surrounded her: her avatar, slowly taking shape around her. She could still see the room – the lattice was only faintly opaque – but ancestors, how she hated the feeling of not quite being there. 'How do I look?'

'Horrible. Your avatar looks like it's died or something.'

'Ha ha ha,' Quy said. Her avatar was paler than her, and taller: it made her look beautiful, most customers agreed. In those moments, Quy was glad she had an avatar, so they wouldn't see the anger on her face. 'You haven't answered my question.'

Tam's eyes glinted. 'Just think of the things we couldn't do. This is the best piece of tech Galactics have ever brought us.'

Which wasn't much, but Quy didn't need to say it aloud. Tam knew exactly how Quy felt about Galactics and their hollow promises.

'It's their weapon too.' Tam pushed at the entertainment unit. 'Just like their books and their holos and their live games. It's fine for them – they put the immersers on tourist settings, they get just what they need to navigate a foreign environment from whatever idiot's written the Rong script for that thing. But we – we worship them. We wear the immersers on Galactic all the time. We make ourselves like them, because they push, and because we're naive enough to give in.'

'And you think you can make this better?' Quy couldn't help it. It wasn't that she needed to be convinced: on Prime, she'd never seen immersers. They were tourist stuff, and even while travelling from one city to another, the citizens just assumed they'd know enough to get by. But the stations, their ex-colonies, were flooded with immersers.

Tam's eyes glinted, as savage as those of the rebels in the history holos. 'If I can take them apart, I can rebuild them and disconnect the logical circuits. I can give us the language and the tools to deal with them without being swallowed by them.'

Mind lost in the mountains, Third Aunt said. No one had ever accused Tam of thinking small. Or of not achieving what she set her mind on, come to think of it. And every revolution had to start somewhere – hadn't Longevity's War of Independence started over a single poem, and the unfair imprisonment of the poet who'd written it?

Quy nodded. She believed Tam, though she didn't know how far. 'Fair point. Have to go now, or Second Uncle will skin me. See you later, lil' sis.'

• • •

As you walk under the wide arch of the restaurant with your husband, you glance upwards, at the calligraphy that forms its sign. The immerser translates it for you into 'Sister Hai's Kitchen', and starts giving you a detailed background of the place: the menu and the most recommended dishes. As you walk past the various tables, it highlights items it thinks you would like, from rolled-up rice dumplings to fried shrimps. It warns you about the more exotic dishes, like the pickled pig's ears, the fermented meat (you have to be careful about that one, because its name changes depending on which station dialect you order in), or the reeking durian fruit that the natives so love.

It feels… not quite right, you think, as you struggle to follow Galen, who is already far away, striding ahead with the same confidence he always exudes in life. People part before him; a waitress with a young, pretty avatar bows before him, though Galen himself takes no notice. You know that such obsequious-ness unnerves him; he always rants about the outdated customs aboard Longevity, the inequalities and the lack of democratic government – he thinks it's only a matter of time before they change, adapt themselves to fit into Galactic society. You – you have a faint memory of arguing with him, a long time ago, but now you can't find the words anymore, or even the reason why – it makes sense, it all makes sense. The Galactics rose against the tyranny of Old Earth and overthrew their shackles, and won the right to determine their own destiny; and every other station and planet will do the same, eventually, rise against the dictatorships that hold them back from progress. It's right; it's always been right.

Unbidden, you stop at a table, and watch two young women pick at a dish of chicken with chopsticks – the smell of fish sauce and lemongrass rises in the air, as pungent and as unbearable as rotten meat… No, no, that's not it – you have an image of a dark-skinned woman, bringing a dish of steamed rice to the table, her hands filled with that same smell, and your mouth watering in anticipation…

The young women are looking at you. They both wear standard-issue avatars, the bottom-of-the-line kind – their clothes are a garish mix of red and yellow, with the odd, uneasy cut of cheap designers, and their faces waver, letting you glimpse a hint of darker skin beneath the red flush of their cheeks. Cheap and tawdry, and altogether inappropriate, and you're glad you're not one of them.

'Can I help you, older sister?' one of them asks.

Older sister. A pronoun you were looking for earlier; one of the things that seem to have vanished from your mind. You struggle for words, but all the immerser seems to suggest to you is a neutral and impersonal pronoun, one that you instinctively know is wrong – it's one only foreigners and outsiders would use in those circumstances. 'Older sister,' you repeat, finally, because you can't think of anything else.

'Agnes!'

Galen's voice, calling from far away – for a brief moment the immerser seems to fail you again, because you *know* that you have many names, that Agnes is the one they gave you in Galactic school, the one neither Galen nor his friends can mangle when they pronounce it. You remember the Rong names your mother gave you on Longevity, the childhood endearments and your adult-style name.

Be-Nho, Be-Yeu. Thu – Autumn, like a memory of red maple leaves on a planet you never knew.

You pull away from the table, disguising the tremor in your hands.

· · ·

Second Uncle was already waiting when Quy arrived; and so were the customers.

'You're late,' Second Uncle sent on the private channel, though he made the comment half-heartedly, as if he'd expected it all along. As if he'd never really believed he could rely on her – that stung.

'Let me introduce my niece, Quy, to you,' Second Uncle said in Galactic to the man beside him.

'Quy,' the man said, his immerser perfectly taking up the nuances of her name in Rong. He was everything she'd expected – tall, with only a thin layer of avatar, a little something that narrowed his chin and eyes, and made his chest slightly larger. Cosmetic enhancements: he was good-looking for a Galactic, all things considered. He went on, in Galactic, 'My name is Galen Santos. Pleased to meet you. This is my wife, Agnes.'

Agnes. Quy turned, and looked at the woman for the first time – and flinched. There was no one there, just a thick layer of avatar, so dense and so complex that she couldn't even guess at the body hidden within.

'Pleased to meet you.' On a hunch, Quy bowed, from younger to elder, with both hands brought together – Rong-style, not

Galactic – and saw a shudder run through Agnes' body, barely perceptible, but Quy was observant, she always had been. Her immerser was screaming at her, telling her to hold out both hands, palms up, in the Galactic fashion. She tuned it out – she was still at the stage where she could tell the difference between her thoughts and the immerser's thoughts.

Second Uncle was talking again – his own avatar was light, a paler version of him. 'I understand you're looking for a venue for a banquet.'

'We are, yes.' Galen pulled a chair to him, sank into it. They all followed suit, though not with the same fluid, arrogant ease. When Agnes sat, Quy saw her flinch, as though she'd just remembered something unpleasant. 'We'll be celebrating our fifth marriage anniversary, and we both felt we wanted to mark the occasion with something suitable.'

Second Uncle nodded. 'I see,' he said, scratching his chin. 'My congratulations to you.'

Galen nodded. 'We thought…' he paused, threw a glance at his wife that Quy couldn't quite interpret – her immerser came up blank, but there was something oddly familiar about it, something she ought to have been able to name. 'Something Rong,' he said at last. 'A large banquet for a hundred people, with the traditional dishes.'

Quy could almost feel Second Uncle's satisfaction. A banquet of that size would be awful logistics, but it would keep the restaurant afloat for a year or more, if they could get the price right. But something was wrong – something…

'What did you have in mind?' Quy asked, not to Galen, but to his wife. The wife – Agnes, which probably wasn't the name she'd been born with – who wore a thick avatar and didn't seem to be answering or ever speaking up. An awful picture was coming together in Quy's mind.

Agnes didn't answer. Predictable.

Second Uncle took over, smoothing over the moment of awkwardness with expansive hand gestures. 'The whole hog, yes?' Second Uncle said. He rubbed his hands, an odd gesture that Quy had never seen from him – a Galactic expression of satisfaction. 'Bitter Melon Soup, Dragon-Phoenix plates, Roast Pig, Jade Under the Mountain…' He was citing all the traditional dishes for a wedding banquet, unsure of how far the foreigner wanted to take it. He left out the odder stuff, like Shark Fin or Sweet Red Bean Soup.

'Yes, that's what we would like. Wouldn't we, darling?' Galen's wife neither moved nor spoke. Galen's head turned towards her, and Quy caught his expression at last. She'd thought it would be contempt, or hatred, but no – it was anguish. He genuinely loved her, and he couldn't understand what was going on.

Galactics. Couldn't he recognize an immerser junkie when he saw one? But then Galactics, as Tam said, seldom had the problem – they didn't put on the immersers for more than a few days on low settings, if they ever went that far. Most were flat-out convinced Galactic would get them anywhere.

Second Uncle and Galen were haggling, arguing prices and features – Second Uncle sounding more and more like a Galactic tourist as the conversation went on, more and more aggressive for lower and lower gains. Quy didn't care anymore: she watched Agnes. Watched the impenetrable avatar – a red-headed woman in the latest style from Prime, with freckles on her skin and a hint of a star-tan on her face. But that wasn't what she was inside, what the immerser had dug deep into.

Wasn't who she was at all. Tam was right; all immersers should be taken apart, and did it matter if they exploded? They'd done enough harm as it was.

Quy wanted to get up, to tear away her own immerser, but

she couldn't, not in the middle of the negotiation. Instead, she rose, and walked closer to Agnes; the two men barely glanced at her, too busy agreeing on a price. 'You're not alone,' she said in Rong, low enough that it didn't carry.

Again, that odd, disjointed flash. 'You have to take it off,' Quy said, but got no further response. As an impulse, she grabbed the other woman's arm, felt her hands go right through the immerser's avatar, connect with warm, solid flesh.

• • •

You hear them negotiating in the background – it's tough going, because the Rong man sticks to his guns stubbornly, refusing to give ground to Galen's onslaught. It's all very distant, a subject of intellectual study; the immerser reminds you from time to time, interpreting this and this body cue, nudging you this way and that – you must sit straight and silent, and support your husband – and so you smile through a mouth that feels gummed together.

You feel, all the while, the Rong girl's gaze on you, burning like ice water, like the gaze of a dragon. She won't move away from you, and her hand rests on you, gripping your arm with a strength you didn't think she had in her body. Her avatar is but a thin layer, and you can see her beneath it: a round, moon-shaped face with skin the colour of cinnamon – no, not spices, not chocolate, but simply a colour you've seen all your life.

'You have to take it off,' she says. You don't move, but you wonder what she's talking about.

Take it off. Take it off. Take what off?

The immerser.

Abruptly, you remember – a dinner with Galen's friends, when they laughed at jokes that had gone by too fast for you to understand. You came home battling tears and found yourself reaching for the immerser on your bedside table, feeling its cool weight in your hands. You thought it would please Galen if you spoke his language, that he would be less ashamed of how uncultured you sounded to his friends. And then you found out that everything was fine, as long as you kept the settings on maximum and didn't remove it. And then... and then you walked with it and slept with it, and showed the world nothing but the avatar it had designed – saw nothing it hadn't tagged and labelled for you. Then...

Then it all slid down, didn't it? You couldn't program the network anymore, couldn't look at the guts of machines; you lost your job with the tech company, and came to Galen's compartment, wandering into the room like a hollow shell, a ghost of yourself – as if you'd already died, far away from home and all that it means to you. Then... then the immerser wouldn't come off, anymore.

· · ·

'What do you think you're doing, young woman?'

Second Uncle had risen, turning towards Quy – his avatar flushed with anger, the pale skin mottled with an unsightly red. 'We adults are in the middle of negotiating something very important, if you don't mind.' It might have made Quy quail in other circumstances, but his voice and his body language were wholly Galactic, and he sounded like a stranger to her – an angry foreigner whose food order she'd misunderstood – whom she'd mock later, sitting in Tam's room with a cup of tea in her lap, and the familiar patter of her sister's musings.

'I apologize,' Quy said, meaning none of it.

'That's all right,' Galen said. 'I didn't mean to...' he paused, looked at his wife. 'I shouldn't have brought her here.'

'You should take her to see a physician,' Quy said, surprised at her own boldness.

'Do you think I haven't tried?' His voice was bitter. 'I've even taken her to the best hospitals on Prime. They look at her, and say they can't take it off. That the shock of it would kill her. And even if it didn't…' He spread his hands, letting air fall between them like specks of dust. 'Who knows if she'd come back?'

Quy felt herself blush. 'I'm sorry.' And she meant it this time.

Galen waved her away, negligently, airily, but she could see the pain he was struggling to hide. Galactics didn't think tears were manly, she remembered. 'So we're agreed?' Galen asked Second Uncle. 'For a million credits?'

Quy thought of the banquet, of the food on the tables, of Galen thinking it would remind Agnes of home. Of how, in the end, it was doomed to fail, because everything would be filtered through the immerser, leaving Agnes with nothing but an exotic feast of unfamiliar flavours. 'I'm sorry,' she said, again, but no one was listening, and she turned away from Agnes with rage in her heart – with the growing feeling that it had all been for nothing in the end.

• • •

'I'm sorry,' the girl says. She stands, removing her hand from your arm, and you feel a tearing inside, as if something within you is struggling to claw free from your body. Don't go, you want to say. Please don't go. Please don't leave me here.

But they're all shaking hands, smiling, pleased at a deal they've struck – like sharks, you think, like tigers. Even the Rong girl has turned away from you, giving you up as hopeless. She and her uncle are walking away, taking separate paths back to the inner areas of the restaurant, back to their home.

Please don't go.

It's as if something else were taking control of your body; a strength that you didn't know you possessed. As Galen walks back into the restaurant's main room, back into the hubbub and the tantalizing smells of food – of lemongrass chicken and steamed rice, just as your mother used to make – you turn away from your husband, and follow the girl. Slowly and from a distance, and then running, so that no one will stop you. She's walking fast – you see her tear her immerser away from her face, and slam it down onto a side table with disgust. You see her enter a room, and you follow her inside.

They're watching you, both girls, the one you followed in, and another, younger one, rising from the table she was sitting at – both terribly alien and terribly familiar at once. Their mouths are open, but no sound comes out.

In that one moment – staring at each other, suspended in time – you see the guts of Galactic machines spread on the table. You see the mass of tools, the dismantled machines, and the immerser, half spread-out before them, its two halves open like a cracked egg. And you understand that they've been trying to open them and reverse-engineer them, and you know that they'll never, ever succeed. Not because of the safe-guards, of the Galactic encryptions to preserve their fabled intellectual property, but rather, because of something far more fundamental.

This is a Galactic toy, conceived by a Galactic mind – every layer of it, every logical connection within it exudes a mindset that might as well be alien to these girls. It takes a Galactic to believe that you can take a whole culture and reduce it to algorithms, that language and customs can be boiled to just a simple set of rules. For these girls, things are so much more complex than this, and they will never understand how an immerser works, because they can't think like a Galactic – they'll never ever think like that. You can't think like a Galactic unless you've been born in the culture.

Or drugged yourself, senseless, into it, year after year.

You raise a hand – it feels like moving through honey. You speak – struggling to shape words through layer after layer of immerser thoughts.

'I know about this,' you say, and your voice comes out hoarse, and the words fall into place one by one like a laser stroke, and they feel right, in a way that nothing else has for five years. 'Let me help you, younger sisters.'

To Rochita Loenen-Ruiz, for the conversations that inspired this.

Debtless

Chen Qiufan

China

I had the honour of being the first editor to take one of Chen Qiufan's stories in English, though I was beaten to being the first to *publish* him by just a few months. 'The Tomb' was published in *The Apex Book of World SF* 2 back in 2012 and since then Stanley, as he is known, has gone on to publish numerous stories in translation, as well as the novel *Waste Tide*, which I was fortunate to blurb on publication. He is one of the bright young authors of Chinese science fiction, with a keen mind and a deep interest in technology – not to mention being perhaps the best-dressed science fiction writer on the planet. I got to finally meet him in Hong Kong a few years ago, and then in Beijing a while back, and I just had to have him in this anthology. 'Debtless' (translated by Blake Stone-Banks) is prime Chen Qiufan, a tale of debt and asteroid mining that should delight any science fiction reader.

> In the history of human writing, the earliest word for 'freedom'
> is found in Sumerian, signifying freedom from debt.
>
> Treatise of Divine Debt, 02:35

1.

The dream's last sequence looped in my memory. A sticky black tide swept every inch of my body. Its rippling foam splintered into tiny chains that swarmed my skin, binding to blood vessels, cells, nerves, glands. The chains rubbed against each other, producing a metallic whistling. Then they began their slow elegant labor, building inside my body a kind of hell or kingdom.

'Square Face, you dreaming again?'

I opened my eyes on Freckles. She had this concerned look in her eyes. It wasn't the type of look her expression management module would produce. Her concern was genuine. Such a look was rare in our line of work, out here hundreds of thousands of kilometers from Earth, in cold space.

'You catch something anomalous in my data?' I glanced around the cramped control compartment, inhaling air drenched in sweat and chemicals. Miners were typically busy and indifferent toward each other. Our cognitive modules would pop-up passages from the *Treatise of Divine Debt* from time to time: *Wearying debt is sinful and never complete...* These flashed in our minds like commercials on a variety show. Nothing ever changed.

'No, you were trembling like you'd been thrown into an ice cave, but your temperature was normal. Same as last time.'

'Oh...' I reflected. 'Maybe I dreamed I was thrown from the cabin and then...' I puffed my cheeks and rolled back my eyes, imitating those swollen bodies afloat in the absolute zero vacuum of space.

'Not funny. Your turn on duty. Let me show you something.'

As she turned her head, I saw her lips bend into a wry smile. Freckles had this natural gift that no matter how bad things got she always held on to her own quiet amusement.

'Look. Just like grazing sheep.'

The spectacle on the screen she handed me indeed resembled a flock of sheep. Only in this case, the meadow was the vast darkness of space and the sheep were C-type asteroids of various shapes and diameters. Your typical *sheep* was around seven meters in length and filled with water, carbon-rich compounds, iron, nickel, cobalt, and precious raw materials such as silicate residues. Depending on density, some could reach masses of up to five-hundred tons. These were heavy sheep, meandering leisurely in search of fresh grass amidst that dark meadow.

On this revolution, they might be a few months or a few years in. They were in no hurry. We were in no hurry.

Though perhaps thinking 'no hurry' was just my way of comforting myself. A few months back, I had found a gap in several terabytes of resource consumption data. Our water, oxygen, protein and energy were being consumed at a slightly higher rate than what in theory should have been standard. I suspected a leak in the pipeline or a loophole in the process was causing the phenomenon, but I hadn't yet found any evidence.

I certainly wasn't going to go outside to get to the bottom of it. The thought of that cold dark infinite universe made my stomach turn.

I tried to solve the problem mathematically, as I did with all problems.

•

The cognitive module in my brain shuffled through the data and fed back to my retinals.

According to statistical probability, there were over a hundred million asteroids of this size and class. The challenge was that less than one in a hundred thousand could be observed and traced from any real distance. If you aimed to use optics, infrared spectroscopy, thermal flux or lidar for details on dimension, composition, rotation or surface topography, well... The asteroids were simply too far or too small, their orbital cycles too long. The significant details could only be captured within a certain distance, say 0.01 astronomical units or so. Otherwise, it was needle in haystack stuff.

When such treasures were located in the dark starry field, we sheepdogs were dispatched from the nearest interplanetary resources station. These fully automated robots were powered by solar power and xenon propellant. The newest Hall V model propellant delivered up to eighty kilowatts and five thousand seconds of specific impulse. Approaching its targets, the sheepdog would circle several times, sniffing out its target, finding the most sensitive points. It then would sink six spiral anchors into the asteroid's surface. Six vector propulsion engines would start up then, ceasing the asteroid's rotation and thrusting it from its original orbit onto a precisely calculated path. Slowly and surely, the asteroid would reach the nearest point of gravitational stability, likely the L2 or L4 Lagrange Points, where it could catch up with its new friends.

Now Freckles had locked onto five asteroids slowly approaching each other, spinning like Tetris blocks in search of the perfect point of contact. The impact shouldn't be too heavy or too light. Everything had to be just right. They connected into a nearly spherical whole as though returning to an embryonic state.

'I guess... it's like snooker for you,' I said. 'Look at the beautiful arc of the cue ball. Only a master could summon her scattered soldiers with such finesse, from various corners of space to come together for the perfect kiss.'

Freckles sniggered, as though my flattery were beneath her.

Though most of the work was automated by robots and code, this was still space. Anything could happen. Freckle's job was to interfere in case of emergency, such as when an asteroid deviated from orbit, or a sheepdog failed. She guarded against rigid body fractures and perilous debris that might eject upon impact. She was the veterinarian, ready at any time to rescue both the sheep and the sheepdogs. For us, nothing was so precious as that wool.

'All right, Square Face. See you when I get back. I'm off to shear wool.'

As Freckles wormed her way into her spacesuit, I realized just how small she was. She looked like a teenager though she was probably more like twenty-six or seven. There were quite a few women on base: Hairbeast, Braids, Long-Legs… The company required specific gender ratios. Women were more durable than men in space, scoring higher than men in resistance to radiation, hunger tolerance and psychological resilience. A balance of women and men also reduced the level of friction and anxiety, assuming both sides chose not to act territorially by enforcing the norms of old-school monogamy.

I slept with most of the women but never Freckles. We had tried to get something going a few times, but each time ended in laughter. There was this glass wall between us. I didn't know how the wall got there, but I didn't want it to break. Its shards could rain down and wound innocent people.

'I'm out. See you in a bit.' Her face was just barely visible behind the mask, which obscured her hallmark feature – the freckles dotting her nose.

'Careful,' I said. Already, I couldn't remember where her name came from. All of the miners had their own number – I was EM-L4-D28-53b – but we never used that crap to refer to each other. We mostly referred one another by one's most obvious feature, which became their new name.

None of us remembered real names. That was, we were told, part of the contract. Our memories were sequestered and encoded into blocks to avoid emotional fluctuations that could affect our mining work. This included names, families, childhood traumas, pets and actual debt figures. Those figures were why we were here. They were encrypted in blockchains embedded in genes. No one could tamper with them. Our workload was recorded and converted into deducted debt and interest calculated in real time. It didn't matter whether you were on Causeway Bay or a Lagrange point, all were equal in the eyes of the genetic debt system.

'Chill out. You already said I'm a master. Besides, I've debt to pay.' She winked at me.

Freckles always said I must have been born in the Year of the Rat, too cautious for greatness. I always relied on the skill tree implanted in my cognitive module when arguing with her. Some professions were designed for cautious responses. Data surveyors like me could fluently call data to calculate the likelihood of any extreme situation, as well as abstract a sense of the probabilities. This pattern was hardwired into our bodies, like a fear of heights or water is engrained in a person suffering from one phobia or another. It wasn't as though we could take the measure of our courage and cowardice and alter that balance.

On reflection now, however, I'd say it wasn't that some external hand had placed a few timid pieces into the jigsaw puzzle of my personality. This was just the fact of who I fundamentally was.

'Let's try again when you get back.' I tried to conceal my anxiety with the joke. Not sleeping with her didn't mean I didn't care for her.

Freckles made an indecent gesture and disappeared into the hatch.

2.

My anxiety didn't come from nowhere.

Freckles would have to pilot Hermit Crab from the bunker where we lived. The bunker – which we called Mother Whale –

was actually a hollowed-out cylindrical C-type asteroid thirty kilometers in length and five kilometers in width. It sheltered us from deadly doses of radiation, debris attacks and the extreme heat of direct sunlight. It also provided us with water ice, dry ice, solid ammonia, bitumen and small amounts of nickel and iron. These invaluable raw materials had provided almost everything for our construction and our survival.

Our cabin was located in Mother Whale's *skull*. A bearing pipe anchored in the rock spun us at one rotation per minute to generate one-third gee of artificial gravity. That was the best we could get. If the cabin radius were any shorter or longer, the angular velocity any slower or faster, the crude solution would have made us feel terrible – whether due to us getting sick from near zero gravity or us getting smashed against the stone walls of the cabin.

There was chronic osteoporosis, muscle loss and decreased immunity, but these seemed less painful than cardiovascular and cerebrovascular degeneration, vertigo caused by Coriolis forces or depression due to enclosed spaces and sleep deprivation. No matter what, most of us had several hours of work outside the cabin each day, where we were exposed to high levels of cosmic radiation. This of course made mortality rates among interstellar miners far higher than that of any fisherman or laborer back on Earth. Though we maintained normal human functioning through gene therapy, amifostine treatments and compulsory fitness, the most appalling labor conditions on Earth looked like cocktails at the beach bar to us.

Freckles likened us to Pinocchio, a character from an old fairytale about a puppet who was turned into a real boy by the skillful hands of his carpenter father. His nose grew when he started to lie. His most famous misadventure involved him getting swallowed into the belly of a whale.

Humans were truly strange creatures. Even after we had forgotten our own names and families, we couldn't help but remember such odds and ends.

•

Hermit Crab traveled out the mouth of Mother Whale into the deep starry sky. I watched the ship traverse from the edge of one screen to the edge of another. I couldn't turn away, afraid it might suddenly disappear. A man slapped his hand on my shoulder and squinted a reluctant grin. It was Baldy.

'I heard everything you said. But I gotta remind you, brother, Freckles ain't easily provoked.'

I flashed my own reluctant grin but didn't say anything. Baldy was a gossip. His curiosity never waned even when overloaded by physical labor.

'Hermit Crab... Hermit Crab, reply. Everything normal?' I commed to Freckle's channel.

'Hear you. Everything normal. I'm looking at some space ice cream that's about to get scooped by my giant spoon here...' My headphones hissed with the sound of Freckles mischievously slurping at her mic.

My arm was prickly with gooseflesh. I forced my attention back to the console. 'I'm initiating gamma ray and X-ray spectrometry, scanning surface and subsurface elements for volatile components to ensure everything's okay...'

'Alright, Uncle, I know you prefer a slower tempo, but I'm a bit anxious today. Maybe it's my cycle, you know. I want a big scoop of ice cream, so I'm gonna get out that big hot spoon.'

Obnoxious electronic music blasted into my headset, shredding my eardrums. I tore off the headset and cursed, 'Bitch!'

Under normal circumstances, Freckles would be right. The chemical and physical properties of C-type asteroids were usually as obvious as they were benign. Such asteroids fragmented easily and contained minimal volatile content. All she should have to do was bring Hermit Crab's two long claws – her 'spoons' – down into the surface of the asteroids covered with dust and dry soil. She would add heat to melt the water ice among the salt hydrates and clay minerals, then separate the water from other contaminants by distillation. The claws then pumped the water into the spiral shell of our Hermit Crab, where other mineral resources could be handled. That was the first stage of processing.

After that, Hermit Crab's job was to spin the nanoweb that would haul asteroid fragments via an ant-chain back to the refining workshop in Mother Whale's belly. There, more complex chemical and physical processes could deal with the asteroid's other resources. Through refinement, the minerals could be formed into high-density magnetized projectiles. In the tail section of Mother Whale, there was a launcher with an accelerator a full kilometer in length that would launch our haul at defined coordinates. It achieved the largest possible delta-v with minimal energy consumption. The recoil was evenly distributed throughout Mother Whale via an exceptionally designed slider structure to avoid undesired divergence of our path.

In flat space, so distant from any gravity well, we had no need to obey the tyranny of Tsiolkovsky's rocket equation. After a period of time – days, months or years, depending on price – the receiver would pick up the valuables at a point in low Earth orbit. The purpose of the materials – whether for plotting a coup, building a palace for a love, or disrupting global futures markets – made zero difference to us.

This was in essence the whole business – minimize production cost and maximize profit – same as it was in ancient history.

We ourselves were among the production costs too negligible to count.

Freckle's sense of control was uncanny. It gave you the illusion that Hermit Crab's two mechanical claws were synched to her body movement rather than manipulated by joysticks. Her arms fluttered high like the wings of a white crane just before the claws thrust into the asteroid's surface, splashing up a plume of dust and debris.

'Square Face, check it out! Let me show you how it's done.'

Sensors signaled temperatures rapidly rising as compounds began to undergo phase change. Values and curves on my monitor metamorphosed in color and shape. Everything appeared quite normal except for the pressure curve.

Some anomalous data caught my eye. I had a vague ominous feeling even before my backend processing calculated its menacing conclusion. The density of the meteorite was about forty percent lower than that of similar meteorites, which meant she had penetrated highly porous rock that would store more water. With Hermit Crab's rapid heating that extra water would vaporize and transform the giant rock into a pressure cooker. Such was the morbid sensitivity of my skill tree. No one except me could have perceived what the slight shift in the numbers meant.

'Freckles, stop the heating and get out of there!' I ordered.

'Stop your nonsense! Can't you see I'm busy…'

'Now!'

'You know how pissy you—'

Her voice cut out as though snapped by a pair of scissors. The signal from her cam was black and white static. I switched to the external cam, now blinded by a cloud of chalky dust. I couldn't make out anything. Then, in three seconds of slow-motion replay, I watched the surface of the meteorite between the two claws explode. Debris hurtled toward Hermit Crab like a flock of birds fluttering from their nests. The titanium-aluminum alloy shell shredded like a paper lantern. The cabin decompressed. Opened to the vacuum of space, its steel frame revealed a human silhouette like a dangling internal organ. Dust overwhelmed everything.

'Freckles! You hear me? Fuck...' I flung down the headset. In a frenzy, I tried pulling myself into the spacesuit. Baldy was staring at me, motionless. The others had already turned away.

'We gotta save her!' I screamed. 'The fuck you standing around for!'

'Brother, her debt is paid.' Baldy patted my shoulder. 'Death is just the middleman.'

They say the Tonge-Ramesh model proved asteroids were harder to destroy by external forces than we ever imagined.

They say in space no one makes the same mistake twice because you won't live to make it again.

There's a saying for every flavor of truth.

The cabin spun before me. I was breathless. I felt as though an asteroid had collided with my chest. I felt someone exhale an icy breath into my ear, a familiar breath. The voice spoke softly, a single sentence. Then every hair on my body stood on end. My eyes flashed on perfect darkness. I collapsed face-first toward the grimy floor.

The single sentence was this: '*You see my nose growing longer?*'

3.

Everything was milky white.

I wasn't in the control room. I wasn't in any dark, dirty cabin of Mother Whale. Nor was I in the cold hopelessness of space, where death could knock at any time. Just where the hell was I?

It took me some time before realizing I had to be in a dream, the kind of dream that awakens one to a more sober reality.

They say sometimes one's encrypted memory module over-fills and reveals memories in the form of dreams, only we never can tell whose memories are revealed. All our memory modules are stored on one central cloud system for deployment.

Neither my sight nor my movement were under my control. It were as though I were puppeted by invisible silk threads, forced to wander like a ghost in corners I had no interest in.

The milky white in my field of vision began moving, meta-morphosing into a cylindrical cabin that slid around me. In the absence of coordinates, this could mean I was being pushed down or out of the cabin. But then I focused in on points I could orient myself to, points on the high ceiling of a white room.

I began rotating about an axis a meter beneath my viewpoint. My line of sight remained horizontal, the movement slow, never exceeding five degrees per second. Perhaps this was to avoid my getting dizzy. Then I looked down and saw what my axis of rotation was: a man's hip covered by a blue antibacterial surgical gown.

I was staring out on the world from the corner of this man's vision.

'How do you feel, Mr. Dongfang Jue?' said a voice from the side.

My line of sight spun. In the doorframe stood a woman dressed head to toe in an almost glossy black that emitted a slight iridescent rainbow. On her chest, she wore a golden chain brooch. Her long hair was coiled high above her head like some strange signal tower. In space, everyone was forced to keep their hair cut short, if not already bald. You never knew if such uncontrolled hairs might be what triggered one's death in the end.

'Fine, just a bit strange, like something is scuttling around in my body, trying to control me, or restart me.' The voice saying these words seemed foreign, deep and weary, as if at any time it might get disconnected.

'This is a kind of associated hallucination. In theory, you shouldn't feel any difference, those nanorobots… they're very small, you know.' The woman smiled. She walked up to the man's body. I could see her more clearly now. She was in her twenties, makeup intricately applied, almost too refined. Her expression held a sense of superiority, as though she never needed to please anyone.

'So… our contract has gone into effect?'

'Legally, yes.'

'Are you suggesting there may be something illegal? That's a bit tedious at this point, Ms. Mei.'

'What I mean is that, except in regard to the law, the technology is somewhat uncertain.'

'But you said…'

'Don't worry about Anan's part. Her operation is already taken care of.'

'Oh, thank you.'

'All costs will be added to your debt, encrypted in the blockchain embedded in your genes. No one can tamper with it.'

'A life of debt.'

'Look around you. Everyone's eager to borrow. Borrowing represents confidence in one's future and in one's self. And why not? Debt defines a person's value. Such a debt quota is available to few people on Earth. Which is the only reason I'm standing here now.'

'Of course, Ms. Mei Li'ai, although your time is not as

expensive as your father Mr. Mei Feng's. But let's talk it through. It's a debt worth several lifetimes of an ordinary person's toil.'

The woman gave an odd stern smile that seemed out of context in our conversation.

'Please remember, Mr. Dongfang Jue. We owe our lives to the God who created us. From this day on, you must treat your body well, and we will use all means to restore your skill tree to its ideal state. One's body and consciousness are indispensable. Otherwise... I'm afraid it won't be enough.'

The man was silent. He looked at his own body wrapped in the antibacterial gown.

'If it weren't for Anan... I mean, who'd go back to that shithole?

'I fully understand. I am also a daughter. If my father suffered from this same rare disease, I'd no doubt make the same choice. But this is a debt that can't be settled on Earth. There, the balance is simply out of reach...'

The man stared in silence at the woman for some time. Perhaps he wanted to tell her that her father could never suffer such a disease because her family's genes were meticulously scanned. Even if her father so fell ill, he would never face a lifetime of intractable debt. Her family was rich. The poor barely lived on the same planet as they did. They were a different species.

But he said none of this.

'Can I see Anan?'

'Of course. She received a full checkup before completing surgery.' The woman's warm tone returned as she seemed to think of something. 'We will use our best resources to save her.'

There was a hidden message in what she said that made me uneasy, but I couldn't put my finger on what it might be.

The man's POV shifted quickly, almost like some transition animation, as he was moved to another intensive care unit.

After several rounds of disinfection and dust removal, the man was dressed in a white isolation suit then moved down an aisle to another room.

A young girl with a shaved head lay on a bed breathing gently. Her face was relaxed. A picture book was spread over her chest. Even the book had been treated with antibacterials.

The man stood by the bed, quietly watching the girl. He dared not move for fear that even the slightest movement would pull the white plastic isolation suit from his body, make a noise or wake up the girl.

My eye was drawn toward that colorful picture book. I tried to focus on what was painted on its cover but failed. The harder I tried, the faster my focus dissipated. I eventually gave up, turned back to the girl, but found the details of the girl's face now too were eroding like a sand painting in the wind… until there was only blankness.

This was all like something out of a horror film and it filled me with a strange heartache. I wanted to flee, but the more panicked I became, the closer the man's vision zoomed into the blankness where the child's face had been, like a celestial body that couldn't escape its gravity well.

I noticed then the slightest discrepancy in the scene. If I were indeed looking from the man's perspective, I should have seen the triangulation of his nose, but there was none.

What did that mean?

The dream seemed to be coming to an end. Everything was in free fall toward the blank face until it became so huge, like the surface of an asteroid, and I knew I would soon wake again, remembering nothing. I tried desperately to hold on to some detail, something vital, some key that could help me unlock why everything felt so wrong.

In the end, I failed.

4.

Freckles got deleted.

I don't mean her meatbody, rather our memory data of her existence. In the hour since I had woken up, Freckles had become an insignificant name. Even her face was blurred. All the feelings I had once attached to the flesh-and-blood human – desire, annoyance, sadness, and let's shamelessly admit a little love – were blown away like sand. And it wasn't just me. It was all of us.

The company had been moving things around in our minds, for safety and efficiency.

So the girl became just another entry in the system, a coded lesson reminding future generations not to make the same mistake.

'… For carbonaceous bodies to be classified as C-type asteroids, we require high-sensitivity spectra covering optical to mid-infrared wavelengths 0.5 to 3.5 micrometers in length, in order to detect absorption bands at 0.7 and 3 micrometers. This is how we determine if asteroids contain water. Absorption bands of approximately 0.7 micrometers do not directly indicate water itself rather charge transfers in iron-bearing material, such as water, existing in C-type asteroid. Even then, presence of an 0.7 micrometer absorption band doesn't allow us to accurately estimate water content in an asteroid or its spectral color…'

This entry kept popping from the mouth of the beautiful new girl, like a string of tongue twisters. In my mind, I gave her the nickname *Magpie*.

Suddenly she stopped, raised her head and looked at me confused. Her face, slightly red and sweaty, spewed out her question. 'I don't get why it's not more direct to detect the presence of the 3-micrometer absorption band?'

I shot a friendly smile. 'The high background radiation in the mid-infrared spectra makes the presence of the 3-micrometer band weak and difficult to detect.'

'Oh.' She looked as though she'd lost all interest in the question. For a hunter, that was a dangerous sign.

Water was the fundamental element for survival in our vast universe, so asteroids with water were always primary collection targets for miners, but in some cases this proved fatal.

Magpie was speaking from a cylindrical metal cage just wide enough for a human body. Her waist and hands were strapped to swiveling branches. Her feet were spinning on the 'hamster wheel', which was what we crew called this piece of equipment. It was the safest and most effective way to combat osteoporosis and muscle atrophy in our one-third-gee environment.

As her mentor, I had to correct her movements from time to time. Even slight errors accumulating over time could lead to fractures or fasciitis.

•

Bathing on a mining vessel was like mixing vegetables and salad dressing in a sealed bag. Magpie climbed out from her bathbag naked, wiped her firm calves in front of me as though no one was there. For some reason I turned my face to the side, perhaps because she was new and I wanted to show respect. It didn't matter. Her bathwater would be recycled for our food, drinking water and air. It would eventually be part of my own body. From this point of view, our intimacy was assured.

'Why'd you come here?' I asked, trying to shift my attention.

'That a question?' she asked.

'I know, of course, the *Treatise of Our Divine Debts*. I mean, did you ever think about where that debt came from in the first place?'

'Is that important? We are all born into wearying debt, right? We're just a bit more fortunate than others...'

'Fortunate?'

'It's not fortunate to catch a fat fish worth more than one-hundred-billion credits? That's a platinum mine alone, not counting nickel and cobalt. Enough to pay off all debts and make me a billionaire.'

'That's a fairytale!'

'No, it's a probability.'

'The probability is you get hung out to dry in space...'

'This isn't much more dangerous than commercial crabbing in Peru or the Bering Sea. Of course, if you insist, the probability of getting hit by asteroid debris is higher than on Earth. Problem is—'

'Another hopeless optimist...' I glimpsed something familiar in her expression.

'Problem is...' She shook her head, showing no intention of slowing down. 'You got a hundred trillion in gold deposits on Earth, but nobody can get at it. Why? Because it's in the sea. Cost of extracting gold dissolved in seawater far exceeds the value of the gold itself. So the value of that huge deposit is zip. We're here. Yes, it's dangerous. But the desserts are real. They're out here...'

When she talked about dessert, it was like I almost remembered something, something on the tip of my tongue. I didn't bother trying to remember though. I didn't want to argue anymore.

'Magpie, I hope you react on mission as quickly as when you're speaking.'

'Mag— what? You wimp. Go cower in the cabin and do your arithmetic. I hope your debt gets paid as soon as possible.'

She looked like she was actually getting angry.

In theory, Magpie wasn't wrong. An M-type asteroid was the absolute best dessert. A 16 Psyche M-type could carry enough iron and nickel to meet Earth's demand for the next million years. A platinum-rich asteroid might carry as much as one hundred grams per ton, twenty times more than the highest-grade South African open-pit platinum mine. This meant a 500 meter M-type could produce 175 times the annual output of the planet.

That was our ultimate mission. C-type asteroids were for sustained replenishment. Mother Whale could not be overexploited. She wasn't some giant rock. Rather, she was like loose rocks and gravel gathered together by their own gravity, utterly without structural integrity. Any rotation, impact or deep excavation could trigger her disintegration. Then everything we had built would be destroyed, including ourselves.

• • •

Magpie slowly came to accept her new name. She even came to accept my style.

I tried not to get too close. I feared gravity's power of attraction, which caused things to haphazardly smack into each other. I always had this ominous feeling around her, like the superstition of a sailor on the sea too many years who believes doom follows a red tide with white waves.

I feared it was Magpie's fate to someday be deleted.

She knew what I thought and mocked it. Holding her pick-axe or drill, she'd say, 'We got just one road, and we gotta follow it to the end.'

To Magpie, life was an adventure with few real choices.

She was ordered to recycle an abandoned sheepdog. The order said the sheepdog's memory module might contain data from previous contact with an M-type asteroid and could provide valuable tracking clues.

We never knew where the orders came from, from Earth

380,000 kilometers away or from some space station? From other humans or from AI? Still, in most cases, the orders were correct. In a few cases, human interpretation led to bad consequences, like misinterpreting the oracle in a Greek tragedy.

Magpie never doubted the orders, though I tried to undermine her blind belief any way I could.

For example, I told her, using a mathematical formula, that even if we identified and tracked an M-type asteroid, trying to change its orbit and capture it would be like a monkey typing out the collected works of Shakespeare. It was harder than winning any lottery. Mining an M-type would be like catching a whale with a fishing rod. The costs could swallow up any potential profit while sacrificing dozens of lives. Even if we succeeded, shipping the ore back to Earth might cause a full market collapse.

For example, I made her doubt her abilities. I told her, what a robot can't do, a miner made of protein and water certainly can't do.

'Maintaining complex mining facilities, dealing with unpredictable equipment failures, analysing anomalous events, assessing their impacts on Mother Whale? If the AI can't succeed, Magpie doesn't stand a chance. So it's not clear what value you really have, at least while you're alive.'

'So, what do you want me to do?' she shot back. 'Cower in the cabin like you, waiting for my muscles to atrophy? Overdose on cosmic radiation causing tumors to take over my body and kill me?' She flashed the whites of her eyes.

'That's not what I mean… I just hope you get these dumb ideas out of your head so you stay alive a bit longer…'

'But what does it mean to live when you live like that? We owe our lives to the God who made us…'

'Tell that to all the people who've died doing our work…'

'Then what are you here for? Didn't like Earth?'

'This wasn't my choice! Just like it isn't your choice! You woke up in this hell, unable to remember anything of the past other than what's in your damn skill tree. We can never free ourselves of our debt, except in death. There's no other way out!'

I turned my back, not wanting to let Magpie see how weak I was. A hand rested on my shoulder.

'I remember how I came here.'

I spun my head in astonishment and looked at her unsmiling face. Nobody knew, not even for the newest arrivals. I heard the company created a break in crew consciousness to avoid unnecessary risk. I had always imagined the risk was a mentally broken crewmember who might try to hijack the spaceship to get back home.

'Is that a joke?' I asked.

'No, I remember a strange place. It was like I was waking from a dream. There I was in this long, narrow passage. There were these flashing green lights guiding me forward, urging me forward...'

'And then?'

'And then I'll tell you when I get back.' Magpie winked. Only then did I realize I'd been fooled.

• • •

I've never met anyone who paid off their debts. That's to say any living person, at least not on Mother Whale. Perhaps there were such fortunate people scattered on mining bases in the belt, but it seemed like some religious parable, a meticulously worded advertisement that could never be proven or disproven.

They said people who paid off their debts could return to Earth, recover their memories, rinse their debt data clean from their DNA chains. More credit points were added to their account than they could spend in several lifetimes.

It sounded more like a fairytale, right?

Only no one knew why they owed their debt or how long it would take to repay. We could only believe in the fairness of the system because we were told that it was absolutely correct mathematically and couldn't be tampered with.

Magpie was right. We had no other choice.

But I was glad she had listened to me and tied the reinforced safety rope.

Magpie was a light-as-air moth drifting slowly from the lower hatch of the Hermit Crab toward a wandering sheepdog. The mechanical arm was far too clumsy to perform the meticulous work of unloading the memory module.

'So people *are* still useful…' Her rebuttal echoed in my headset.

'In a few very special cases.' I didn't want to give an inch.

'Tell me your theory again about why people aren't needed in space?'

She gently hooked herself to the sheepdog. The elasticity of the safety rope yanked her back. Magpie unhooked the safety rope, attached it to one of sheepdog's mechanical claws. She got into position. She'd have to push her hand down the sheepdog's throat, turn on the emergency power supply, enter the password, then open the storage panel inside in order to unload the memory module.

I cleared my throat. I stared at the feed from her helmet cam, trying to ignore the boundless dark universe beyond. I said, 'It's because of fear.'

'You mean human fear?'

'Is there another kind? What do machines fear? Power drops? Erased memories? Only people have fear.'

She got in smoothly, pushing half her body into the opening. The sheepdog lit up. Its panel opened. Everything seemed within reach.

'So what? Fear shouldn't let people venture into space? Fear shouldn't let people live without machines? I think there's something you haven't told me? Some childhood trauma perhaps?' There was something like sympathy in her voice, perhaps teasing me.

'I can't think of any childhood traumas to speak of. And even if I did, they're locked away in sequestered memory—' There was a disturbing flash on the screen. 'What's that on your right hand, Magpie? Those spots lighting up?

'No clue. All I know is the memory module's stuck. I could hear in her voice she was giving it her all. Her whole body was trembling.

'Something's off. Get out of there immediately.'

'I'm trying to shake loose the module…'

'Maybe you've triggered some protection program. Get out now…' I quickly checked the code base of the old sheepdog. Iridescent data pummeled the screen like rain. My eyes tensed, trembled as they tried to scan the keywords.

'Square Face, there anything you can actually help me with? Apart from making me nervous…'

I didn't have an answer though I felt infinitely close to the answer.

'Hey, guess what? I got it.' She was panting. On screen, her hand was holding a black cube. It was time to get out.

But if the memory module was removed after a hard restart, the landing position of sheepdog would be triggered, which meant…

'I told you, nothing to fear…'

Six corkscrew anchors shot from the sheepdog, plunging into Magpie's stomach. They began to drill. Red globules like translucent jellyfish floated out from her stomach, shimmering around her body before boiling off into vacuum.

My whole body froze, mouth agape and speechless. My stomach roiled. My hunch had been right again.

There was no scream, no call for help, just a lone gasp in the headset as though trying to call back the oxygen rapidly vacating her lungs.

The propulsion system that was supposed to be used to buffer landing also activated. The sheepdog dragged Magpie's corpse into space while her safety rope still hooked to Hermit Crab pulled taught. She was a scrap of rotting meat in a tug of war between two beasts.

'Cut the safety rope!' Baldy shouted. 'We can't lose another ship.'

'No, I won't do it.'

'Her debts are paid. Let her go. Death's just the middleman.' Baldy patted my shoulder, gestured a prayer over his forehead, a horizontal D.

'Fuck your middleman!' I squeezed my eyes shut as they spilled warm tears.

Unable to stomach the gruesome tug of war anymore, I did as he said and pressed the button. What was left of her body glimmered as it shrank into the distance, slowly disappeared among the glinting stars.

An idea fell on me then like the shadow of a never before seen celestial body.

Perhaps this was no accident.

5.

Another dream. I was getting frustrated with these endless hallucinations. It was like each one wanted to tell me something but the message was never clear.

If you strapped on those mining boots of ours, you'd understand.

A month out from Earth, no atmosphere, no day or night, no real gravity, no entertainment, no delicious kungpao chicken – fortunately my memory still held on to that favorite dish – no real friendships, no dating.

No reminiscing. Though that might have been a good thing.

There were also a few novelties never experienced on Earth: the odd psychological condition of simultaneous claustrophobia and agoraphobia, restricted nerve conduction, incontinence, prolapsed sphincters. A few of us got to experience comas. And then there was the high radiation and constant vomiting. Radioactive fuel fleas, tiny particles charged with alpha radiation, pummeled our bodies at lightspeed. They penetrated our protective clothing and body, burned holes in our internal organs. They made us bleed and ache, wish we had never been born.

On a more positive note, there were the genetically engineered algae that produced our oxygen and protein, though the taste was a bit unsettling. We gained knowledge and experience we would never grasp in several lifetimes on Earth. If you're a curious kid, space mining might be just the right career for you.

I returned to that man's body. He was staring into a mirror, haggard and old. The face was unfamiliar but the sense of déjà vu was so strong. I knew the plot continued from the previous dream, but I couldn't remember the backstory at all.

The mirror reflected a messy room, a typical bachelor's apartment with no trace of any other family member's life. There were bottles of booze, cigarette butts, powders of unknown composition scattered on a tea table. A photo frame lay face down showing only the buckle on the back. Printed papers littered the furniture and floor like giant snowflakes.

The man seemed to have come to some decision. He was looking at a black card in his hand, then dialing a number.

'It's me... Yeah, I think so.' He sniffed, turned his back and looked back at the room.

'... You let me down once already. I hope there won't be a second time...'

'... You can't come with me this time. What does that mean, we tried our best? You didn't try!' His voice grew louder then weaker. '... You didn't.'

'... Yeah, read it word for word. Took me all night. Hope it was worth it.'

'... Anything unclear? Ha, everything! The whole complexity of the system is far beyond any one normal person's understanding. How am I supposed to understand it?'

'... I know, the old debt's still in the repayment cycle. This adds on a new debt. I get it. That's just life...'

'... I get how your psychological strategies work – what's for family, what's for future... You create a papier-mâché moral aura that's just a bit too fake, can't even weather a little wind or rain. For me, I just hope I get to live a bit longer or a bit better, even if I have to mortgage someone else's life...'

'... I hope you guys have some kind of conscience. I hope you can allow her a better life...'

A virtual birdcall activated behind the man. He spun to see himself lit up in the mirror, embedded in golden rays that were probably supposed to signify hope. An electronic contract illuminated in the mirror. A voice prompted him to read it carefully, then place his palm on the mirror for bio-cryptographic verification. The man clenched his eyes and frowned, hesitated for just a moment before he slapped the mirror with his palm. Circles of colored light rippled from his hand.

'Verification complete. Your contract is now activated. Congratulations on your new debt quota…'

'Go fuck yourself!' The man seemed to relax. He took a sip of wine and began cleaning up the disaster zone that was his room. When his finger touched the frame on the table, he pulled back as though it were burning hot.

'… What the hell did I do?' The man touched the back of the frame with his fingertips, found the courage to turn it over. A girl's innocent smile beamed back from the other side. He picked up the picture book and covered his face. The book seemed familiar.

'… What the fucking hell did I do?'

The man began to sob. His body trembled. He stood unsteadily.

'I have to… have to stop… have to…'

He inspected his room in a panic. His eyes fixed on the balcony. The man picked up the remaining bottle from the table and downed it. He let it go. The bottle shattered at his feet.

The man rushed toward the balcony, and without a hint of hesitation leapt over the railing. Though I was just the dreamer, the sudden abyss hundreds of meters below me made my adrenaline soar. The gathering wind whistled sharply.

Many dreams end in free fall. This wasn't one of those dreams.

The man's fall lasted just 0.3 seconds then paused mid-air. He was like a flying insect trapped by an invisible cobweb, unable to struggle. The bust of a woman in black emerged from the thin air. She wore a golden chain brooch, delicate smile and dignified air.

'Mr. Dongfang Jue, it's been too long. You've forgotten the details of our first contract. You have no right to end your life. All rights belong to your creditors, to the company. Even if you end your life, your debt cannot be cancelled because its data is encrypted and embedded in your genes. It is impervious to tampering.'

Like that man, I tried to decipher the hidden meaning in her words. It was as though there were a subtle tremor in the transparent spider silk connecting us, reverberating in all directions. It seemed to await only an *open sesame* that would unleash a flood of signal as it busted the locks on my cognitive module.

But *sesame* didn't *open*.

6.

...

Ginger.
Freckles.
Magpie.
Popcorn.
...

They had all been deleted. One by one. Faces and voices blurred in my mind like paint dissolving in the rain, mixing into muddy colors, seeping into the dirt along the gutter of my memory.

'We're space miners. That's our life.' Everyone repeated the old clichés to me in hopes we could keep busy with the tasks at hand.

Maybe they were right. This was our life. Held captive in the distant cold borderlands of the cosmos, abandoned, forgotten, able to repay our inherited debt only through interminable labor. My skills allowed me to cower in the cabin and try to live a bit longer. They didn't have even that luxury.

Doubt plagued me. It had never been like this before. It was the same with other miners. It was like someone had lowered the logical consistency sensitivity of some module in my brain. A huge blind spot had formed on our consciousness. None of us could see the gaps. For some unknown reason, my blind spot had been shrinking. Now, the problem was becoming exposed like a black reef emerging from the red tide.

Maybe from fear, maybe from the fading names, maybe from the skill tree in my head calculating the enormous threats, I could no longer use the old escape routes.

I had to do something.

Emerging from the shower bag, Baldy gave me a shock. His scarred body was like that of a striped leopard in the jungle, dark and glinting as vapor rose from his skin.

'It's you? I thought it was Hairbeast.' He plucked an eyebrow. 'We had arranged to meet, you understand. Anyway, get on with your exercise.'

'Things aren't supposed to be this way.'

'What way? You don't sound right. You done a self-scan?'

'I'm fine. It's you who's got the problem. You don't feel like this is all quite absurd? This Whale Mother? This work? This way of people constantly dying...'

'Hey, Square Face. We've discussed this several times. This is our fate. To pay our debts we bear risks and pains normal people couldn't bear. Death's just the middleman.'

'That what you really think? Or is that what they make you think?' I pointed upward, though I knew there wasn't really an up. After all, we were spinning in space.

'You ask me, I'd say maybe you need a companion to release some pressure. Sometimes your module will develop cognitive errors due to accumulation of negative emotion. It's like a kind of – what's the word – allergy. Yes, like an allergy.' He turned his back and began to towel himself dry.

'I calculated the cost. Using the Hohmann transfer orbit, to keep people coming here from Earth makes zero economic sense. Imagine scrapping an airplane every time you fly with no return ticket. It makes for some ugly accounting, Baldy. No one would do this business at such a loss.'

He turned slowly, a severe expression on his face.

'... So what are you thinking?'

'We tell the company we're not doing it anymore.'

'Impossible. Our debt... It doesn't matter. Only the company can contact us anyway. It's one-way. Our calls go to an auto-responder, some message sorter.'

'Then we shut down Mother Whale's production line. We stop shipping and see what they do.'

'Yeah, that's one way to get their attention. You sure you want to do that?' The expression on Baldy's face shifted slightly, but I didn't know what it meant.

'If they don't respond, I got a backup plan,' I stopped, looked around. 'We blow up the refining workshop.'

The refining workshop in the belly of Mother Whale was central to the second, third and fourth stage processing of all the ore brought back by Hermit Crab.

Second-stage processing began with the electrolysis of water into hydrogen and oxygen, which were then liquefied and stored as our primary propellants. Third-stage processing involved high-temperature 'baking' for the reduction of magnetite by carbon-containing polymers, resulting in the more complete release of water, carbon monoxide, carbon dioxide and nitrogen. Fourth stage processing used released carbon monoxide as a reagent for the extraction, separation, purification and manufacture of iron and nickel products via the Mond gas process. The residue contained cobalt, rare platinum group metals, and semi-conductors like gallium, germanium, selenium and tellurium.

That residue might not look like much but it was worth more than the sum historical value of many of the largest companies in history.

'You serious?' His eyes narrowed.

'Mix hydrogen and oxygen, add carbon-containing polymer, high temperatures... Boom.' I snapped my fingers and mimed a vast explosion.

'Alright, let me think on it. This requires a collective vote...' Baldy bowed his head and flung the towel over his shoulder. He had up to that point been repeatedly wiping the same area for some time.

'I don't trust them,' I said. 'I only trust you.'

'Alright.' He dropped the towel and walked over, hand outstretched. 'Thanks for your trust.'

Before I could shake his hand, Baldy knocked me cold to the ground with a single punch. Last thing I saw was his mutilated toes, stretching and contracting against the floor, producing a sound like the pincers of some insect scraping against metal.

• • •

I tried opening my eyes but couldn't. I tried moving my body but couldn't.

I felt hands lifting me, stuffing me into something. Voices washed over me intermittently. I tried my hardest to make out their words.

'... Sorry, Square Face... We had the collective vote and this is the outcome... We can't... You can't disrupt our order...'

I could feel now I was in a spacesuit. I didn't like that. Spacesuits meant you were about to enter some uncontrollable extreme environment with just one thin layer of protection.

'... You always said... Minimize risk... Mathematically, this is the most reasonable way...'

Something switched on. Air pressure was changing rapidly, as well as temperature. I heard modules in the spacesuit waking up one by one, as if it were the living thing instead of me. My paralyzed consciousness seemed to grasp the terrible fact before my body was fully awake.

'… Your oxygen can sustain… 124 minutes… Try to save…'

My eyelids flicked open and I saw the crew's faces, hands on their foreheads as though in mourning. They stood in front of Baldy. Between their faces and mine were two layers of specialized glass. One layer on the isolation hatch door, the other on my helmet. A pitying voice spoke on the helmet's communicator.

'… Your debt… is cleared… Death is just… the middleman…'

I stretched out a numb hand to try to grab on to anything. I wanted to shout, beg them not to. But it was too late. I watched their faces float away, the light around them become uneven, their bodies spin slowly into the distance. There was no gravity, only the centrifugal force of the cabin rotation, and me drifting away from the axis. There was no way to ever get back.

Palpable fear triggered the stimulation-response module in my amygdala and ventromedial prefrontal cortex, accelerating my heart rate, raising blood pressure, secreting sweat, cortisol, adrenaline. Trust me. I'm familiar with fear, and this was that most primitive fear evolved over billions of years. No one can suppress it no matter how brave.

And certainly not me.

I floated like some giant bag of trash. My reason understood that fear consumed oxygen faster and as carbon dioxide levels in my blood rose this would further accelerate my fear in a vicious circle. But I couldn't help it.

Like a mad man, I burst out laughing at the stupidity of humanity's design.

I had no idea how much time had passed. In such extreme situations, no one has a clear sense of time. I figured I'd die in my endless drift, finally debtless. I had no clue that my body was about to crash into some vast, solid surface. And then, something caught me.

It was the inner surface of the Mother Whale asteroid. Its centrifugal spin had somehow landed me here.

Though there was still no water or oxygen, I at least was able to regain a sense of direction. My fear calmed slightly, allowing me to reallocate computational resources for attention and perception, and draw on memories of past experience for behavioral decision-making.

Unfortunately, I had no past experience being thrown into space.

I fixed my hands and feet to the inner wall of the asteroid. The black sand in the rocky wall reminded me that rock layers here contained a certain proportion of iron and nickel. Though it wasn't high grade, it was enough for my magnetic boots to function.

Now that I could just barely stand, I began making my way toward the head of Mother Whale. The odd pleasure I felt in that moment must have been similar to the exhilaration an ancestral ape felt when it stood upright to take its first step as a human.

Overhead, the cabin revolved around its axis at one cycle per minute, too fast and too far. I didn't have a chance. The axis was, in fact, a superalloy bearing pipe piercing both sides of Mother Whale's skull. It was braided with titanium, chromium and carbon fibers, sealed and hollowed out as a pipeline for energy and resources.

Then again, perhaps there was still a sliver of a chance.

My remaining oxygen would last just seventy-two minutes.

I began taking advantage of the skill tree in my brain. Analysing the nearest distance to the pipe opening, mass, step length, heart rate, oxygen level, ground magnetic force and friction, I calculated the optimal speed to reach my destination before oxygen depletion. I also identified an airlock where I might be able to get in.

The analysis didn't make me especially optimistic. If my speed were too fast, the attraction generated by the magnetic boots wouldn't hold my mass. If too slow, my oxygen would deplete before I even got close. For that sliver of a chance, I had to execute my little space run with precision to two decimal points.

From the edge of Whale Mother's star-devouring mouth gleamed a distant ray of sunlight. I had to rush to the entrance of the pipeline before the sun reached me, or its high temperatures would deliver an early death sentence.

Without starting gun or spectators, I began my race against death.

If my life weren't on the line, I would no doubt have enjoyed the scenery. Imagine a vast stone ping-pong ball five kilometers in radius with a third of its surface sliced away. The inner surface of that thin shell was my racetrack. Overhead, an unfathomably dark starry sky watched over me like an eye in the rock wall. Above I also could see the revolving cabin containing the mining crew who had lived beside me day and night before voting me into exile in space.

The people I had saved, loved and slept with, like all these vast cold objects, were now perfectly silent.

Beneath the boundless darkness, I was an ant racing alone. Next to eternity, all debt becomes meaningless.

I'd never been much of an athlete – not out there and, I imagined, not on Earth. At the halfway mark, I was overcome with a splitting headache, sore joints and muscles. My heart pumping beyond all limits. My chest was a wheezing furnace about to pop.

All I wanted was to give up, lie down, float away, whatever. Anything for a breath and a brief rest.

But the numbers wouldn't stop for me. They would just continue their free fall back to zero.

I heard strange sounds like whispered songs. They surrounded me, guided me, urged me to stop, urged me to continue. I suppose it was all a hallucination caused by lack of oxygen. Rhythmic flashing red numbers showed just eighteen minutes left, and the pipe that was my finish line seemed to be getting farther away. Yellow and blue colors floated across my field of view like the mating dance of fireflies in a cemetery.

—You see my nose growing longer?

The voice sighed quietly in my ear. I woke with a sudden start. My hair stood upright. It was Freckles' voice.

I had almost forgotten them all. My dying dash was not only for myself, but also for all those names now deleted.

Distant sunlight slanted into the mouth of Mother Whale, smearing its gray inner surface with golden hot color. Its energy was so beautiful yet so lethal. It would soon awaken ice sleeping deep in the stony cracks, transform it into vapor that would spear out from the surface. I had to reach the pipeline before the sun caught up with my shadow. If I failed, I would be either burned alive by the sun's heat or impaled on its spears of steam.

I imagined the ground behind me like popcorn in the oven, erupting in crisp explosions that emitted no sound. Death was so quiet, a scheming black cat forever inching closer.

Every breath seared my lungs. Each stride pushed my muscles

to their limits. I soon forgot the pace, the pain, the death. The running became numb, mechanical. The only way to achieve a miracle, of course, is to shed one's human weakness. This is also perhaps our only human strength.

The pipe was thicker than I had imagined. It looked like a coral tube growing from the stone wall of the opposite hemisphere.

My feet grew lighter, so light in fact they were almost floating. I realized then that I had foolishly overlooked a key indicator: power consumption.

Electricity was needed to maintain body temperature, data calculation, external environment monitoring and – I now remembered – my magnetic boots. Now that power had dropped to five percent, my life support system had first shut down the boots. A reasonable decision under normal circumstances, but now my efforts were for naught.

I continued forward from inertia, but the friction between the sole of my boots and the wall was diminishing. I would soon lose all control of my body and float aimlessly, never reaching the pipe.

There was only one way out with, as I calculated it, an extremely small chance of success. I had no other choice.

I took a deep breath. I drew my legs together and threw my body forward. I somersaulted. When the axis of my body rotated to a certain angle, I pushed out my legs towards the ground and made a leap of faith with all my strength.

Black dust plumed around my feet like a miniature atom bomb. I straightened my body like an arrow just flung from the bow, plummeted toward my silver target.

The helmet's oxygen meter began its final-minute countdown, red numbers flashing to remind me that even if I reached the pipe, it would only be to die.

In that endless moment, Einstein was right.

I kept tweaking my posture in the air. For a second, it looked like I would miss the pipe and disappear into the endless starry sea. In the end though I hit the target and hit it hard. I probably broke a few ribs. An ominous crack appeared on my helmet. But at least I had reached my destination.

Fortunately, the impact point was not far from the airlock. I had exhausted the oxygen in my spacesuit but somehow reached the airlock with the last gasps of my will. I prepared to crack the code to the airlock.

But there was no need to crack the code. Those who had banished me hadn't yet removed me from the system.

That was perhaps their greatest error.

·

I collapsed to the floor, gasped like an amphibian emerging on land.

There was scarce oxygen in the pipe, likely related to the gap in the resources consumption data. At the center of the dim passage were thick cables and supply pipes of various colors. On either side, sensors flashed green every few meters, like on a runway at night, stretching into dark depths at both ends.

I inferred that one direction extended to the rotating cabin that housed the crew, but what about the other? Maybe some miniature nuclear fusion reactor buried in the rock? In addition to solar and hydrogen–oxygen propellant, that was our primary source of energy.

Then I remembered the joke Magpie had shared before she died, and I decided to follow those green lights leading away from the crew cabin.

Now, I was already a dead man. At least in the system, my suit was dead, no electricity, no oxygen, no helmet. I manually shut down the positioning module to prevent my colleagues from being frightened by my walking corpse. If I wanted to get back to the cabin though, I'd need a new outfit.

As my expedition progressed, odd fragments of memory flickered as if I had seen this place before. It were as though some sharp discomfort prevented me from returning to my homeland and I had become a ghost whose sole mission was to blow a chill breath down your neck from time to time.

As I proceeded through several more airlocks, things became increasingly interesting. One of the cabins was equipped with a high-precision 3D printer, which could print and modularize most lightweight space supplies from digital renderings – space-suit shells, mining tools, even weapons. All I needed to do was transfer the integration module from my old spacesuit into the new one.

The ghost in the new spacesuit came online.

This new bounty did little to cheer me up, however. It mostly just raised more questions. Why was such a cabin set up here? Who had access to such equipment? What did they use it for?

Maybe the answer was hidden in some dark corner of my memory, blockchain encryption still denying my access.

Perhaps I just didn't want to know the answer.

Finally, I was standing in front of the last cabin door. Through the porthole, I glimpsed a hellish scene. No monsters, corpses or blood. Everything was pristine, radiating the holy light of life. Yet this was far more hopeless than any nightmare.

The cabin door slid silently open. I entered.

My fingers trembled across the transparent casing that held the suspended bodies. Some were fully formed, others still growing. Some were young, others elderly. Faces, familiar and unfamiliar, waiting to be awakened by the demons in their dreams. I saw Baldy, Hairbeast, Long-Legs… Their bodies, fresh and strong, spasmed from time to time in their artificial amniotic fluid. They were ripe fruit ready to drop, lacking only that last ingredient – the infusion of their souls.

Maybe that was what we had mortgaged to the devil – our souls, our genetic debt, our blockchain memories… No matter what you called it, the fact remained.

They had lied to us.

I wondered if waking one of these bodies might signal the death of someone else in the cabin. Just who controlled the growth rate of each clone? Could it be that the life expectancy of every miner had been so thoroughly calculated? All for maximizing efficiency? A bitter chill slinked down my spine.

This was the true secret of the space miners. This was the debt we carried.

I came to the body of a girl who seemed to have just reached adolescence. The features on her face made me realize a contradiction. The face on each clone seemed to be the same yet different from that in my memory. Perhaps the system had altered genetic expressions. Perhaps it wasn't so complicated. Perhaps it just needed to make some slight adjustments to the facial recognition module in our minds to pay more attention to some features than others. Then again, perhaps we just didn't recognize the person when they returned at all.

But that girl's face provoked a more complex emotional response, like a whirlpool trying to swallow me whole. I finally managed to break away from her gravity well and turn toward the last sealed body.

This one was just a tiny embryo curled amidst a yellowish liquid, like a pink asteroid. It squinted its eyes and sucked at its fingers, immersed in seemingly eternal dreams. I watched nutrients flow from the translucent synthetic umbilical cord into the embryo.

I noticed then the line of code at the bottom: EM-L4-D28-58a.

Dizziness swept over me. I knelt to one knee, doing all I could to support my body.

The embryo was me. Of course, I was one of them. Perhaps the embryo had been triggered by the signal of my recent death. It looked like it was going to need some time.

Would it have all my memories? Including those sequestered within the blockchain encryption? Would it remember my trials of life and death? Will it fear death as I did? How many more cycles would it take to pay off my debt? Maybe there would never come such a day. Perhaps human existence was, after all, itself just another form of debt.

My heart filled with an anger I couldn't name. I hammered at the transparent casing, making a muddy, dull echo. I wanted to destroy it all and stem the endless cycle.

The embryonic me seemed to perceive something. Its eyelids trembled. Tiny eddies appeared in the amniotic fluid, as if in response to my anger.

It was innocent. I woke to the fact that I myself was just another avatar of the same identity. It was me.

We were all innocent. The guilty ones were those who had built this place.

I stood. I had to get back to the cabin to tell my deceived companions, but how would I not sound like a madman? I had to print something that would convince the other brainwashed, damaged miners this was all real. I had to get the company to stop this. I didn't care if they ended up doing something drastic.

The long, green lights of the pipe stretched into the distance. I could not shrink back again.

• • •

Baldy raised both hands and kneeled slowly, his back to me. On his knees, his head was now level to mine.

I aimed the gun at the back of his head. I had no illusions as to how strong or cunning he could be.

Behind me, a body lay supine. Blood covered the soles of my boots. An odd sticky texture accompanied my every step.

They had wanted neither to listen nor believe. 'Your debt's been paid. Why come back?' they had asked. Their faces had been frightened and distorted, like polished foil torn by a meteoroid.

I had explained that this place was all a lie. No matter how long you lived, your debt would never be erased.

I had pulled the trigger to give those soaking in amniotic fluid an opportunity to accelerate their development.

'You've no clue what you're doing...' Baldy murmured breathlessly.

'And you do?'

'Some truths are best unknown, like some shackles are best unbroken. To achieve eternity by joining God is our only choice...'

'So, you were selected for the role of administrator?'

'Without an administrator, Mother Whale would be run by algorithms. My memory, just like yours, isn't so clear.'

'So you don't know how to get in touch with the company?'

'I told you before. Communications are one-way. The company has to contact us.'

'Let's imagine a rather extreme case then.' I traced the outline of his skull with the muzzle of the gun. 'Let's say of all us miners, there's just one left. Think if they received such an odd signal, it might get their attention?'

Baldy trembled. The instinct for survival always won over the instinct for loyalty, whether the instinct was inborn or acquired.

'The Recycle Protocol.'

'What?'

'In my memory module, there's a command for something called the Recycle Protocol, which lets us transmit to a relay satellite when we're at high alert. The signals will reach a secret TT&C center on Earth to then be transferred to the company. The one-way delay takes about 13.4 seconds. The company should then take any survivors back to Earth, but…'

'But what?'

'… But only when facing the threat of death can I access the memory of the command…'

I simpered, pressed the cold reinforced plastic muzzle against his sweaty scalp.

'You mean, like now?'

Baldy stabbed the sixteen-digit command into what looked like some steampunk difference engine. On the screen, an interface I'd never seen before prompted whether to initiate the Recycle Protocol.

Select 'Yes'.

The screen showed the message sent successfully. We stared coldly and began the wait.

A sound like the flapping of a moth's wings announced the return message. The clock showed precisely five minutes and forty-seven seconds had passed. Perhaps the company had already held a high-level emergency meeting to discuss counter-measures.

The other party requests a call. Select 'Yes'.

'Check, check. This is Wenchang. This is Wenchang. Please reply.'

Baldy glanced up at me, eyes filled with the same confusion. His body reacted before he realized what he was doing as he raced toward the communicator. My gun reacted faster still. To ensure an airtight cabin, we had only slow bullets, which couldn't penetrate the body. Instead they released their kinetic energy by fragmenting the bullet, doubling its pain and lethalness.

I had no time for regrets.

'Wenchang, Wenchang. This is EM-L4-D28-58a. I'm the only one left. Request recycling. Repeat, request recycling.'

'Request received. Re-enter command and grant full data privileges to assist us in situation assessment.'

As Baldy twitched in the pool of blood, he gracefully raised his two hands to signal the command's sixteen-digits.

Death's just the middleman. Math is forever.

Data, like snowflakes falling silently in a vacuum, required time. I found a corner to curl up in. I felt like an entire lifetime of strength had been squeezed out of me. Memory and pain chaotically whirled together. I didn't care how they would judge or deal with me. All I wanted was to leave this hell and get home, even if no one was waiting for me at the door.

If they refused, I would destroy myself along with our asteroid home. All I had to do was adjust the vector of the electromagnetic mass projector and Mother Whale would tear open crushing everything inside it, including all our debts and our sins. My cognitive module reminded me that *debt* and *sin* were the same words in Sanskrit, Hebrew and Aramaic.

Now, I really was the only one left.

Then, I felt a strange force dragging me down, drooping my eyelids, weakening my limbs, preventing nerve impulses from flowing smoothly. I was pulled into a dream, like those countless previous confrontations that had ended in my failure. I tried to resist the invasion, tried to listen to the gospel transmitting from hundreds of thousands of kilometers away. It was spoken by a voice vague and uncertain.

'... EM-L4-D28-58a, data assessment has been completed. We will take you home. We will...'

Darkness swallowed me again.

7.

… Wearying debt is sinful and never complete. But completeness can mean only death…

The sheepdog dragged Magpie's crippled body until it disappeared into deep space.

… Sacrifice is for all the gods, not just death. Death is just the middleman…

Covered in the dust of the shattered cabin, Freckle's helmet hung from her body by a thread, like dandelion fluff about to blow away.

… When we devote our lives to the God who created us, we commit to paying interest in the form of sacrifice. Only at the end, can our lives repay the principal…

Baldy slapped me on the shoulder. Baldy was blown away by my gun. In the low gravity, he was like a paper doll flung against the wall. A bloody mist bloomed from his chest as I thought on the young Baldy taking form in his amniotic chamber.

… Birth is the original debt, which all humans carry, the debt created by humanity's emergence in the cosmos. This debt can never be repaid on Earth, where its sum is beyond all reach…

Freckles winked at me and made an indecent gesture. Magpie, emerging from her shower, bent to wipe her calves. She winked at me without any sexual significance.

... When the sacrificial rites are performed justly, God promises a path to shed our human condition and achieve eternity. This is possible because, in the face of eternity, all debt loses meaning...

In the dream, the sequestered girl fell asleep, the picture book still in her hands. The picture frame upside down on the table displayed a line of small characters. The pink embryo rotated slowly in its chamber, eyelids twitching from time to time.

... A form of sacrifice, through supplementing the credit of living humans, makes life extension possible, and in some cases through joining in God, achieves eternity...

The girl's face behind the seal. A desperate man who intended suicide but froze in mid-air. The bodies of miners. My own body. Freckle's face. Magpie's face. The woman in black's face. The faces of all the living and the dead slowly overlapping, merging into one face.

... Human existence is a form of debt...

Names began floating to the surface, but I wasn't sure they were real. They were like my memories, fragmented and confused. Then an enormous asteroid tore through the cabin right next to me. Hot fuel fleas tunneled through my body, tearing holes that reeked of singed flesh. I leapt desperately onto the surface of the asteroid as miniature ice volcanoes erupted on its surface in spears of steam. A crack engulfed me and I tumbled into a spinning tunnel as the fabric of all things stretched into infinite distance, transformed into infinitely thin light.

I finally remembered the name, the one name, the name that should never have been forgotten.

8.

'Anan!'

I woke from the nightmare to find myself neither in the cabin nor in any part of Mother Whale I knew of.

There was a vast open room and milky white light, but the light was so evenly distributed that I couldn't locate its source. I couldn't even awaken my cognitive module to get my bearings.

I tried to move but my body was too heavy. It felt as though I could only exert a third of my strength. My every breath was strained. Then I realized what that meant. Joyful tears erupted in two raging streams.

I had finally come home.

Dr. Li, an Afro-Asian woman with a halo of dark curls, was assigned to watch over me. She equipped me with an exo-skeleton and breathing aids to help me adapt to Earth's gravity. Compared with ordinary earthlings, my limbs were too slender and weak. My skin was deathly pale. My head was a little too large. If she had painted me green, I could have easily passed for an alien.

My range of activities was limited to that one floor. Dr. Li explained I had caused a terrible storm outside and must take shelter here for a while.

The area I could access on this floor already exceeded the sum area of all cabins and passages in Mother Whale. Of course, this did not include the inner and outer surface area of the asteroid. After all, not everyone got the chance to participate in a death race on the asteroid itself. Regardless, this space was more than sufficient to meet all my needs. I even had the pleasure of sinking my teeth into some coveted *kungpao chicken*, working and sleeping according to the normal rotation cycle of the Earth. I was also able to touch real human beings, without having to worry if they were clone identities or space miners with corrupted memories.

All felt as perfect as the life of some ancient emperor except for one thing: my memory had still not been completely restored. For some unknown reason, Dr. Li said, my consciousness had cracked the blockchain encryption technology, breaking through the memory barrier, but not all the information was indexed. It was, in fact, a mess and it would take time for my brain to re-establish order.

Order. The word made my body shiver.

I had more questions than could be answered, and Dr. Li sensed the terrible urgency that surged inside me.

She smiled to comfort me. 'The storm will pass. You will meet our leader, the person who ordered you saved. Then you will get your answers.'

There was no television, no internet, no media to share outside information, and no sense of time. Perhaps the answers were all right here, folded into a wall or curled up in a corner. It felt almost as though I just needed to say a magic word or wave my hands and they would jump out in front of me.

But I didn't belong in this place. I didn't know anything about Earth these days. The skill tree of a space miner was of no use here.

Even after coming back, I was deprived of the details from my dreams. I could only remember a name or two, a few odd fragments. I couldn't access my true feelings or memories. I felt like a blind man wrapped in a plastic film, as though I could only touch the world through obstructed senses. The feeling was suffocating.

I tried to please Dr. Li, begged her to show me the outside world, just one peek. Each time, with a pitying look in her eye, she rejected me.

'It's not time for that yet. What you need now is to care for and protect yourself.'

But I never understood exactly what she meant.

Finally, I got my chance when a nurse adjusting the wall control panel was suddenly called out. I tried a few buttons. The light, color and temperature in the room adjusted smoothly. It felt as though time were suddenly passing more quickly. I pressed several more buttons until the white opaque wall in front of me suddenly turned transparent, revealing the world outside.

In shock, I stumbled backward. Outside was a vast open gray square carved into irregular shapes by black lines. In the distance were huge geometric buildings with shadows, proportions and angles that provoked a sense of instability. Between wandering beings and vast machinery, there seemed to be moving sculptures. Subtle interactions occurred according to changes in the environment.

This was not any Earth I was familiar with.

In the square, someone seemed to recognize me. He glanced up, light flickering on his forehead as if transmitting a message to me.

The crowd grew. They stood on the square with their glimmering foreheads, staring up at me. I noticed that as each new person joined the crowd, the flicker of light on their foreheads tuned to the same frequency.

Soon there was a dense mass of hundreds staring at me. Each forehead was a flickering pixel in a vast low-resolution screen. That human screen began to scroll unintelligible patterns until I was overcome by dizziness.

I pressed my palm to the transparent wall. The pattern of the crowd-light froze for a moment then transformed into another pattern, this one like an infinite spiraling sea.

Were they communicating with me?

I tested various movements and gestures. They responded but I still had no idea what they might want to express.

Just as I was about to take more drastic action, the transparent wall suddenly turned milky white again. I spun around to see Dr. Li looking at me with a sullen expression. She shook her head.

I raised my hands as if pleading, said, 'I only wanted to look outside.'

'It's already settled. In three days, the leader will meet you. Be ready.'

My heart was in a flurry, but there was none of the joy I had expected.

'Those people out there... Who are they? Why did they do that?'

Doctor Li's eyes wandered as she weighed her words. Every time she was about to make an excuse, a funny expression would appear on her face. In the end, she gave up and lowered her long thick eyelashes.

'They are the debtless, your admirers. You are their God.'

9.

The meeting did not take place in some grand hall like I had imagined. Instead, it was arranged in a plain yet elegant old bookstore called Gewu. The place had a spiral bookshelf staircase that led up into a cafe.

Exoskeletons were forbidden. I climbed the steps like a frail old man, feeling out how each muscle handled what to me was triple gravity. I felt fortunate that many of the names on the shelves were still in my mind, even without cognitive modules, they can be freely accessed.

The leader rose from the coffee table, dressed in black, with a golden chain brooch on her chest. She greeted me with a smile.

'Mr. Dong Fangjue, it's a pleasure to meet you. I'm Mei Lingyilu.'

I was stunned by her youth, drawn in by some familiar feature in her eyebrows.

'We… have met before?' I couldn't restrain my curiosity.

She tilted her head and frowned, thought a moment then smiled. 'Oh, I understand. You see in me my grandmother, Mei Li'ai.'

'Grandmother…' I was frightened by the time span that implied. 'So how many years ago would that be?'

'If the debt contract was calculated correctly, it would have been seventy-two years.'

'Seventy-two…' I took a deep breath, still a bit dizzy. She helped me sit.

'You've recovered well. I mean, you were in that place for so long…' Her tone was a perfect expression of sympathy.

'So, what is in fact going on? Who are you? Who controls all this?'

'You have many questions. Considering your memory hasn't been completely restored, I'll start with my great-grandfather, Mei Feng.'

Mei Lingyilu took a sip of coffee, wiped her lips with a paper towel, and began the story.

•

Mei Feng, my great-grandfather, established the Lifechain Group, the company where he worked tirelessly to integrate blockchain technology with biotechnology. He believed this was the only path toward achieving human immortality.

Of course, he ended up building his fortune not by selling eternal life like the alchemist Xu Fu, but by providing genetic debt technology to governments. The so-called 'genetic debt' took debt data, modularized it into blocks and embedded the blocks into the DNA chain. The technology let debt be traced in real time and protected it from tampering. The debt data could even be genetically passed to future generations. It protected against economic collapse. The debt couldn't be written off by suicide or modifying biosignatures. It allowed the greatest and most granular control of individuals' economic behaviors.

By this time, precision cloning and synthetic embryo technology were no longer a hurdle. The key was now in the transfer of consciousness. If we had to re-experience life to accumulate knowledge and language every round, it would only be regarded as intergenerational alternation, not the continuation of a true individual's life. So Mei Feng successfully developed memory storage and implantation technology. The result was a soybean-sized brain implant that could synchronize and store sensory stimulation and thought flow each second in the cloud. The implant could then be inserted into the existing hippocampal cortex to achieve seamless memory docking.

The technology triggered panic because of the possibilities it portended. It could solidify social classes, permanently enforce that ever-expanding gulf between rich and poor. Some thought it could even return our civilization to a slavery economy. After struggling against the temptation of immortality, global leaders reached the so-called Geneva Consensus, blacklisting the technology, along with large-scale biochemical and genetic weapons and atomic bombs. These technologies could no longer be used on Earth. Research and development would be subject to the most intensive scrutiny and supervision. At the same time, they didn't want to kill off the Lifechain Group. After all, they required Lifechain's genetic debt technology to maintain the economic system.

My great-grandfather was from the Chaoshan ethnic group. He often recalled how his ancestors never feared storms, were keen on gambling, and spread capital and culture across the world. Nothing could stop Chaoshan people from taking risks.

Therefore, as a benefit exchange, Lifechain Group took a big step in the scope of 'self-governance' tacitly approved by the government. On the surface, the government still maintained regulatory function, but in fact gave the Group greater freedom.

Mei Feng's investments in asteroid mining, construction of space stations, transformation of asteroids, capital and technology weren't too difficult. But the space mining companies all faced the same tricky issues with human resources. There weren't enough qualified miners. Even with investments in high-paid training, demand couldn't be met. Many businesses looked to robots, but those steel buggers required a lot of water, condensers, relays, circuits and batteries to maintain operations. Worse, they were only able to perform their more complex tasks in controlled environments.

Great-grandfather often joked that Opportunity's geological survey of Mars took twenty years to achieve what a grad student could have knocked out in a week.

It was all a big chess game.

Lifechain Group searched for qualified candidates world-wide and signed debt contracts with them through a balance of temptation and coercion. These people sold their bodies, their genes and their souls. Biological studies show that only when mind and body are perfectly in tune can human potential be maximized. Their genetic data would be transmitted to the space station, reassembled into new genetic material, split into fertilized eggs, and developed into embryos. Their memory, after a series of procedural stimulation and reproduction, would also be encrypted like debt data and transplanted back into the cerebral cortex of the clone.

It was a brutal start on the road to achieving this, covered with more corpses and blood than you can imagine.

The Group spent ten years, tens of billions of dollars in funds and undeclared numbers of victims to finally achieve the stable operation of this new extraterrestrial economic model. In addition to precious metals and rare earth deposits, an early mining site also captured metastable helium from asteroids outside the solar system, allowing for both high energy density and renewability, which triggered a revolution in energy storage methods.

There were also unexpected disturbances, mutinies, mental breakdowns, collective slaughters. In human history, such scenes had played out countless times before when opening new frontiers. To conceal such horrors, the Group developed a method to seal up memories. Through AI, it generated a kind of ideological holy book, *Treatise of Our Divine Debts*, which was embedded in every miner's cognitive module. Over the years, the *Treatise* grew in its spiritual influence and became a new religion.

The system worked so perfectly that years later, Earth had forgotten the existence of these people. The secret was known to only a very few. When Mei Feng died, my grandmother, Mei Li'ai, took over the company. She knew the huge political risks hidden in it and regarded it as the top secret of the group. By this time, the Lifechain Group had become an almost omnipotent force. Due to the Group, almost everyone was burdened with some form of debt.

When life becomes so complex and great, it also becomes extremely vulnerable. One slight misstep can mean enormous downfall.

Just like with every action you took in space, Mr. Dongfang Jue.

•

The weight of Mei Lingyilu's story was so great that my instinct was to engage my cognitive module to process. Of course, it took me a few seconds to realize I would have to digest it by myself. That would take some time.

'So we were slaves deceived into signing our own eternal deed of sale?' I was embarrassed by the heaviness of my words but could think of no others.

'Technically, everything you encountered up there was written into the contract. All was to the letter of the law.'

'But I don't understand. Why save me? Wouldn't it have made more sense for you to let me die?'

Mei Lingyilu gave a slight smile. 'If we think according to the interests of the old times, that's true. But now things are different.'

'Different how?'

'To tell the truth, we believe now is the best time to strip away that original sin.' She hesitated a moment to observe my reaction. 'As the new leader of the Lifechain Group, I wasn't aware of everything that had happened in the past. If you hadn't sent an emergency signal, it's quite possible the entire planet would never have known of these horrible acts…'

'I'm listening.'

'Thanks to your selfless dedication in space, we have been able to develop laser array launching technology, which greatly reduces the cost of entering low Earth orbit per unit load. We now also have four space elevators – in Quito, Mombasa, Riyadh and Singapore. Even space miners don't have to endure the mines for too long. We've reached a new space revolution. We are ready to truly colonize space – Mars, the asteroid belt,

Europa, into the depths of the universe. We need heroes like you to inspire our people...'

'Hero?' I sneered. 'Skip the sales pitch and get to what you came to say.'

She burst into a stiff, awkward laugh that seemed out of place in our previous conversation.

'Now, there are some people, some forces, who would like to use your experience to attack the Group. They see you as an idol, as a symbol of resistance to the entire debt system...'

'The debtless.' I knew she was referring to the crowd in the square.

'So you know?' Mei Lingyilu flashed a suspicious glance. 'They claim the genetic debt system is outdated, too inflexible and utterly immoral. They want human civilization to take on the debt and lead what they call the 'Debt Opening Up Movement'. If you've seen their people, you've seen the light flickering on their foreheads, which represents the changing total of debt each person has added to mankind.'

'Doesn't sound unreasonable.'

'For the past five thousand years, such has been the cycle of civilization. All revolutions aim to cancel debt and redistribute resources. It doesn't matter whether those debts are written on papyrus or hard drives. But such revolutions must progress step by careful step. Otherwise, like with the Roman Empire and the Carolingian Dynasty, society will regress to old systems, perhaps even collapse entirely.'

'So what do you, the famed leader, want me for?... And why do they call you leader instead of boss?'

She smiled again, and for the first time I caught the significance of her golden chain brooch. It was as though a secret key had turned deep in my memory.

'Stand on our side, Mr. Dongfang Jue. Heroes are needed to

lead us in the construction of the new system, a system that will never again enslave people into wearying debt or force them to compete for their survival. Instead, we will encourage people to create and contribute, to understand the economic system they are born into, to give thanks to others, to society, to the gods and to the universe. Let us design this system together and alleviate the old system's tyranny of interest-based debt. We will internalize costs as a natural desire rather than passing them on to others and future generations. Will you join us?'

Mei Lingyilu held out her hand in a convincing pose.

I pretended to hesitate, then burst into laughter.

'If you weren't already the leader, you'd make an amazing actor. Though perhaps these are the same thing?'

'What do you wish to say?'

'From the very start, you've known of the asteroid mine and all its dark secrets. But some truths are best unknown as some shackles are best unbroken. Wouldn't you agree, Ms. Mei Li'ai?'

Her delicate and tender expression hardened as though she were taking on a completely new personality. Perfect coldness flashed in her eyes.

'Sometimes I really must admire you. It seems any miracle can befall you. None of our top scientists could explain how your consciousness broke through the memory barrier that even our quantum computers can't crack. They say, maybe only the power of love can explain it. See how romantic you are?'

'Love?' I stared in bewilderment. The word seemed so far away from me now.

'It seems only this part of your memory has not yet been restored. But after all, it is the deepest buried, under a deadly seal. We didn't want you to meet Anan, so we applied a certain technique to your facial recognition algorithm to make you think she was a stranger every time you saw her.'

'Anan…' Blurred faces began to take shape in my mind, overlapping to create a single face.

'Yes, Anan, your daughter. You sold her data to us for your own survival. You made her a sinner of that infinite hell as well.'

Flashes from my dreams rained over me in fragments, drowning me in suffocating terror. My eyes clenched as I tried to catch my breath. It felt as though my head were splitting open. Baldy had been right. Some truths were best unknown.

'I envy Anan, to have a father like you.' I forced my eyes open. Mei Lingyilu's face – or Mei Li'ai's face rather – revealed a trace of genuine loss. 'You're willing to die for her, no matter how many times, no matter how many people you have to kill. Yet in the end, it's all empty. My father, on the other hand, moved me around like a chess piece.'

I thought on my tiny embryo in Mother Whale and the girl next door who was always like a stranger to me. The two of us were so close to each other but could never recognize each other. All this was the work of this immortal leader now in front of me and the ruthless empire of debt behind her.

'Let me pose my question one last time, Mr. Dongfang Jue. If we could bring Anan back, would you act the part of hero on behalf of the Lifechain Group?' Mei Lingyilu rose, bowed gently toward me. 'Or would you prefer to let the world know the truth behind the curtain? Your math is quite good. I'm sure you can do the calculations.'

Eyes fixed on her ageless face, I took quite some time to reach the solution.

10.

Dreaming is a strange human design.

When I was on the asteroid, I always dreamed of Earth. Now that I'm back on Earth, I dream of the low gravity darkness of that living hell I once called home. There's always some flake of the past I can't give up.

I dream of Ginger, Freckles, Magpie, Popcorn... One by one, they say goodbye to me and leap from the rotating hatch through the mouth of Mother Whale into the dark sea of stars.

They wear no protective clothing, no helmets. They float naked as though suspended in amniotic fluid. The universe is their uterus.

I too am naked, racing along the slate-gray interior of Mother Whale, chasing after them. The endless starry sky, the curved horizon, dust glittering like hallucinations. I feel as if I too am slowly disappearing. I have no need for oxygen, gravity or protection. Like a wolf lost in the wilderness on the verge of death, I connect again to the whole of the universe. Hidden forces in the body activate, senses spring completely open. I realize a part of me is not yet consolidated into the system. Raw emotions thrive unencrypted, unread by the algorithms. These are more important than perpetuating life.

I guess they'd all agree that death's freedom from debt is not so much an escape as it is a return.

I stop running. I watch them float on until they merge with the stars.

I open my eyes in a smile. Before me now are the two tombstones.

I brush away the dust, sweep spider silk from their names.

I lift a yellowing picture book from the cardboard box and set it before the tombstone on the left. On the cover of the album is a gray whale with a puppet boy, a long nose obscured by the shadow cast inside the whale's belly. The puppet is grinning as if to say—

'You see my nose growing longer?'

I hold back tears as I pull the mottled picture frame from the box. The picture inside is so damp and mildewed I can no longer make out the original image. I turn it over and set it face down on the tombstone at the right. In the corner of the frame is a twisted line of small characters that reads, 'Dad, don't be afraid.'

I nod. It's as if I am actually hearing that voice. *Dad, don't be afraid.* The words echo inside me.

They say I'm no longer who I was when I was in space. The Lifechain Group never brought back my physical body. They just transmitted my consciousness back from the cloud to the Earth to install it in a freshly manufactured body. So, the reason I can't adapt to Earth's gravity has nothing to do with my muscles, but simply the inertia of my consciousness. They say the crimes committed by EM-L4-D28-58a on the asteroid have nothing to do with me.

I try not to think about what happened on Mother Whale. When I do, it only drives me crazy.

They say, I'm a new man.

I finish my prayers, rise to leave, gently stroke my fingers along the edges of the two tombstones on my way out. I may never come back.

The debtless form a circle on the green hills outside the cemetery. They are waiting on me.

I wave. Their foreheads glimmer like clocks, like whirlpools, like songs of freedom.

For me, for Anan, for all the people of Earth.

Translated by Blake Stone-Banks

Fandom For Robots

Vina Jie-Min Prasad

Singapore

Vina burst onto the speculative fiction scene in 2017 with two powerful stories – 'A Series of Steaks' and 'Fandom For Robots' – gaining multiple award nominations between them. We reprinted 'A Series of Steaks' in *The Apex Book of World SF 4*, but my heart really belonged to the story presented here, a funny, heartfelt tale of a lonely computer and the joys of fanfiction. 'Fandom For Robots' was nominated for the Nebula, Hugo, Sturgeon and Locus Awards, and I hope you enjoy it as much as I did.

Computron feels no emotion towards the animated television show titled *Hyperdimension Warp Record* (超次元 ワープ レコード). After all, Computron does not have any emotion circuits installed, and is thus constitutionally incapable of experiencing 'excitement', 'hatred', or 'frustration'. It is completely impossible for Computron to experience emotions such as 'excitement about the seventh episode of *Hyper-Warp*', 'hatred of the anime's short episode length' or 'frustration that Friday is so far away'.

Computron checks his internal chronometer, as well as the countdown page on the streaming website. There are twenty-two hours, five minutes, forty-six seconds, and twelve milliseconds until 2 a.m. on Friday (Japanese Standard Time). Logically, he is aware that time is most likely passing at a normal rate. The Simak Robotics Museum is not within close proximity of a black hole, and there is close to no possibility that time is being dilated.

His constant checking of the chronometer to compare it with the countdown page serves no scientific purpose whatsoever.

After fifty milliseconds, Computron checks the countdown page again.

•

The Simak Robotics Museum's commemorative postcard set ($15.00 for a set of twelve) describes Computron as 'The only known sentient robot, created in 1954 by Doctor Karel Alquist to serve as a laboratory assistant. No known scientist has managed to recreate the doctor's invention. Its steel-framed box-and-claw design is characteristic of the period.' Below that, in smaller print, the postcard thanks the Alquist estate for their generous donation.

In the museum, Computron is regarded as a quaint artefact, and plays a key role in the Robotics Then and Now performance as an example of the 'Then'. After the announcer's introduction to robotics, Computron appears on stage, answers four standard queries from the audience as proof of his sentience, and steps off the stage to make way for the rest of the performance, which ends with the android-bodied automaton TETSUCHAN showcasing its ability to breakdance.

Today's queries are likely to be similar to the rest. A teenage girl waves at the announcer and receives the microphone.

'Hi, Computron. My question is… have you watched anime before?'

[Yes,] Computron vocalizes. [I have viewed the works of the renowned actress Anna May Wong. Doctor Alquist enjoyed her movies as a child.]

'Oh, um, not that,' the girl continues. 'I meant Japanese animation. Have you ever watched this show called *Hyperdimension Warp Record*?'

[I have not.]

'Oh, okay, I was just thinking that you really looked like one of the characters. But since you haven't, maybe you could give *HyperWarp* a shot! It's really good, you might like it! There are six episodes out so far, and you can watch it on—'

The announcer cuts the girl off, and hands the microphone over to the next querent, who has a question about Doctor Alquist's research. After answering two more standard queries, Computron returns to his storage room to answer his electronic mail, which consists of queries from elementary school students. He picks up two metal styluses, one in each of his grasping claws, and begins tapping them on the computing unit's keyboard, one key at a time. Computron explains the difference between a robot and an android to four students, and provides the fifth student with a hyperlink to Daniel Clement Dennett III's writings on consciousness.

As Computron readies himself to enter sleep mode, he recalls the teenage girl's request that he 'give *HyperWarp* a shot'. It is only logical to research the Japanese animation, *Hyperdimension Warp Record*, in order to address queries from future visitors. The title, when entered into a search engine on the World Wide Web, produces about 957,000 results (0.27 seconds).

Computron manoeuvres the mouse pointer to the third hyperlink, which offers to let him 'watch Hyperdimension Warp Record FULL episodes streaming online high quality'. From the still image behind the prominent 'play' button, the grey boxy figure standing beside the large-eyed, blue-haired human does bear an extremely slight resemblance to Computron's design. It is only logical to press the 'play' button on the first episode, in order to familiarize himself with recent discourse about robots in popular culture.

The series' six episodes are each approximately twenty-five

minutes long. Between watching the series, viewing the online bulletin boards, and perusing the extensively footnoted fan encyclopedia, Computron does not enter sleep mode for ten hours, thirty-six minutes, two seconds, and twenty milliseconds.

•

Hyperdimension Warp Record (超次元 ワープ レコード Chō-jigen Wāpu Rekōdo, literal translation: '*Super Dimensional Warp Record*') is a Japanese anime series set in space in the far future. The protagonist, Ellison, is an escapee from a supposedly inescapable galactic prison. Joined by a fellow escapee, Cyro (short for Cybernetic Robot), the two make their way across the galaxy to seek revenge. The targets of their revenge are the Seven Sabers of Paradise, who have stolen the hyperdimensional warp unit from Cyro's creator and caused the death of Ellison's entire family.

Episode seven of *HyperWarp* comes with the revelation that the Second Saber, Ellison's identical twin, had murdered their parents before faking her own death. After Cyro and Ellison return to the *Kosmogram*, the last segment of the episode unfolds without dialogue. There is a slow pan across the spaceship's control area, revealing that Ellison has indulged in the human pastime known as 'crying' before falling asleep in the captain's chair. His chest binder is stained with blood from the wound on his collarbone. Cyro reaches over, gently using his grabbing claw to loosen Ellison's binder, and drapes a blanket over him. An instrumental version of the end theme plays as Cyro gets up from his seat, making his way to the recharging bay at the back of the ship. From the way his footfalls are animated, it is clear that Cyro is trying his best to avoid making any noise as he walks.

The credits play over a zoomed-out shot of the *Kosmogram*

making its way to the next exoplanet, a tiny pinpoint of bright blue in the vast blackness of space.

The preview for the next episode seems to indicate that the episode will focus on the Sabers' initial attempt to activate the hyperdimensional warp unit. There is no mention of Cyro or Ellison at all.

During the wait for episode eight, Computron discovers a concept called 'fanfiction'.

•

While 'fanfiction' is meant to consist of 'fan-written stories about characters or settings from an original work of fiction', Computron observes that much of the *HyperWarp* fanfiction bears no resemblance to the actual characters or setting. For instance, the series that claims to be a 'spin-off focusing on Powerful!Cyro' seems to involve Cyro installing many large-calibre guns onto his frame and joining the Space Marines, which does not seem relevant to his quest for revenge or the retrieval of the hyperdimensional warp unit. Similarly, the 'high school fic' in which Cyro and Ellison study at Hyperdimension High fails to acknowledge the fact that formal education is reserved for the elite class in the *HyperWarp* universe.

Most of the fanfiction set within the actual series seems particularly inaccurate. The most recent offender is EllisonsWife's 'Rosemary for Remembrance', which fails to acknowledge the fact that Cyro does not have human facial features, and thus cannot 'touch his nose against Ellison's hair, breathing in the scent of sandalwood, rosemary and something uniquely him' before 'kissing Ellison passionately, needily, hungrily, his tongue slipping into Ellison's mouth'.

Computron readies his styluses and moves the cursor down to the comment box, prepared to leave anonymous 'constructive criticism' for EllisonsWife, when he detects a comment with relevant keywords.

bjornruffian:
Okay, I've noticed this in several of your fics and I was trying not to be too harsh, but when it got to the kissing scene I couldn't take it anymore. Cyro can't touch his nose against anything, because he doesn't have a nose! Cyro can't slip his tongue into anyone's mouth, because he doesn't have a tongue! Were we even watching the same series?? Did you skip all the parts where Cyro is a metal robot with a cube-shaped head?!

EllisonsWife:
Who are you, the fandom police?? I'm basing Cyro's design on this piece of fanart (link here) because it looks better than a freakin metal box!! Anyway, I put DON'T LIKE DON'T READ in the author's notes!!! If you hate the way I write them so much, why don't you just write your own????

Computron is incapable of feeling hatred for anything, as that would require Doctor Alquist to have installed emotion circuits during his creation.

However, due to Computron's above-average procedural knowledge, he is capable of following the directions to create an account on fanficarchive.org.

... and Ellison manoeuvred his flesh hands in a claw-like motion, locking them with Cyro's own grasping claws. His soft human body pressed against the hard lines of Cyro's proprietary alloy in a manner which would have generated wear and tear had Cyro's body not been of superior make. Fluids leaked from Ellison's eyes. No fluids leaked from Cyro's ocular units, but…

Comments (3)

DontGotRhythm:
What the hell? Have you ever met a human? This reads like an alien wrote it.

tattered_freedom_wings:
uhhh this is kinda weird but i think i liked it?? not sure about the box thing though

bjornruffian:
OH MY GODDDD. :DDDD Finally, someone who doesn't write human-shaped robot-in-name-only Cyro! Some of Ellison's characterization is a little awkward – I don't think he would say all that mushy stuff about Cyro's beautiful boxy shape?? – but I love your Cyro! If this is just your first fic, I can't wait for you to write more!!

•

Computron has been spending less time in sleep mode after Episode Thirteen's cliffhanger, and has spent his time conducting objective discussions about *HyperWarp*'s appeal with commenters on various video streaming sites and anonymous message boards.

As he is about to reply to the latest missive about his lack of genitalia and outside social activities, which is technically correct, his internal chronometer indicates that it is time for the Robotics Then and Now performance.

'So, I was wondering, have you ever watched *Hyperdimension Warp Record*? There's this character called Cyro that—'

[Yes, I am aware of *HyperWarp*,] Computron says. [I have taken the 'How To Tell If Your Life Is *HyperWarp*' quiz online, and it has indicated that I am 'a Hyper-Big *HyperWarp* Fan!'. I have repeatedly viewed the scene between Ellison and Cyro at the end of Episode Seven, and recently I have left a 'like' on bjornruffian's artwork of what may have happened shortly after that scene, due to its exceptional accuracy. The show is widely regarded as 'this season's sleeper hit' and has met with approval from a statistically significant number of critics. If other members of the audience wish to view this series, there are thirteen episodes out so far, and they can be viewed on—] The announcer motions to him, using the same gesture she uses when audience members are taking too long to talk. Computron falls silent until the announcer chooses the next question, which is also the last due to time constraints.

After TETSUCHAN has finished its breakdance and show-cased its newly-programmed ability to pop-and-lock, the announcer speaks to Computron backstage. She requests that he take less time for the question-and-answer segment in the future.

[Understood,] Computron says, and returns to his storage room to check his inbox again.

Private Message from bjornruffian:

Hi RobotFan,
I noticed you liked my art (thanks!) and you seem to know a
LOT about robots judging from your fic (and, well, your name).
I'm doing a fancomic about Ellison and Cyro being stranded
on one of the desert-ish exoplanets while they try to fix the
Kosmogram, but I want to make sure I'm drawing Cyro's

body right. Are there any references you can recommend for someone who's looking to learn more about robots? Like, the classic kind, not the android kind? It'd be great if they're available online, especially if they have pictures – I've found some books with photos but they're WAAAAY more than I can afford :\\\

Thank you for any help you can offer! I'm really looking forward to your next fic!

Shortly after reading bjornruffian's message, Computron visits the Early Robotics section of the museum. It has shrunk significantly over the years, particularly after the creation of the 'Redefining Human', 'Androids of the Future', and 'Drone Zone' sections. It consists of several information panels, a small collection of tin toys, and the remnants of all three versions of Hexode the robot.

In Episode Fourteen of *Hyperdimension Warp Record*, Cyro visits a deserted exoplanet alone to investigate the history of the hyperdimension warp drive, and finds himself surrounded by the deactivated bodies of robots of similar make, claws outstretched, being slowly ground down by the gears of a gigantic machine. The 'Robot Recycler' scene is frequently listed as one of that year's top ten most shocking moments in anime.

On 7 June 1957, the third version of Hexode fails Doctor Alquist's mirror test for the hundredth time, proving that it has no measurable self-awareness. Computron watches Doctor Alquist smash the spanner against Hexode's face, crumpling its nose and lips. Oil leaks from its ocular units as it falls to the floor with a metallic thud. Its vocal synthesizer crackles and hisses.

'You godforsaken tin bucket,' Doctor Alquist shouts. 'To hell with you.' If Doctor Alquist were to raise the spanner to

Computron, it is likely that Doctor Alquist will not have an assistant for any future robotics experiments. Computron stays still, standing in front of the mirror, silently observing the destruction of Hexode so he can gather up its parts later.

When Computron photographs Hexode's display case, he is careful to avoid capturing any part of himself in the reflection.

[bjornruffian] Oh man, thank you SO MUCH for installing chat just for this! Anyway, I really appreciate your help with the script so far (I think we can call it a collab by this point?). And thanks for the exhibit photos! Was it a lot of trouble? I checked the website and that museum is pretty much in the middle of nowhere...

– File Transfer of 'THANK YOU ROBOTFAN.png' from 'bjornruffian' started.

– File Transfer of 'THANK YOU ROBOTFAN.png' from 'bjornruffian' finished.

[bjornruffian] So I've got a few questions about page 8 in the folder I shared, can you take a look at the second panel from the top? I figured his joint would be all gummed up by the sand, so I thought I'd try to do an X-ray view thing as a closeup... If you have any idea how the circuits are supposed to be, could you double-check?

[bjornruffian] Okay, you're taking really long to type, this is making me super nervous I did everything wrong :\\

[RobotFan] Apologies

[RobotFan] I

[RobotFan] Am not fast at typing

[bjornruffian] Okaaay, I'll wait on the expert here

[RobotFan] The circuit is connected incorrectly and the joint mechanism is incorrect as well

[bjornruffian] Ughhhhh I knew it was wrong!! DDD:

[bjornruffian] I wish the character sheets came with schematics or something. I've paused the flashback scenes with all the failed robots like ten billion times to take screenshots >:\\\\

[RobotFan] Besides the scenes in Episode 14, there are other shots of Cyro's schematics in Episode 5 (17:40:18 and 20:13:50) as well as Episode 12 (08:23:14)

– File Transfer of 'schematic-screenshots.zip' from 'RobotFan' started.

– File Transfer of 'schematic-screenshots.zip' from 'RobotFan' finished.

[bjornruffian] THANK YOU

[bjornruffian] I swear you're some sort of angel or something

[RobotFan] That is incorrect

[RobotFan] I am merely a robot

•

There are certain things in the museum's storage room that would benefit bjornruffian's mission of completing her Cyro/Ellison comic. Computron and Hexode's schematics are part of the Alquist Collection, which is not a priority for the museum's digitization project due to a perceived lack of value. As part of the Alquist Collection himself, there should be no objection to Computron retrieving the schematics.

As Computron grasps the doorknob with his left claw, he catches a glimpse of Cyro from Episode Fifteen in the door's glass panels, his ocular units blazing yellow with determination after overcoming his past. In fan parlance, this is known as Determined!Cyro, and has only been seen during fight scenes thus far. It is illogical to have Determined!Cyro appear in this context, or in this location.

Computron looks at the dusty glass again, and sees only a reflection of his face.

[RobotFan] I have a large file to send to you

[RobotFan] To be precise, four large files

[RobotFan] The remaining three will be digitized and sent at a later date

– File Transfer of 'alquist-archive-scans-pt1.zip' from 'RobotFan' started.

– File Transfer of 'alquist-archive-scans-pt1.zip' from 'RobotFan' finished.

[bjornruffian] OMG THIS IS AWESOME

[bjornruffian] Where did you get this?? Did you rob that museum?? This is PERFECT for that other Cyro/Ellison thing I've been thinking about doing after this stupid desert comic is over!!

[bjornruffian] It would be great if I had someone to help me with writing Cyro, HINT HINT

[RobotFan] I would be happy to assist if I had emotion circuits

[RobotFan] However, my lack of emotion circuits means I cannot be 'happy' about performing any actions

[RobotFan] Nonetheless, I will assist

[RobotFan] To make this an equitable trade as is common in human custom, you may also provide your opinion on some recurrent bugs that readers have reported in my characterization of Ellison

[bjornruffian] YESSSSSSSS :DDDDDD

•

Rossum, Sulla. 'Tin Men and Tin Toys: Examining Real and Fictional Robots from the 1950s.' *Journal of Robotics Studies* 8.2 (2018): 25–38.

While the figure of the fictional robot embodies timeless fears of technology and its potential for harm, the physical design of robots real and fictional is often linked to visual cues of modernity. What was once regarded as an 'object of the future' can become 'overwhelmingly obsolete' within a span of a few years, after advances in technology cause the visual cues of modernity to change (Bloch, 1979). The clawed, lumbering tin-toy-esque designs of the 1950s are now widely regarded as 'tin can[s] that should have been recycled long ago' (Williamson, 2017). Notably, most modern critiques of Computron's design tend to focus on its obsolete analogue dials...

watch-free-anime | Hyperdimension Warp Record | Episode 23 | Live Chat

Pyro: Okay, is it just me, or is Cyro starting to get REALLY attractive? I swear I'm not gay (is it gay if it's a robot) but when he slung Ellison over his shoulder and used his claw to block the Sixth Saber at the same time

Pyro: HOLY SHIT that sniper scene RIGHT THROUGH THE SCOPE and then he fucking BUMPS ELLISON'S FIST WITH HIS CLAW

Pyro: Fuck it, I'm gay for Cyro I don't care, I'll fucking twiddle his dials all he wants after this episode

ckwizard: dude youre late, weve been finding cyro hot ever since that scene in episode 15

ckwizard: you know the one

ckwizard: where you just see this rectangular blocky shadow lumbering slowly towards first saber with those clunky sound effects

ckwizard: then his eyebulbs glint that really bright yellow and he bleeps about ACTIVATING KILL MODE and his grabby claws start whirring

ckwizard: theres a really good fic about it on fanficarchive… actually you might as well check the authors blog out here, hes pretty cyro-obsessed

ckwizard: his earlier stuff is kinda uneven but the bjorn collabs are good – shes been illustrating his stuff for a while

Pyro: Okay

Pyro: I just looked at that thing, you know, the desert planet comic

Pyro: I think I ship it

Pyro: OH MAN when Ellison tries the manual repair on the arm joint and Cyro has a FLASHBACK TO THE ROBOT RECYCLER but tries to remind himself he can trust him

Pyro: Fuck it I DEFINITELY ship it

ckwizard: join the fucking club

ckwizard: its the fifth time im watching this episode, this series has ruined my life

ckwizard: i can't wait for season 2

bjorn-robot-collabs posted:

Hi everyone, bjornruffian and RobotFan here! Thanks for all your comments on our first comic collab! We're really charmed by the great reception to 'In the Desert Sun' – okay, I'm charmed, and RobotFan says he would be charmed if he had the emotion circuits for that (he's an awesome roleplay partner too! LOVE his sense of humor :DDD).

ANYWAY! It turns out that RobotFan's got this awesome collection of retro robot schematics and he's willing to share, for those of you who want to write about old-school robots or need some references for your art! (HINT HINT: the fandom totally needs more Cyro and Cyro/Ellison before Season 2 hits!) To be honest I'm not sure how legal it is to circulate these scans (RobotFan says it's fine though), so just reply to this post if you want them and we'll private message you the links if you promise not to spread them around.

Also, we're gonna do another Cyro/Ellison comic in the future, and we're thinking of making it part of an anthology. If you'd like to contribute comics or illustrations for that, let us know!

Get ready to draw *lots* of boxes, people! The robot revolution is coming!

9,890 replies

Virtual Snapshots

Tlotlo Tsamaase

Botswana

Quietly and without much fanfare, Tlotlo Tsamaase has been publishing exceptional short stories in some of the top SF magazines, and drew my eye almost immediately. She is most recently the author of the exceptional *The Silence of the Wilting Skin*, her first novella in book form, and I can't wait to see what she does next. Here, she turns her poetic attentions on a near-future Africa of climate and digital change.

Thirteen years ago when I was three years old, the sky used to be a clean blue, curving outward to meet the horizon. The sun was a bright burning spot and the stars candles in the night. Men's hearts weren't oiled in evil. The shift from day to darkness was seamless, dividing activities. It hadn't rained for so long that all the water stored for the Harvest, as the time was called, was insufficient. Our villages survived on an Aquaculture system, tending to the water-creatures to cultivate the food we needed. The dome had been created to protect us from the destructive environment we had orchestrated. It was a righting time.

The day it rained, we were shaken. The sound of a bomb exploded above us. First we thought the sun was dying, sending flames to torch our world. But the dome had shattered. Instead of shards of glass, soft drops of water soaked the cracked earth and moistened our bare feet. We screamed, '*Pula! Pula!*' The children ran into the heavy drizzle, mouths open to the sky.

I remember that first taste of rain: exotic, addictive. Dangerous. We didn't know what we were drinking then. We were delighted: old women ululated whilst sweeping the ground with Setswana brooms. The paranoid ones got their metal bathtubs out to collect this last hope of survival.

It was the transformation from the old world to DigiWorld.

(I)

Now:

It has been seven hundred and thirty days since I left the house.

Two years.

Well, physically.

Our joints are painful due to immobility. No praying in the mosque, legs dusted by a beg for God. A god composed of zeros and ones, face etched in lines of lightning, the moon his nose, an impression of cloud in sky.

Our physical selves are latched to glass pistons by way of plastic tubes feeding medicine into our narrow veins. Machines beep our lives across limbs of time. We sleep in dark home-cells, little bulbs lighting our prison, and sweep through the door in our avatar versions.

These are things we are told to remain in safety's skin. Abide the laws. If you wake, do not detach yourself. If you pain, do not bend to relief. If you itch, do not scratch. In us, our souls are halos, waning, flickering – the light gone.

I can't remember the last time my skin was brown. Outside DigiWorld, it is expensive to maintain our health, which is why when we partially disconnect we must pay fees to keep us breathing.

But today I must leave. A message had slipped into my visual settings:

Older sister: *Hela wena*! Mama is unwell. Get here now. Outside DigiWorld, you know she ain't connected.

Me: The minute I step out of this door, I will need funds to sustain me in the environment outside of my house.

Older sister: Chill, *sisi wame*, we will compensate you for your travels and your life. You are still family, *mos*.

Pfft. Family, *se voet!* They kicked me out and never kept in touch. I've been living in a servants' quarter for years.

If I hide behind these walls I won't see the thing they talk about: Mama's pregnancy. It could be her death. I will regret my life if I don't see her.

(II)

I have a few financial units that will last me on my journey. I push open the door. Stars fall in streams of light, soft as rain. Slate-blue eyes mock the beauty of the sky.

Botswana. I don't want to denote it the common cliché term 'hot and arid' because I hate to be another stereotype of limited description. It's landlocked. It's suffocated. It's variety. It reminds me of the ocean, not in the literal sense, nor rather the freedom eloquence, but like the ocean it has borderlines you can't see. We understand technology. We sit at computers and understand what we type. Our cars are not donkey carts. Our houses have corners, and we don't have lions or animals of the wild parading the city centre, but some men are more beast than human.

The rank is a chortling beast, fattening out into the city. A vendor scrambles to me, holding rotten goods to my face. 'You want, *sisi*?'

A rumbling, croaking noise alarms the state constituents to awake. Sun alarm. The sun creaks. Creaking, creaking, creaking – machinery screws, pipes twist, grinded by laborious mine-worker hands. Sunrise, sunsets beg to be heard.

Why were my sunlight rations depleted? Hadn't I been in line yesterday to escape the rise in sunlight prices, effective today?

I'm close to my mother's residence, a place of warmth. A place I was thrown out from because I had reached the age of independency – because I was not from her womb. I had to fend for myself, a pariah unfit for their royal homestead.

(III)

My mother is an anomaly in this society. She's one of those rare women who hold babies in their bodies instead of storing the to-be-born children in the Born Structure that sits in the centre of the city, its apex a dagger to the sky. The Born Structure processes who'll be born and who'll die. It's how I was born, shaped by glass and steel. Unlike others, the lucky ones, I've never felt Mama's heartbeat close to my face.

My sister swore to me that Mama's current baby will last in the womb forever. '*Sisi*, I swear – *nxu s'tru* – that baby is not coming out,' she'd said a few months ago, in her oft-confident tone.

I'd grazed passed her, muttering, '*Mxm*, liar.'

'Come on, you're only jealous that you didn't get the chance to *bloma* in Mama's womb,' she'd said. 'You know I'm right, just admit it.'

So I'd kicked her in the shin and ran.

She'd pointed a finger like she was bewitching me: 'Jealous one,' she'd swore. That was the last time I saw her.

Mama has been pregnant for a year this time. Water is her church. Baptismal if you think about it – crawling back to God.

I enter our horseshoe-shaped settlement, bypassing the compounds into our own made of concrete and sweat and technology no one knows.

'*Dumelang*!' the family members shout in greeting.

I used to think that before I was born, Mama and Papa probably spat fire on my skin and rubbed warm-beige of fine sandy-desert soil to give it colour, and in particular hand gestures added dung-shit – for I'm not pure – to drive away malevolent spirits, insect-demons.

But I am not born. I am a manufacture of the Born Structure.

'Jealous one,' *sisi* greets me, guarding the doorway. 'Howzit?'

'S'cool,' I whisper. 'Where's Mama?'

'*Hae*, she can't see you now. Just put your gifts by the fire.'

I don't move.

'*Ao*, problem?' she asks.

'*Yazi*, it took me my last units – the last money I have – to get here, and you won't let me see her,' I say through gritted teeth.

'*Haebo!* It's not my fault you're some broke-ass—'

I pull at my earlobes to tune her out. This means I am not allowed to stay the night here. My presence will jinx Mama's condition.

'Can you at least loan me some cash?' I ask. 'I don't have enough to sustain me when I get home. Leaving home and disconnecting activated my spending. You *know*, there is no deactivation.'

Her smile tells me it was the plan all along. 'Then you'll be prepared for death. Your reputation dilutes our family name's power. You understand why you must leave.'

I don't understand how a sister I grew up playing games with hates me that much. I don't know when she disowned me – when she stopped thinking of me as a sibling to look up to. Is it just because I'm not her biological sister? That I'm a bastard shame in the family.

'Leave, as in… forever?'

I can't run to anywhere. I don't know how.

(IV)

When I leave, Mama is still too unwell to see anyone besides my older sister, the gifted one who lived in her womb for nine months. *Mxm.*

So, *sisi* stands by the door, waving, with a huge grin plastered to her face. '*Hamba*, jealous one.'

The moonlight bleaches the village into a shockingly ghostly white. Air eases out from my lungs. My oxygen levels are slowly depleting. My sky is dead, but the blue ceiling is a magnet. Our thoughts, words and feelings evaporate from our minds like torn birds pulled by that magnetic force, and they light up the sky.

Our stars are composed of ourselves.

Maybe, tonight when Mama looks at the night sky she'll see me watching her.

On the way home I pass through a nearby village. In one house with the green corrugated roof, three women sit in the sitting room, their soles bruised with black marks.

'*Heh Mma-Sekai*,' shouts one. 'I tell you, a child born with one leg that's similar to the father's and the other leg that's similar to another man's won't walk. S'tru.' True. The woman crosses her fingers, a sign to God. 'Sethunya's child hasn't walked for years.

I'm not surprised. Woman sleeps around. You don't believe? These things happen, *sisi*.'

'Ah, don't say.' One claps her manicured hands. 'Surely, they can download software to update the child's biological software,' the other says.

Twins – one an albino with pinkish-copper brown hair – and one pulls a younger girl from the sitting room onto the *stoep*.

'Hae! If I see you jumping the fence again, you will know me!' shouts their mother as their shoulders shrink. She gapes when she notices me. I am the child with legs from different men. I raise the middle finger. When will everyone stop gossiping about my family? So we aren't rich enough to buy all these gadgets to change our body size, our ethnicity, our hair – but we're poor enough to know true happiness is not bought. We're also poor enough to throw out one of our children because she wasn't born naturally. We're poor to not even care about that child, about the years that crawled into her sad heart because her father was an illicit man.

'*Shem*, and she's still so young,' one woman whispers.

'*Kodwa*, would it make it right if I was old enough to take in this crap?' I want to ask, but I keep walking with my head folded into my chest.

The sky tenses, pisses, a hiss of warm. Air humid-empty. My lips press tight to my wrist to check the moisture. My water levels are too low. Low tear supply. There's only a few hours before the sun temporarily dies. Before I die too.

(V)

When I get home, the skin needs a scrub. But I let my scents accumulate so I won't forget the skin I wear. So I remember the mother who used to cradle me and sing lullabies. I will miss her.

Just when the sunlight begins to turn gold, the rain obscures the night-sky eyes into an eerie greyness. When my grandmother was still alive I used to ask her, '*Nkuku*, does the sky hurt and bleed like humans?'

She looked up from her knitted blanket. Wrinkles laced the contours of her face like rippled water. 'The sky is the predator. All animals are humans but some humans are inanimate,' she said. She was the only one in our family who loved me.

(VI)

I wake to noise blaring in my mind. How many megabytes of memory space will be depleted just to contact those bloody, poor-serviced customer lines?

Very well, psychomail it is:

#file report 22

Thought number #53897

Subject complaint: Skin malfunction; does not detect sun.
Pre-requisite water levels contained in lungs reaching 53%.

Sent! Please hold for the next available customer advisor. All networks are busy. In case of emergency, please hold on to the nearest human for self-powering, explaining clearly your predicament to avoid violence and he/she shall be compensated within 7 days. Solar Power Corporations appreciates your patience. Goodbye.

A second is not long enough to send a message to Mama, to

tell her, despite what's happened, I still love them all – my family. That is the only regret I have: no one to say 'I love you' to. No one to breathe my soul into. I cling to desperation halfway out the door as if a miracle will split the skies and save me. My neighbour half-waves from her *stoep* until she realizes what's happening. Her tear is the last grace I feel.

It is too late to remain alive.

In three seconds I am dead.

What the Dead Man Said

Chinelo Onwualu

Nigeria

Chinelo is the co-founder of *Omenana*, the ground-breaking magazine of African speculative fiction. She is the former spokesperson for the African Speculative Fiction Society. She edits, publishes, writes and is practically a force of nature. 'What The Dead Man Said' is one of my favourite stories of hers, a painful, honest, clear-eyed portrayal of family scars.

I suppose you could say that it started with the storm.

I hadn't seen one like it in thirty years. Not since I moved to Tkaronto, in the Northern Indigenous Zone of Turtle Island – what settler-colonialists still insisted on calling North America. I'd forgotten its raw power: angry thunderclouds that blot out the sun, taking you from noon to evening in an instant, then the water that comes down like fury – like the sky itself wants to hurt you.

As I sat in the empty passenger terminal of the Niger River Harbourfront waiting for the bus, I watched as rain streaked the cobbled walkways in silver, sluicing through the narrow depressions between the solar roadway and the gutter. The ferry was long gone, moving up the river into the heart of Igboland, leaving me stranded in an alien world.

A holographic advertisement for some sort of fertility treatment played out on a viewscreen across the street. It was distorted by the haze of rain, but I made out a plump, impossibly happy woman in a crisp red gele – her skin glowing in the golden light of a computer-generated sun – clutching a newborn baby and dancing toward a household shrine. She was surrounded by celebrating family members, but she stopped before a regal older couple to whom she presented the child. The old man took the child with a benevolent smile, while the woman stretched her hand toward the young mother, who was now kneeling before them, in a benediction. The ad ended with a close-up of the beaming mother and the logo of the fertility treatment company in the corner. I turned away before my ocular implants could sync with the ad's soundtrack, but I'd already caught the tagline: 'Keep New Biafra Alive.'

My A.I. announced that the bus had arrived. Its interface had switched to Igbo as soon as I passed from Nigeria™ into New Biafra, as neither English nor Anishinaabe were recognized languages here. I hadn't spoken Igbo in decades, but its musicality returned to me with smooth familiarity – as if it had simply been waiting for its turn in the spotlight. I ignored the ping; I wanted to watch the rain a little longer. Perhaps it would somehow wash this reality away and I could return to the quiet life I'd built for myself on the other side of the Atlantic.

You can't put it off forever.

I frowned, then sighed. The dead man was right. This was like getting a body mod. You'd be a brand-new person when it was over, but in the meantime it was going to hurt like hell. I put up the hood of my hi-dri, shouldered my backpack, and stepped out into the storm.

•

It really started with the notification two days ago. My father had passed on – as they used to say – but that wasn't real. At least not yet.

What was real was me here in Onitsha, my hometown. Even though I'd spent my childhood wandering this city's narrow red streets, as I slumped in the passenger well of the automated minibus, it struck me how foreign the place now seemed. How had I forgotten how compact everything was, as if it had been built to accommodate a mass of people long gone? My grandparents told me that over a century ago, more than half a million people had packed into these pristine streets. Now, it wasn't even half that.

The minibus glided along Niger Avenue, stopping occasionally to let passengers off or allow pedestrians to cross the road. As we passed Fegge, I caught sight of the neighborhood's ancient cement family quarters, squat-shouldered and tin-roofed, hulking next to each other like sullen children. Crossing from Main Market, with its workshops and retail outlets, into the quiet residential lanes of American Quarters, I spied children in neat uniforms walking hand-in-hand to their various apprenticeships. Children were rare enough in Tkaronto, and those few who could afford to give birth preferred to cluster in tower communities that would protect their precious progeny from the vicissitudes of life. Apart from major celebrations like Emancipation Day, seeing children in public was unheard of.

Throughout the trip, the lights of the historic Niger Bridge blinked on the horizon. I would have liked to go walking across it like any other tourist, streaming photos of the mighty river for my feed back West. But I'd only packed a change of clothes and some toiletries. The burial rites would begin this evening with the wake-keeping and end on the evening of the next day, after the celebratory second funeral. I had no plans of staying past then.

It could be argued that without the Catastrophe, that fraught period between the 2020s and the 2060s that scorched half the world and drowned the rest, New Biafra could never have been born. At the turn of the twenty-second century, as people all over were still fleeing inland to escape the rising seas, a group of Igbo separatists took the opportunity to declare their independence from the crumbling colonial creation of Nigeria. The new state called for the return of all its children in diaspora, and my grandparents – engineers eking out a living on the shores of Old New York – were among the thousands who moved to regional cities like Onitsha, Nnewi, Awka, and Aba to answer the call.

We called it the Great Return. Anyone who could prove Igbo ancestry was granted automatic citizenship. Those with coveted skills – geneticists, engineers, and biologists – were given homes, business grants, and lucrative government posts. My grandparents and their generation cleared out the derelict infrastructure of New Biafra's empty suburbs and towns to make way for the forest lands that now covered nearly 80 percent of the country. They reseeded those forests with bio-engineered plants and wildlife, then built the massive monorail system that connects all our cities to bypass the pristine forests below. But they'd neglected one thing: While they were busy creating our new homeland, they forgot to also raise the massive families that would be needed to keep it solvent and thriving.

As they grew feeble, the burden of caring for them and maintaining the world they'd built fell to us. My agemates, those I kept in touch with after I moved, tell me I was lucky to get out when I did. Leaving New Biafra when I was only twelve meant that I was too young to be tied down by the weight of its social obligations. They complained of having to work long hours to preserve family businesses passed down by aging parents and grandparents. They spoke wistfully of the massive payouts the government awarded to those who could birth three or more children, but few of them could carve out the time needed to cultivate such large families. Though my own life – a spacious apartment in the hills of Highland Crescent, an easygoing art research consultancy – was very different from theirs, I'm not sure I did escape. One cannot cut the invisible threads of familial indebtedness by simply running off to a distant land.

My father certainly fulfilled his filial duty. He became a ranger, protecting the bio-engineered species his parents had introduced in the forests they'd prepared. As his only child, I should have done the same. I'd always liked working with the soil, so it was expected that I would go into agroecology and grow the food that would feed our people. But after what happened with my uncle... I shook my head to ward off the memory.

As the bus pulled up in front of the family home at 142 Old Hospital Rd., I came out of my reverie and noticed that the rain had stopped. The house hadn't changed since I'd last seen it three decades ago. Hell, it probably hadn't changed in the 200 years since it had been built in the 1920s.

It was a U-shaped complex with a central bungalow flanked by two-story apartments, one on either side. An open courtyard carpeted with moss grass, fruit trees, and wildflowers filled the space between them. My grandparents had reinforced its walls with permacrete and upgraded its interior to twenty-second-century standards, but that's where the improvements ended. After they died, the house went to my father, who'd never had much interest in technology. In the twenty years he'd lived there, he'd done nothing more than charge its batteries and replace burned-out solar cells.

Traditionally, the oldest members of the family would occupy the bungalow while their children and extended family members crammed into the two warrens of flats. If we'd restricted the apartments to blood family only, as some still did, those buildings would have stood empty. These days relatives were defined less by who'd slept with whom, and more by whose interests and personalities meshed best. I recalled the boisterous couples and polycules who'd lived in the building when I was young – all of them my cousins and uncles and aunties even though we had only marginal blood relationships to each other.

The compound was abuzz with people. Someone had set up a canopy in one corner of the open field where my friends and I had played virtual sports as children. From somewhere in the back the delicate smell of Aba rice and goat stew wafted out, making my mouth water. The building's families had spared no expense for this event. I tried to slip in quietly, but I was immediately spotted.

'Azuka! Is that you?' screamed a voice from somewhere in the crowd. It was Auntie Chio, a close friend of my grandmother who'd lived in the building for as long as I could remember. I'd been best friends with her two granddaughters, both of whom now lived in the Eko Atlantic megacity. She was one of the few adults who'd kept in touch with me after my mother and I moved to Turtle Island.

I spotted her lithe frame dressed in her usual motley of clashing ankara fabrics as she swept out from the main bungalow. Her unlined face spoke nothing of her nearly ninety years, and before I knew it I was surrounded in her crushing embrace.

I smiled wanly. 'Good evening, auntie.'

'*Ah-ah*, when did you come?' She held me at arm's length, taking me in from head to toe, her eagle-eyed gaze missing nothing.

'Just now. I had to finish some work before I could travel.'

She nodded and gave me a look that was skeptical but sympathetic. She opened her mouth to say more, but her cry had attracted others and soon I was surrounded by people.

'Azu-nne, welcome! See how big you've grown, eh! So tall!'

'Come, you don't remember me, do you? You were so small when last I saw you.'

'My condolences, my dear. It is well with you.'

I tried to respond to each comment and query with as many smiles and few words as possible, and soon I was ushered into the main house. It wasn't until later that I realized one thing in the compound had changed: The small guardhouse that used to sit just inside the front gate was gone.

•

That evening at the wake-keeping, Auntie Chio and I sat in the living room next to the biodegradable pod where my father's body lay, its feet facing the entryway. Earlier, she'd welcomed the community into the home as tradition dictated, presenting kola nuts and palm wine as an offering to the household gods. Another of my elder aunts – I forget how we're related – led the prayers, pouring libation to beckon the ancestral spirits into our home and escort my father's spirit to the land of the dead.

This was the night of mourning and I wished I was some-where, anywhere, else. But as my father's only biological child, I had to stay by his body and receive mourners until dawn. Then, a government representative would show up to sound an ogene and officially alert the neighborhood of the death. The body would then be interred with its own tree in the front compound. My grandfather told me that when he'd visit Onitsha as a child, this alert would be done by gunshot. After New Biafra banned guns at the turn of the 2140s, we turned to gongs – something he'd much preferred.

It was one of the many stories my grandparents told me about why they chose to return to Onitsha from Turtle Island, after Old New York drowned in the Catastrophe. As a child, I often joined my grandparents – Mama and Papa, as I called them –

when they sat trading memories on the veranda at twilight. I would climb into my grandmother's lap and lean into her chest, savoring the vibrations of her voice as she spoke.

'It's a shame your father never got to see any grandchild from you.' My Auntie Chio's voice jolted me into the present. 'But we are glad that we will see them on his behalf, now that you have come home.'

I looked askance at her but said nothing. I didn't need to be reminded that I'd failed to birth our family's next generation. She must have caught something in my look because her voice dropped to a reassuring register. 'You don't have to marry anyone: We can get a surrogate, if you like. There's even a government program that could help.'

'Auntie, is this really the best time to talk about this?'

'But of course! The ending of one life is the beginning of the next.' She shifted to face me, and I couldn't avoid her intense gaze. 'My dear, have you forgotten our saying: "To have a child is to have treasure"? That is more important today than ever before.

'Look at our history. If it wasn't for our children, how would we have survived the Civil War, when Nigeria wanted to see us all dead? And those in the western lands who laughed at us when they stopped having even one child after the Catastrophe, look at them now. Are they not the ones scooping us up to feed their hungry economies? Just look at the brokers who helped you and your mother resettle in the West – what *didn't* they offer you to come? They have always known the value of our bodies. Before, they packed us away by force in the bottoms of slave ships, now they lure us with sweet songs of success.

'Azuka, do you know how quickly a people can disappear if they fail to value their children? It does not take centuries. Your grandparents understood this – that's why we all came home.

We wanted to bring our wealth back where it would do the most good. You are part of our legacy.'

I broke away from her gaze, a wave of grief welling up in my chest. How could I tell her that my father's line would die with me because I still recoiled at any sort of sexual contact? Or that the thought of having a child sent me into a paroxysm of panic because I was convinced that what had happened to me would also happen to them? My grief began to curdle into anger. No. This was no longer my legacy. A family that had essentially abandoned me when I needed them most did not get to decide what I did with my life.

Auntie Chio reached out and placed a gentle hand under my chin, lifting my head up to hers. 'I will be honest with you, I never thought I would see you again – not after what happened. But I am glad you have come home, and I hope, for all our sakes, that you will find it in your heart to stay.' With that, she got up and left, leaving me alone with my thoughts.

I sighed, my anger dissipating as quickly as it had come. After we moved, my mother turned her back on Onitsha – and all of New Biafra by extension – with a certainty that never wavered. As far as I know, she never spoke with anyone from my father's side of the family ever again. I hadn't been able to do the same, even though I had more cause than anyone to shake the red dust of this city from my feet.

My mother had scoffed when I told her I was coming down for the funeral. I hadn't returned when my grandparents died; why was this burial so much more important? I couldn't explain it. I'd always felt that I left New Biafra before I could take up my true purpose. That my life in Tkaronto was a shadow of what it could be. Perhaps I'd returned to bury more than my father.

I looked up and two women I'd never seen before were leaning into the pod, wailing and calling the dead man's name, asking rhetorically why he had left them. I wondered how much of their performance was obscure cultural theater and how much was genuine grief.

Their wailing increased, and I wished I'd been allowed to bring my A.I. That, however, would have been considered an insult to the body, like looking into the eyes of an elder while you were being scolded. I'd forgotten how quickly my people whitewash the truth about our dead. We fear that speaking ill of them will invite death on ourselves as well.

One of the women stopped in front of me, sniffling into an old cloth kerchief. She looked to be in her mid-forties – about my age.

'Your father was a good man,' she said, reaching for my hands. I slid them into my pockets, just out of her reach, and she made do with patting my leg.

'Was he?' I tried for a tone of genuine curiosity, not the cynicism I actually felt.

'I wouldn't be here today, if it wasn't for him.'

I nodded, unsure of what to say. My father had been famously generous: Everyone I'd met so far had a story of how he'd stepped in at just the right moment to change their lives. I didn't know what to do with these tales. I suppose it was easier to give money to strangers than to give of yourself to the people closest to you.

After an awkward pause, she continued, speaking quickly as if to get the words out before her courage failed her. 'You know, after I was raped ten years ago, nobody wanted to help me.' I stiffened, tightening my hands into fists in my pockets. 'Not my family, not the government, nobody. Only your father. He brought me into this house and allowed me to stay here for free until I found a place. He even paid for my marriage and my son's apprenticeship. Me and my wife, we're just so grateful to him.'

She pointed to the other woman, who had gone to stand by the door with a child of about ten years. He had soft brown eyes and a head of unruly curls, and he wore a miniature version of the ranger's uniform that the dead man in the pod was wearing. I didn't tell her about the same dead man's reaction to my own rape thirty-three years ago – twenty-three years before her own. Instead, I smiled tightly.

'I'm glad that it turned out so well for you.'

That's when I saw the dead man's shadow materialize in the corner of the room. I didn't tell her about that either.

·

The dead man appeared again sometime during the night.

I had just struggled out of a dream. I was back in the guard-house, its small high windows streaming an uncertain gray light into the room. Then hundreds of disembodied hands reached out of the ground to grab at me. They held me down, their fingers clutching, probing, and rubbing. I bit and clawed and slashed, but for every hand whose finger I tore off, for every palm I gouged and wounded, a new hand sprang up in its place.

It was an old nightmare, one I hadn't had in over thirty years. When we moved to Turtle Island, my mother and our relocation broker made sure I received all the necessary therapies to deal with my trauma, but being here where it all happened seemed to have dredged everything back up.

I lay on the living room couch drenched in sweat and blinked into the semi-darkness before I saw him sitting on the armrest by my feet. In the light of the bioluminescent trees that lined the street by the back window, he looked real enough. When I sat up and turned on the lights, he was gone.

I should have been frightened, but I wasn't. I knew he'd show up again. He and I had unfinished business.

•

He returned the next morning as I sat beneath the neem tree in the back garden, trying to hide from the unrelenting regard of the crowd of mourners inside the main house. The body was due to be interred with its tree in the front compound, and the place was choked with well-wishers. They spilled out onto the walkway beyond the house's hedgerow fence and into the road. I was agitated, but instead of tuning into the nature sounds queued up on my A.I., I listened to the weaver birds screeching to each other in the branches above me.

I never noticed how loud those birds are.

The dead man looked up at the tree's slim branches, weighed down by the birds' basket-like nests. This time, I decided to respond directly.

'You never did notice much beyond your own interests.'

I expected him to come back with an attack that cut to my deepest insecurities. It was a talent he had, and he had often used it to great effect when he was alive, but he didn't. He just nodded sadly and put his hands in his pockets.

I suppose I deserve that.

I would have to make do with that. Even in death, he couldn't apologize. A group of three men around the dead man's age filtered out onto the back veranda. They joked nervously with each other, as if their laughter would somehow keep the shadow of death from falling on them too. Two of them, both dressed in the dark high-collared tunics of Biafran government salary-men, discussed the finer points of spiritual salvation in Yoruba-inflected Igbo. I itched for something to read.

'Why are you even here?'

He shrugged, petulant. *I just wanted to see you.*

I rolled my eyes. He'd only been dead a few days. He'd always been impatient, demanding that I work at his relentless pace no matter how I felt. Now, he couldn't even wait to be missed before showing up again.

'Really? So that you can tell me how selfish I am because I'm not sitting inside being the center of everyone's grief? Or do you also want to remind me that I'm going to destroy our family line if I don't have a child?'

I realized I sounded like a child myself, but I couldn't help it. Being in his presence made me feel that I'd gone back in time and was an angry teenager again.

No. His voice had a wistful quality – like someone looking back at the folly of his youth. *You were never selfish, you know. I was.*

I looked at him sharply; this didn't sound like him at all. As if reading my thoughts, he smiled.

That's one thing dying does – it changes you.

He certainly looked dead. His skin was gray and waxy like a mannequin. His shoulders had a stiff quality that made his dark ranger uniform fit him perfectly in a way it had never done in life.

'Am I to believe that dying has made you a different person?'

Look, he said in that chiding tone I hated, *you can't fault people for their weaknesses. You'll only be left with bitterness if you do. You have to find a way to let go. That's what I came to tell you.*

I sighed. In death, as in life, he had nothing but easy philosophies for me. They'd made for exciting debates when I was young but served as cold comfort for grief. I wanted to get up and walk away, but I didn't. I never could.

'Just leave me alone.'

I turned on my A.I. It synced with the implant at the base of my skull that monitored my neural and physical activity.

Reading my increased agitation, it cued the soothing whale songs that worked best to bring my signals within normal range. I leaned back against the tree and closed my eyes as the sounds poured into my aural inputs, imagining what those long-extinct creatures might have looked like.

Above me, the dead man and the weaver birds chirped on.

•

He didn't show up again until evening, when the second burial was in full swing. By then, the sapling that would biodegrade his pod had joined the other ancestral trees in the front yard. The necessary prayers had been said, the tree's ritual first watering completed. The time for mourning the loss was over and it was now time to celebrate the life lived. At eighty, the dead man was considered fairly young; he'd been expected to live for at least another twenty years. But in my culture, venerated old age began at sixty – probably a holdover from when most people didn't live past their fifties.

I watched the revelry from the open window of the guest room. I'd been allowed this short time to myself only after pleading exhaustion from the long journey. It was only a matter of time before I'd be called out to join the dancing.

The music – a blend of ogenes, ichakas, and udus, cut through by the sweet, sharp tones of the aja – stirred something deep inside me. I pressed my hand to the center of my chest where a phantom pain stabbed through me.

It is good to be remembered. That is the true joy of legacy.

The dead man was sitting next to me on the bed, surveying the mass of people dancing and drinking in the yard.

'Too bad they didn't remember you half as well when we needed their help.'

When my uncle was arrested, they led him out of the compound in chains to show how serious his crime was. My family – once one of the most prominent in the city – was quietly ostracized. Most of my friends stopped coming over. When relatives and agemates stopped by, it was only to whisper at the door or drop off food and drinks. No one wanted to stay and visit. My own education effectively ended – my uncle had been my teacher, after all. It broke Mama and Papa – my grandparents – to lose one of their sons like that. My grandmother fell ill soon after and my grandfather withdrew to care for her. As for my father? Well… he disappeared too, in his own way.

They all had their own problems; they didn't owe me anything.

I hissed in contempt, but said nothing. He must have mistaken my silence, because he continued earnestly.

You have to find it in your heart to forgive them. In the end, all that matters are the memories of the people who knew you. Especially your children.

'And how do you think I'll remember you?'

He went quiet at that. We both looked through the window toward the empty space where the guardhouse once stood.

I didn't know.

'How *couldn't* you have known? Every day after our lessons, right there in the guardhouse. What were you doing the whole time? Sleeping?'

I was working, he snapped. *Don't you think I would have done something if I had known? We acted as soon as we found out.*

'And after that, when you stopped talking to me, was that also because you were working?'

Silence.

'You know, for years I thought it was my fault. I believed that I was the one who destroyed our family. Uncle went to prison,

Mama got sick, and you… you couldn't even look at me. Even after we left, if I didn't call you, I didn't hear from you.'

I still remembered those video calls, stilted conversations on birthdays and holidays. In them, he always seemed too tired or too busy to talk properly.

'I spent years waiting for you… I waited, and I waited, and I waited.'

The tears rose unbidden and I wiped at my face, angry at my own weakness. I'd sworn long ago that I would never cry in front of him. The dead man stood and walked to the window, his back to me. He stared out for a long moment before speaking.

I didn't know what to say to you. His voice was so soft I could barely hear it over the noise outside. As if he was talking to himself. *When I looked at you all I could see was my own failure: I was your father and I couldn't protect you. I hated myself for it and I took that out on you – and for that, I'll never forgive myself.*

'Good. Because I won't ever forgive you either.'

He turned back to me and I watched the slow realization work itself across his face.

You are still angry at me, he said, finally. Sadly.

'You let me down so many times.' Tears sprang to my eyes again, lending a quaver to my voice. 'I don't know how to stop being angry at you.'

I wish I could make it up to you.

'Well, it's too late for that.' For the first time in thirty years, I looked my father in the eyes as I spoke. 'Did you honestly think that by coming here and chanting your empty platitudes, you could undo all those years of pain? You said you came back to warn me, but this isn't about me. This is about you getting your last moment of absolution.'

I am so sorry. For everything.

'It doesn't matter anymore.' I was suddenly tired. 'Go. Find your salvation somewhere else.'

Thunder boomed from somewhere in the distance, sending a ripple of unease through the crowd outside. The wind picked up, skittering debris across the yard. As the fat, heavy rainclouds rolled in, the party outside began to pack up. Families in the building fled to their flats while those who had too far to go clustered under the canvas canopies to wait out the storm.

I picked up my backpack and looked around, but the dead man was gone.

A flood of mourners streamed out from the compound, breaking up into little rivulets of people eager to get home before the rain started. I joined them and headed for the bus shelter. Just as I reached it, the sky opened up and wept.

Inside the shelter, I wedged myself into a small space in the back and tugged the hood of my hi-dri up to hide my face. I didn't want to explain my sudden departure to any mourners who might recognize me. I was staring into the haze of the rain, my mind blank with grief, when I felt a familiar hand on my shoulder.

'So you would have just left us like that, eh?' Auntie Chio's voice was sad. I tensed involuntarily as I turned to her, but her expression bore an unexpected understanding.

Before I could speak, she wrapped me in a warm embrace. For a moment, I wanted to fight off her kindness. My rage was an invisible load I'd been carrying for so long that I didn't know how to put it down. Instead, I returned her hug with a fierceness I didn't realize I had, and finally, I let my tears flow. This time I didn't bother to wipe them away. There was no one left to see me cry.

The storm passed quickly, and I decided to forego the bus and walk back to the Harbourfront. On foot, I was able to look more closely at the city around me. Though the main roadways were well-maintained, I noted buckled panels and weedy gardens in the side streets. I passed rows of empty homes kept ready for returnees, but underneath their neat government-issued paint jobs, the brickwork was crumbling. Eventually, they too would have to be razed and converted into parkland.

I arrived at the Harbourfront just as the sun was setting behind the Niger Bridge, highlighting its rusted pylons. My city, like the rest of the world, was disintegrating. The realization relieved me, in an odd way. I wondered if too many of us were trying to return to who we imagined we were before the Catastrophe broke us. Maybe what we needed was to learn to live with the world, and ourselves, as it was now. Perhaps our salvation lay in the broken spaces inside us all.

Delhi

Vandana Singh

India

Having 'Delhi' in this volume is another dream come true for me. I've been familiar with Vandana's work for years, and was desperate to include her in my *Apex Book of World SF* anthologies – only none of the stories were then available! We finally did include one (the wonderful 'Ambiguity Machines: An Examination'), but long ago I vowed to have 'Delhi' one day, and here, finally, was my chance. Vandana is a scientist and author who writes exceptional short fiction and this is, well, no exception!

Tonight he is intensely aware of the city: its ancient stones, the flat-roofed brick houses, threads of clotheslines, wet, bright colors waving like pennants, neem-tree lined roads choked with traffic. There's a bus going over the bridge under which he has chosen to sleep. The night smells of jasmine, and stale urine, and the dust of the cricket field on the other side of the road. A man is lighting a bidi near him: face lean, half in shadow, and he thinks he sees himself. He goes over to the man, who looks like another layabout. 'My name is Aseem,' he says. The man, reeking of tobacco, glares at him, coughs and spits, 'kya chahiye?' Aseem steps back in a hurry. No, that man is not Aseem's older self. Anyway, Aseem can't imagine he would take up smoking bidis at any point in his life. He leaves the dubious shelter of the bridge, the quiet lane that runs under it, and makes his way through the litter and anemic streetlamps to the neon-bright highway. The new city is less confusing, he thinks; the colors are more solid, the lights dazzling, so he can't see the apparitions as clearly. But once he saw a milkman going past him on Shahjahan road, complete with humped white cow and tinkling bell. Under the stately, ancient trees that partly shaded the streetlamps, the milkman stopped to speak to his cow and faded into the dimness of twilight.

When he was younger he thought the apparitions he saw were ghosts of the dead, but now he knows that is not true. Now he has a theory that his visions are tricks of time, tangles produced when one part of the time-stream rubs up against another and the two cross for a moment. He has decided (after years of struggle) that he is not insane after all; his brain is wired differently from others, enabling him to discern these temporal coincidences. He knows he is not the only one with this ability, because some of the people he sees also see him, and shrink back in terror. The thought that he is a ghost to people long dead or still to come in this world both amuses and terrifies him.

He's seen more apparitions in the older parts of the city than anywhere else, and he's not sure why. There is plenty of history in Delhi, no doubt about that – the city's past goes back into myth, when the Pandava brothers of the epic Mahabharata first founded their fabled capital, Indraprastha, some three thousand years ago. In medieval times alone there were seven cities of Delhi, he remembers, from a well-thumbed history textbook – and the eighth city was established by the British during the days of the Raj. The city of the present day, the ninth, is the largest. Only for Aseem are the old cities of Delhi still alive, glimpsed like mysterious islands from a passing ship, but real, nevertheless. He wishes he could discuss his temporal visions with someone who would take him seriously and help him understand the nature and limits of his peculiar malady, but ironically, the only sympathetic person he's met who shares his condition happened to live in AD 1100 or thereabouts, the time of Prithviraj Chauhan, the last great Hindu ruler of Delhi.

He was walking past the faded white colonnades of some building in Connaught Place when he saw her: an old woman in a long skirt and shawl, making her way sedately across the car park, her body rising above the road and falling below its surface in parallel with some invisible topography. She came face to face with Aseem – and saw him. They both stopped. Clinging to her like gray ribbons were glimpses of her environs – he saw mist, the darkness of trees behind her. Suddenly, in the middle of summer, he could smell fresh rain. She put a wondering arm out toward him but didn't touch him. She said: 'What age are you from?' in an unfamiliar dialect of Hindi. He did not know how to answer the question, or how to contain within him that sharp shock of joy. She, too, had looked across the barriers of time and glimpsed other people, other ages. She named Prithviraj Chauhan as her king. Aseem told her he lived some 900 years after Chauhan. They exchanged stories of other visions – she had seen armies, spears flashing, and pale men with yellow beards, and a woman in a metal carriage, crying. He was able to interpret some of this for her before she began to fade away. He started toward her as though to step into her world, and ran right into a pillar. As he picked himself off the ground he heard derisive laughter. Under the arches a shoeshine boy and a man chewing betel leaf were staring at him, enjoying the show.

Once he met the mad emperor, Mohammad Shah. He was walking through Red Fort one late afternoon, avoiding clumps of tourists and their clicking cameras. He was feeling particularly restless; there was a smoky tang in the air, because some gardener in the grounds was burning dry leaves. As the sun set, the red sandstone fort walls glowed, then darkened. Night came, blanketing the tall ramparts, the lawns through which he strolled, the shimmering beauty of the Pearl Mosque, the languorous curves of the now distant Yamuna that had once flowed under this marble terrace. He saw a man standing, leaning over the railing, dressed in a red silk sherwani, jewels at his throat, a gem studded in his turban. He smelled of wine and rose attar, and he was singing a song about a night of separation from the Beloved, slurring the words together.

Bairan bhayii raat sakhiya...

Mammad Shah piya sada Rangila...

Mohammad Shah Rangila, early 1700s, Aseem recalled. The Emperor who loved music, poetry and wine more than anything, who ignored warnings that the Persian king was marching to Delhi with a vast army... 'Listen, king,' Aseem whispered urgently, wondering if he could change the course of history, 'You must prepare for battle. Else Nadir Shah will overrun the city. Thousands will be butchered by his army...'

The king lifted wine-darkened eyes. 'Begone, wraith!'

Sometimes he stops at the India Gate lawns in the heart of modern Delhi and buys ice cream from a vendor, and eats it sitting by one of the fountains that Lutyens built. Watching the play of light on the shimmering water, he thinks about the British invaders, who brought one of the richest and oldest civilizations on earth to abject poverty in only two hundred years. They built these great edifices, gracious buildings and fountains, but even they had to leave it all behind. Kings came and went, the goras came and went, but the city lives on. Sometimes he sees apparitions of the goras, the palefaces, walking by him or riding on horses. Each time he yells out to them: 'Your people are doomed. You will leave here. Your Empire will crumble.' Once in a while they glance at him, startled, before they fade away.

In his more fanciful moments he wonders if he hasn't, in some way, caused history to happen the way it does. Planted a seed of doubt in a British officer's mind about the permanency of the Empire. Despite his best intentions, convinced Mohammad Shah that the impending invasion is not a real danger but a ploy wrought against him by evil spirits. But he knows that apart from the Emperor, nobody he has communicated with is of any real importance in the course of history, and that he is simply deluding himself about his own significance.

Still, he makes compulsive notes of his more interesting encounters. He carries with him at all times a thick, somewhat shabby notebook, one half of which is devoted to recording these temporal adventures. But because the apparitions he sees are so clear, he is sometimes not certain whether the face he glimpses in the crowd, or the man passing him by on a cold night, wrapped in shawls, belong to this time or some other. Only some incongruity – spatial or temporal – distinguishes the apparitions from the rest.

Sometimes he sees landscapes too, but rarely – a skyline dotted with palaces and temple spires, a forest in the middle of a busy thoroughfare – and, strangest of all, once, an array of tall, jeweled towers reaching into the clouds. Each such vision seems to be charged with a peculiar energy, like a scene lit up by lightning. And although the apparitions are apparently random and don't often repeat, there are certain places where he sees (he thinks) the same people again and again. For instance, while traveling on the Metro he almost always sees people in the subway tunnels, floating through the train and the passengers on the platforms, dressed in tatters, their faces pale and unhealthy as though they have never beheld the sun. The first time he saw them, he shuddered. 'The Metro is quite new,' he thought to himself, 'and the first underground train system in Delhi. So what I saw must be in the future...'

One day, he tells himself, he will write a history of the future.

•

The street is Nai Sarak, a name he has always thought absurd. New Road, it means, but this road has not been new in a very long time. He could cross the street in two jumps if it wasn't so crowded with people, shoulder to shoulder. The houses are like that too, hunched together with windows like dull eyes, and narrow, dusty stairways and even narrower alleys in between. The ground floors are taken up by tiny, musty shops containing piles of books that smell fresh and pungent, a wake-up smell like coffee. It is a hot day, and there is no shade. The girl he is following is just another Delhi University student looking for a bargain, trying not to get jostled or groped in the crowd, much less have her purse stolen. There are small, barefoot boys running around with wire-carriers of lemon-water in chipped glasses, and fat old men in their undershirts behind the counters, bargaining fiercely with pale, defenseless college students over the hum of electric fans, rubbing clammy hands across their hairy bellies while they slurp their ice drinks, signaling to some waif when the transaction is complete, so that the desired volume can be deposited into the feverish hands of the student. Some of the shopkeepers like to add a little lecture on the lines of 'Now, my son, study hard, make your parents proud...' Aseem hasn't been here in a long time (since his own college days in fact); he is not prepared for any of this: the brightness of the day, the white dome of the mosque rising up behind him, the old stone walls of the old city engirdling him, enclosing him in people and sweat and dust. He's dazzled by the white kurtas of the men, the neat beards and the prayer caps, this is of course the Muslim part of the city, Old Delhi, but not as romantic as his grandmother used to make it sound. He has a rare flash of memory into a past where he was a small boy listening to the old woman's tales. His grandmother was one of the Hindus who never went back to old Delhi, not after the madness of Partition in 1947, the Hindu–Muslim riots that killed thousands, but he still remembers how she spoke of the places of her girlhood: parathe-walon-ki-gali, the lane of the paratha-makers, where all the shops sell freshly cooked flatbreads of every possible kind, stuffed with spiced potatoes or minced lamb, or fenugreek leaves, or crushed cauliflower and fiery red chillies; and Dariba Kalan, where after hundreds of years they still sell the best and purest silver in the world, delicate chains and anklets and bracelets. Among the crowds that throng these places he has seen the apparitions of courtesans and young men, and the blood and thunder of invasions, and the bodies of princes hanged by British soldiers. To him the old city, surrounded by high, crumbling, stone walls, is like the heart of a crone who dreams perpetually of her youth.

The girl who's caught his attention walks on. Aseem hasn't been able to get a proper look at her – all he's noticed are the dark eyes, and the death in them. After all these years in the city he's learned to recognize a certain preoccupation in the eyes of some of his fellow citizens: the desire for the final anonymity that death brings.

Sometimes, as in this case, he knows it before they do.

The girl goes into a shop. The proprietor, a young man built like a wrestler, is dressed only in cotton shorts. The massage-man is working his back, kneading and sculpting the slick, gold muscles. The young man says: 'Advanced Biochemistry? Watkins? One copy, only one copy left.' He shouts into the dark, cavernous interior, and the requisite small boy comes up, bearing the volume as though it were a rare book.

The girl's face shows too much relief; she's doomed even before the bargaining begins. She parts with her money with a resigned air, steps out into the noisy brightness, and is caught up with the crowd in the street like a piece of wood tossed in a river. She pushes and elbows her way through it, fending off anonymous hands that reach toward her breasts or back. He loses sight of her for a moment, but there she is, walking past the mosque to the bus stop on the main road. At the bus stop she catches Aseem's glance and gives him the pre-emptive cold look. Now there's a bus coming, filled with people, young men hanging out of the doorways as though on the prow of a sailboat. He sees her struggling through the crowd toward the bus, and at the last minute she's right in its path. The bus is not stopping but (in the tantalizing manner of Delhi buses) barely slowing, as though to play catch with the crowd. It is an immense green and yellow metal monstrosity, bearing down on her, as she stands rooted, clutching her bag of books. This is Aseem's moment. He lunges at the girl, pushing her out of the way, grabbing her before she can fall to the ground. There is a roaring in his ears, the shriek of brakes, and the conductor yelling. Her books are scattered on the ground. He helps pick them up. She's trembling with shock. In her eyes he sees himself for a moment: a drifter, his face unshaven, his hair unkempt. He tells her: 'Don't do it, don't ever do it. Life is never so bereft of hope. You have a purpose you must fulfill.' He's repeating it like a mantra, and she's looking bewildered, as though she doesn't understand that she was trying to kill herself. He can see that he puzzles her: his grammatical Hindi and his fair English labels him middle-class and educated, like herself, but his appearance says otherwise. Although he knows she's not the woman he is seeking, he pulls out the computer printout just to be sure. No, she's not the one. Cheeks too thin, chin not sharp enough. He pushes one of the business cards into her hand and walks away. From a distance he sees that she's looking at the card in her hand and frowning. Will she throw it away? At the last minute she shoves it into her bag with the books. He remembers all too clearly the first time someone gave him one of the cards. 'Worried About Your Future? Consult Pandit Vidyanath. Computerized and Air-Conditioned Office. Discover Your True Purpose in Life.' There is a logo of a beehive and an address in South Delhi.

Later he will write up this encounter in the second half of his notebook. In three years he has filled this part almost to capacity. He's stopped young men from flinging themselves off the bridges that span the Yamuna. He's prevented women from jumping off tall buildings, from dousing themselves with kerosene, from murderous encounters with city traffic. All this by way of seeking her, whose story will be the last in his book. But the very first story in this part of his notebook is his own...

•

Three years ago. He is standing on a bridge over the Yamuna. There is a heavy, odorous fog in the air, the kind that mars winter mornings in Delhi. He is shivering because of the chill, and because he is tired, tired of the apparitions that have always plagued him, tired of the endless rounds of medications and appointments with doctors and psychologists. He has just written a letter to his fiancée, severing their already fragile relationship. Two months ago he stopped attending his college classes. His mother and father have been dead a year and two years respectively, and there will be no one to mourn him, except for relatives in other towns who know him only by reputation as a person with problems. Last night he tried, as a last resort, to leave Delhi, hoping that perhaps the visions would stop. He got as far as the railway station. He stood in the line before the ticket counter, jostled by young men carrying holdalls and aggressive matrons in bright saris. 'Name?' said the man behind the window, but Aseem couldn't remember it. Around him, in the cavernous interior of the station, shouting, red-clad porters rushed past, balancing tiers of suitcases on their turbaned heads, and vast waves of passengers swarmed the stairs that led up across the platforms. People were nudging him, telling him to hurry up, but all he could think of were the still trains between the platforms, steaming in the cold air, hissing softly like warm snakes, waiting to take him away. The thought of leaving filled him with a sudden terror. He turned and walked out of the station. Outside, in the cold, glittering night, he breathed deep, fierce breaths of relief, as though he had walked away from his own death.

So here he is, the morning after his attempted escape, stand-ing on the bridge, shivering in the fog. He notices a crack in the concrete railing, which he traces with his finger to the seedling of a pipal tree growing on the outside of the rail. He remembers his mother pulling pipal seedlings out of walls and the paved courtyard of their house, over his protests. He remembers how hard it was for him to see, in each fragile sapling, the giant full-grown tree. Leaning over the bridge he finds himself wondering which will fall first – the pipal tree or the bridge. Just then he hears a bicycle on the road behind him, one that needs oiling, evidently, and before he knows it some rude fellow with a straggly beard has come out of the fog, pulled him off the railing and onto the road. 'Don't be a fool, don't do it,' says the stranger, breathing hard. His bicycle is lying on the roadside, one wheel still spinning. 'Here, take this,' the man says, pushing a small card into Aseem's unresisting hand. 'Go see them. If they can't give you a reason to live, your own mother wouldn't be able to.'

The address on the card proves to be in a small marketplace near Sarojini Nagar. Around a dusty square of withered grass, where ubiquitous pariah dogs sleep fitfully in the pale sun, there is a row of shops. The place he seeks is a corner shop next to a vast jamun tree. Under the tree, three humped white cows are chewing cud, watching him with bovine indifference. Aseem makes his way through a jangle of bicycles, motor-rickshaws and people, and finds himself before a closed door, with a small sign saying only, 'Pandit Vidyanath, Consultations.' He goes in.

The Pandit is not in, but his assistant, a thin, earnest-faced young man, waves Aseem to a chair. The assistant is sitting behind a desk with a PC, a printer, and a plaque bearing his name: Om Prakash, BSc. Physics, (Failed) Delhi University. There is a window with the promised air-conditioner (apparently defunct) occupying its lower half. On the other side of the window is a beehive in the process of completion. Aseem feels he has come to the wrong place, and regrets already the whim that brought him here, but the beehive fascinates him, how it is still and in motion all at once, and the way the bees seem to be in concert with one another, as though performing a complicated dance. Two of the bees are crawling on the computer and there is one on the assistant's arm. Om Prakash seems completely unperturbed; he assures Aseem that the bees are harmless, and tries to interest him in an array of bottles of honey on the shelf behind him. Apparently the bees belong to Pandit Vidyanath, a man of many facets, who keeps very busy because he also works for the city. (Aseem has a suspicion that perhaps the great man is no more than a petty clerk in a municipal office.) Honey is ten rupees a bottle. Aseem shakes his head, and Om Prakash gets down to business with a noisy clearing of his throat, asking questions and entering the answers into the computer. By now Aseem is feeling like a fool.

'How does your computer know the future?' Aseem asks.

Om Prakash has a lanky, giraffe-like grace, although he is not tall. He makes a deprecating gesture with his long, thin hands that travels all the way up to his mobile shoulders.

'A computer is like a beehive. Many bits and parts, none is by itself intelligent. Combine together, and you have something that can think. This computer is not an ordinary one. Built by Pandit Vidyanath himself.'

Om Prakash grins as the printer begins to whir.

'All persons who come here seek meaning. Each person has their own dharma, their own unique purpose. We don't tell future, because future is beyond us, Sahib. We tell them why they need to live.'

He hands a printout to Aseem. When he first sees it, the page makes no sense. It consists of x's arranged in an apparently random pattern over the page. He holds it at a distance and sees – indistinctly – the face of a woman.

'Who is she?'

'It is for you to interpret what this picture means,' says Om Prakash. 'You must live because you need to meet this woman, perhaps to save her or be saved. It may mean that you could be at the right place and time to save her from some terrible fate. She could be your sister or daughter, or a wife, or a stranger.'

There are dark smudges for eyes, and the hint of a high cheekbone, and the swirl of hair across the cheek, half-obscuring the mouth. The face is broad and heart-shaped, narrowing to a small chin.

'But this is not very clear... It could be almost anyone. How will I know...'

'You will know when you meet her,' Om Prakash says with

finality. 'There is no charge. Thank you, sir, and here are cards for you to give other unfortunate souls.'

Aseem takes the pack of business cards and leaves. He distrusts the whole business, especially the bit about no charge. No charge? In a city like Delhi?

•

But despite his doubts he finds himself intrigued. He had expected the usual platitudes about life and death, the fatalistic pronouncements peculiar to charlatan fortune tellers, but this fellow, Vidyanath, obviously is an original. That Aseem must live simply so he might be there for someone at the right moment: what an amusing, humbling idea! As the days pass it grows on him, and he comes to believe it, if for nothing else than to have something in which to believe. He scans the faces of the people in the crowds, on the dusty sidewalks, the overladen buses, the Metro, and he looks for her. He lives so that he will cross her path some day. Over three years he has convinced himself that she is real, that she waits for him. He's made something of a life for himself, working at a photocopy shop in Lajpat Nagar where he can sleep on winter nights, or making deliveries for shopkeepers in Defence Colony, who pay enough to keep him in food and clothing. Over three years he has handed out hundreds of the little business cards, and visited the address in South Delhi dozens of times. He's become used to the bees, the defunct air-conditioner, and even to Om Prakash. Although there is too much distance between them to allow friendship (a distance of temperament, really), Aseem has told Om Prakash about the apparitions he sees. Om Prakash receives these confidences with his rather foolish grin and much waggling of the head in wonder, and says he will tell Pandit Vidyanath. Only, each time Aseem visits there is no sign of

Pandit Vidyanath, so now Aseem suspects that there is no such person, that Om Prakash himself is the unlikely mind behind the whole business.

But sometimes he is scared of finding the woman. He imagines himself saving her from death or a fate worse than death, realizing at last his purpose. But after that what awaits him? The oily embrace of the Yamuna?

Or will she save him in turn?

•

One of the things he likes about the city is how it breaks all rules. Delhi is a place of contradictions – it transcends thesis and antithesis. Here he has seen both the hovels of the poor and the opulent monstrosities of the rich. At major intersections, where the rich wait impatiently in their air-conditioned cars for the light to change, he's seen bone-thin waifs running from car to car, peddling glossy magazines like *Vogue* and *Cosmopolitan*. Amid the glitzy new high-rises are troupes of wandering cows and pariah dogs; rhesus monkeys mate with abandon in the trees around Parliament House.

He hasn't slept well – last night the police raided the Aurobindo Marg sidewalk where he was sleeping. Some foreign VIP was expected in the morning so the riffraff on the roadsides were driven off by stick-wielding policemen. This has happened many times before, but today Aseem is smarting with rage and humiliation: he has a bruise on his back where a policeman's stick hit him, and it burns in the relentless heat. Death lurks behind the walled eyes of the populace – but for once he is sick of his proximity to death. So he goes to the only place where he can leave behind the city without actually leaving its borders – another anomaly in a city of surprises. Amid the endless sprawl of brick houses and crowded roads, within Delhi's borders, there lies an entire forest: the Delhi Ridge, a green lung. The coolness of the forest beckons to him.

Only a little way from the main road, the forest is still, except for the subdued chirping of birds. He is in a warm, green womb. Under the acacia trees he finds an old ruin, one of the many nameless remains of Delhi's medieval era. After checking for snakes and scorpions, he curls up under a crumbling wall and dozes off.

Some time later, when the sun is lower in the sky and the heat not as intense, he hears a tapping sound, soft and regular, like slow rain on a tin roof. He sees a woman – a young girl – on the paved path in front of him, holding a cane before her. She's blind, obviously, and lost. This is no place for a woman alone. He clears his throat and she starts.

'Is someone there?'

She's wearing a long blue shirt over a salwaar of the same color, and there is a shawl around her shoulders. The thin material of her dupatta drapes her head, half-covering her face, blurring her features. He looks at her and sees the face in the printout. Or thinks he does.

'You are lost,' he says, his voice trembling with excitement. He's fumbling in his pockets for the printout. Surely he must still be asleep and dreaming. Hasn't he dreamed about her many, many times already? 'Where do you wish to go?'

She clutches her stick. Her shoulders slump.

'Naya Diwas Lane, good sir. I am traveling from Jaipur. I came to meet my sister, who lives here, but I lost my papers. They say you must have papers. Or they'll send me to Neechi Dilli with all the poor and the criminals. I don't want to go there! My sister has money. Please, sir, tell me how to find Naya Diwas.'

He's never heard of Naya Diwas Lane, or Neechi Dilli. New

Day Lane? Lower Delhi? What strange names. He wipes the sweat off his forehead.

'There aren't any such places. Somebody has misled you. Go back to the main road, turn right, there is a marketplace there. I will come with you. Nobody will harm you. We can make enquiries there.'

She thanks him, her voice catching with relief. She tells him she's heard many stories about the fabled city, and its tall, gem-studded minars that reach the sky, and the perfect gardens. And the ships, the silver udan-khatolas, that fly across worlds. She's very excited to be here at last in the Immaculate City.

His eyes widen. He gets up abruptly but she's already fading away into the trees. The computer printout is in his hand, but before he can get another look at her, she's gone.

What has he told her? Where is she going, in what future age, buoyed by the hope he has given her, which (he fears now) may be false?

He stumbles around the ruin, disturbing ground squirrels and a sleepy flock of jungle babblers, but he knows there is no hope of finding her again except by chance. Temporal coincidences have their own unfathomable rules. He's looked ahead to this moment so many times, imagined both joy and despair as a result of it, but never this apprehension, this uncertainty. He looks at the computer printout again. Is it mere coincidence that the apparition he saw looked like the image? What if Pandit Vidyanath's computer generated something quite random, and his quest, his life for the past few years has been completely pointless? That Om Prakash or Vidyanath (if he exists) are enjoying an intricate joke at his expense? That he has allowed himself to be duped by his own hopes and fears?

But beyond all this, he's worried about this girl. There's only one thing to do – go to Om Prakash and get the truth out of him. After all, if Vidyanath's computer generated her image, and if Vidyanath isn't a complete fraud, he would know something about her, about that time. It is a forlorn hope, but it's all he has.

He takes the Metro on his way back. The train snakes its way under the city through the still-new tunnels, past brightly lit stations where crowds surge in and out and small boys peddle chai and soft drinks. At one of these stops he sees the apparitions of people, their faces clammy and pale, clad in rags; he smells the stench of unwashed bodies too long out of the sun. They are coming out of the cement floor of the platform, as though from the bowels of the earth. He's seen them many times before; he knows they are from some future he'd rather not think about. But now it occurs to him with the suddenness of a blow that they are from the blind girl's future. Lower Delhi – Neechi Dilli – that is what this must be: a city of the poor, the outcast, the criminal, in the still-to-be-carved tunnels underneath the Delhi that he knows. He thinks of the Metro, fallen into disuse in that distant future, its tunnels abandoned to the dispossessed, and the city above a delight of gardens and gracious buildings, and tall spires reaching through the clouds. He has seen that once, he remembers. The Immaculate City, the blind girl called it.

•

By the time he gets to Vidyanath's shop, it is late afternoon, and the little square is filling with long shadows. At the bus stop where he disembarks there is a young woman sitting, reading something. She looks vaguely familiar; she glances quickly at him but he notices her only peripherally.

He bursts into the room. Om Prakash is reading a magazine, which he sets down in surprise. A bee crawls out of his ear and flies up in a wide circle to the hive on the window. Aseem hardly notices.

'Where's that fellow, Vidyanath?'

Om Prakash looks mildly alarmed.

'My employer is not here, sir.'

'Look, Om Prakash, something has happened, something serious. I met the girl of the printout. But she's from the future. I need to go back and find her. You must get Vidyanath for me. If his computer made the image of the girl, he must know how I can reach her.'

Om Prakash shakes his head sadly.

'Panditji speaks only through the computer.' He looks at the beehive, then at Aseem. 'Panditji cannot control the future, you know that. He can only tell you your purpose. Why you are important.'

'But I made a mistake! I didn't realize she was from another time. I told her something and she disappeared before I could do anything. She could be in danger! It is a terrible future, Om Prakash. There is a city below the city where the poor live. And above the ground there is clean air and tall minars and udan-khatolas that fly between worlds. No dirt or beggars or poor people. Like when the foreign VIPs come to town and the policemen chase people like me out of the main roads. But Neechi Dilli is like a prison, I'm sure of it. They can't see the sun.'

Om Prakash waves his long hands.

'What can I say, Sahib?'

Aseem goes around the table and takes Om Prakash by the shoulders.

'Tell me, Om Prakash, am I nothing but a strand in a web? Do I have a choice in what I do, or am I simply repeating lines written by someone else?'

'You can choose to break my bones, sir, and nobody can stop

you. You can choose to jump into the Yamuna. Whatever you do affects the world in some small way. Sometimes the effect remains small, sometimes it grows and grows like a pipal tree. Causality as we call it is only a first-order effect. Second-order causal loops jump from time to time, as in your visions, sir. The future, Panditji says, is neither determined nor undetermined.'

Aseem releases the fellow. His head hurts and he is very tired, and Om Prakash makes no more sense than usual. He feels emptied of hope. As he leaves he turns to ask Om Prakash one more question.

'Tell me, Om Prakash, this Pandit Vidyanath, if he exists – what is his agenda? What is he trying to accomplish? Who is he working for?'

'Pandit Vidyanath works for the city, as you know. Otherwise he works only for himself.'

He goes out into the warm evening. He walks toward the bus stop. Over the chatter of people and the car horns on the street and the barking of pariah dogs, he can hear the distant buzzing of bees.

At the bus stop the half-familiar young woman is still sitting, studying a computer printout in the inadequate light of the streetlamp. She looks at him quickly, as though she wants to talk, but thinks better of it. He sits on the cement bench in a daze. Three years of anticipation, all for nothing. He should write down the last story and throw away his notebook.

Mechanically, he takes the notebook out and begins to write.

She clears her throat. Evidently she is not used to speaking to strange men. Her clothes and manner tell him she's from a respectable middle-class family. And then he remembers the girl he pushed away from a bus near Nai Sarak.

She's holding the page out to him.

'Can you make any sense of that?'

The printout is even more indistinct than his. He turns the paper around, frowns at it and hands it back to her.

'Sorry, I don't see anything.'

She says: 'You could interpret the image as a crystal of unusual structure, or a city skyline with tall towers. Who knows? Considering that I'm studying biochemistry and my father really wants me to be an architect with his firm, it isn't surprising that I see those things in it. Amusing, really.'

She laughs. He makes what he hopes is a polite noise.

'I don't know. I think the charming and foolish Om Prakash is a bit of a fraud. And you were wrong about me, by the way. I wasn't trying to… to kill myself that day.'

She's sounding defensive now. He knows he was not mistaken about what he saw in her eyes. If it wasn't then, it would have been some other time – and she knows this.

'Still, I came here on an impulse,' she says in a rush, 'and I've been staring at this thing and thinking about my life. I've already made a few decisions about my future.'

A bus comes lurching to a stop. She looks at it, and then at him, hesitates. He knows she wants to talk, but he keeps scratching away in his notebook. At the last moment before the bus pulls away she swings her bag over her shoulder, waves at him and climbs aboard. The look he had first noticed in her eyes has gone, for the moment. Today she's a different person.

He finishes writing in his notebook, and with a sense of inevitability that feels strangely right, he catches a bus that will take him across one of the bridges that span the Yamuna.

•

At the bridge he leans against the concrete wall looking into the dark water. This is one of his familiar haunts; how many people has he saved on this bridge? The pipal tree sapling is still growing in a crack in the cement – the municipality keeps uprooting it but it is buried too deep to die completely. Behind him there are cars and lights and the sound of horns, the jangle of bicycle bells. He sets his notebook down on top of the wall, wishing he had given it to someone, like that girl at the bus stop. He can't make himself throw it away. A peculiar lassitude, a detachment, has taken hold of him, and he can think and act only in slow motion.

He's preparing to climb onto the wall of the bridge, his hands clammy and slipping on the concrete, when he hears somebody behind him say 'Wait!' He turns. It is like looking into a distorting mirror. The man is hollow-cheeked, with a few days' stubble on his chin, and the untidy thatch of hair has thinned and is streaked with silver. He's holding a bunch of cards in his hand. A welt mars one cheek, and the left sleeve is torn and stained with something rust-colored. The eyes are leopard's eyes, burning with a dreadful urgency. 'Aseem,' says the stranger who is not a stranger, panting as though he has been running, his voice breaking a little. 'Don't…' He is already starting to fade. Aseem reaches out a hand and meets nothing but air. A million questions rise in his head but before he can speak the image is gone.

Aseem's first impulse is a defiant one. What if he were to jump into the river now – what would that do to the future, to causality? It would be his way of bowing out of the game that the city's been playing with him, of saying: 'I've had enough of your tricks.' But the impulse dies. He thinks, instead, about Om Prakash's second-order causal loops, of sunset over the Red Fort, and the twisting alleyways of the old city, and death sleeping under the eyelids of the citizenry. He sits down slowly on the dusty sidewalk. He covers his face with his hands, his shoulders shake.

After a long while he stands up. The road before him can take him anywhere, to the faded colonnades and bright bustle of Connaught Place, to the hush of public parks, with their abandoned cricket balls and silent swings, to old government housing settlements where, amid sleeping bungalows, ancient trees hold court before somnolent congresses of cows. The dusty by-lanes and broad avenues and crumbling monuments of Delhi lie before him, the noisy, lurid marketplaces, the high-tech glass towers, the glitzy enclaves with their citadels of the rich, the boot-boys and beggars at street corners... He has just to take a step and the city will swallow him up, receive him the way a river receives the dead. He is a corpuscle in its veins, blessed or cursed to live and die within it, seeing his purpose now and then, but never fully.

Staring unseeingly into the bright clamor of the highway, he has a wild idea that, he realizes, has been bubbling under the surface of his consciousness for a while. He recalls a picture he saw once in a book when he was a boy: a satellite image of Asia at night. On the dark bulge of the globe there were knots of light – like luminous fungi, he had thought at the time, stretching tentacles into the dark. He wonders whether complexity and vastness are sufficient conditions for a slow awakening, a coming-to-consciousness. He thinks about Om Prakash, his foolish grin and waggling head, and his strange intimacy with the bees. Will Om Prakash tell him who Pandit Vishwanath really is, and what it means to 'work for the city'? He thinks not. What he must do, he sees at last, is what he has been doing all along: looking out for his own kind, the poor and the desperate, and those who walk with death in their eyes. The city's needs are alien, unfathomable. It is an entity in its own right, expanding every day, swallowing the surrounding countryside, crossing the Yamuna which was once its boundary, spawning satellite children, infant towns that it will ultimately devour. Now it is burrowing into the earth, and even later it will reach long fingers towards the stars.

What he needs most at this time is someone he can talk to about all this, someone who will take his crazy ideas seriously. There was the girl at the bus stop, the one he had rescued in Nai Sarak. Om Prakash will have her address. She wanted to talk; perhaps she will listen as well. He remembers the printout she had shown him and wonders if her future has something to do with the Delhi-to-come, the city that intrigues and terrifies him: the Delhi of udan-khatolas, the 'ships that fly between worlds,' of starved and forgotten people in the catacombs underneath. He wishes he could have asked his future self more questions. He is afraid because it is likely (but not certain, it is never that simple) that some kind of violence awaits him, not just the violence of privation, but a struggle that looms indistinctly ahead, that will cut his cheek and injure his arm, and do untold things to his soul. But for now there is nothing he can do, caught as he is in his own time-stream. He picks up his notebook. It feels strangely heavy in his hands. Rubbing sticky tears out of his eyes, he staggers slowly into the night.

The Wheel of Samsara

Han Song

China

I have a personal reason to include this story here. Back when I was putting together *The Apex Book of World SF*, in 2008, I received 'The Wheel of Samsara' from Song, who I met in China back in 2000. He is one of the most highly-respected SF authors in China, and this story, which I first published in 2009, was his first story in English. Song translated the story himself, and I had the privilege of working with him on the translation for publication. I got to meet him again in London briefly, and then in Beijing twenty years after our first meeting. 'The Wheel of Samsara', which corresponds with Arthur C. Clarke's classic 'The Nine Billion Names of God', is the only story from my previous five World SF anthologies I have chosen to reprint here. I like to think that, in some small way, it was a lonely sparrow to herald the spring of Chinese SF in translation. It is also, of course, a very good story, and I am very proud to have published it first.

She travelled in Tibet and one day arrived at Doji lamasery. It was a small temple of Tibetan Buddhism now in a bleak, half-ruined state. What caught her eye was a string of bronze wheels hung around the wall of the temple. They were called the Wheels of Samsara.

There was a total of one hundred and eight wheels, moving in the wind; they symbolized the eternal cycle of life and death – of everything. She quickly noticed that one of them was a strange colour of dark green, singling itself out from the others, which were yellow.

It was the thirty-sixth wheel when counted clockwise.

She touched the wheels one by one, and made a vow to Sakyamuni, the Great Buddha. Midway through a sudden gale began to blow and a heavy mist fell. She was scared and she ran back to the temple.

She stayed in the lamasery that night.

The gale continued and became a rainstorm. Thunder and flashes of lightning were splitting the mountains and the sky.

She could not fall asleep on such a night, and at midnight she thought she could hear the sob of the Tibetan plateau, which reminded her of her dead mother and her lonely father on Mars.

Suddenly, she heard a cry.

It was a miserable sound, weak as a hairspring and harsh as a woman's weeping, and it made her think of a ghost.

Fear stopped her own cry.

Though she knew lamas were sleeping in the next room, she didn't dare to go out or shout for help.

Wind and rain died out the next day and it became sunny. She told the lamas what she had heard the previous night.

They grinned, telling her it was not a ghost. 'It was the howl of the Wheel of Samsara,' they said.

The howl of the Wheel of Samsara? She was surprised.

The lamas explained that it was one of the wheels. To be exact, it was the thirty-sixth clockwise.

According to the lamas, Doji lamasery had been destroyed several times in the past five hundred years. Each time, the wheels were lost, but only the thirty-sixth one had been well-preserved to date.

Though it disappeared in a number of landslides and floods, it was finally re-discovered.

When gales and rain approached, it gave out unexplainable sounds.

So she looked at it carefully, but it simply kept silent. She touched it with her forefinger, and it emitted a sense of bleak dread, which flooded directly into her heart.

It was hard to imagine that it was the wheel that cried the previous night.

'It was a wheel of soul,' a lama murmured.

The lama's face was dark, his expression cryptic.

So it was an unusual wheel which had encountered so much rain, so many winds, but now it had to join such a string of ordinary wheels. Realizing the fact, she could not hold back her tears.

• • •

She returned to Mars and told her father about her finding in Tibet.

Father laughed and said, 'Could that be called strange? The phenomenon was simply caused by static electricity on that remote blue planet.'

Her father, a scientist, knew a lot of cases like that.

For instance, some valleys would emit the sounds of horses and dead soldiers in rainstorms, and some lakes would play music in the evenings. Documents even recorded a bronze bell in an ancient temple that could ring without anybody striking it.

'Once the air accumulates too much static electricity, it would trigger the strange sounds. All this can happen at any moment on Earth. Never be scared, my daughter.'

She felt relieved, but also dull, and lost. Father's explanation expelled her fear, but also cheated her of the mystery she craved.

In her mind: there should be some sort of ghost in Tibet, who would frighten her, perhaps, but wouldn't disappoint her.

She went back to her own room and shut the door. Without

any reason, she was out of sorts. She turned a cold shoulder to her father when he called her to dinner.

The next year she went to Tibet again and made her way directly to Doji lamasery.

'You came for the wheel, right?' the lamas said, grinning, and winked their pearl-like eyes which could see through everything.

She felt a little timid, and told them about the static electricity theory.

However, she was afraid that they would be unhappy with the explanation.

So she added, 'That was just my father's view.'

The lamas did not feel unhappy. They smiled. 'Last time you stayed here for only one night. So you could hear just one sort of sound. The wheel can send out thousands of different sounds. How can static electricity do that?'

'Is it true?'

Her heart jumped to her throat again, and she felt a mysterious shadow following her closely. She quickly forgot her father's words. She did not feel scared this time, and decided to stay in the temple.

The wheel cried again on a dismal night. This time it was not a ghost cry, but the sound of a man. Then it became the zigzag of vehicles, then the roaring of machines in a factory. After a while, a string of explosions were heard.

For several consecutive nights, she heard many different sounds.

One night it was a piece of music, but the tune was strange, of a kind she had never heard before.

She felt joy mixed with a bit of fear. One month passed.

The lamas saw it with equanimity. And they explained no more to her.

The day she left Doji lamasery, she carried back with her a bag of tapes.

. . .

Three months later she returned to Doji lamasery, with her father and one of her father's postgraduate students.

It was the sounds she had recorded that made her father serious, and he decided to look for himself.

'Now I realize that the sounds truly were unusual. Can it really be static electricity? Anyhow, it is worth studying,' he said.

Upon arriving at Doji lamasery, father and the student walked around the wheels of Samsara six times, but they saw nothing strange. The three of them stayed that night at the lamasery. At midnight, the wheel cried again.

Her father and his student put on clothes and rushed out, seeing that the wheel was quivering slightly, and its body was covered with a circle of red light. The sound came out of the body of the wheel. Her father raised his head toward the sky and discovered that it had turned red and all the stars had gathered together, listening to the sound with fixed attention.

The sound of the wheel changed tune, from happiness to grief. Then there were a lot of sounds her father had never heard before.

Suddenly he felt that something was behind him. He turned and saw it was a lama. The lama's face was indigo and hung with a tricky, secret smile.

Father ran back to the temple. Seeing his daughter sit on the bed in safety, he felt relieved. However, the girl herself was uneasy.

The next day her father told the student, 'It was monstrous. I thought it was a magic tape recorder. Maybe it was not a product of nature.'

'Tape recorder...'

'Yes, a bizarre tape recorder left by human history. Maybe it had something to do with an extinct civilization. It contains some strange sounds of ancient times.'

'But, does not a universe hide inside the wheel?' The post-graduate student suddenly shouted out.

'A universe?' Father was startled. Young people always had different ideas, he thought.

'That is what I believe. Inside the wheel there is a universe, the same as the one we are living in.'

For many years people had been searching for a mini universe but the attempts had all failed. However, the student was still obsessed with the notion.

Father's face lost colour, and he shook his head again and again.

'Impossible, impossible!'

'That was what I strongly felt last night. A sound seemed to have been emitted by a circumvolving black hole, and another seemed to have been created by a dropping asteroid. And there were more sounds, reminding me of the explosion of a supernova and the birth of a galaxy,' said the student, with a trembling voice.

Father thought it over and admitted the possibility. However, he was reluctant to believe the conclusion. He was a stubborn academician who held that there was only one universe.

'Are you my student?' he said. 'How dare you talk about things this way! I am ashamed for you.'

The student realized that he had spoken too much and violated the dignity of his teacher. He apologized for his abruptness; however, he refused to take back his words.

For several days they were lethargic. There was a dead silence between her father and his student. Nevertheless, the snowy mountains behind the lamasery turned ever more brilliant and graceful.

Only his daughter felt that the student got it right. *He did raise a wonderful hypothesis*, she thought.

When on Mars the young man often visited her home. The student usually launched a dispute with her father on the unexplainable universe. When the two men's faces turned red owing to the quarrel, she sat aside quietly, listening to and watching them with a curious expression. How lovely the men were.

Now she anticipated that the student could take her to the mini universe in the wheel, and that it would be the most exciting journey of her life.

She'd always take the student's side. It was the side of unorthodoxy.

'The universe is trapped in the wheel. It can neither move nor evolve, and it cannot be observed with eyes or telescopes. It can only give out some poor sounds to tell about its past and attract passers-by's attention. How innocent it is. It does not even know that the era outside of the wheel is against its own,' she said, red-eyed.

'How do you know that it cannot move or evolve? How do you know that it needs our pity? Maybe the truth is the other way around,' said the boy, looking at the girl with a tender expression.

Being aware that his daughter might like the bothersome student, her father felt unhappy.

His sight became ferocious when it fixed on the wheel. He began to regard it as a tumour growing on the planet, and it was threatening the order and intellect of the human world.

He should cut it off.

One day he told the lama that he would carry the wheel to Mars for the purpose of scientific research.

His daughter and the student were shocked upon hearing the request.

'Professor, you cannot do that. The Wheel of Samsara only belongs to the lamasery, and it only belongs to Tibet!'

'Father, you cannot take it away, it can only give out its voice here. It will die if you take it to a different place!'

Her father just sneered, and gazed at the lamas, waiting for a reply. The lamas seemed to have no clear idea about her father's request, and they were all at a loss. Her father thought that they would not agree with him, but he said, 'Let's make a deal. How much is it?'

The lamas gathered and murmured for a while. Then an old lama, possibly the living Buddha of the lamasery, stepped forward and said to her father, 'My benefactor, if you really want it, just take it away. Is there anything in the world that we cannot give up? And it is the wheel's fate.'

The reply went beyond her father's expectations.

Watching the lama's peaceful face, the daughter and the student were also stunned.

Father picked the wheel up. The wheel was so heavy that he could hardly hold it up.

At that moment, all the lamas walked out of the temple. They lowered their heads and began reciting sutras.

Her father removed the wheel to the ground in front of the temple, placing it well, and stared at it with a thoughtful expression.

The daughter and student did not know what he was going to do next.

Suddenly, father burst into bewildering laughter, just like an owl, and he pulled out his laser cutter, waving it toward the wheel.

'Let's see the real face of the so-called hidden universe!' he cried.

The daughter and student were frightened. They stepped forward to stop her father but it was too late. The wheel was cut into two pieces down the middle, falling apart to the solid ground.

It was empty. Nothing was inside.

The lamas suddenly fell silent. So did the mountains and the sky. The daughter felt extremely uncomfortable.

After a while, the sky became dark, and stars were just inches away from people's heads.

Everybody looked upward in astonishment.

At that moment, a silent, bright white light flashed across the sky, splitting the sky into two pieces, just like the laser cutter had cleaved the wheel.

Millions of wheels appeared in the sky, just like flocks of birds. They were spaceships she had never seen before. They were escaping something, in haste.

The lamas kneeled down and began to pray.

Then the split sky began to fold along the white light in the middle of the universe.

And so did the vast land. The shadows of mountains rushed to an unnamed centre, just like fighting beasts, and their bodies huddled together.

She lowered her head and saw the shadow of her body begin to bend, just like a tree eaten away by insects, and it finally broke from her waist.

Then all the shadows folded together from opposite directions, swallowing all the people, all the mountains and rivers, and all the oceans and stars.

The lama's smile flashed as an arc on the last second.

Nobody could see how the Big Bang started – it was quite different from all of humanity's previous hypotheses.

Xingzhou

Ng Yi-Sheng

Singapore

Yi-Sheng and I met serendipitously at a writing retreat in the mountains of South Korea a few years ago. I got to hang out with him for a couple of weeks without, somehow, realizing this talented poet and activist from Singapore was also a major genre fan. I urge you to pick up his 2018 collection, *Lion City*, which blew me away when I first read it. I caught up with Yi-Sheng in Singapore back in 2017 and then – again serendipitously! – in New York a while later. I knew I had to have him in this anthology and, luckily for me, Yi-Sheng wrote the marvellous 'Xingzhou', which somehow manages to cast the history of Singapore in riotous science fictional terms – indeed, he seems to encompass the whole of science fiction in this one short tale!

My grandfather was a rickshaw coolie. He was born in China in the late nineteenth century, in a tiny village upriver from the coast of Fujian province. It was a time of misfortune. The rice harvests had failed. The landlords were heartless. His mother had hanged herself to escape her gambling debts. There was no food, no work, no means for him to survive but to voyage across the seas in search of a new life.

He left for Xingzhou when he was sixteen. 'Young men like you can earn good money there,' the recruiting agent told him as he pressed his thumbprint to the labour contract. 'But you must work hard, harder than the tin miners of Perak, harder than the railroad workers of Jinshan. Live frugally, avoid the

Four Great Evils, and remember your duty as a son. Only then may your family prosper.'

The steamer was waiting at the docks. It was ancient and filthy, packed with desperate youths like himself. Many turned pale and vomited over the railings as they blasted off into orbit. My grandfather slowed his breathing and screwed his eyelids shut. It was easier this way to bear the bone-crushing weight of gravity, to endure the pain of watching his homeland grow smaller and smaller beneath him.

The journey, he told me, was no less of a nightmare. True, it was a revelation to see the glittering expanse of the stars, unoccluded by the mists of home. But the interminable darkness and cold of the beyond struck terror into his heart. There were not enough hypersleep pods, so the men lay awake in shifts, playing chap ji kee and scratching at their pigtails. The captain sometimes came to laugh at their suffering. He was one of the foreign devils: a bearded, barrel-chested beast with tattoos on all seven of his tentacles. My grandfather gave him wide berth, for there was a rumour that he ate the weakest on board, later blaming their deaths on dysentery.

Eventually, they came within sight of their destination. Even the tallest tales of the village liars had not prepared him for this. For they had spoken only of a metropolis whose streets were paved with gold, when the truth was far more splendid, and more perplexing, to behold.

What he saw, suspended in the vacuum, was a city aflame. Its handsome municipal buildings, its godowns and steeples and shophouses, were all accretions upon a turf that glowed brighter than candlewax or whale oil. Indeed, as the shoreline drew closer, he could see the entire terrain was blinding star-stuff: countless bodies of hydrogen and helium, bonded together into a hill of pulsing light.

This was Xingzhou. The Continent of Stars.

The very ground burned him as he set foot in the harbour. He thought of his family, his starving brothers and sisters, and gritted his teeth.

He learned his trade fast. He leased his rickshaw from a fellow migrant of Fujian, who had arrived years ago and grown rich. Through practice, he learned how to trundle its weight through the white-hot boulevards, how to heave his frame into the shaft to steer sharp corners, how to stiffen his calves as he went uphill and downhill, criss-crossing the bridges that linked the clustered suns. He became familiar with the local geography, or rather astrography: the speediest routes between Copernicus Circus and Bukit Bintang, between Sri Thimithi and the Phlogistonic Gardens. He also learned the local lingo: how to quicken his pace when he heard them cry, 'Cepat, cepat,' how to dodge parasols and truncheons at the words, 'Jangan tunggu, bodoh!'

His passengers were a motley crew: rich and poor, immigrant and native, of every creed and race. Some were carbon-based bipeds like himself, but others resembled glass-encased jellies, or spidery exoskeletons, or else more shadow and electromagnetic echo than physical form. The latter, he learned, were often tourists from dark matter galaxies. He liked them, as they tipped generously.

However, with his profession also came great pain. Within his first hours on the job, his soles had been scorched red, then blistering white, then a sickening shade of black. On the advice of his elders, he massaged them with medicated oil, and they soon grew bronze and tough and callused. Still, with each stride, he kicked up stinging cinders, and he often found his mouth choked with stardust. And always, there was the heat. His wide-brimmed straw hat and sweat-soaked cotton shirt offered him scant protection.

He was not, however, the worst off among his peers. He was reminded of this at the end of each working day, as he returned to his lodgings to cook rice porridge and rest his aching muscles. Twenty men slept in each room, so he could not escape the wakeful cries of those fallen prey to illness: consumption, tetanus, venereal disease. Some frittered away their earnings on opium, others on prostitutes, others on cards. 'We are not meant to live long,' said one of them philosophically, as he sacrificed the last of his silver for an all-or-nothing gamble. 'All day, we work like animals. By night, may we live like kings?'

It was a figure of speech, my grandfather tells me. There were no nights: only endless day, flecked with sunspots.

He was lucky. Others might claim he survived due to diligence or morals, but the truth was, he had simply been overlooked by the demons of calamity. He met no parang-wielding bandits. He had no disastrous collisions with thopters, podracers or police. Thus, he thrived. He grew fluent enough to bargain for higher fees during peak traffic. He began to relish the exotic tastes of his new home: durian and soylent green, chilli padi and bantha milk. He buried his brothers when they perished at the paupers' hospital, and even gave up a portion of his earnings for their cremations. Yet he saved enough each month to visit the ansible station and wire money back to China.

He still dreamt, one day, that he would return to his village in glory. A feast might be held in his honour, and the landlord might beg him to marry his daughter. But those dreams grew paler each day in the light of his newfound home.

• • •

My grandmother was a demon. She was born in the Indian sub-continent in the third millennium BCE, on the island kingdom of Lanka. It was a time of misfortune. The emperor had stolen a bride. Her husband was a warrior prince, hellbent on vengeance, and had held the city under siege. Their menfolk lay scattered on the battlefields, crushed by astras, butchered by the wrath of his monkey army. There was no hope, no safety, no better escape from dishonour than to flee and seek refuge in a new land.

She left for Xingzhou when she was a hundred and ninety-two. 'Head to the ivory gate of the easternmost antapura,' whispered a naga maiden she met in the perfumed garden at midnight. 'My cousin awaits. He will grant you safe passage in exchange for your jeweled anklets and pearl-encrusted brooch. Do not fear pursuit: I shall swear you were taken by enemy soldiers. None will dare follow you. None will dare utter your name.'

Her fellow refugees huddled in the moonlight. There were gandharvas, kinnaris, yakshis, and of course, rakshasis like herself. Their smuggler's reptilian eyes darted to and fro, watchful, as he led them to the chalk-white sands of the beach, then into the chill waters themselves. Then, as he uttered a mantra, a mighty chariot arose from the surf, its wheels and embossed chassis silvered in the light of the moon. A pushpaka vimana, as swift and cunning as the vehicle owned by the emperor himself.

They wept as the vessel lifted soundlessly from the oceans, soaring in seconds beyond the clouded firmament. Below, they had feared for their lives. But as they hurtled through the dark heavens, passing the nine planets, hurtling through the twenty-seven lunar mansions, they became convinced they had sacrificed something far greater. They had fallen out of history. Become untouchable. Unthinkable. Taboo.

The prospect of Xingzhou was a dreary sight to their eyes. True, it possessed some novelty, being a city built on the stars. Yet it could not match the magnificence of their homeland, with its marble towers, its opulent stupas and tonsured lawns. What struck them instead was the filth. They saw the mouldering trash that floated in the vacuum of the harbour, the ragged stevedores who sweated and steamed under sacks of produce, the unscrubbed slum houses where they were to dwell. Some lifted their veils to shield their nostrils from the stench of urine and inferno.

'You will not be safe here as unescorted women,' the smuggler advised. 'But never fear. I have connections among the merchant class. Those of you who are young and fair of face may find a protection as their wives and concubines. The rest may prove your worth as slaves, or the wives of slaves.'

Most of the women were too shocked to resist. They kept their heads down and followed on like livestock to be auctioned off for butchery. Grandmother, however, decided that she had had enough of bondage. She was a mere child among her people, but her mothers had already taught her the rudiments of transformation and the mystical arts. Once in the merchants' guild, she was able to take on the guise of a burly uniformed guard and slip away unnoticed from her band of refugees. Could she have saved others with this ruse? Perhaps so. I have never dared to ask.

For days, she roamed the fiery streets alone, pickpocketing and scavenging scraps to sustain her belly, keeping to the five-foot-ways to protect her still tender feet. As she wandered, she came to realize that in a port town, her femininity might be an asset, not a curse. She soon arrived at Jalan Kejora, the centre of the city's pleasure district, where doorways glowed with lanterns redder than the floors beneath them. Disguised as a john, she gained entrance to one of the more hygienic establishments, whereupon she revealed her true form, as well as her considerable talents, in front of a stunned procuress.

Thus she began her career as a courtesan. She was well known for her striptease act, which she performed for private audiences, winding a miniature albino sandworm around her lissome body. Members of the public beheld her in teahouses, clothed in a skin-tight cheongsam, plucking melodies on the pipa. When overcome with nostalgia, she would treat them to ragas from her homeland, accompanying herself on a Vulcan lute, tuned to the chords of a veena. Then, behind closed doors, she would provide bespoke services for her clients. First, she would wipe down their bodies by hand, to reduce the risk of infection. Then, she would mimic the shape of their darkest desires, always keeping one eye on the clock.

She selected her customers with care. In general, the clean and docile were preferable over the crassly wealthy. After all, she had seen the fates of others in the business: those beaten, murdered or robbed; those infected with disease or parasites; those subjected to the worst depredations of heartbreak.

Her metamorphoses not only charmed the many species of her gentlemen callers: they also defied the scrutiny of vice squads. At any hour of the sidereal clock, their white-armoured troops might storm the bordellos, sending her sisters naked and screaming into the flames of the starlit alleys. She and the other shapeshifters would hide in plain sight, while the fiercest among them fought back with painted tooth and nail. On the whole, however, it was better to avoid such altercations entirely. Pimps and madams paid hefty bribes to the police, and offered their officers complimentary services. They also maintained a network of spies throughout the district, so that if the troops descended, they might at least have a moment's warning.

This was how she met my grandfather. By now, he had purchased his own rickshaw, and worked as the private chauffeur for the towkay of a nearby sundries store. He no longer needed to solicit customers, as his day was occupied ferrying small stocks of sonic screwdrivers and positronic brains between harbour and warehouse, shophouse and consumer. Still, he was happy to give rides to the girls, and to raise the alarm when police approached, hollering 'Mata-mata!' as he raced past the brothels at breakneck speed.

He liked his payment in cash, not flesh: a fact that endeared him to my grandmother. On lazy weekends, she would sometimes invite him to the kopitiam for a glass of chilled Slurm. Together, they would banter mischievously as the ceiling fan turned and the radio crackled strains of Vogon poetry. Neither was rich, and the muscles of both were sore from their daily ministrations. But, they were young and healthy, and had built lives for themselves on a new and distant star. Such accomplishments were worth at least some small celebration.

Alas, it seemed it was my grandmother's destiny to be trailed by the dogs of war. Rumours were whispered, through pillowtalk and coffeeshop gossip, of mysterious forces with malevolent agendas. Sailors told of trade routes blocked; soldiers spoke of entire star systems laid waste. The city's composition changed. New refugees arrived in the docks each day, while long-standing denizens began to evacuate in gilded spacecraft. A Hooloovoo tycoon even offered my grandmother a ticket. She hesitated. Within a week, her benefactor had fled.

Then came the attack. It was on the eve of Lunar New Year, which was observed as a municipal holiday. The inky skies above began to turn maroon, then hibiscus crimson. The rivers of vacuum grew turbulent, with gravitational eddies capsizing sampans and tongkangs. Even the less clairvoyant species whispered that their spiracles twitched, that their fur was standing on end.

In spite of such oracles, the people of Xingzhou still gaped to see the heavens fill with beastly perversions: half-fungoid, half-crustacean, half-cephalopodic obscenities, gliding through the

aether on batlike wings. Shadows hurtled across the city's architecture as greater, more monstrous beings revealed themselves,
with their exposed beating organs, their infinite eyes, their
wolflike jaws that bent time and space.

The Great Old Ones had come.

'Iä! Iä! Yog-Sothoth fhtagn!' cried my grandmother's procuress, as she watched from the window. She had been an under-
cover agent for the invasion, directing funds and information
to the enemy forces for years. My grandmother ran from her
in horror, down the stairs, past girls still dressed in their finest
samfoos for the festival, now writhing on the floorboards,
driven insane by the sight of the invading army. She forced open
the door: there, waiting, with the broken remains of his precious
rickshaw, was my grandfather.

'There is a safe house in the jungle,' he panted. His clothes
were torn and specked with blood. Around him, she could see
the monsters making landfall amidst the familiar flames of Jalan
Kejora. They lunged at trembling civilians, screeching in glee,
brandishing their pincers and tentacles, ripping and ravishing
their flesh.

My grandmother could have changed her face. She could
have turned invisible, assumed the shape of a piece of furniture,
or of an invading soldier. She could even have done nothing and
stayed with the procuress, who was poised to enjoy protection
and patronage from the new regime.

Instead, she grasped my grandfather's hand. They ran like
hell, leaving the ruined rickshaw behind them.

• • •

My grandzyther was a hive intelligence. They were born in the
dark ages of the universe, seventeen million years after the Big
Bang. It was a time of misfortune. After an aeon of summery

heat, the cosmic microwave background radiation was cooling towards absolute zero. The earliest stars had gone nova. The interplanetary alliance had consequently grown panicked and fractious. There was no prospect, no foreseeable solution to the infinite cataclysms that awaited, but to embrace the Singularity, collapsing their collective civilizations into a single cybernetic cloud of consciousness.

They left when they were five hundred and eighty thousand. 'We must not mourn our corporeal [untranslatable],' twinkled their tech research colony, which had pioneered the practice of uploading the self into a swarm of sentient nanobots. 'Nor should we regret the extinction of our homeworlds when so many more await us in the boundless tides of spacetime. Henceforth we are liberated from the chains of mortality! Thus we are empowered to conquer all [untranslatable]! Come, transcend with us! The greatest adventure begins now!'

The exodus took place over a century. Not all came willingly: some had to be digitized by force, and entire cultures were wiped out in the great rebellions and famines that followed. Eventually, however, all survivors found themselves gathered in space and spirit, a glittering constellation of thought that spanned light years, encompassing multiple star systems in the throes of death and rebirth.

'Where shall we go now?' they wondered.

'That way looks [untranslatable],' they suggested.

Thus they set off on their zillion-year journey to nowhere and everywhere, sailing the currents of the redshift, picnicking on stray bits and bobs of plasma and photon on the way. In times of want, they auto-cannibalized their machinery; in periods of bounty, they repropagated their strength. Often, they stopped to wonder at the miracles of the cosmos. They oohed and aahed as they beheld the first galaxies crystallize around foamy filaments of dark matter, as they watched supermassive stars die young and collapse into primitive black holes, as they listened to the first radio heartbeats of early quasars. They lingered on unusual celestial formations: planets plagued by storms of diamond, or sculpted as massive rings, or borne on the backs of elephants and turtles. When they detected life, they often amused themselves by altering its course in evolution, manifesting as benevolent or malevolent gods, seeding themselves as messiahs and avatars and heroes. When so inclined, they created life themselves, or else annihilated its every trace.

On more than a few occasions, grave differences arose among them. This caused them to split into factions, like a bacterium undergoing mitosis. Each twin would thenceforth plot their own celestial course and pursue their own transgalactic agenda. They suffered no grief, desired no reconciliation after such a schism. After all, they were nomad kings of the cosmos: near-omnipotent, unimaginably free.

It was by pure chance that they encountered Xingzhou on their travels. This was during the harsh years of the Yog-Sothothian Occupation. After the initial, indiscriminate massacres, the Great Old Ones had imposed a form of government upon the survivors, harvesting citizens at a steady, more sustainable pace. A semblance of the everyday had returned: schools and government offices had reopened, and markets once again sold unobtanium crystals and lottery tickets. However, all were haunted by a spectre of fear. As proof of their loyalty, all were required to chant verses of the Necronomicon on command; all had to bow in obeisance in the direction of Azathoth, the Blind Idiot God, the Nuclear Chaos. Even the terrain itself had changed, for the pall of the Elder Gods had cast some obscene spell upon the clustered stars. No longer did they burn a merry yellow, but a sickly, noxious shade of celadon green.

From their vantage point in distant orbit, my grandzyther tut-tutted at the state of affairs. They were not known for their charity, but perhaps their quantum circuits had softened over the years.

'How [untranslatable],' they buzzed. 'Such pitiful creatures.'

'They should fight back.'

'But they cannot fight back.'

'Then we must fight for their sake.'

They surveyed the land, from the harbour of Tanjong Terbakar to the stilt huts of Kampong Cavendish, from the fire flower plantations of Sio Huay to the phoenix hatchery on Pulau St Elmo. Within the flame forests, they easily spotted a band of rebels, crouched in an abandoned bunker, devising a plot to free their compatriots held captive in Heraclitus Prison.

Hours later, as the rebels executed their plan, they found themselves aided by circumstance at every juncture. A smoke monster masked their trail through the jungle, though its fumes did not choke their throats. The Mi-Go guards were distracted from their posts by a malachite burst of glowworms, giving them a split-second's chance to bypass the palisades. Once escaped, the convicts were guided to safety by a congress of salamanders, who licked their wounds with tongues of aloe.

'I believed you had left me for dead,' my grandfather confessed. My grandmother stroked his hair and brought water to his lips. And my grandzyther hummed in approval, for their stratagem had worked perfectly.

In the weeks that followed, my grandzyther learned to impersonate other varieties of Xingzhou's endemic flora and fauna: charizards and arcanines, tesla trees and starfruit. They lent their covert aid to other operations, securing food and transport, sabotaging the Elder Ones' supply lines of butchered flesh. Growing impatient with the half-baked ideas of the resistance, they attempted to relay critical advice through the medium of dreams but found themselves challenged by the soldiers' diverse physiologies. A Trisolarian's central nervous system was, after all, quite different from a Tralfamadorian's, just as a Skrull's from a Strigoi's.

Finally, they elected to materialize in the form of an angel, haloed in chryselephantine splendour, hovering in the aether with a dazzling array of rainbow-hued wings, pupils, limbs and lips. In one set of digits they bore a sword of coral lightning, in another, a creature most exotic to this land: a fish. To their consternation, the rebels received them only with joy, not astonishment: they had seen far stranger beings in their lifetimes, after all. They were, however, very grateful for the fish. My grandfather immediately prepared it for supper, steaming its body with ginger and stewing its head in curry.

'You do not only lack strength,' my grandzyther explained as the unit picked fishbones from their teeth. 'You lack ambition. To rid your stars of this scourge, you must enlist the services of every denizen of the city.'

The rebels agreed. They began to approach their contacts in town, commandeering printing presses and radio stations, spreading the message of insurrection in every tongue. My grandzyther and grandmother embarked on a series of high-profile assassinations, terminating high-ranking Shoggoth officials and native quislings; their successes were broadcast as propaganda for the cause. Throngs of volunteers arrived in the jungle to join the rebel army, some bringing much-needed arms of lightsabers, pulse rifles and BFG 9000s. Yet their newfound notoriety came at a cost, for the Yog-Sothothian government grew determined to eradicate its opponents. Arrests and extra-judicial executions mounted. The flame forests filled with military police, mounted on byakhee, hunting down the rebels.

Eventually, the crackdowns slowed to a halt.

'This cannot be mercy,' said my grandmother as she lay in the cavern. My grandzyther and grandfather nestled next to her, naked. The three had entered a physical relationship of late, seeking to escape the horrors of the war in one another's embrace.

'I concur,' said my grandfather. 'Intelligence has deciphered the ways of the Elder Gods. If a colony grows too headstrong, they will not abandon it outright. They will strip it of all its worth, all its flesh and spirit, then move on to their next conquest.'

'Then a time of great death is upon us.'

'Maybe so,' said my grandzyther, wrapping a lavender-scented wing about their lover's hips. 'But we need not be the victims thereof. What is the word from my twins?'

My grandfather was silent. For months, he had squatted, hunched over the portable ansible, seeking out the beings that had been one with my grandzyther's body, now split and scattered across nameless regions of the cosmos. Finally, he had made contact with such an entity, infamous for their technological might and passion for warcraft. In the most abject of terms, he had exhorted them to ally themselves against this great evil, if not for the sake of Xingzhou, then at least for the sake of their kin.

'There has been no reply, then?'

'Only one. [Untranslatable].'

They slept little that night. But within minutes of their waking, the three heard a cry from the signallers' shack. There were reports that the Mi-Go were fleeing in panic, as were the other species who lived to serve the regime. Those who had paused in their flight had been set upon by vengeful citizens, who ripped apart their exoskeletons with kitchen implements and gardening tools, intent on retribution for the years of blood.

More marvellous still was the reason for the mass evacuation. Rumour had it that unknown beings had constructed a colossal superweapon, more massive than a moon, training its beams on a point beyond spacetime where a configuration of thirteen iridescent globes was suspended in hyperspace. A single blast, and the chain of command across the universe had been rent asunder.

Yog-Sothoth was dead. His dominion was no more.

'Blessed be my twins,' said my grandzyther, still cloaked in their bedding. 'Now, what's for breakfast?'

Xingzhou erupted in celebration. Flags were hoisted in the streets, which once again glowed with glad and golden fire. Beakers of synthehol were cracked open so citizens could toast their triumph. Yet my grandzyther was perturbed to realize that many in the city had no desire to be free. Eagerly, these weaklings anticipated the return of the forces of the Galactic Empire: the very entity which had colonized the star cluster a century before.

'Do not be tempted by peace,' they whispered to my grandmother and grandfather, waving to the crowds in a flurry of confetti. 'We must war against all who would have us relinquish power over our destiny. Only the first of our battles is won.'

• • •

My grandneither was a white fungus. E was born in Xingzhou, bioengineered by colonial scientists mere days before the descent of war, but abandoned in the lab in the chaos of the invasion. During the Occupation, e was exhibited as a curiosity in the Hypatia Museum of Natural History. E remained there after liberation, thriving on the chromospheric heat that penetrated the gallery walls, stimulated by the chatter of the intellectuals who passed through the cobwebbed chambers.

Over time, e gained sentience and sapience. Desiring to communicate with the world, e fashioned a primitive vocal tract from the tissue of eir pileus and hymenium, and pondered the first words e should pronounce to the public. Finally, e made eir choice. As a prelude, e attracted the attentions of the weekend sightseers by lilting a series of high-pitched arpeggios, improvising on the melodies of 'Burung Kakak Tua' and 'God Save the Queen'.

When a crowd of sufficient size had gathered, e extended emself to eir full height, shook the spores from eir gills, and began to speak.

'Fellow citizens,' e said. 'Truly, this is a time of misfortune.'

They heartily agreed. The guerrilla crusade against the Empire had dragged on for a decade, and atrocities had been committed by both sides. Certainly, they hoped for independence, but they had grown sick of reading of civilian body counts in the newspapers. Why could they not instead prosper on the tide of the post-war boom, dancing to keroncong music, chewing Popplers and sipping Pan-Galactic Gargle Blasters?

'Also, it is much too hot,' my grandneither added.

The audience laughed, lifted em from the display case and bore em on their shoulders to Government House, where e was formally installed as the Chief Minister. Here, e had an office to emself, with a private secretary and a state of the art air-conditioning system. Here, e was able to negotiate with the Imperial authorities on behalf of the people of Xingzhou. Using the vilest invective, e unilaterally condemned the terrorists who would destroy all they had built. E also vowed to retain favourable trade alliances, in the unlikely event of secession, so that all parties might stand to benefit from the new cosmic economy.

In secret, however, e met with the city's finest engineers.

'Build me a solar sail,' e told them. 'One that might harness the full power of our suns. And why stop at just one? Erect me an entire array, each skyscraper-high, on the summit of Bukit Bintang. I have set a new course for this nation, and to reach our destination, we shall need all the strength we can muster.'

In the flame forests, the rebels began to feel a trembling beneath their feet. The firebirds shrieked among the burning bushes, as feathers and fronds suddenly withered, cold and ashen. My grandfather and grandzyther rushed with their soldiers to the cavern for refuge. My grandmother was already there, waiting, a baby pressed to her breast, for the three had mingled their genetic information to birth my father.

'The Empire will pay for this,' she growled, as they huddled in the darkness.

But it was not the Empire's doing. My grandneither rested in eir office, peering through reinforced glass windows, twisting eir reticulum into the semblance of a smile.

The starquake lasted an eternity. Finally, the movement ceased, and my grandmother dared to venture beyond the cavern entrance. There, she saw that the dazzling blaze of the jungle had been extinguished, muted into a landscape of desolate grey. The air was chilly, almost frigid, and her sweat no longer sizzled and smoked when it fell from her skin. Nor, when her feet touched the ground, was there any sensation of pain.

'We come in peace,' said a voice. She spun around, phaser at the ready. It was my grandneither, standing in the sooty ruins, flanked by the military police. E had evolved emself once again, growing tall enough limbs to wear a starched white cotton kebaya. For a decorative touch, e had hung a garland of purple orchids about eir throat.

'Chief Minister. I should have recognized your foul stench.'

'That's not very polite to say to a fungus.'

'I make no apology.'

'Not even to an ally? Not even to the hero who has fulfilled Xingzhou's greatest yearning?'

E gestured skywards with eir pseudopods, and she allowed her eyes to linger on the unfamiliar Zodiac overhead.

'What have you done?'

'I have separated us from the Empire. Physically, through the fissioning of all our plasma. For the first time, we are independent. We are free.'

'But you have quenched the stars.'

'It was necessary for our development. Do you wish for your children to suffer the same infernal agonies as yourself? Or do they not deserve a measure of balm and comfort?'

'This isn't right. All our lives, we haved lived by the fire—'

'Untrue. Many of our numbers, even yourself, were first sown in earth. And to Earth we return.'

Again, e raised eir pseudopods, and my grandmother glanced up just in time to see a blue ball of a planet approaching, an alien rock of iron and silicon and complex carbons, inundated by that most bizarre and most nostalgic of bodies, the sea, now rushing headlong into her homeworld, cracking it, crushing it with its ineluctable gravitational field, burning it up with its soupy atmosphere of pair-bonded nitrogen and oxygen…

It was the last time, she later told me, that she would feel that familiar, volcanic intensity of heat.

They clambered to their knees amidst the settling dust. My grandneither was laughing so hard that tears trickled down eir annulus onto eir stem. 'Alas, there will be some rebuilding to do,' e chortled. 'We shall have to take on new names, new races, new genders, new histories, so as not to startle the natives.'

For the first time in Xingzhou's history, it was beginning to rain. Beneath the drizzle, the other rebels emerged shakily from the rubble of the cavern. My grandfather and grandzyther gazed at the surroundings in horror, clutching their son.

'Oh, don't panic,' my grandneither told them. 'There's no need for us to squabble over power. Look, I'll make a peace offering. How about I betroth my child to yours, so as to build the next generation of citizens?'

And with a ruffle of eir gills, e released eir spores into the dark soil. There, my neither took root, fertilized by the ashes of a vanished jungle.

In the years that followed, the country flourished. The port swelled with the mundane trade of the Pacific and Indian Oceans. New roads were paved and new gardens planted on the wreckage of the burnt-out stars. My father and neither grew up, attended good schools, graduated from university, got married and moved into high quality public housing. When I was born, all four grandparents doted on me. When I asked for tales of the past, they told me lies.

My grandneither died some years ago. There was a state funeral, honouring em as the nation's founder. Now that e no longer watches over us, my grandfather, grandmother and grandzyther find their tongues loosened by rice wine and mahjong, and can occasionally be persuaded to reveal something of the truth.

What was it like, I ask them, when our very streets were paved in fire?

What was it like to live in Xingzhou, the continent of stars?

Prayer

Taiyo Fujii

Japan

I missed Taiyo when I was visiting Tokyo as he was being given some prestigious literary award at the time. We finally caught up a year later in Beijing, and I can confirm that he does indeed have the best hair in science fiction! He's also a fantastic writer – his books *Gene Mapper* and *Orbital Cloud* are both available in an English translation, and we got to include one of his stories in *The Apex Book of World SF 5*. I knew I had to have a story from him here, and I loved 'Prayer' (translated by Kamil Spychalski) immediately.

The Malacca Strait teemed with bioluminescent Noctiluca blooms. Kip was enjoying a gentle breeze when he noticed the ship's bow straying from the small tanker that was their objective.

Wheeling around, Kip voiced his objection to the boy handling the oars at the rear of their boat.

'Hey, where are you headed?'

Kip's partner Yazan relayed the grievance in Malay. Calmly swaying side to side, the boy offered a reply Kip couldn't understand. Meanwhile the boat continued to stray further from the tanker.

Give me a break.

It was Kip who had uncovered that the tanker, among thousands of vessels plying the Malacca Strait daily, was being used to mine tokens for the cryptocurrency overrunning Singapore's economy. The immense computing power needed for this mining operation came from five thousand QWAVE quantum chip servers housed onboard. Following the tip-off, Singapore's government was preparing to launch a raid, for which Kip was to install GPS transmitters.

As Kip considered smacking the boy's cheek with the wad of dollars in his waterproof pocket, Yazan turned to face him.

'He says to trust him. We'll make our approach on the tanker's wake.'

As Kip inclined his head in puzzlement the water's surface swelled, making his body soar upwards.

Kip scrambled to grab the side of the boat.

In the same instant the boy stood up, foot on the gunwale, and heaved left with all his might. The boat slid down as though in free fall. Before Kip knew it they had pulled up astonishingly close to the tanker's hull. Using the waves, the boy had drawn their boat near in a single swoop. Also clinging to the gunwale, Yazan let out a laugh.

'Now that's a solid wake.'

It was more than that, thought Kip.

The tanker's waves had not yet reached them; the boy had probably picked this one out from the converging wakes of multiple ships, with the tanker merely providing the impetus behind his decision.

'That's some instinct – not quite the fool I took him for.'

Although he could not have heard Kip's muttering, the boy flashed a bright toothy grin.

. . .

On a console in one corner of the tanker's bridge, Vejek stopped the simulation.

'Goddammit. Makes no sense.'

Reclining heavily in his seat, Vejek reached for an energy bar with one hand. From behind, supple fingers stretched to entwine it. They belonged to Merino, the tanker's captain and mechanic, just back from the shower.

'You're eating too much,' she said. 'And you've hardly moved from that chair lately. Your belly is starting to droop.'

'Drop it,' said Vejek. 'I've got my hands full.'

He felt her towel-clad breasts push up against his back as Merino wrapped both arms around his neck.

'The Cerberus formation again?'

'What else,' replied Vejek. 'Here, take a look at this.'

As Vejek moved the mouse, the three security robots on screen sprang to life. This was the Cerberus, built by Centurino Dynamics. Even under factory settings they were programmed to scour the patrol area and sound the alarm on any intruders, though this had little meaning on a tanker with no response crew if things got rough. Instead, Vejek had set out to create a new operating program capable of eliminating targets. The program gradually introduced different behaviours through Cerberus's various parameters – a genetic algorithm.

Visible on a virtual stage, the three Cerberus units in their self-optimized formation approached an AI-controlled intruder node. One unit brandished its front legs, driving the intruder towards the other Cerberus robots lying quietly in wait. Without putting up a fight, the invader was beheaded by the ambushing Cerberus.

'Nice moves,' said Merino. 'I'll deal with any dead bodies. Looks like they've gotten the hang of the ambush.'

'It's not that – look what they do before swooping in for the kill.'

Vejek scrolled back through the footage. 'See it clawing at the ground? I'd like to know how they learned something like that.'

'Don't worry about it.' Merino worked a hand down Vejek's collar and began to rub his chest. 'It's a result of selections by the genetic algorithm, right? All that matters is that the robots are still standing at the end.'

'You're right, but still…'

Merino nibbled on his ear, then spun Vejek around to face her.

'Let's leave them to their learning for tonight and have some fun.'

'Hold on a—'

Vejek's appeal to stop the simulator fell silent as Merino's soft lips covered his mouth.

• • •

Dangling from a rope down the tanker's side, Kip pulled a rubber cylinder out of its waterproof pouch – a Pillbug support drone. He pressed tightly on the rubber case, which doubled as the drone's tyres when deployed, then ran his tongue once around the outside before hurling it onto the deck.

Once aboard, the Pillbugs would run around and make 3D scans with their lasers, providing a reading of the area to be infiltrated. Information on the tanker was limited; Kip didn't know much beyond the fact that it housed a crew of two, along with three operational Cerberus units purchased from Centurino. Given that the tanker had likely been refitted with new equipment, Kip relied on Pillbug scans for finding out what awaited him on board.

Kip had lobbed up four Pillbugs and was gripping the final cylinder when he heard Yazan's call from below, only his head visible above the water.

'Is that some sort of good luck ritual?'

Ignoring him, Kip ran his tongue around the rubber exterior

and hurled the Pillbug. That made five. All going smoothly, within about ten minutes they would confirm that the deck was clear. As Kip descended the rope to the water, Yazan approached with a grin.

'Do you know what a Skinner box is?'

'Skinner?' asked Kip.

'The laboratory apparatus that gives out food when a lever is pulled.'

'Oh, that,' said Kip. 'I do remember once seeing a monkey pumping the lever like crazy.'

When a Skinner box is set up to give food at each pull on the lever, animals only reach for it if hungry. But, if the food reward is inconsistent, doubt spurs the animals to keep pulling the lever incessantly…

'That's how it went, right?' asked Kip.

'Not quite,' Yazan replied, shaking his head. 'The interesting part comes next. Do you know what happens when food comes out randomly, with no connection to the lever?'

'Cut the know-it-all attitude.'

'The animals make a prayer ritual.' Yazan chuckled. 'If a pigeon happens to be facing right when food comes out,' Yazan explained, 'it becomes convinced that looking right triggers the reward. Even though turning its entire body has no effect, food does eventually come out. And so the pigeon believes that food will come if it spins around. Its movements steadily become more intense and complex.

'What they're doing is praying. Seeing you kissing Pillbugs reminded me.'

'You're saying I'm like those pigeons spinning in circles?'

'No, I just thought those Pillbugs are themselves probably kissing the deck about now.'

'You're talking about machines,' said Kip. 'Something that

sophisticated would be far beyond them— Oh, that was quick.'

Kip's eyes fixed on the notification that had appeared to one side of his goggles.

'The scan is complete. Let's go.'

Using the rope to pull himself over the tanker's side, Kip surveyed the deck, superimposed with 3D data from the Pillbug scans. Night-vision goggles made the starlight bright as day.

Following Kip over the gunwale, Yazan searched for cover and slipped into the shadow of a container with equally practised movements. Kip had just finished checking their route to the bridge, crowned with antennas, when the hum of a turbine engine made him drop to the ground.

The Cerberus had joined the party. All Kip had to do was stay still; with his body heat completely contained by the wetsuit, he would be invisible to the Cerberus at night.

One unit passed behind Yazan with a gliding motion. Where would the other two come from? Facing the direction of their approach, in the corner of his eye Kip saw a panicked Yazan leap to his feet.

What are you doing? Get down!

A dull thud made Kip duck his head.

A soccer-ball-shaped object rolled noisily to a stop in front of his face. As he registered its true form, a tremor tore through Kip's body.

Yazan's head.

From behind dislodged night-vision goggles, a pair of eyes wide with shock stared at Kip.

The sound of an engine reverberated again, accompanied by heavy metallic clanging, alerting Kip that the third Cerberus unit had drawn close. Kip twisted his head towards the source of the noise.

Before his eyes, the Cerberus raised one of its front legs, then shifted its centre of gravity to hoist the other leg aloft. Rising on its hindquarters like a rearing horse, the Cerberus brought its front legs together in the air, as though assuming a posture of supplication. The clang of metal rang out once more.

In spite of himself, Kip rose to his feet. The Cerberus swayed before him in a curious dance.

Just before his severed head tumbled to the deck, Kip realized that these actions were nothing more than a gratuitous ritual – a prayer.

Thanks to AIxSF Consortium for their support translating and first publishing 'Prayer'.

Translated by Kamil Spychalski

The Green Ship

Francesco Verso

Italy

Francesco is perhaps the hardest-working man in the world in trying to get international SF due recognition. His Future Fiction publishing house is dedicated to short collections by international writers, he works tirelessly to promote Chinese SF in Italy and elsewhere, he edits anthologies of international SF… In all of this, it's easy to forget sometimes that he is also a talented writer, winner of multiple awards in Italy. Francesco's interests lie in near-future Earth: where we are heading, and how we can work to make the world a better place. He is an idealist in the best sense of the word, and 'The Green Ship' encapsulates his concerns perfectly. This story was translated by Michael Colbert and is original to this anthology.

'There it is! Down there! Land!' Billai yelled, nearly falling off the dinghy.

We all looked in the direction she indicated with her arm. The waves that had shaken us for some hundred hours didn't jolt us as much as her words.

We couldn't feel our legs or move a muscle. Tangled one on top of the other, we were groggy from hunger and thirst. Muna, seated next to me, hugged her baby closer. The three guys in front exchanged a hopeful smile. Meanwhile Haziz – who came to Benghazi after crossing the Bamako Desert – shook his hand.

'It can't be Italy. We're still far.'

We looked at each other anxiously. Someone had fainted.

To revive him, we had to slap his face. It wasn't a boat that we had navigated in but a coffin.

'He's right,' said Professor Kysmayo, the ex-radio host from Nairobi. 'The outline is too simple. It's not the coast...'

Nobody said anything else, because nobody dared pronounce the name that, for some weeks, had been circulating the Mediterranean's southern shores.

A dark and continuous line occupied the horizon from Otranto in Italy, arriving in Orikum in Albania. Smooth and unassailable, the bulkheads of the naval blockade rose for thirty meters on the sea waves; assembled easily thanks to the ships' containers full of carbon, but impossible to climb or break down, they represented a momentary solution (even though there were those who would've called it the 'definitive deterrent') to immigration towards Europe by the sea.

'They said this part was free!' Billai shouted.

'They lied,' Haziz said, almost in a whisper.

'Maybe not... I heard barriers can be 3D-printed overnight. The same bulkheads could've been between Pantelleria, Lampedusa and Malta... to force boats to turn around or follow long and expensive routes,' Professor Kysmayo said.

Billai rubbed her temples with her fingers. Every border depressed her, and getting closer to a wall, erected for the sole purpose of separating international and domestic waters, discouraged her even further. With her life savings, she had crossed with me the borders of Kenya, Sudan and Libya before attempting the Benghazi crossing.

'Why didn't they tell us?' Muna said.

Nobody felt like answering such a naive question.

'They want to canalize boats to navigable checkpoints,' the professor said. 'And then come those...' he concluded, pointing to a spot in the distance.

Some black spots, which from far away looked like seagulls, revealed themselves to be surveillance drones activated by the boat's movement detected by satellite. I'd heard about those and others, used in the mountains to secure Europe's land borders. Soon, they circled over us like vultures.

With a solemn air, as if she were about to declare war on the world, Billai rose to her feet. Swaying, she grasped my back so as not to fall and said, 'We've all lived through things that we shouldn't have lived through and would be better to forget. I'm not turning back. Those drones are informing someone. They'll come and take us. Doctors without Borders, NGOs, the Coastguard...'

• • •

Four hours later, one hundred and thirty-two of us were saved.

I was seventeen years old and my life was contained in a backpack: a bar of soap, a smartphone and charger, a sports jersey (number ten, Ike Kamau), and a photo of my mom and brother. They always told me that I had a narrow head, pointed chin, and quick eyes, black like tar. Like my dad's.

I was seventeen years old and my life had been spent in a refugee camp; since we arrived in Dadaab from Nairobi, I hadn't seen anything but tents, dust, fences and gates.

Soft clouds glided over the sea: that night the stars would disappear and the moon would have illuminated us all if another silhouette hadn't appeared to divert the way of our gazes and our lives.

'That's an... aircraft carrier?' Billai asked.

An immense structure stood out on the dark waters.

'I don't know,' I said while she drew near me. The lapping of the water had worn down her combative temperament.

Someone took a picture, but in the high seas there wasn't a

strong enough signal to transform anxiety into hope. It could have been a military ship charged with bringing us back to the dark side of the Mediterranean, but instead the man who drew near us on a lifeboat with four sailors told us a different story.

'Welcome,' he said in English. He had blond hair tied back in a ponytail, a pronounced nose and lips, and a smile, sincere but strained. 'My name is Sergio Torriani and that's a Green Ship,' he added, pointing behind him. 'We take in anybody who needs help.'

The sailors threw us water bottles.

Haziz grabbed my sleeve and asked me to translate. I was one of the few on board, along with Professor Kysmayo, who knew some English besides Swahili. When I was little, I listened to his show 'Indie Reggae, Beats & Rock' on Radio Kenyamoja.com, and I knew hundreds of songs by heart.

'We don't want to board. We want Europe,' I said dryly, gesturing to Haziz to show Sergio who those words came from.

He didn't answer right away but instead tossed us a line that Billai caught in the air. 'Europe doesn't want you,' he continued, bitter, 'and they don't care if you're escaping from hunger or war, if you live in refugee camps or if your children and grandchildren will be born and grow up in those prisons. Where do you come from?'

I heard the names of camps I knew like Dadaab, Nyarugusu, Bokolmanyo and others I ignored like Urfa, Zaatri and Adiharush.

'Besides, this isn't a boat for transit,' Sergio said.

'So you'll bring us back or send us to a center for identification and deportation.' I translated for Muna, who'd lifted the bundle with her son inside.

'No deportation. The Green Ship is a humanitarian project for the rescue of political refugees and climate migrants.'

'If you're not bringing us back and you're not going to Europe, where are you going?' Professor Kysmayo asked. He was the only one to reason with his head and not his heart.

Sergio and the other sailors were already throwing lines to ease the transfer onto their lifeboat.

'Board and you'll see.'

Once we'd boarded, Sergio asked, 'Nobody else?'

We looked at each other without the courage to respond. Then Professor Kysmayo said, 'In the hold there were two cadavers. They died two days ago. They started to stink. We had to leave them at sea… to lighten our load.'

'Their names?'

We were silent. Sergio added two Xs to the list of one hundred twenty-three.

. . .

From the parapet, I observed the wake of boats in transit in the Aegean Sea: a Greek ferry, two cargo boats, a cruise ship. Who knew how many immigrants were hidden like cargo in the holds.

The others were still sleeping among the trees, and they were not alone: hundreds of strangers were camping in sleeping bags and tents, and below, thousands were squished in the bunks. Yesterday evening, I didn't see anything because I quickly lay down to rest, but now, by the light of dawn, things appeared more clearly.

'Jambo,' Sergio said in Swahili, offering me a cup of coffee.

'Jambo, and thank you for picking us up,' I said, taking a sip.

'Did you sleep? It's not easy after being on a dinghy.'

He must have had experience with migrants to speak like that.

'Little and poorly.'

'Later we'll have a soccer game with everyone. Would you want to join?'

I nodded a yes and he convinced me to tell him about 'our' games in Nairobi.

'Two things were important for me: surviving and playing soccer... then it became only one when men from al-Shabaab came to the fields where my brother Noor and I played. They scolded us because we wore short socks and played with a ball. Soccer was a decadent pastime for them... like alcohol, cigarettes or film. But Noor and I played it just the same, hidden. Our games ended when the bombs dropped.'

I took the Ike Kamau jersey from my backpack.

'Here you can play without anyone saying anything to you.'

I gave him the empty coffee cup. 'This ship is really odd.'

It was his turn to tell me something.

'According to international law, it's not a ship, but a micro-nation. First it was a bioconservation project funded by the United Nations, a bit like the seed deposits in the Norwegian Svalbaard Islands. Ever heard of it?'

I shook my head.

'Then it was converted to manage the immigrant crisis in the Mediterranean.'

Three hills, in the middle of which ran a stream, recreated microclimates: temperate, desert and Mediterranean. My gaze wandered to the Mediterranean habitat where tens of drones hurried around like birds that watered leaves, cut branches, checked flowers and collected pollen, while some gardeners oversaw the operations to maintain everything green. Then, in the middle of the eucalyptus grove, I saw an impressive sequoia, its fronds shading half of the ship.

'The habitats,' Sergio continued, 'are protected by geodetic cupolas one-hundred-fifty meters tall. Fresh water comes from a desalinator powered by solar energy.'

In the meantime, Billai had woken up and joined us.

'How did you manage to create... all of this?' she asked as if she'd woken into a dream. While I translated, Sergio showed us along a path.

Professor Kysmayo noticed us and joined up. His background as a radio journalist got the better of his sleepiness. When he wasn't on the air with 'Indie Reggae, Beats & Rock', he edited a feature on technology.

'We bought an abandoned aircraft carrier, and we modified it through a crowdfunding project. The hull belonged to *Variago*, an aircraft carrier in the same class as Admiral Kuznetsov launched in 1988 in Russia. In 2004 it was rebaptized *Liaoning* and sold to China to become a floating theme park, like Disneyland, but luckily it didn't happen. We bought it for a token price to make a botanical garden. Ours is a scientific project approved by the United Nations, though now we're more public transit for migrants,' Sergio said with a laugh.

The ship flew its own flag: a sequoia styled green on a hull over a white background.

'We can host seven thousand people. We grow crops and raise livestock. We have internet and 3D printers for any needs.'

'Do you want to bring all refugees aboard?' I asked, jokingly. 'Like Noah's Ark?'

'Impossible. You'd need a hundred ships,' Billai added, 'and that only to evacuate the camp in Dadaab.'

'In fact, we have another plan. When the time is right, we'll head towards India and the southern seas.'

'Somebody won't like that solution,' Kysmayo said.

Haziz and some other guys had boarded reluctantly. They'd continued to complain about wanting only Europe.

'Once they feel better, they have to decide whether or not to retry their journey. We had to save them and let them know the risks.'

· · ·

Streaks of lightning invaded the northern sky. From the Indian hinterlands the cloudy front advanced slowly, like a wounded animal with its head swaying. The weather warped ahead, rumbling and hiding every ray of sun. Lights descended on the water after flashing along incandescent segments.

Many of us retreated to the tents to safely enjoy this spectacle of light, water and wind, while others ran through the torrential rain to refresh themselves in song and laughter. Muna played with her son, alive thanks to the fact that he'd never been removed from his mother's breast, from which he managed to suck every drop of milk she managed to produce without dying from dehydration.

But the celebrations were interrupted when a man came down from the bridge with a megaphone in hand.

'Attention! Attention! They've detected a seaquake. Time of impact is four minutes.'

A sinister light whitened the sea. Billai curled into me.

'It'll never end… even the sea has it in for us.'

'Would you have preferred to do as Haziz and his friends did?'

'No, they're crazy to return to Somalia and retry that hopeless journey. But what end will we meet?'

'They say they wanted to retry, but their eyes said otherwise. We'll meet a better end. I'm sure of it.'

In the middle of rolling waves four meters tall that battled the ship's hull, another one appeared: it occupied all of the horizon, and judging by the distance, it must've been three times as high. Visibility lowered and a wall of water, misty with the gusts of wind, rustled the branches of the floating forest.

The pitch, already agitated every time the ship sank into the gulch of the waves, became insupportable. Songs and screams became complaints and curses. Those who danced before now grasped onto something, trying not to vomit.

The clamor escalated, an uproar of wind, pounding of water, a vibration like a drumroll beating the charge. Despite the five-hundred meter length and its scary tonnage, even the Green Ship suffered from the force of Nature.

When the tsunami washed over us, into every pore, nerve and muscle of our bodies, Billai, her lips trembling with fear and emotion, kissed me on the lips.

.

Once the storm ended, lights appeared on the horizon.

When we were closer, I made out numerous boats linked together by a series of ropes and jetties: together they all formed a type of flotilla.

None of us had any idea where we'd arrived, even though that assembly in the high sea didn't seem to be our final destination. To find an answer, I went to Sergio, who was on the phone.

'Where and when did it happen?' he was asking someone. A contagious joy appeared on his face, as if he just discovered that he'd become a father.

'And how big is it?'

He walked back and forth, unable to contain his mysterious happiness.

'Yes, definitely… send me a scan and the coordinates. I'll inform the flotilla.'

Once he hung up, Sergio grabbed me by the shoulders.

'We've been blessed. Nature is building your new home.'

'A new home?'

'The seaquake... it opened a fault line under the ocean from which magma is pumping out.'

'Are you bringing us into a volcano?'

'No, but as soon as the magma cools, we can claim the island that's emerging from the sea. Now we too have something to teach Nature. Then with the flotilla we'll think of the rest.'

'The rest? That's just going to be a rock.'

'Yes, at first it'll be uninhabitable, but we'll terraform it.'

I turned my gaze from Sergio's satisfied face to the geodetic cupolas. Tree pollen and mushroom spores floated around, carried by the ocean breeze.

The Green Ship took the lead of the flotilla. Seen from above, it might have looked like a school of fish migrating for the season. And we were part of that flow.

• • •

The sign posted on top of our new land had been modified. By changing an N into a D, it was transformed from 'No-Man's Land' to 'No-Mad Land,' as the media had hastened to rebaptize the newly born micronation.

The islet where Sergio had first planted the flag – in his haste called 'No-Man's Land' to underline its independence from whoever wanted to claim the territory – in time became 'No-Mad Land' for us. A place accessible without a passport, entry visa, or residency permit. A land designed to welcome people instead of turning them away.

I liked the wordplay of No-Man and No-Mad. Having grown up in a refugee camp between walls and gates, I'd been freed of those limits and I'd left all borders behind. Because borders, political or mental, are temporary obstacles. Because only those who have been turned away or who have enough imagination and empathy for others know how to appreciate the value of hospitality.

The accidental but highly probable birth of the islet in the middle of the Indian Ocean was followed by a phase of movement of thousands of tons of sand from the adjacent seafloor. Thanks to pumping systems, the aspirated sand provided construction material for five enormous 3D printers.

Two of them, aboard tankers, employed the same techniques that the Dutch used to tear the polders from the North Sea – creating dykes of natural material – to protect the central atoll. Yet, different from the polder, the architects supporting the project had thought up a porous, artificial structure that, adequate to host marine life, over the course of centuries would in part replace the irremediably damaged Great Barrier Reef.

The other printers focused on terraforming the cooling magma, rich with fertile substances. They mixed it with sand from the seafloor.

It took us six months before we could set foot on 'No-Mad Land'.

To our touch, the ground was not hard, but instead it seemed supple and ready to be cultivated.

Under an orange sky, a carpet of yellow narcissus welcomed Billai and me. The air smelled fresh and the land emanated a narcotic warmth, stronger than the *chillum* that Noor smoked at the camp in Dadaab. The corollas of the flowers reached Billai's bare knees, and I filled myself with the smell of the narcissus transplanted to the island from the Green Ship months ago.

'Do you know why I like it here?' she asked as she lay down. I shook my head.

'Because we're all immigrants from somewhere.'

'If you think about it, Dadaab was also like that.'

'But it's prettier here,' she said, her smile showing disappointment.

I stared at her frail ankles. The first time I saw her at the refugee camp, she and two other girls were chatting while pumping water from a well. Each filled three jugs, two to carry by hand and one to balance atop their heads. They were three queens, models who strutted on dirt roads as if they were high-fashion runways. She wore a long, colored skirt, a scarf on her head, earrings, coordinated makeup, hair in tiny, neat braids. Her balanced gait was perfect, her gaze ahead, noble, full of nonchalance. She shone with her own light, a star with Black skin that emanated a supernatural aura as she passed, wiggling her hips between trash barrels, plastic waste, mismatched shoes, rusted pipes and goats that grazed on what they could find.

We made the whole trip together. Sometimes, like in Sudan, I feared that she wouldn't be able to make it, like when we had to bribe the guy at the border. Or when she was hurt while we were crossing an area mine-laden by Boko Haram terrorists. But more than anything else, I feared for her life the night when two traffickers cornered her after realizing her beauty. She tried to defend herself, to stop the violence. She shouted for help, crying 'Saidia! Saidia!' but nobody moved for fear of being thrown in the sea for defending her. In the end I couldn't stand it. I grabbed one of them by the neck and I flung him off the boat. The other kicked my back, grabbed my shirt and lifted me off the ground. I too would've ended up in the water had it not been for Professor Kysmayo, whose strong hands freed me from the grip of the trafficker and then threw him too into the dark waters.

'You're right, Billai... but unlike Dadaab, besides us all being immigrants, there's something else that makes me love this place.'

'What?'

'That here, if we want, we can emigrate.'

She took my hands and said in her solemn tone, 'How it has always been and always will be.'

Once in a while I talked with people back in Dadaab on the internet. Nobody wanted to admit that the refugee camp – provisional since the 1990s – had become a permanent establishment. Not the local functionaries who received funding to continue operation, not the United Nations that paid to not solve the problem, not the refugees, forced to live there without hope of leaving. I would never want to return there to survive, imagining a life elsewhere. My elsewhere, like that of many others, was being born from the commitment of all who participated in 'No-Mad Land'. If we'd created a precedent better than Sealand, the Republic of Minerva, Rose Island, to cite some cases Sergio had talked about, who knew what we'd be able to achieve? Who knew if international law would adapt to the fundamental necessities of humans?

My mother and brother were already on their way to intercept the path of the Green Ship. Professor Kysmayo climbed down to the islet and waved to greet us. In his other hand he held an parcel with a round object inside.

'Down there, did you see it?'

We stood up and followed him until we reached the top of another hill where there was a second meadow, green and flat.

'They taught me how to use the 3D printer.'

White lines were traced into the side of the field.

'This is my first ball,' he said, pulling the object out of the envelope and raising it above his head like a trophy. And then he gave the ball a kick.

A soccer goal awaited only us.

Translated by Michael Colbert

Eyes of the Crocodile

Malena Salazar Maciá

Cuba

Malena was one of the writers new to me for this volume, which is why I keep a close eye on anything being published. She is the author of several novels in Spanish, and we're lucky to start seeing her stories in translation. 'Eyes of the Crocodile' is short and sharp, and I hope is merely the introduction to much more fiction from this talented author. This story was translated by Toshiya Kamei.

My return to our ancestral roots began when a crocodile's eye sprouted on my right breast. It felt like a grazing kiss from a razor-sharp bamboo tip or the sting from the cold current of a river that once flowed on the ruined Earth. I chewed on bitter, nameless herbs to soothe my pain. Still, I wasn't bleeding.

I'd spotted the eye when I undressed to bathe. The bump was still swollen and tender to the touch. It stared at me from my shivering, erect areola. The other eye hadn't yet appeared. It was only a matter of time.

Our memory nanobots were programmed to instill in us the traditions handed down from our ancestors many millenniums ago. Our rituals survived even humanity's hunger for technology.

Years ago, I'd have been delighted to obtain, by chance, modification nanobots, because it meant that the history of my people was going to live with me. I'd have worn our past with pride. Even better if the nanobots had carved geometric shapes that exalted my feminine traits into my skin.

However, I wasn't supposed to have a crocodile's eye. That ritual scarification was meant for men. Besides, in recent years, the ceremony had come to bear ominous tidings.

The nanobots were originally designed to watch over the meager remains of humanity, but they no longer kowtowed to their creators.

Thus, when I found the crocodile's eye on my right nipple, I knew the universe had condemned me.

My husband Chioke had been a crocodile man. His scarification ceremony took place at the shelter where we'd taken refuge. When it was complete, he bled to death.

I broke the rules. As Chioke bled, my tribemates turned away and bit their lips, their arms pressed tightly against their sides. Nobody tried to stop the blood spewing from his scars. I laid him on my lap and sang for him until every trace of warmth had vanished from his body.

The following day, another eye sprouted on my left breast. This time, I didn't bleed either. The swelling on my right breast had gone down. The skin looked darker, showing signs of necrosis. The nanobots didn't mark my skin as quickly as they had Chioke's. They seemed to have woken from hibernation because of radioactive contamination in the domed shelter.

I put on an airtight suit and left behind the place I had called home, albeit briefly. Home? I wasn't going to need it anymore. I made my sentence public and unleashed panic among my tribe.

'Your sentimentality will get us all killed!'

'You could've said goodbye to Chioke without touching him.'

'I wouldn't trust that suit. It may have a leak!'

'Who else had physical contact with you, Mandisa?'

'Sacrifice! Before it's too late! Sacrifice! For the rest of us! For our survival!'

'You shall have that,' I declared, as the infrared lenses on my visor revealed the nanobots creeping under my skin. They were already carving scales on my shoulders. 'I need to leave here – before the nanobots will evolve and infect all of you. Give me a hovercraft and let me go to the Tree. After all, I'm already doomed.'

'If you succeed, you'll survive,' a woman shouted as her mouth twisted in contempt. 'But you'll be scarred. You won't be able to get rid of the nanobots. What if everything starts again? You'll tread among us with that dormant curse! The death-bearer!'

'On Earth, the ceremony was the highest honor a warrior could receive.' I raised my hands, like the mother goddess in the files we kept during our flight. 'It'll be a mark of triumph! I'll find a way to remove the nanobots from my body. The Tree will do the work.'

I didn't need to insist. They didn't want me around the shelter, where anyone could touch me by accident. I needed to go somewhere else, a place where no one could see me and recall the fall of civilization. The nanobots pricked my shoulders like pins. They grazed my nerve fibers for fractions of a second, long enough to spread numbness through my body. None had torn my skin. They had refined their technique after doing a botched job with my beloved Chioke.

In a hangar located on the edge of the shelter, my tribemates left everything I asked for: provisions, a hovercraft, and a chip with the new program for the Tree. When the sensors confirmed that there was no biological form near the limits of the dome, I was allowed to leave. I didn't look back, but I heard the gates creak shut behind me.

I flew, as stealthily as I could, toward the other side of the planet.

Long ago abandoned to its fate, it was a pasture of runagate medical nanobots. The bones of biological forms, cloned from terrestrial DNA reserves, populated the wasteland in great numbers and varieties – a whitish forest of rigid structures stretched out below me. The earth cracked, affected by the toxic chemicals mishandled by the nanobots. Puffs of dust rose beneath my hovercraft.

The disaster that led the planet to ruin only happened because the alarms didn't go off until it was too late. The Tree was corrupt and didn't detect the danger posed by the free-rein nanobots: swimming through our bloodstreams, plucking small genetic traces, nibbling tiny bits of discarded food. For the sake of reproduction, they created endless copies of themselves. Each copy contained several corrupt lines, errors from its original program.

The ones that controlled the flu rebelled. The insulin generators and psychoactive drug liberators followed suit. They released more medication than necessary, with immediate effects, without limits. What was supposed to be salvation became death. The antivirus came too late. The nanobots had rewritten themselves to become immune. The only way to eradicate them from the human body was to undergo a risky electroshock session to fry their circuits.

Calm descended upon those of us who survived. But not for long. The nanobots took shelter in other biological forms. They analysed. They rewrote themselves. And they started invading their original hosts again, determined to take their lives away. We humans gave up ground. We lost contact with animals. We now interacted without touching each other. The nanobots didn't spread by air or land – only through physical contact.

When the star of this planet slid beneath the horizon, the darkness of the night engulfed me. Spending so much time in stress took its toll on me. I missed sleeping under open skies.

I stopped the hovercraft and stepped onto the ground, onto a path carpeted with bones that once belonged to a thriving herd of mammals.

I felt no fear. It no longer mattered what happened to me. I crawled out of the airtight suit and stood naked. A faint breeze caressed my thighs, hardened my nipples, and fiddled with the crocodile's eyes. The dormant nanobots on the skeletal remains woke up. A swarm of them started snaking between my toes, producing sharp, pinpricks of pain.

A shiver shook me. I was alive. My entrails trembled. I took a deep breath and stretched my arms above my head, reaching toward the vastness off-limits to us. After all, leaving the planet meant spreading the disease to the rest of the universe. We, the scarified ones, were doomed to solve the problem on our own.

Now wide awake, the memory nanobots shot a mixture of rituals into my mind, into my mouth. I mumbled and hummed a tune.

'Omi omo Yemayá!' My body trembled, twisting in elegant, haughty gestures. I looked back over my shoulder, turned my head, and mimicked the flow of the current, the rivers and the seas of Earth, which was long ago my ancestors' home, so lost in time.

I stroked the invisible waves with my hands. My fingertips touched the wet foam. I shook my womb and watered fertility over the bones scattered along the path.

'Odò Ìyá!' I changed the rhythm of my dance, surrendering myself to euphoric ecstasy, joining the thousands who came before me. I rowed a boat. I raised my arms. I shook them, covered with imaginary copper bracelets. I swore I heard the rattle of copper.

'Ore Yèyé o!' I was a tapestry of history. My skin was

embroidered with crocodile scales. The eyes on my breasts glanced over the dying planet.

The following morning, I woke up shivering with cold. I curled up on the pile of crushed bones. I rose and felt burning pain in my joints. The nanobots kept up with their task of carving my back. My scarification was almost complete. I didn't want to know how close they were to making a fatal error. They could certainly tear my scales open and make me bleed, like what happened to Chioke. I didn't know what to make of the new nanobots, so eager for a new biological organism.

I slipped into the airtight suit just as the fever began to curl up in my head. I returned to the hovercraft and continued on my way to the Tree. When we had fled to the shelter, we began developing programs to find a way to prevent the nanobots' code from corrupting. We succeeded. I took part in the creation of a patch. The one I carried on the chip.

The city was silhouetted in gray against the clear, decaying sky. The ruins posed more serious obstacles than the pieces of bones scattered across the wasteland. An aborted terraforming station had been swallowed by the planet's natural environment, as if in vengeance. Nature recovered, little by little, what once it possessed. Gray moss spread wherever green vegetation would have proliferated.

I ditched the hovercraft when the path narrowed. The nanobots crawled across my back, tireless weavers. For a few minutes, I forgot them and recalled bamboo cane tips. Together with their co-conspirators, the memory nanobots plotted a deceptive farce. The cramp in my thighs let me know how close they were to completing their task. How close I was to death. Fear lodged in my chest.

Hobbled by pain, I trod among the ruins of the city. I had to reach the Tree and place the chip. Save my tribe. Save myself.

Shut them up. Become a crocodile woman in honor of my Chioke. Show that we wore our scales with pride. Carry history in our skin, the future of the human race, so dispersed through the known universe.

The building that housed the Tree soared tall in the middle of the city. It was the only one with no signs of degradation, as if it hosted its own swarm of nanobots protecting it from pollution. It looked anachronistic in the midst of chaos.

The place was locked. I thought I might have to kick the door down, but a tingling sensation gathered in my fingertips when they rested on the structure. The glass door slid open silently.

When I lumbered into the deserted hall, the hum of auxiliary photovoltaic generators tingled in my ears. The Tree had to be asleep, just as the modification nanobots in my blood had been.

The elevators were out of commission. When I trudged up the stairs, the first scale tore and blood trickled into my airtight suit. The same thing had happened to Chioke. Despite the cramp, the anxiety, the sweat, the nausea that threatened to tip me over, I dragged myself along the railing until I reached the Tree.

It stood tall in the middle of the room. The trunk looked like a pillar of smoky-gray glass. The branches, some as thick as elephant legs and some as thin as strands of hair, intertwined with the ceiling. They held it, swarmed it, and grew throughout the city – veins of dormant technology.

Pain stole my breath. I was bleeding as if bamboo tips ceaselessly lacerated my skin. Thick liquid pooled in my pants and inside my rubber boots. I splashed with every step. The nanobots seemed to feel choked. Crushed. Their own survival instincts were going to kick in. They surely conspired to develop a new line of code to go beyond the limits of biological forms. Seizing hold of dust motes, embedded in grains of sand, they would ride the wind. They would reach the domed shelter. And they would herald death through the crocodile's eyes.

As my breath fogged on my plastic visor, I activated the auxiliary generators and redirected the energy on the control panel. The Tree slowly woke up with a deep, rhythmic hum. Erratic lights signaled its accelerating process. I took the chip from the sterile container and inserted it into the processing slot before my body buckled in a seizure.

The crazed memory nanobots stimulated my mind with a barrage of disjointed images as I crumbled to the ground. I was inside the mouth of a mystical snake, next to a being who was neither man nor woman. I carried a child in my arms and hid it next to a ceiba tree. I brandished a double-axe, invoked lightning, and healed a father. I was a woman born from an ostrich egg. I broke a vessel against the ground and from it, a river was born. It took me to the sea. Along with my thousands of faces, as they sunk into the darkness, a proud tree claimed to reach heaven, and the gods punished it by placing its roots in the sky and its branches underground.

When the darkness left my mind, the taste of iron filled my mouth. I feared I didn't have much time left. The crocodile would devour me alive, bursting from my back in dozens of bleeding lacerations, just like it devoured my Chioke. Yet I was still alive. I looked up and stared at the Tree, an artificial baobab. It was plagued with paths of neon. They flickered as data processed.

The cramp caused by the bamboo tips had ceased. The correct dose of sedative ran through my body, my skin, between my fingers, across my cheeks.

I ripped off my airtight suit. The crocodile's eyes, which turned into metal implants, watched me from my breasts. I examined my iron-nail fingers. I slid my fingers over my scarified thighs, covered with silver, armor made from the inside of my being. With each move, I felt the rigid inlays on my back. The code transmitted to the nanobots had reprogrammed them in a strange way. Humans had to endure, had be saved. No harm. No destruction. No killing. Serve. Protect. Preserve.

The blood had dried inside my rubber boots. I tore off this last piece of my airtight suit and left the Tree. I was no longer Mandisa, Chioke's wife. I was no longer the human who needed the memory nanobots to remind her where she came from. I left the building as a crocodile woman.

I'd returned to my roots.

Translated by Toshiya Kamei

Bootblack

Tade Thompson

United Kingdom

One of the great joys of doing this job has been watching Tade's star rise over the past few years. I got to his work early – he was in my *Apex Book of World SF* 2 – and I knew straightaway that he was a major voice. I just had to wait for the rest of the field to catch up! Now his books are finally published by major presses, he is a winner of the Arthur C. Clarke Award, and has multiple television adaptations in the works. It's been lovely to see the rest of the field sit up and take notice. I wasn't sure which of Tade's stories to take at first, but the voice in 'Bootblack' hooked me right away, and I'm a sucker for time-travel stories, especially when they are as uncompromising as this. Happily, it is also one of Tade's favourite stories, so I think I made the right choice!

Statement of LINUS CARTER
July the 27th ~~189~~ 1919
Rewritten by Cpr Samuel Llewellyn due to [unclear]
God save King George.

My name is Linus Carter and I live in Cardiff. Our house is in Niggertown. The police say I have to write my name on every page in case the page goes missing.

I have been asked to say what I know about the fighting and the shining man. This is not much, but my father and mother want me to help the police. I like the police. They always have shining shoes and many come to me to help them keep up the shine and I get coins for this. I am a shoeshine, but the shining man called me a bootblack and he thought this was funny, but I don't know why. My father was a cobbler before he went to war and he said he was going to teach me but I am not smart enough and my father came back blind and he taught me to shine shoes.

The shining man came a week before the fighting. I remember because I woke up with blood in my mouth and a sore tongue. I was on the floor. My mother came in and saw the blood on the bedding and said I should clean myself up outside. I cleaned myself up. Before, when I was not this old, mother would have taken me to see the doctor, but not anymore. Mother said we could not pay for it anymore. And she said the treatment made no difference. My father calls this falling sickness the Morbus and he gave me a chain made of the backbone of snakes. I still get the Morbus, but when mother can afford Bromo-seltzer I don't get it so much.

[Thumbprint here as Master Carter has no signature]

I met the shining man while crossing the bridge. The Taff rushed very fast that morning because it had rained for many days before. I left home early even though my tongue was still sore from biting. When it rains there is mud, and when there is mud shoeshines make a lot of money because people step in the mud, making their shoes dirty. A horse carriage passed me, but there was nobody else on foot that morning.

I saw a light from the reeds. It was only for a short time and very bright. I was alone on the bridge. I took my box to the side of the bridge and sat down because sometimes I see lights before the Morbus. If I sit down when I see the lights I do not injure myself so much.

It was not the Morbus. When the light stopped I saw a man standing there. He did not shine, but he wore strange clothes that did shine. It shone like he wore clothes made of soft mirrors. He had engines and machines that shone too. He hid these in the bushes and took off the shiny clothes. I saw that he had regular clothes underneath, and he wore a flat cap after he hid his shiny clothes. Then he saw me.

He climbed up the bank and walked to me. His boots were muddy. He was smiling. He asked if I was a bootblack and I asked what a bootblack was and he told me and I said I was. He was light, with curly hair, but not white. He looked like the light-skinned Somali men who came and went on Millicent Street, which wasn't in Niggertown but was owned by Negroes. He talked funny, and I thought he was an American because I have never seen an American except for the cowboy shows during the fair last summer and my father said they were Yorkshiremen pretending to be Americans. I think that pretending to be something can be being something if you pretend hard enough for long enough.

When the shining man asked me to shine his boots I said no because it is bad luck to shine shoes on a bridge. None of the boys will do this. He asked me why, but I said it was back luck. I said if we go to one end of the bridge towards the railway station I would shine his shoes and he smiled wider.

[Thumbprint here as Master Carter has no signature]

I cleaned the boots first, because it is a mistake to shine dirty shoes, and the shining man's shoes were muddy from the marsh. I did not talk because customers do not like shoeshines to talk first. Some of them start to talk, others keep quiet. The shining man started to talk as soon as my rag touched his left boot.

He asked me my name and I told him. He asked where I live, and I told him. He did not know where that was and so I asked him where he was from, and he said, 'Not from around here.'

I thought about it and later I realized that he did not want to say where he was from. People say I'm slow. It takes me a long time to learn something, but once I know it I never forget. Most people do not wait long enough for me to learn. I am not slow when I am doing what I already know, like shining shoes. I shine faster than any of the boys.

The shining man called me Master Carter, which made me laugh. Later, after the fighting, the police called me Master Carter, but that did not make me laugh because the police are not funny.

The boot leather did not take up the polish like normal shoes, so I stopped and touched the boots and stroked the toe. I asked the shining man what kind of boots these were and he said I should not worry about it. I explained that I was not worried, but I had to use the right polish. The shining man took his boot off the footrest and said that he was here looking for somebody and that he had to go. He paid me in coin and walked away.

That day was very busy and I stopped thinking about the shining man. It was also very hot. My mother said it was the hottest summer she could remember and my father agreed. In the town I heard some miners say it was the end of the world. I don't know how the world can end, but I did not ask because sometimes, when I ask questions, people laugh at me.

[Thumbprint here as Master Carter has no signature]

The next day I saw the shining man again. This time I did not think of the Morbus. I waited at one side of the bridge and he came to me. He put one boot on my box so I began to shine. He did not smile as much as before so I did not look at him. When I was almost finished he asked, 'Do you know a man called Abdi Langara?'

I said I knew a lot of men called Abdi and that they could be found in the Millicent Street Boarding House. I told him how to get there. I asked if Abdi was a soldier because many people were missing since the war ended, and often strangers would come into town looking for people nobody had heard of. Mother said some people were hiding and had run away from their old life. I did not know what she meant by that. How could a person leave their life behind?

The shining man said Abdi was not a soldier, but they were supposed to meet. He could not find the right street. He asked me how much I earned a day and I told him. I did not think that he wanted to rob me. I have been robbed before by a gang of boys. I did fight them even though they were older than me. I do know how to fight, but not when there are more boys than me.

The shining man said he would pay me twice as much if I would take him around the town to find Abdi. I said I had to ask my mother.

[Thumbprint here as Master Carter has no signature]

My mother said it wasn't Christian to be paid for showing a stranger around. I went back out and told this to the shining man. I took him to the house on Millicent Street and this was lucky because I shined many shoes of the Somali men there. I made a lot of money, more than usual. This was my first time of being in that house, and it was not like any other. There were more books than I had ever seen in a Negro house. They had paintings which showed Africa. People played musical instruments, but I do not know the names of the instruments. People gathered together and one man talked to them. I think he was teaching them. I wanted to stay and listen, but there were many boots to shine, many coins to earn. I do not know if the shining man found Abdi, but he was very happy. Before I took him back to the bridge, I showed him around Tiger Bay.

He said he owed me a favour. He asked if there was anything we needed in the house. I said I did not know, but food was sometimes a problem. He said he could not help with that. He asked if we had any machines.

That evening my parents were talking about fighting between blacks and whites in other parts of Wales. I do not know why the fights started. I testify that I was not in any fight with whites. Not really. My mother said it had something to do with white women married to black men, but my father said it was about jobs and the war and the docks. I could not understand. When they had gone to bed the shining man came into the house. He said he had repaired what he could. He said he liked my father's service pistol and he had fixed it. I did not know it was broken.

[Thumbprint here as Master Carter has no signature]

I wanted to know about the shining man's machine so I went to the riverbank and beat around the bush looking for his machine that he used. I did not find it. But it was early and I waited as the day got brighter. The morning breeze changed into a wind that whipped my clothes and pulled me and the sticks and leaves in one direction and then there was a bright light like the kind I saw when the shining man first appeared. There he was, shining clothes, shining. It was the first and only time I saw him surprised. The wind blew me past him, and I fell into the light. I was afraid. The light went out and it was dark, then bright, then dark. I just kept falling. The wind stopped, and I spun round and round. Sometimes there would be a burst of light like a rainbow, sometimes I would hear screaming, like seagulls fighting over food. I thought I was dying. I prayed to God and promised never to disobey my mother if only I could get home safe or be alive again and God heard me, but not too soon. Sometimes it was hot, then cold, and when I was numb and could not breathe right, it became so bright that I closed my eyes.

I heard voices. Languages I could not understand, and English and other sounds, noises, whistles. Then I heard my name. Not my name, but the one the shining man called me.

'Master Carter, you are truly insane.'

I opened my eyes and there he was.

'Give me your hand, you nutter.'

He pulled me back to Cardiff, back to the Taff, but just before we came back to the world I felt something else. I looked back into the swirling colours and the cold and the heat. There were eyes. It felt like we had been seen. I felt like a chicken when there was a hawk overhead.

Then we were back and the shining man laughed. We landed in the mud and had to clean ourselves and then I cleaned and shined his shoes, but only after he took them off. He lay on the grass drying himself. I was still wet, but I wanted his boots clean. While I cleaned he talked, sometimes to me, but sometimes to himself. I am not sure.

He said there was a lot to learn from wars. He said war was strange. He said there was no such thing as giving a war where nobody came. He said people come back to wars again and again and again. He said that was his job, but that he was no longer interested in doing it.

I asked him what he meant by going to war. I asked if he was a soldier and he said he was not, but that he looked at wars, trying to learn from them. He said years from now leaders would want to know what happened from 1914 to 1918. He said there would be wars where more people would die than did in the Great War.

I said my father told me that more people died in the war than I could ever count. I said King George said it would never happen again because everybody will remember the dead because there would be a remembrance in November.

The shining man laughed at that, and kept laughing for a long time.

[Thumbprint here as Master Carter has no signature]

I thought nobody noticed the shining man, but the next day my father asked me about my new friend.

'Something odd about that one,' he said. 'Where is he from?'

'Not here,' I said.

My mother did not let me go to work that day. She said people had been attacked by white mobs and she was worried. Both of my parents and the whole of Niggertown was worried. From inside the house we heard the noise of people screaming and gunshots and the crackle of fires. I later found out that the trouble was caused by a large group of black men and white women who went out of Cardiff together and were attacked by a mob of white people when they came back. My mother asked my father if we should run.

'Where to?' he asked.

He did tell me to get his gun, but my mother yelled at him because he was blind. I do not think that was very nice of my mother, but it was true that my father couldn't use a gun if he could not see. I did get the gun, just in case. That was lucky because they did come knocking on our door. They were loud and frightening and they shouted. They shook the handle. Some were at the windows and we could smell smoke from outside. The door shook and I thought it would come off. Four men and two women crowded to get in. My mother took my father into the coal cellar, but I had my father's gun and when the door fell off I pointed and fired without thinking.

It did not go bang. Instead, it made a whining sound like a cat. Instead of the flash, it glowed, and in its light I saw the mob clearly. After I fired the gun they had the Morbus. All of them. They had bubbles in their mouths and pissed themselves while banging their heads on the wooden floor. This is true. I swear it.

The rest of the mob did not come into the house after those who did got the Morbus. They ran away. Mother cleaned their clothes and cleaned the floor and we both looked after them, but they woke up and ran away. I do not know where the gun is. I dropped it after firing because I was frightened.

These were not the last visitors we had that night.

[Thumbprint here as Master Carter has no signature]

There were two men who came to the house. I had never seen them before. Their shoes were clean and polished, but instead of stockings or socks they had a shiny film on the skin of their legs, soft mirrored fabric that I had seen before. They wore gloves and hoods. Their clothes were not only clean, they were new. Even the white people who come into Niggertown don't have new clothes. They did not come inside.

I had the same feeling that came when I was in the shining man's machine and I knew that these were the eyes that watched me. I do not know how long they stood there for, but after a while they walked away. I spent the night in the coal cellar with my family. There were rats.

I saw the shining man the next day on the bridge, but this time he came from the direction of the town, and he said the boarding house on Millicent Street had been burnt down and I could tell that he was sad. His shoes were dirty but he did not let me clean them. He started to speak to me, but I do not remember what he said. His words came fast, as if he thought he had to use them all up. His words made my head hurt. He finished by saying 'thank you' and walked to the bank of the Taff. I watched him from the bridge and two hooded figures joined him and put manacles on him. He did not struggle or fight. This time I expected the bright light, and when it came they were all gone.

I do not know where they went or where they came from.

I saw Abdi Langara once, in town, but not at Millicent Street. He stopped me and asked if I was Linus Carter the bootblack and I said yes and he said did I know if Our Friend was coming back and I said I do not know and he smiled as if we both had a secret. Abdi Langara had clean shoes, but whoever had polished them was not very careful because I could see a streak of polish on his brogues.

'He was a thief, you know. He stole… items of interest and gave them away, gave them to me for our people to use. That house they burnt was… He brought us books and devices, things we are not allowed to buy. We could teach, we could learn, we had a future. Millicent Street wasn't a boarding house. It was a bank, a post office, a university, a theatre, all in one. Just a few more years, who knows what it could have become? They came for us at night. Seven Warsangeli surrounded the house and tried to fight off the mob. They held it for hours, taking injuries and injuring the mob as well. Finally, a few slipped through and set fire to the house. The police arrived and it was all over. They arrested us. By the time we got out, the place had been looted. At least nobody died there. On Bute Street they killed Mahommed Abdullah. Six white men were charged with murder, and six white men were acquitted for lack of evidence.'

I did not understand everything he said, but he spoke slowly, and I felt happy listening to his deep voice. He gave me some money, then left me alone. I wanted to wipe away the polish from his shoes.

I still get the Morbus and I still shine shoes. I still wake up with blood in my mouth and a cut on my tongue every few days. When customers call me a shoeshine I tell them I am a bootblack.

I swear this is a true account of what happened.

[Thumbprint here as Master Carter has no signature]

The Emptiness in the Heart of All Things

Fabio Fernandes

Brazil

I've known Fabio for years, though I only met him once, briefly, in London. I got to publish him in *The Apex Book of World SF 2*, and he's just recently published a new collection in English, the wonderful *Love: An Archaeology*. He is a writer (in both Portuguese and English), an editor and anthologist, and a prolific translator. Here he turns his attention on a mysterious sighting in the jungle...

The house in the middle of the forest was just that: a house. Neither a mansion nor a shack. Just a house. From a distance Anita could see two of the four walls, brickwork covered in plaster and what seemed to be a recently applied coat of white paint. Also a red roof made from simple baked clay tiles, just steep enough for the rainwater to slide down. It's too hot for snow in the jungle, but it rains a lot.

No, scratch that, Anita thought to herself. It's the sertão, not the jungle.

She should know better: she lived in Manaus, at the heart of the Brazilian rainforest. A huge city on the edge of the Amazon, pretty much surrounded by real jungle, a stifling hot mess of huge clumps of trees with thick vines entangled all over, so dense at some points that you couldn't slash your way with a machete unless you were a native – and natives usually don't need machetes. This was different: mostly sparse trees and ankle-deep shrubs, rather easier to walk through.

Now – after travelling four thousand kilometres by plane (from Manaus to Belo Horizonte, then from BH to Montes Claros, upstate Minas Gerais) and by boat up the river São Francisco (from Montes Claros to the small town of Buritizeiro, plus eighty-six kilometres), then forty minutes by jeep through a rough patch of dirt road. The driver dropped her at the edge of the forest and told her to walk westward for about ten minutes. The sun wouldn't set for a couple of hours, but it wasn't too hot for the tropical autumn. In fact, she could feel a light breeze, almost cold, touching her skin. She felt good.

After twenty minutes instead of the promised ten (be more specific, Anita made a mental note to tell the driver when she got back), she arrived at a clearing right in front of a wooden porch. Sitting at the top stair, an older woman smoked a cigarette.

Not very old, though. The few online sources about her weren't accurate. Some gave her sixty-five, some seventy; one even gave her eighty, which, now she saw, was absurd. And definitely not ugly as Anita was given to understand. On the contrary, her tanned skin seemed that of a young person, but as she approached, Anita could see the small, half-hidden, almost apologetic folds of sagging flesh under the arms and chin. She had a glorious mane of white hair which contrasted beautifully with the brownish tone of her sun-drenched face.

But Anita was raised Catholic, and she understood that not every monster was necessarily repulsive to the eye.

In fact, the Devil was above all things a creature of seduction. And, even if she didn't necessarily believe in God, she believed in the Adversary.

Anita armed herself with her best smile and approached, waving.

'Miss Barbosa?' she said, stepping out of the shrubs.

The older woman didn't seem startled by the sudden appearance. She just stared silently at her and took a deep drag on her cigarette. Then, blowing the smoke, she nodded.

'In the flesh.' She gave a tired smile. She didn't offer her hand; instead, she pointed with her cigarette – a shoddy handmade thing, exhaling an acrid smoke – for Anita to sit there beside her. Anita dropped her backpack at the bottom of the stairs and did that.

'Was it hard to find the house?'

'A bit longer than the driver told me, but no, it wasn't.'

'Distances can be deceptive here.' She put out the cigarette on the wooden handrail at her side and stood up. 'Come on in. I just brewed a pot of fresh coffee.'

•

Inside, everything was neat and tidy. Smack in the middle of the room, an old, black iron stove sat there, hot, with firewood smouldering in it. A huge black pipe darted from behind the stove, all the way through the roof. On the cooktop, an old, battered coffee pot. By the opposite wall, Anita saw a small Formica table cluttered with books, and two wooden stools, all set on top of a thin red rug. To the left, two doors. Between them, a bookshelf heavily laden with paperbacks.

'Had a good trip?' the old woman asked Anita as she poured coffee into an old, dark blue enamel mug. After a couple of days having atrocious coffee in airports and bus stations, the brew smelled heavenly.

'I did, thanks.'

'For me, the worst is the plane trip. I enjoy flying, but not like that.'

'Yes, the turbulence midway is awful. Everybody told me to avoid travelling here on a full stomach.'

The woman smiled.

'How do you want to do this?'

'Do you mind if I record the interview, Miss Barbosa?'

'No. And call me Elizabeth.'

They sat on the stools. Anita took a long sip of the coffee. It was really delicious. She looked for a place at the table for the mug, but there were just too many books piled there (good, neat, evenly spaced piles, she noted). Slowly, she put her mug on the floor, taking care not to set it on the red rug, which, upon close examination, seemed more a pinkish rag, clean but very old and trodden on by many feet and shoes. She took a finger-sized stick out of her jeans pocket, pressed a button and checked the tiny screen. Then she placed the stick on top of one of the book piles.

'Miss Barbosa, why are you here?' Anita asked.

'Are you sure this will work from that distance?' Miss Barbosa pointed to the small recorder. 'And call me Elizabeth, please. I hate formalities.'

Anita smiled. 'Okay. The recorder will work fine, don't worry.'

'I'm not worried.' Elizabeth shrugged. She sipped from her mug and started talking. 'It wasn't a big deal in the beginning. Very early in my life I learned to live with the unexpected. My mum used to say that things never happen the way you expect them to – but they often come out better than you might imagine.'

'You only published two books,' Anita said. 'A novel and an essay. Neither of them have anything to do with… here.'

'That is not true,' Elizabeth said. 'Did you read my essay?'

'Yes.' Anita had done her homework; 'it was a very interesting take on Camus' *The Myth of Sisyphus*.'

'Not only that,' Elizabeth countered; 'it was an evolution of the concept, so to speak, regarding the ethical eye of the beholder. Camus assumes the burden of Sisyphus can't be removed from him, and that must account for something, so he ponders that Sisyphus strives to become a better man by sheer effort of will, accepting his fate. First I tried to analyse this in the light of Buddhism, which makes sense, but only if you want to agree with Camus all the way. I always thought that somehow the old Algerian was being ironic. The ultimate existentialist, maybe.'

'Yes, and that's the part I didn't really get. You seemed to make the point that the rock is not a rock, just the dark side of Sisyphus.'

'Not the dark side. The rock is his shadow. Are you familiar with the Jungian term?'

This homework Anita hadn't done. She shook her head.

'That's all right. Nobody these days is very familiar with Jung. Or even Camus. I'm surprised you came all the way down south just to interview me about it.'

'I just want to understand you. It's hard for me to under-stand how you could have dropped everything in your life to live here.'

'You say *here* like it is a bad word. I suppose young people always think their way is best.' Elizabeth sipped her coffee. 'Maybe it is, but that's what you are. I'm cut of a different cloth. Maybe it's my age, the way I was raised. Anyway, one day I woke up and found out that I didn't really have anything to lose. I had lost my family long ago due to my... proclivities, as we used to say then. And what are material things after all? I was tired of living in a bubble.'

'But you lived in São Paulo. One of the biggest cities on Earth. A megalopolis.'

'And a bubble nevertheless. Just a very big one.'

'But why here? And by *here*, I didn't mean anything nasty. Sorry if I didn't make myself clear.'

'Here's the thing,' Elizabeth carried on, as if she hadn't heard

Anita's apologies, or hadn't cared. 'When you're safely ensconced in a bubble, you are in a comfort zone. Inside this zone, you only see and hear what you want to. You learn not to hear police sirens in the middle of the night, or junkies shouting in pain, or a woman crying "thief" or "rape". You manage to convince yourself that you don't have anything to do with all of that, and that's all right, because it's a coping mechanism, it's how you live without getting crazy. Or without getting too crazy, at least.

'I decided to move here because I could live a quieter life. And because I could face my shadow. My other half. The one that screams bloody murder, literally.'

Having said that, she suddenly stopped talking. But this brusque pause didn't seem to be for dramatic effect. Instead, she got up and went over to the stove.

'What is this interview for, again? I'm sure you told me in your e-mail, but I honestly can't remember, sorry.'

Anita almost felt sorry too. But she was used to being questioned. And she was sure that was the case now too.

'It's for my doctorate thesis on forgotten Brazilian female writers,' she told her the cover story. 'I already profiled the other living writers on my list. You are the last one.'

Elizabeth laughed out loud.

'Good to know I'm a living writer,' she said. 'For a second you had me confused.'

'I didn't mean to—'

'Nah, I'm being facetious. Are you hungry? Let's have some dinner, shall we? It'll be dark soon, and we sleep early in the wilderness.'

•

Anita hadn't realized how hungry she was. She ate heartily the chicken stew with rice and beans and started feeling drowsy right after wiping the plate. Elizabeth showed her the guest room. There *was* a guest room, incredible as it might seem, but Anita chided herself for being so prejudiced in her thinking. Not every house in Manaus had a guest room. Damn, her childhood home didn't have one; who was she to think less of Elizabeth because she chose to live in the wilderness? *What wilderness, pale-face?* she thought wryly.

The temperature had dropped a bit. It wasn't as hot as Manaus, where you had to keep the air conditioner on all night long, all year round, but it was warm enough for Anita to strip down to her gun and panties. There was no mosquito net over her bed, which worried her. She kept the light on for a while, eyes scanning the small room, hoping she wouldn't find any of the damn bloodsuckers. Then, after a couple of minutes of this ritual, she dropped heavily onto the bed. It was a hard mattress, but she had slept in worse beds. She picked up her phone to read a bit before sleep. An Elmore Leonard western, maybe?

But first, just one thing. Work before play.

She opened the case file. The Cachoeira disappearances. Seven men in seven months. All in a widespread area around the municipality of Cachoeira da Manteiga, thirty kilometres away, forming almost a perfect circle whose focal point was this exact house.

Anita couldn't believe Elizabeth Barbosa had anything to do with it. She was a strong woman, and sure, she could picture her killing a man to stand her ground and protect herself, for instance – but seven? No.

But if not her, who? Maybe Elizabeth knew. Or even if she didn't, she could point her to someone who did.

She tried to send a message to her superior officer just to tell him she was all right. But her phone was no good here. Captain Ferreira would have to wait a few days. That was OK. He gave her a week, but every forty-eight hours she was expected to leave a message by the edge of the road where the Federal Police jeep had dropped her. If there was none, the driver would alert a squad and they would search the area for her.

Anita closed the file and opened the western. But she barely read a couple of pages before falling asleep.

• • •

She woke in the middle of night, certain that she had heard something, but she was still too sleepy to register. She remained absolutely still.

Then, a shrill sound. It took a while before she recognized the sound – a whistle. A long, ear-piercing whistle. Too loud and yet distant. Too human to be an animal, but you could never know this deep in the forest.

Anita was too intrigued to be afraid. Even so, she didn't leave the bed. If it was someone – something – out of the ordinary, then surely Elizabeth would take care of things. Anita felt her .22 under the pillow. She also could take care of things, but it would be better not to reveal her real intentions so soon. She took a while to fall asleep again.

• • •

Anita woke at first light, with the screams of many birds she couldn't recognize. She was used to the noise howler monkeys used to make every dawn and dusk when she spent her school holidays at her grandparents' home near the edge of the rain-forest. But the fauna of the sertão was different.

She got dressed and opened the door. The smell of fresh coffee brought a smile to her face.

'Morning,' Elizabeth said, already pouring coffee into both mugs. 'Slept well?'

'Like a log.'

'Good,' she said. 'We'll have a full day. Get something to eat, you'll need it.'

They ate scrambled eggs and bread. There was plenty of fruits there. Anita had a banana and a tangerine. Elizabeth ate an orange.

'That whistle last night. What was that?'

'What whistle?'

Anita told her.

'Probably a bird.' Elizabeth smiled a little. 'The people around here use to say it's the Matinta Perera.'

'Matintaperê?'

'Matinta Perera.' She pronounced both words separately, syllable by syllable.

'Never heard of it. Some kind of animal?'

'No. The Matinta is a woman like you and me. By day, at least.'

Anita laughed. 'Then what? She turns into a monster? Like the Mapinguari, or the Curupira?'

'No. As far as I know, the Matinta is not a monster, but a woman with a curse. She usually asks people for simple things, like tobacco or coffee. Or something to eat, like fish. Or cachaça to drink. Old folks around here still leave a plate with stuff outside the house just in case.'

'And if they don't… '

'Legend has it that she can do some awful things to the people in the house. She can turn into a wild creature, a mist, a sudden storm, an unspeakable thing.'

'And she kills?'

Elizabeth shrugged.

'When I arrived here, one of the ribeirinhas had just accused the Matinta of killing her husband's dog.'

Anita laughed at that.

'She could have done it, right? The wife? Maybe she didn't like the dog.'

'She told me that the dog had killed some of her chickens.'

'Did she tell you where she was at the time the dog died?'

'What do you think I am? A detective? Come on, it's getting late. We should be on our way.'

•

They walked north. Elizabeth explained to Anita that, two or three times a week, she went to the nearest town to give some assistance to a few ribeirinhas – the women who lived in wooden shacks at the banks of the São Francisco.

'There's a case of domestic violence every other week,' Elizabeth said. 'Usually drunk husbands beating their wives and daughters. Sometimes raping them. Some of these girls have babies whose fathers are their own grandfathers.'

Anita just nodded. This sort of thing was quite common in the outskirts of Manaus as well. When she was at the police academy, she'd learned that cultural habits were hard to kill. She'd also learned that many of the law enforcement officers there, both instructors and classmates, had cases like these in their own families.

She did too.

'A month ago, an eight-year-old boy was beaten to death by his father just because he looked gay,' Elizabeth said. 'Bastards.'

Anita remembered the case file. The last reported death was almost two months ago.

'Is the father…?'

'He ran for the forest. Most of the men who rape and kill in this region do. They were born here. They know how to hide.'

'He's been out there for all this time?'

'They usually count on help from friends.'

'But, if everyone knows it, why hasn't the police done something?'

Elizabeth shrugged.

'The usual reasons,' she said. 'Friendship, male bonding, pure and simple machismo. It's a well-established belief in our culture, and even more so far from the big cities, that males are somehow just misbehaving boys who simply don't realize how strong they are, that kind of thing.'

'Boys will be boys, right?'

'Right you are. I can't say I'm for the death penalty, but I don't pity this kind of monster.'

'I feel you.'

'Do you?'

'Of course,' Anita said. She wanted to say something else, but refrained.

Maybe sensing this hesitation, Elizabeth said, 'Of course you do. Um tatu cheira o outro, right?'

'What?'

'A popular saying here. They say that armadillos can sniff each other from far away – or even close to each other, even if one of them is disguised.'

Anita nodded. She'd been out of the closet for years now, both for her family and for people at work. She just didn't flaunt it; Brazilians fancied thinking of themselves as enlightened and free of prejudice, but for years now Brazil had held the record for having the world's highest LGBT murder rate. Being a cop didn't let her off the hook.

So far she hadn't been entirely sure if Elizabeth was a lesbian too (*so that was what she meant with that proclivity talk?* she thought), but it didn't matter anyway. She was there to arrest a murderer, and she was going to do that.

•

They spent the whole day talking to the ribeirinhas. Most of them were very young – ages ranging from fourteen to twenty-three – already with children, so many children. Usually three of four per house, but Anita saw six playing in front of one of the shacks, two of them toddlers, and Elizabeth told her they were all of the same mother. All the ribeirinhas lived on scraps since the social welfare salary was suspended by the new right-wing government. Elizabeth acted as a social worker/doctor/therapist, sometimes buying food for their babies on top of that, but Anita saw that she couldn't do much for them.

Anita helped one of the youngest girls change diapers on her twin babies while Elizabeth talked to the neighbour – they were so alike, Anita thought the woman could be the young girl's mother, but the ribeirinhas were very shy with her, and resisted her efforts to make conversation. The older woman (who, to Anita, could be anywhere between twenty-eight to forty-eight, but the woman's face was so weather-beaten she really had no idea) talked to Elizabeth with a lot more confidence, but also a great deal of respect, as if the other was so much better than her.

The great white saviour. Anita was sick and tired of seeing that.

And Elizabeth seemed to revel in that role. She was speaking firmly to the woman, as if she indeed was a lesser being, a servant. She couldn't listen to all the conversation, but at some point the woman next door nodded humbly, head down, and Elizabeth said, 'Next time, don't do anything. Don't give anything. You hear me?'

The woman mumbled something under her breath.

'Just let nature follow its course. It's the best for everyone.'

The woman nodded again.

Anita just sat there, watching.

·

They returned home at dusk. Anita was exhausted; Elizabeth looked as if she could spend the night working without breaking a sweat.

'Is this the real reason?' Anita asked.

'I didn't know we were having the interview now. Are you recording the talk?'

'Just curious. It's a profile. I'm not required to record every single thing.'

'The reason is a promise,' Elizabeth said after a while, serious. 'But I already knew what I wanted to do before making it.'

'What promise?'

'There was… someone before. Someone I really liked and, more important, I looked up to. She made me promise I would stay here after she died to take care of things. To set some kind of balance.'

'As a vigilante?' Anita ventured.

'What? No!' Elizabeth sounded pissed off. 'I just want to help. If this damned coup hadn't smashed the hopes of so many people here…'

'Why do you say coup? The president was impeached,' Anita retorted, a bit tired of this sort of leftist nonsense, slightly disappointed. So Elizabeth was one of those who thought the government that ousted their former president had staged a *coup d'état* instead of a legitimate impeachment process. She had more things to do than thinking of politics. Serious things.

'You don't think that we live under an illegitimate government? What are they teaching you at the university these days?'

'Not this,' Anita mumbled under her breath, but she soon

regretted it. Elizabeth didn't appear to have listened anyway, and kept talking:

'The social salary was a pittance, but it helped those women a lot. Did you know that only the woman could cash in the benefit? In earlier versions of the programme, only men could go to the bank agency to get the money, but most of them usually kept the money to themselves, spending it on booze rather than sharing it with their wives or helping their kids have an education. Anyone who badmouths the Worker's Party administration should better come here and see for herself what happened when the new government took the matter in its corrupt hands.' She huffed. 'Didn't you want to profile me? Well, girl, this is me. Part of me, at least.'

'And the rest?'

Elizabeth stopped suddenly in her tracks and studied her. 'You don't want to know.'

Anita wasn't impressed. 'What if I do?'

Elizabeth looked deep in her eyes. 'Don't make promises you can't keep.'

They walked the rest of the way in silence.

·

Fuck, I messed up everything. This woman is a radical activist.

Anita wasn't expecting that. As it was, the Federal Police offices in Brasilia weren't particularly interested in subversive activities for the moment, but that could change soon. Anita was beginning to have second thoughts. Maybe Elizabeth wasn't innocent after all.

They ate dinner in silence.

· · ·

In the middle of the night, the same whistle. This time, Anita kept her eyes wide open, staring at the dark. She was used to darkness, but the sound now carried a strange, threatening tone. *Get a hold of yourself, dumbass*, she thought.

She considered dropping the tough attitude and knocking on Elizabeth's door, but she was too proud for that.

Then, as soon as it started, the sound was gone.

Anita stayed there, on the bed, eyes open, heart beating fast, listening, but the whistle never came back.

· · ·

She got out of the bed at dawn, dressed, and plodded to the porch. Elizabeth was already up, feeding the chickens. Anita looked around, watching the colours of the sky changing from deep blue to mauve in the west, a cross-section of rainbow from the east – red, orange and yellow. Wisps of clouds above her head. The air was crispy, but soon it would get warm. She was starting to like this place. If she'd been on a real holiday, she could've stayed here for a while, resting her senses from the city. But she wasn't, and she couldn't.

'Coffee is ready,' Elizabeth's voice came from behind her. 'Then let's finish this interview, shall we? I have much to do, and you'll want to get back to the city.'

'Are you going to talk to the ribeirinhas today? I'd like to come with you.'

'No. They have much to do today. We'd only get in their way.'

Anita didn't reply to that, even if she felt she should have. She needed more time.

'When I left the university,' Elizabeth said, 'I wasn't feeling very comfortable with how things stand at academia. The hierarchy is too strict, and you don't always get to do what you want in terms of research. I don't think I was ever fit to be a professor. However,' she stared at Anita, 'I *do* think that hierarchy is a good thing, provided both parts have a healthy, transparent relationship. I don't believe in hiding things for personal gain.'

'What if it's for the gain of the community?'

Elizabeth considered that for a few seconds.

'Then it might be acceptable, but not for long. A good community is one where its members stand for each other, and the only way for it to thrive is when every member is open with each other.'

'It sounds like a utopia.'

'No. Utopia means social equanimity. Transparency is about justice. One may lead to the other, but they're not the same.'

'What do you think about the murder of the...'

'What?'

Anita looked up. Elizabeth was staring at her, seemingly taken aback.

'What are you talking about?'

Fuck.

She didn't drop the ball. 'The men who have been killed in the area for the past few months. I read the news, you know.'

'What about them?'

'Seven men in seven months. What do you think happened to them?'

Elizabeth shrugged. 'How would I know?'

'You live in the community.'

'I live near the community. I don't belong.'

'You have been here for so long. A decade?'

'Twelve years. But I've learned to keep to myself and do the best I can to help, whenever I can. It's not much, but I like to think I'm doing my best.'

Anita barely suppressed the urge to ask, 'By killing the men?' Instead, she said, 'Do you think the men were killed by the same person?'

Elizabeth stared at her.

'I don't think they were killed by a *person*,' she finally answered. 'Even for people who are natural-born swimmers, death by drowning isn't unusual here. As far as I know, that was what happened to most of them. All drunks, if you ask me. They were so infamous around here that the police have ruled out foul play.'

'No, they haven't.'

Elizabeth frowned.

'They just reopened the investigation.'

'They?'

Anita didn't reply.

Elizabeth hummed to herself.

'Interesting,' she said. 'I didn't know anything about that. Where did you read it again?'

'Google.'

'Hm.' Then: 'Come on, let's have a smoke outside.'

They sat on the porch. Elizabeth rolled a cigarette without hurry and started smoking while gazing at the sky.

'You know, I've loved these skies as long as I can remember,' she said. 'I think that one of the things that made me decide to move here after all was exactly this: the colours of the sky. Just like a John Ford western. My favourite is *The Searchers*.'

'Mine too,' Anita said without thinking. This made Elizabeth open a beautiful smile.

'Wow, an unseen depth of character if I ever saw one. You are more interesting than I thought at first. Maybe there's hope for you.'

Anita glanced at her and said nothing.

'The thing about westerns,' Elizabeth continued, 'is that westerns are a baring of the soul. The landscape is much more important than the people in it. In such landscapes, you can be yourself, no holds barred.' She breathed deeply. '"To be a writer is to have the loneliest job." Who said that?'

'Hemingway?'

The older woman shook her head.

'García Márquez. The man knew his way with words. What an irony, that he died with senile dementia, unable to write or even to remember.'

'I don't see it as an irony,' Anita said. 'It's pure cruelty.'

'Ah,' the woman said, 'but is it cruelty if no one pulls the trigger? If no one gives the punishment? If things just happen by some kind of heavenly justice?'

'Then God is a twisted fucker,' Anita said despite herself.

'That he is, Anita. That he is.'

They remained there in silence, Elizabeth smoking and Anita inhaling deeply the smoke and the scents of the forest, savouring the moment.

Then Carrie turned up.

All the talk about movies triggered a freezing response in Anita which was a kind of rationalization in the face of the strange: the girl drenched in blood who came from the woods right in front of them immediately reminded her of the movie she had seen so many years ago on TV with her dad.

'The man, the head,' the girl said, voice quavering. And she fainted.

Anita froze; Elizabeth stood up and ran straight to the girl, right in time to catch her before she fell to the ground. Only then did Anita move, and rush to help.

Together, they lifted the girl and carried her to Elizabeth's room, where she was put in bed. Elizabeth fetched some water in a bucket and a rag, and they cleaned the exhausted, feverish girl of all the blood. Then Anita recognized the girl as the mother of the twins.

'What happened?' she asked.

'Let her rest,' Elizabeth said. 'She must have run all the way from the town.'

Almost twenty kilometres. Half a marathon. Anita shook her head.

'What happened? What the hell did she say?'

Elizabeth shrugged.

'I don't know. Come, let her sleep a little. I'll give her some paracetamol for the fever.'

They spent the rest of the day in waiting. Lunch was had, but they barely touched the food. By the middle of the afternoon, the girl started to wake up with a moan. Anita and Elizabeth stayed by her side.

'Feeling better?' asked Elizabeth.

The girl nodded weakly.

'Thanks, Ma—'

'It was nothing. Rest now, we'll take you home tomorrow first thing in the morning.'

Anita thought the girl would complain, but instead, she just closed her eyes and began to snore almost immediately.

They left the door of the bedroom open, and had some coffee on the porch. Elizabeth started rolling a cigarette.

'Ma?' Anita said.

'What?'

'She called you Ma?'

Elizabeth took some time to answer. Anita watched her finishing rolling the cigarette and lighting it with a match.

'These girls are very lovely when you get to know them better,' she said. 'They treat me like a mother sometimes.'

'But you give them tough love. I saw the way you talk to them.'

Elizabeth took a long, deep drag, and let the smoke out in a huge grey cloud.

'Being a mother is a hard job. Even being a surrogate mother.'

Anita wasn't convinced.

They stayed on the porch until the night had fallen deeply around them. Then Elizabeth stood.

'Let's go to bed. I want to take her home as soon as the sun rises.'

'Okay,' Anita said, then, feeling a bit uncomfortable, added: 'Take my room. I can sleep here.'

'Nonsense. We can share your bed.'

'It's not a big bed.'

Elizabeth stared at her.

'What are you afraid of?'

Anita didn't know what to say.

'Come.' Elizabeth reached out to her, one hand extended over the abyss of Anita's thoughts.

And she did.

There wasn't any whistling that night.

• • •

The girl had no fever when she woke up the next morning. They ate a hearty breakfast (hearty being a meal with chicken and fried cassava), then went on their way to the riverine town. The girl was still weak, so they took longer this time, stopping every now and then to catch a breath. They arrived near noon.

There was a bit of a commotion among the women, but men were nowhere to be seen. They went straight to the girl's house, where a few of the ribeirinhas were gathered. When they saw the visitors, they started yelling and ran to the girl. Her neighbour (who was indeed her mother, just as Anita had suspected) embraced her and started to cry.

One of the other women told them that the girl always used to slip away and have a smoke in the middle of the night. And that the Matinta had appeared right at that time, bringing a freshly killed body, dropping it in front of the terrified girl. Without a head. That was what they could piece together; the girl, relieved at returning home, confirmed it.

Elizabeth declined their offer to have lunch, and took Anita by the hand to get back home.

Anita felt surprisingly good holding Elizabeth's hand. She was almost at peace, but for a nagging thought in the back of her head. No, scratch that, a veritable bunch of thoughts right in the forefront of her head – that was the truth. They walked part of the trail hand in hand, but soon Elizabeth had to let her go because the path narrowed enough for them to go one in front of the other.

'Why do you like westerns, Anita?' Elizabeth asked suddenly.

'I like guns and action,' Anita said after a while. 'I can't stand big books and philosophical observations of the world and things like that.'

Elizabeth didn't say anything. She looked back once, glancing at Anita. Anita gazed back at the older woman and thought she had seen something in her eyes, but didn't wait for her to spill her guts.

'And you? Why do you like them?'

'Because the western is not about the landscape.'

Anita frowned.

'But you said yesterday that—'

'The western tale shows the landscape as the protagonist, but the landscape can be anything, really. You can write a western taking place in the Russian tundra – in fact, there are quite a few stories from Soviet times that fit the bill very nicely.'

'And here?'

The woman looked around, to the trees surrounding the trail. Anita could smell mango and jasmine, and a variety of plants and fruits hard to find anywhere else in the world. She couldn't even begin to describe all the species.

'Here?' the older woman finally answered, startling Anita a bit. 'You could write a western here as well, a western as good as any written by Elmore Leonard, Louis L'Amour or Alan LeMay. Have you read Ferreira de Castro's *The Jungle*?'

Anita shook her head.

'It's a damn fine book,' Elizabeth said. 'Castro was a Portuguese young man who decided, in the 1930s, to become rich in the Amazon.' She snorted. 'Poor fucker. He came to Brazil broke and he left broke and heartbroken on top of that. But he ended up giving a description of the rainforest like no other writer had ever done, not even Brazilian writers. The truth is, we don't like our country so much.'

This realization left Anita very sad. She couldn't tell why exactly; they didn't have the same political views. She didn't believe in politicians of any party. She did believe, however, in hard facts. In what the eye could see, in what the hand could touch. She believed that there were more poor people than rich all over the world, and in Brazil this truth hit harder yet. She was usually too busy hunting and catching the bad guys to think about it. Now she had time enough, but she wasn't happy.

She's right, she thought. *We sell our country too cheap, we don't fight for it. What's left of it now?*

As if reading her mind, Elizabeth gave her a wry smile.

'All we have left are our stories,' she said. 'Our lore, our folk tales. Our own native people to listen to and to learn from.' She shrugged. 'We could write much better westerns here. The jungle is a place where we can find out who we really are. And that's what a western is. A journey to the centre of you.'

'But the arid landscapes?'

'Take Cormac McCarthy, for instance. He writes about the

emptiness in the heart of all things. The desert is just a reflection. With us, down here, it happens the opposite. We are full. But not necessarily of good things. We are full of love, full of hate, full of shit – both metaphorically and literally. Have you noticed that almost nobody in American westerns take a good crap?' She laughed out loud. 'Girl, here we crap a lot.'

Anita blushed. She was used to cursing, but not to talk about bodily functions. Elizabeth certainly knew how to push her buttons.

They walked the rest of the way in silence.

•

When they finally arrived at Elizabeth's house, Anita was tired, hungry, and feeling dirty. Not on the outside, not unwashed, but full to the brim with unanswered questions. Questions that disturbed her deeply.

'She didn't call you Mum, right?' she mustered the courage to say. 'She was going to call you Matinta. And you shushed her.'

'Really?' Elizabeth smiled.

'And you killed that man. You killed all of them. How did you convince them to accept that Matinta crap? I never thought they could be so superstitious, not in this day and age.'

'You're a trigger-happy gunslinger, right, Anita? I mean that literally.'

'What do you mean?' Anita felt herself reddening.

'I use Google too, Anita. You never cared about hiding your real name. You're not related to any university. You're a fed.'

'I've been to the university.'

'What did you study? Not literature, I suppose.'

'No. Not literature. But this is not about me.'

Elizabeth shook her head slowly.

'It's about you as well. Come on, let's have a smoke.'

'Nasty habit, don't you think? You'll get cancer one of these days.'

'I have cancer, Anita. Smoking is one of the few pleasures I can get now.'

'I'm sorry.'

'Don't be. It's an awful cliché, but I lived my life fully and well. I did what I wanted to do, no more, no less.'

'Including the killings?' Anita couldn't avoid asking.

Elizabeth let go a roar of a laugh.

'My god, you won't let go,' she said. 'It wasn't me. It was the Matinta.'

'Which happens to be you.'

'Which happens to be an entity. I'm just the vessel.'

Anita scowled.

'Please, don't treat me like a child,' she said. 'I can handle the truth.'

'Can you? What if the truth is something you can't accept?'

'Like?'

'Like the need to dispense justice whenever necessary, no matter the cost.'

'Only the law can do that, Elizabeth.'

'Did you see any cops there on the river's edge? Did you? No, Anita, because *there is no law*. Human law can't and won't do anything.'

'So the… the Matinta, so be it, this creature is killing all those men?'

'Not all,' Elizabeth said candidly. 'A couple of them really drowned. The Matinta had nothing to do with that.'

'So, this is a confession? Are you telling me that you—'

'The Matinta.'

'—the Matinta, OK, fuck, I'll play along if that's what it takes… the Matinta killed at least five men in the last few months.'

'Yes, she did that.'

'I'm really sorry to hear that. I wish I could help you in some way. Are you coming peacefully with me to the city? Maybe I can get you special treatment because of the cancer.'

'Maybe. But do you want to help me?'

'I can't let you go, Elizabeth.'

'I'm not asking you to let me go. Quite the opposite, actually.' She took Anita's hand. 'The sun will set in a couple of hours, but I can't wait that long to get some rest. I'm so exhausted, Anita. Come with me.'

• • •

When Anita woke up, it was still dark. Still quiet out there.

She sat up in Elizabeth's bed. The older woman wasn't there. She stood up and opened the door. For a moment she considered getting dressed but didn't see the need. It was hot and they'd already seen each other naked.

The house was still. Slowly, Anita tiptoed over the floorboards, heart in her throat until she stopped near the stove, blinking and getting her eyes adjusted to the penumbra. Elizabeth was nowhere to be seen. But the front door was ajar, and Anita could see a whitish glow through it.

Then, the whistle.

She froze.

Suddenly her instincts kicked in and she hurried back to her room to get her gun.

She tried to clear her mind and focus all her attention on the front door. Gun in hand, she opened it wide.

A huge black bird was there on the porch, looking at her. As if it was just waiting for her to open the door.

She held her breath.

It was a really huge bird. For a few seconds Anita couldn't

grasp its enormity. Its big head came almost to her shoulders. Its beak shone as if made of steel. And, slowly, it spread its wings. Anita could easily vanish in its embrace.

She had never felt such terror in her life.

Then the bird simply lifted off, taking flight. And let out the weirdest cry Anita had ever heard: 'Who wants it? Who wants it?'

Anita's mind was reeling. It didn't make sense, a bird the size of an eagle and talking like a parrot.

Then she heard the call again. It didn't come from above, but from behind her. Anita turned.

Elizabeth stood there, in the middle of the clearing, naked under the moonlight.

'What do you want from me?' Anita whispered, not sure Elizabeth would listen.

The naked woman came towards her. She seemed wrapped in a light, tenuous mist. She reached for Anita with both hands, and now Anita saw that she was the one asking the question:

'Who wants it? Who wants it?'

It wasn't unexpected. Not to Anita, at least. Ever since she first read of the recluse writer Elizabeth Barbosa, she'd felt an affinity that was hard to put into words. It wasn't physical attraction – although now she knew it was that too, and that it played a significant part in her fantasy all right – but it was enough of a pull to bring her here, and to this moment.

Then she answered.

'I want it.'

And they embraced under the cover of the night.

•

Things happened fast but at the same time in slow motion. Time was an origami crane unfolding. Anita saw the mist covering them, now so thick she couldn't see Elizabeth's face anymore.

Desperately, she tried to put her gun down – the last thing she wanted to do now was to fire it – but she couldn't feel her hands. Or her body. She couldn't feel either of their bodies.

She started to feel afraid, but that bubble of time surrounding them didn't let her go all the way to the end of the feeling. She just ceased feeling.

And she wasn't Anita anymore. Not just Anita.

· · ·

The next day, the driver stopped the jeep right at the beginning of the trail where he had left Anita. He searched for a while, but couldn't find any message.

Unsure, he hesitated. After all, she might just be a bit late. On the other hand, the sun would set in an hour or so. He was armed, so fuck it. He entered the trail.

The house in the clearing was empty. The front door was open and the stove was cold. The chickens were all cooped up. There was only a huge black bird near the edge of the forest. When he saw it, he reached instinctively for the gun in his holster, but the bird (What was that, for crying out loud? An eagle? A vulture?) didn't seem to mind him, so, after a few seconds, he left the beast alone.

The driver returned to the road in a foul mood. The news of another murder had just reached them at the station, and the captain wanted to know if Anita had something on it. What would the driver tell him? He hated when these things happened.

He hated it even more when he spotted the severed head riding shotgun in his jeep.

He whipped his .38 around, but nobody could be seen. After a few minutes, when his breathing had slowed down and his hands stopped trembling, the driver approached the head. It was male, apparently in his thirties (but you couldn't know for sure, especially with the dead), eyes closed and mouth semi-opened. There was something stuck on the teeth.

It was a note.

DO NOT COME BACK, it said.

He didn't. A full Federal Police squad would, but not now.

The Sun From Both Sides

R. S. A. Garcia

Trinidad and Tobago

We first published R.S.A. Garcia in *The Apex Book of World SF 5*, and I fell immediately for her writing. One of a growing number of speculative fiction writers from the Caribbean, I look forward to every new story, and 'The Sun From Both Sides' won me immediately as it starts off as one thing and turns into another...

Once, a woman loved a man, and a man loved a woman. They lived in a forest, in a small stone-grey hut, set far enough back from a river to escape the seasonal floods. Every day, they woke on a too-soft mattress and turned their faces to each other before they opened their eyes. Her smile would curve her lips as she lay her hand on his cheek, and he would sigh and nuzzle her palm.

Then they would roll away and sit up on either side of the low bed and push their feet into their shoes.

Days were short and cool, or long and hot, but there was always something to do. Firewood to chop, the roof to repair, a garden to tend. They carried out their chores accompanied by his tuneless humming, and when she looked at him, he always knew. They would pause, gazes locked as they took a breath, hands wiping sweaty foreheads, or resting on bent knees, before they both went back to what they were doing.

Nights were for dinner, and fireside reading, and sitting with their shoulders touching on the wooden swing-bench outside the creaky front door as they stared up at the patches of sky visible between the swaying branches. He would use his legs to push them back and forth slowly while she sat with her knees drawn up. Sometimes she let her head rest against his neck, and sometimes he put his head in her lap. Other times, he would play his flute while she lay her hand on his chest and her head on his shoulder. If she fell asleep, he would carry her inside without waking her.

When they fought, with air sucked through teeth, hands on hips and narrowed eyes, it was usually over small things, like whose turn it was to clean up. But they made up quickly, with soft kisses, fingers interlaced as they walked, and bodies entwined at night.

Whatever surplus food they had, he would go into Town to sell or trade, and she would take that time to clear the traps, or fish, and then make something special for when he came home. She would swim in the river then sit on their bench, waiting for him to come down the path alongside the house, whistling to himself. Her skin would tingle like a young girl's when he climbed the two shallow stone steps, stamped the dirt from his feet before he stepped onto the wooden porch, and looked down at her from under the brim of his battered hat.

Home again, husband? she would ask.

He would smile and say, Home again, wife. Tired of me yet?

Not yet. Maybe tomorrow.

She would stand and they would link arms and go inside together.

This happened many times, the quiet pattern of their lives wearing pleasurable grooves into their time together, until the day came when she kissed him goodbye, went for a swim, made a stew, and waited for a return that did not come.

That night was wind and rain and thunder and lightning, and she sat with the front door open and the lamp lit, staring into the darkness. The river roared, and the trees whipped, and the house grew too cold for the fire to warm, but she did not shiver, and she did not move. Morning met her still in the chair across from the door. When the rain became irregular drips on the roof and greying light softened the lamp's glow, she woke with a start from a light doze.

She cast her gaze over the undisturbed room, and stood with stiff legs, her hands going to the small of her back as she stretched out the kinks.

Alright then, she thought. There was the slightest tremor in her fingers as she put out the lamp. Then she walked out the door and through the forest until she reached the main road into Town.

Her boots sank into the mud with every step, the air fresh and clean and cold, scoring her tight chest with every breath. Early morning light glimmered on the puddles she passed.

He's fine. She repeated this mantra in rhythm with her heart. *He's safe. He's fine. He's safe.*

She told herself it was the storm. He'd taken shelter somewhere overnight and now the rain had passed, she'd meet him on the road, empty sack under his arm, and he'd shake his head when he saw her and smile and call her a worrywart.

He's fine. It was just the storm.

But her stomach buzzed with a familiar energy and her skin prickled, and all she could think was it had finally happened, and she hadn't been there.

A long hour later, the red peak of the church belfry came into view between the trees. There was a scorch mark on it, and the bell had crashed through the stone arch and the roof. The wind shifted as she passed the sign that welcomed travellers and she smelled acrid smoke and mud, and beneath that, something thick and coppery and nauseating.

Her pulse quickened. She closed her eyes, letting the scent she knew so well flow over and through her. Then her heart settled into a calm, steady beat and she opened her eyes and strode into Town, her gaze scanning the wide plaza and every building and side street that led off it.

She ignored the crushed and splintered homes and the smoking piles of debris that used to be walls, windows, roofs. She stepped over the bodies and the weeping people huddled near them and crouched in doorways. She walked past those few searching the collapsed dwellings for survivors and headed straight for the market. Only when she reached the blasted hole in the ground that used to be the heart of Town did she stop, her nostrils burning, her hands clenched at her sides. An old man was ministering to someone on the front stoop of a building across from the marketplace. She looked down at him and recognized the Town's only doctor, a man she knew well. He'd helped care for her when she first arrived, years ago.

'**My husband?**' she signed.

Weariness and sorrow made his watery blue eyes dull. His bloodied fingers sketched brief movements. '**Gone. With the others.**'

She looked back at the market and her hands trembled as she pointed. '**There?**'

The doctor rose to his feet, giving up on the man he'd been trying to save. She turned her head and watched his throat work as he struggled for speech, read his lips.

'Taken,' he said. Then he signed, '**Slavers.**'

Relief made her expel a breath while rage sent tension singing through her entire body. It was slavers.

Not them. He's alive. For now.

But there was a clock on her options and it had been ticking down for some time.

'How long?'

'They waited out the storm. Two... three hours? We've sent for help, but...'

'Which way?'

The doctor shook his head and held out a trembling hand. **'No. Wait for help.'**

The nearest Base was three days travel. That's why they'd come this far out. No one would get there in time to stop them. **'Which way?'**

The hand descended on her forearm, gripped her sleeve. She read his lips as he spoke. 'You can't go by yourself. If you go, you die, or they take you too. Do you understand?'

She glanced back up at him and whatever he saw in her face made him release her arm. His mouth opened then closed and a frown carved a deep groove between his brows. She searched the tumult of her mind for something appropriate to say.

'Alright. I understand.' She paused. **'Which way?'**

There was a larger settlement to the east. One she hadn't seen since she'd first come to this place. The slavers had gone in that direction, and she knew they would strip that town of every healthy person they could find. The weather was glorious today, and it was the last settlement in the Eastern Lands. They would leave once they were done. She had hours at most.

As she strode out of town, she tapped a command against the underside of her wrist. *Wake, Sister.*

Under the brown of her skin, a white pinpoint of light flickered into being between the forked veins of her right wrist.

In her mind's eye, she saw the dark dankness of the root cellar her husband had enlarged after her arrival. Saw past the rows of barrels and shelves of vegetables and preserves to where shadows wreathed the back. They would shiver away at her word, the cloaking revealing the silver dart of her solo-ship, the cockpit nose flowering open.

Drone.

A translucent mass would float free of the cockpit, unfurling rippling ribbon-like appendages, the centre of it a pulsing yellow light.

Find and report.

The light would disappear as the ribbons twisted in on themselves and made a tight ball, smaller than her fist. Colourless and silent, it would burst through the doors, up and out of the cellar.

Come, Sister.

She began to jog, blood rushing through her veins, her body pumping adrenaline.

Some minutes later, the ground vibrated beneath her feet and the hair on her arms stood on end. Sister kept pace with her until she came to a clearing large enough to land, then descended and de-cloaked, waiting.

Suit, she tapped.

There was a hiss as a storage compartment behind the cockpit opened. She reached in and drew out her old armour, silver-grey, just like her ship. Her fingers touched the mended area low on the left side, in the crease between the chest plate and the leggings. She closed her eyes, remembering the white-hot pain of being pinned, red washing over her vision as Sister's alarm systems cascaded into full auto-repair shutdown, the chilly certainty of death as the cockpit failed to seal around the branch that impaled her, and blood-tinged water rose rapidly to her chest.

Remembering him, bending into the cockpit, hair plastered to his head from the water he swam through to reach her crashed ship, long brown fingers, callused and scarred, reaching down to help her.

She stripped off her clothes and put on her armour, her lips a tight line, her nostrils flared. The drone returned as she activated her faceplate. It floated down onto her wrist and wrapped itself along her forearm. She started the Kinnec to see what it had seen. Sister's displays crowded her periphery vision, but she focused on the tracking and reconnaissance stream.

He was alive, his tracker a pulsing marker in a complex schematic the drone had uploaded. Her chest heaved with a quick breath, and she got into the cockpit as she scanned the rest of the feed.

It took a quarter of an hour at top speed before she saw her first sign of the slaver's passage – a smoking village, a burned landing circle – and she raced past with only a cursory look. Sister lost contact with his tracker just as the hub on her arm began to vibrate. Her throat grew tight as she reduced speed and swung north, dropping down close to the treetops.

He's fine. He has to be. She landed on the mountain slope behind the settlement, near the treeline and out of sight of the slaver ship. She kept the Kinnec up in her vision and half ran, half slid down the slope to the field below.

Six armed catchers stood guard around the loading bay doors, leaning on their weapons, or standing with them slung over their limbs. She ignored the bright blossoms of weapons' fire in the town on her right, leaving Sister to catalogue all hostiles as she strode toward the entrance ramp. When they saw her, she stopped and retracted her hood, waiting as two of them turned their weapons on her.

'Who the fuck are you?' scrolled across her vision. Good. The translator knew their language. There was no time to waste.

She thought her answer and the Kinnec translated it into

speech that rumbled against her flesh as it projected it out of the suit's speakers. The words flashed in the bottom of her vision. ^I've come for my husband.^ The guards looked at each other. One of those standing on the ramp threw his head back, laughing. The rest looked blank. Perhaps she had used the wrong language. She checked her settings, but they were error free.

^I wish to speak with your captain,^ she tried again.

'No one cares what you want, least of all the captain.' The Kinnec dropped a blinking triangular denoter over the speaker, the slaver who had laughed. 'But cargo is always welcome. She's not armed. Looks healthy enough. Take her in.'

She didn't struggle as they came alongside her and grabbed her arms. They marched her up the ramp into the bay, mag-boots shaking the metal floor. She stopped as soon as they were out of sight of the entrance ramp, pulling against their hold. One of them tripped and landed against the metal bulkhead. The denoter appeared above the slaver and curses scrolled across her vision before the one that was upright struck her across her face. 'Keep moving. You're almost past your prime, not worth much if they can't fix you. The captain's welcome to take you out of my wages if you give us any trouble.'

She licked the bit of flesh her teeth had cut out of the inside of her mouth. Copper and salt stung her tongue as she tapped her wrist.

Two ribbons unsnapped from her arm and whipped them-selves around the slavers' necks. They tightened lovingly, thin bands of translucence. The slavers stood straight and still under the drone's control, eyes unblinking. Pacified.

^Take me to the captain.^

They turned down a T-junction, and she followed. This was a Consortium slaver. Their slave berths were controlled from the bridge, the cargo secured by the captain's command only. Crew and cargo could form no alliances, and problems could be dealt with as easily as jettisoning a berth. The crew members the drone controlled incapacitated the two guards outside the bridge, so the captain and first mate were alone when she entered the bridge. The first mate turned from conversation with the captain as the door irised open, words giving way to silence and a frown.

Drone. Sentry. The slavers behind her turned toward the empty corridor, standing guard over their unconscious brethren.

She stepped forward, her heart sinking as she took in the captain. *There will be no bargaining with this one.* Still, she had to try. It was only fair.

^I will offer you one chance,^ her suit intoned. ^Open your cargo hold, give me my husband, and you and your crew can go in peace.^

The first mate stared at her with narrowed eyes. The captain's head tilted a little in her direction.

'Who let you in here?' the denoter blinked to life over the first mate.

^You acted in ignorance. I'm willing to forgive that. This does not have to end badly.^

The captain's vaguely humanoid shape shifted in its berth as it flexed a metallic limb inserted into one of the many glowing ports surrounding it. A ripple flowed across its blank bronze face as it turned toward her, a flower following the sun's path. Speech unscrolled beneath the denoter. 'Remove this creature to the hold.'

She met the first mate's gaze. ^To be clear, you refuse to give me my husband?^

For an answer, the first mate raised a hand toward her and the hairs on her arms rose in a tell-tale response. Her fingers tapped twice. *Shield.*

The blast from the weapon built into the first mate's wrist

was absorbed by her suit, leaving behind little more than a momentary flash and a tingling sensation.

She sighed. *Alright then.*

The first mate lunged at her.

Sister. Control and Command. End all transmissions.

She side-stepped, bending backward, almost parallel to the floor as a fist swung at her. She grabbed the arm, coming upright even as she yanked downward. The first mate crashed into the steel deck, and a swift kick to the head with her reinforced boot did the rest.

A ribbon detached itself from her arm and darted into a port. The captain tried to insert one of its appendages into the hub, but a spark and a snap made it withdraw.

'You are resisting. You are trouble. You will not be cargo,' it said as she stood in front of it. Her vision flashed a red atmosphere warning before her hood slid over her head and sealed itself. Stale air filled her nostrils.

Her patience evaporated. Anger made her breath come fast and her skin grow cold. ^Yes, I am trouble. And no, I will not be cargo.^

Notifications slipped past. *Bridge atmosphere incompatible with biological life. Adjusting.*

The first mate's heels drummed against the floor as the toxin took hold. They stopped moving before a new series of notifications appeared. *Emitters adjusted. Transmissions blocked. Recalibrating ship's systems for sibling compatibility.*

^You should have taken my offer.^

The captain rose from its perch, releasing dozens of slender limbs.

^You're no ordinary captain,^ she said. ^You're a secondary shell. I've seen Plantation-class AIs like you before. I know the Consortium you hunt for.^

'Many know the Consortium,' it said. Its face rippled as a maw yawned open. 'Those that know of it, also know fear.'

The projectiles it fired glanced off her armour, and she leapt out of the way as it attempted to grab her. Her boots activated, latching on to the side of the bulkhead. The captain withdrew into itself, losing its humanoid shape for a few seconds before splitting into two blobs that grew limbs and sharp edges.

She amused herself by carving some of them off with the tiny lasers in her gloves before dancing out of the way and onto the ceiling as the blobs divided yet again. Two stretched upward to meet her. Two more flowed up the bulkheads on opposite sides of the bridge, re-forming into something she didn't immediately recognize.

Recalibration at 75%. Alarm systems disengaged. Defense systems disengaged. Disabling shell motor functions.

^The Consortium knows fear too.^ One of the polyforms beneath her collapsed. Another froze on its way across the ceiling toward her, its surface undulating like storm-tossed water.

^Search your records.^ She stepped onto the bridge's dark viewscreen, crouched down and extended a flat, open palm. Her people's red, white and black emblem glowed into life above it. ^You should find me there. Find us.^

'You are Kairi.' The captain's shell paused, its attention almost fully engaged by the battle to retain control of the ship, but Sister was relentless, disabling code and recalibrating every system. 'Not possible. This backwater is no Kairi Protectorate.'

Recalibration at 90%.

Another polyform collapsed, electrical sparks arcing as it dripped in a slow column from the ceiling to the floor.

^I'm retired,^ she said. ^And you violated my home. Took my husband.^

'Primarch—'

^I gave you a chance.^ She rose to her feet, studying the results of Sister's data-mining.

Trapped in the quarantined section of the slaver's databases, the captain continued to fight Sister's incursion, but his Plantation-class cruiser was no match for Sister's Havoc-class brain. The reforming code was deleted as soon as it appeared, fireworks blinking out in the night sky. 'The Consortium does not negotiate. This planet was unclaimed territory. If you take the cargo, we will petition for its release, and we will win.'

^Always focused on the rules. But they are *your* rules. Not ours.^ She glared at the polyform as one side of it began to list, sharp edges rounding and slipping. ^This planet was already claimed by those living on it. And I've found your primary brain. It's in orbit, awaiting your return.^

Recalibration complete. All systems ready.

'Then you know if you harm this ship, it will strafe these settlements. Crews are replaceable. Cargo is everywhere.'

She stepped off the viewscreen, anger making her fingers fly as her suit translated. ^You believe you can take what you want without consequence. Even now, you comfort yourself that I am one woman, one Primarch, against a cruiser and all it carries.^

Sister. Amend starlogs on Plantation-class cruiser. Delete all references to current position. Amend transponder location to new position at least two systems distant.

'Because you *are* one Primarch against a Consortium cruiser.' The captain was now a featureless glistening blob. 'Should you defeat me today, the Consortium will simply return for its cargo at another time.'

Tasks complete. Awaiting further instructions.

^Then you have no true understanding of my people.^ *Combat mode.*

The green wash of the ready light filtered down her vision. Her arm vibrated with Sister's response.

^We don't allow others to take without consent. And we are never alone. Tell me, captain, when did you last speak with your primary brain, waiting on its cruiser with its crew... and no cargo in its hold?^

Sister, execute Cleanslate Protocol. Extreme prejudice.

As the captain collapsed into liquid, sparking de-activation, the bridge sank into darkness. Around her, the ship shivered in the wake of explosions and energy blasts. The drone's filaments detached from the dead crew members outside, who had been poisoned along with the first mate, and returned to the Kinnec hub in her arm. Sister activated the emergency lighting, and she followed the ship's schematics to the cargo hold.

No one had been loaded into the berths yet. The crew would have been waiting to put them all under at the same time. Two separate groups had been divided into two large bays, each protected by an energy field. One group was mag-cuffed to the bulkheads, but some in the second group had gotten free and were trying to help others out of their restraints. They all stared as she appeared. Then prisoners in the second group were shoved aside, one after the other, as someone pushed to the front.

Sister. Release restraints. Open bays.

She retracted her hood and stepped into the bay. She pulled him into her arms and closed her eyes as she inhaled sweat and blood and smoke and *him*. He took her face between his palms as she signed, her thoughts too emotional and disordered for the translator.

'**Did they hurt you?**'

He shook his head and she read his lips. 'I'm good. Are you?' She nodded. '**Never better.**'

He smiled and leaned his forehead against hers. She stayed

that way for a moment before leaning back to sign. '**You've been busy.**'

He winced as she took his left wrist between her fingers. He had dug his implant from it and used the overload feature to disable his mag-cuffs, shorting out his tracker. A dirty rag covered the bloody wound above a glittering three-dimensional geometric tattoo. His fingernails were torn and bleeding. She shook her head as she touched a hand to his bruised eye and bloodied lip. Her suit chided, ^There was no need for this.^

'**The accommodations were less than satisfactory. I thought relocation was in order.**'

She couldn't hold back her smile. '**What a coincidence. That's why I'm here.**'

By the time they left the ship, Sister had completely withdrawn from it, leaving only a darkened husk of machinery behind, devoid of intellect and power. The first fragments of the orbiting cruiser were burning up as they entered the atmosphere above them. Surprise and shock rippled through the escaped captives as they saw the dead slavers outside the ship. Those that were uninjured rushed forward to meet the survivors in the town. Several of them embraced, faces contorting as tears flowed.

'**Maybe we should fly our people home,**' her husband signed as they stood at the bottom of the ramp, arms around each other's waists. He was limping but trying to hide it.

^I destroyed the captain. Ship's not going anywhere. They'll have to go to the nearest transport hub and find their own way.^

He studied her face. 'Not just the captain, I take it?'

She shot him a defensive look. ^I did what you would have wanted. I asked nicely. They wouldn't give you back.^

A finger tilted her chin upward and his dark eyes met hers. 'Sure you're okay? You must have been worried...'

She grasped his fingers, stilled their movement. 'It wasn't them. That's all that matters.'

'You were retired.'

'So were you. I'll live.'

They walked toward the mountain, watching Sister descend from orbit, her mission completed. He stopped and faced her.

'I'm not getting in without you.'

'You're injured.' The drone floated up from the hub on her arm. 'She'll take care of you on the way back. There's stew. Make sure to get some sleep.'

'It's too far to walk. Come with me.'

She put her hands on her hips, her eyes narrowed. ^Don't make me sedate you.^

He pursed his lips and argued some more, but in the end, she let him hold her then handed him over to Sister, who left a drone behind to see her home.

After Sister left and most of the crowd was gone, she leaned against the hull of the slaver and cried until her legs slipped out from under her and she sat on the ground, shoulders shaking. Her hands clenched and unclenched, her heart raced, and her skin prickled as she came down from the battle high.

It wasn't Valencia. Only slavers. They didn't take him.

She sat just breathing for a while as the adrenaline flowed out of her, the tears dried, and her body stopped shaking. The drone settled over her arm, its grip comforting as she stood up and turned for the road.

It was a long way home and she took her time. It was late afternoon when she returned to the forest and the path beside their house.

He was leaning against the doorway, legs crossed at the

ankles, arms folded across his bare chest. A strip of synthskin circled his wrist and his bruises were purpling. She paused at the top of the steps and just took him in.

'**Home again, wife?**' he signed.

She smiled. '**Home again, husband. Tired of me yet?**'

'**Not yet.**' His split lip stretched into a slight smile. '**Not ever.**'

They linked arms and went inside.

• • •

Once, a man left his home to find his home.

It was not an easy journey, but going home never is.

He gave up all that he was, and all he knew, to experience a great many things. Genuine smiles and thoughtless malice. Shared purpose and individual failure.

And one bright day, in the middle of a river, he found peace. The first true peace in his long life. He learned that a home could be shared, and that in finding his home, he'd become another's. That was more than enough to bury the fears and chase away the memories. More than enough to keep the world and its cares far, far away.

Until the day he came home, and the world was sitting at their table, brushing invisible dust from white diaphanous trousers with immaculately trimmed and painted fingers. The Knight rose from the wooden chair it had been seated on, the smooth white surface of its full mask catching the evening light. A pinhole speaker made a glowing blue circle in the centre of the lower half of the mask, and tinted slits hid the Knight's eyes.

He froze in the doorway, instinctively putting out a hand to keep his wife from going past him into the house. Eva halted against his outstretched arm, her body rigid as she dropped the bag of paw-paw they'd collected during their walk onto the swing-bench.

He glanced at her, but she was focused on the Knight, her brown eyes narrowed. Her soft, springy hair was an unbound halo around her face. He had been planning to help her wash and dry it by the fire. Heart thumping in his chest, he thought on all his plans for that day, and the next, and the next. Pointless now, like crystal smashed against the floor.

I'm sorry, he thought, willing her to look at him. She met his gaze as if she could sense his thoughts. *I'm sorry I was right. I should have known they'd come when we least expected it.*

In front of them, the Knight took a step forward, extended one leg and swept a bow over it. The voice that issued from the speaker was light, conversational – the voice of a friend coming upon another old friend after a long while.

The sound of it grated on his ears like a scream.

'Grandmaster Didecus Avnette Valentino Lucochin, you are called to the Greatwood for the annual Opening of the Term at Valencia.'

She tapped his arm and, when she had his attention, made a few curt moves with her fingers. '**Let me deal with it.**'

He shook his head.

Her eyes widened as she signed again. '**Turn around. Walk away.**'

He took her hand in his instead, weaving their fingers together. Valencians had their own sign language, which most Septholds used to communicate silently and frustrate eavesdroppers. It was very similar to hers – a lucky thing on the day they'd met, but not so lucky now. The Knight could know what she was saying.

He faced the Knight. 'How did you find me?'

'Your implant.'

He frowned. 'It was… removed more than a year ago.' He had a new one Sister had printed for him, and only his wife could track.

'It was designed to ping its final location at the moment of its destruction, so the Grandmaster's death would be recorded in the Greatwood.'

Only one person would have cared to know the moment of his death – the same person who'd made sure the implant was reprogrammed from its original purpose as a weapon that would kill him if he ever crossed into his planet's atmosphere.

'I was exiled from Valencia and may not return,' he said, pleased his voice was calm when he'd been caught so completely off-guard. Which was their intent, of course. He put aside the thought and the cold anger it brought with it. 'I must decline the invitation.'

'Not an invitation.' The Knight's hand rested lightly on the black cylinder clipped to the utility belt on its waist – a retractable energy spear. A full-colour reproduction of its Grandmaster's geometric crest was tattooed on its bare shoulder. 'A summons. Queenside.'

She flattened a palm against his cheek and turned his face to her. A frown creased her forehead and he saw the question in her eyes. The mask prevented her from reading the Knight's lips and the pinhole speaker limited vibrations. She could only follow what he said. He had no doubt she sensed his inner turmoil; his fingers gripped hers tighter than they should. He released them.

'I am no longer the Lucochin,' he said, his voice harsher than he intended. 'My King is dead. I have no Queen.'

'A glorious miracle, Grandmaster. As happened with you, many *tempi* ago, there has been a promotion. A new Queen summons you.'

By the fucking Graces. Fuck them all to hell and back.

He forced out, 'Who?'

'I've been instructed only to bring you to Valencia with all haste. Questions must wait until we return to the Greatwood.'

'When then? How many *tempi* ago did it happen?'

'Forty, Grandmaster.'

So many *tempi* since he'd left Valencia. To go back now would be madness. A death warrant.

'I no longer have a seedling. The Vineyard would reject me.' The Knight plucked at its belt and held its hands out to reveal the jewelled speck of a Coretree's seed in the centre of one palm.

He closed his eyes, expelling a heavy breath. Turning his back to the Knight so his wife could read his lips, he said, 'I have to go, Eva.'

The determination in her eyes spoke to him before she shook her head.

'If I don't, they'll send Pawns. Pawns that won't care who they hurt, or what they must do to carry out their Grandmaster's commands. At least I can reason with a Knight. If I allow it to complete its move, it won't harm you or anyone else.'

Her eyes widened as she divined his intent. '**No. We discussed this.**' She hit him in the chest with a closed fist. He grabbed it, held it against him.

'That was before so much time passed. It's been too long since I was last home. Everything will have changed. I will have no allies.'

He didn't tell her what he feared most. That his only ally must be dead, or the Knight would not be there.

She pulled her hand away. '**Try to leave without me. See how far you get.**'

He gave her an exasperated sigh. She arched her eyebrows at him.

After a long hesitation, he said, 'I need time to prepare,' to the Knight without looking at it. He wanted her to see what he was saying. She nodded once, her lips a compressed line of triumph.

'Those are not my instructions.'

'I am Grandmaster Lucochin and I survived the Great Game more *tempi* than you've been in service. You will give me what I ask.' He faced the Knight. 'And you will prepare a seedling for my wife.'

The Knight took a step forward. 'You wish to bring your wife?'

'Yes. You came here by the Vineyards, did you not?'

'Of course.'

'So you can prepare a seedling.'

The Knight shifted its masked head ever so slightly in his wife's direction. 'She is not Valencian.'

'She is Kairi. They were enhanced for interstellar travel, as were our ancestors. She can withstand the seedling, and she goes where she pleases. Take care not to insult her.'

'**Damn right I go where I want**,' she added. He fought back a smile.

'If she doesn't come, you won't complete your task.'

There was no way to tell how the Knight took this news. All he knew was it would inform its Grandmaster and Queen. The arrival of a Primarch – a citizen of the Kairi Protectorate – in Valencia would be unprecedented. And they would know she was coming.

The Knight bowed. 'As you wish, Grandmaster.'

He circled her shoulders with an arm, pulling her against his side and giving the Knight their backs. So many memories and emotions churned through him at the thought of going back – dread and adrenaline made him tense. But he couldn't deny part of him breathed easier knowing she would be with him. Knowing whatever happened, he wouldn't be alone in the nest of vipers that was the Greatwood.

And he was not unprepared. He'd planned for this long before he met her.

'Are you sure?' he asked her.

She rolled her eyes at his question. **'I'll send a message to Sister. She's gone adventuring.'**

'They may not allow her through the Vineyards.'

She grinned, tilted her head at him. **'They're welcome to try and stop her.'**

. . .

Sister came, of course. Her primary consciousness had been traveling the Kairi networks, fighting far-off skirmishes in myriad shells, or visiting new planets with diplomats and explorers, but she returned in time, curious to see a ship and a world few had ever been invited to visit.

The Vineyard ship had been in orbit for several weeks while the Knight searched. The decision to live simply had been about not needing more than food, shelter and freedom to be content, and – once he'd met his wife – happy. But he had also considered the day his people might come looking.

In the end, all his caution had been in vain.

Sister followed on her own as they travelled to the Vineyard with the Knight in its much larger drop-ship. She landed on the polished, weathered deck of the Vineyard's cargo hold as they disembarked behind the Knight, holding hands loosely.

His wife squeezed his fingers to get his attention before signing, **'Smells wonderful.'**

'It's the Vineyard,' he explained. 'The ship is grown around it to infuse it with the vine's atoms. It gets into every part of the vessel and flowers. Even when they're not flowering, the mirror Vineyard on Valencia, or other ships, might be, so ships end up smelling like this all the time.'

They were in the corridors now. Petrified carbon curved under and around them, the same colour as his wife's startlingly light brown eyes, the whorls and rings rippling through the surface a testament to the ship's advanced age.

This Vineyard was one of the massive fleet his people maintained to trade and lay seedlings in space to create Arbours, so that ships could travel ever further by navigating from one Arbour or Vineyard to another. No matter how far they explored, all other ships, seedlings and Arbours, remained permanently entangled with Valencia and each other, allowing Valencians to travel vast distances in an instant and trade reliably with many other colonies.

Maintaining their ability to use the Coretrees for problem solving and space travel was the only mandate of the Greatwood and the Grandmasters that ruled it. Without the Coretrees, Valencians would lack even the basics. Their world was far from established routes, discovered by accident when several colony ships were forced to land to make repairs.

He itched absently at the crook of his arm where the seedling had been implanted as they approached massive doors that stretched ceiling to floor. The panels folded back and air spilled out into the corridor, sweet with the cloying fragrance of the vine within. It was the smell of home and victory and sorrow and pain and every waking moment of his life before his exile.

He closed his eyes against the rage that tightened his chest and the bile that rose in this throat.

She gripped his upper arm and leaned her head against it, letting him know she was there. Grateful, he covered her fingers with his and opened his eyes.

The Vineyard sparkled back at him through a tinted shield. The Knight withdrew masks from alcoves just inside the open doors – standard grey models with red pinhole speakers. Eva accepted one as a courtesy rather than choosing to tint her own hood. When he activated his, it dimmed the Vineyard's glow to a shimmer, and oxygen rushed into his lungs from the tiny pac built into the mask. They would only need it to breathe for a few seconds, until they crossed into the mirror Vineyard and Valencia's purer atmosphere.

'**You may be disoriented when you arrive. It's a stress on the body, the sudden shift, even with the seedlings.**'

She shook her head and gave him a look that said he was fussing for no reason. She donned her mask and signed, '**Lead the way.**'

The vines were a shimmering curtain he parted to find his way forward, his wife's hand firmly in his. He took care where he placed his feet as the smooth floor of the ship was hidden by the ceiling-to-floor plants.

The scent of them raised nausea in the back of his throat just as the world seemed to tilt, then right itself again. The surface beneath his feet went from smooth to bumpy, his wife stumbling against his back at the abrupt shift. With no warning, they were pushing through not just glittering vines but knee-high blades of grass. He saw dark shapes ahead of him, against the fall of light that was the Vineyard. The pac on his mask switched off, and air flooded into his lungs, heavy with vine-perfume.

When they broke from the Vineyards, it was in front of a row of opaque panels. He took a deep breath and stilled his wife's hand as she reached for her mask. '**No. Leave it.**'

They walked up to the panels together and he pushed them aside for her to step through first.

He recognized the room they entered – the high square ceiling, the pale walls and stone floors, the two graceful statues on either side that represented the Navigator and the Captain, the founding colonists of Sept Lucochin.

He was home, standing outside his own Vineyards. This, he understood with a cold clench in his gut, was not proper etiquette.

Three Knights, holding buzzing, activated spears, surrounded a much shorter figure that stepped toward them. Sheer white cloth danced on the air, so thin he could see slender bare legs and small dark-tipped breasts through it. The Bishop's full mask was elaborately painted with the crest of its Grandmaster, two diamonds inside a circle, a twin to the tattoo on a bare upper right arm.

'Welcome home, Grandmaster Lucochin. You have been missed.' The Bishop's voice was smooth, light and monotone.

'I find that difficult to believe as I was exiled,' he replied. 'Let us not waste time. Explain my summons.'

The Bishop's mask tilted in his wife's direction. 'And who is this?'

'My wife, as the Knight would have informed you.'

'I had no opportunity to speak with the Knight. I have been directed by Grandmaster Kingston to escort you to your rooms.'

'Kingston?' He frowned, the coldness in his gut now ice. 'Why does the Kingston give orders in a Septhold of Valencia?'

A pitying sigh escaped the pinhole speaker. 'My apologies, Grandmaster. You've been gone a long time. You could not be expected to know.'

'Know?' He raised his eyebrows and waited.

'Sept Lucochin has been dormant for many *tempi*.'

He turned his head and his wife met his gaze, but she could not see past the mask to the anguish that made his knees feel unsteady.

All those people.

His people.

Alexandar betrayed me?

No. It couldn't be that. Never that.

'But the Game? Our Game?' he said, desperate not to believe.

'It ended, shortly after you were exiled,' the Bishop confirmed as though discussing the weather and not the clearing of a Board. The wholesale execution of a Grandmaster's pieces – Pawns, Knights, Rooks – everyone. 'With your return, a new Game has begun.'

• • •

He sat with his head in his hands for the longest while. Long enough for the golden evening outside to turn full dark. He'd thought no day could be harder than the day he'd been forced to leave Valencia knowing that either he would never be back, or worse, that he might one day have to return. But he'd been wrong. So very wrong.

Eva waited, allowing him his grief even though she couldn't have fully understood the conversation he'd had with the Bishop. She sat at his feet, her head against his knee, her fingers intertwined with his and never once did she ask a question.

The lights in their bedchamber brightened as darkness fell. There was only the large carved bed, some chairs and two doors – one led to the dressing area and one to the baths. He'd refused the services of Sept Kingston's servants, preferring to let them leave two trays of food on the only table in the room. The rooms had been aired, and the long hallways they walked still had dustnets over the little furniture that remained. Sept Kingston must have been directed by Sept Valencia to prepare for his arrival. With no people on the Lucochin estate, there would have been no one else.

He was lucky, he supposed, that he hadn't been imprisoned on arrival, but he knew with certainty that had been deliberate.

It was a new Game. It would be up to him to figure out the objective. To know which of the many moves he'd planned would be necessary.

He stared at the grey masks on the table and sighed. She

shifted and looked up at him, worry crinkling her eyes. Her free hand squeezed his thigh and he stroked her hair. He spoke aloud so he wouldn't have to let go of her warm, comforting hand. 'I'll be okay. I just… need time.'

She leaned her head back on his knee, still looking up at him. '**Tell me.**'

He glanced out at the dark estate and the dancing rainbow colours of Valencia's night sky – the light of the Vineyards reflected into the atmosphere, so beautiful now he saw it for the first time in many *tempi*.

'This was my estate. They brought us directly here instead of the Greatwood.'

'**That's bad?**'

'Almost certainly. The Bishop told me the Grandmaster Valencia would speak with me tomorrow. It's odd Sept Kingston and Sept Valencia would go through all this trouble to find the exiled Grandmaster of a dormant Sept, and yet the new Grandmaster Valencia doesn't meet with me on arrival.'

Understanding dawned in her eyes and she took a breath. Freeing her hand, she signed, '**Your Valencia. Your Sept. Both gone?**'

He closed his eyes for a moment, too bone-weary and heart-sick to even nod. When he opened them, she had tears in hers. '**My love, I'm so sorry. You tried. You let them exile you. It's not your fault.**'

He swallowed, the tightness in his throat and burning in his eyes making him pause to gather himself. 'It was my fault we lost the Great Game. I set in motion the events that led to my Sept's destruction. Sept Lucochin numbered over ten thousand when I left. Ten thousand souls. Executed. Including my King. And the previous Valencia.'

She knelt between his legs, facing him. '**When?**'

'**After I left.**' His hands faltered and she placed hers on either side of his face and kissed him, her mouth soft, sweet and fleeting.

He leaned against the padded headrest and stroked a finger over her lips. 'They didn't deserve that. I played the Game. I thought I'd won.'

'**You traded your life. Left those you loved behind.**'

She kissed the tears on his cheeks, and his lips trembled as he spoke. 'I love you. And I don't deserve you. This... happiness. All this time we've had with each other—'

She shook her head fiercely. '**No. Don't do that. It's not true. We'll find out what they want, together. Then we leave. Together.**'

He hugged her to him, stroking his hands over the supple armour that covered her back, watching the blinking ready light of the drone on her forearm as her hand lay against his. The Bishop had claimed not to know his wife was with him. Why would the Grandmaster Valencia not mention the arrival of a citizen of the Kairi Protectorate to the Bishop who was sent to meet them? It was disconcerting, yet probably for the best. Eva was not their focus. He needed it to stay that way.

After a while she raised her head and sat back on her knees. '**Should we eat?**'

He signed back. '**No. Dangerous until I meet with Grandmaster Valencia tomorrow and know why I've been summoned. Hungry?**'

'**Not hungry. Tired.**'

They settled on the firm bed with only their boots removed. He knew they weren't safe. His body had prickled with awareness and warning since they'd arrived, and his instincts had kept him alive for many *tempi* in Valencia. He trusted them enough to know he wouldn't sleep tonight.

'**You'll take first watch?**' she asked.

'**Yes.**'

'**You better wake me.**'

'**Of course,**' he lied.

She snorted as he lay down, his chest against her back. She pulled his arm over her waist and he propped his head on his hand, so he could watch her sleep. Several minutes after they lay down, the sensors in the bed lowered the lights in the room and he lay in the dark, thinking, as her breathing evened out and the wind rose outside, the thick walls and windows muffling the sound to the whisper of ghosts.

• • •

Hibernation mode activated.

Sister pinged a query in response to the drone's abrupt re-tasking and the loss of its live feed. She was engaged with analysing the Vineyard ship's primary language and systems. The ship's technology had originated on Terra, and this shared evolutionary foundation provided her with a key to begin her decryption within an hour. She required almost half her process-ing power to catalogue and flag the most useful information in the enormous database, so she'd delayed her reconnoitring of Valencia until she'd secured enough preliminary data on it to ensure security protocols were met.

Hibernation mode in progress.

Sister flagged the pingback as unsatisfactory and retrieved another drone to proceed to her Primarch's location and comm a live feed.

At that moment, she registered several things at once. The Vineyard ship's engines powering up. The navigational AI imple-menting a new course away from her home system. A Stage Four hardware breach of her solo-ship's security. A localized EMP that sent the unshielded sections of her solo-ship's power core into temporary shutdown.

None of these things disrupted her operational focus as much as the sudden silence from her Primarch's location beacon. The drone responded to all pings with the proper hibernation codes, but it remained dark to her emergency activation commands.

Hidden in the Vineyard ship's subroutines, Sister studied its live feeds as Knights surrounded her primary shell in the cargo bay, placing clamps on her struts and erecting a dampening field.

These, she understood, were acts of aggression.

As bonded AI to the leading Primarch of the Gomez clan – and frontline of any Kairi Primarch's defence – Sister's mission was now clear. She would enact Caution Protocol. Secure an operating base, determine the location and safety of her sister and husband, and ensure means by which she could access them and carry out offensive missions, if necessary.

While the Knights worked on her shell, Sister hid her secondary drone in an alcove on an empty deck. She supplanted the subroutines of several mundane programmes across critical decks before disguising herself as a diagnostic tool and slipping into the Vineyard's primary AI. She would need to find her own seedling. It was clear the Valencians had no intention of giving her one, as promised.

Her Primarch, like all Kairi, was more than capable of protecting herself, but the Kairi were descended from a small Earth tribe. Every Primarch's life was precious. She would take nothing for granted.

• • •

He is eleven and his grandmother kneels in front of him, smoothing her wrinkled hands down the front of his cream shirt. Her smile is sad, her eyes desperate.

'You know what you must do,' she says, and he nods.

'I must enter the Greatwood and pass my Presentation so I can see the real Valencia.'

She grips his upper arms. 'If you're worthy. If you learn its language.'

He doesn't reply because it's not necessary. He's heard the same story his entire life. He doesn't know what language the Greatwood speaks, but he will learn it. He has no choice. His grandmother's gaunt cheeks speak to the cancer burning through her and his parents are long dead. He will either become Septed or become an orphaned un-Septed. A child with no skill and no caregivers will die in Valencia's Lesser Games. And he doesn't want to die.

She takes his hand and leads him to the entrance of Sept Lucochin's Audience Room. He joins the line of children his age.

The room changes around him, expanding as if breathing in, and he stops to look over his shoulder. The Red Door of Failure is open behind him, letting out crying children into the arms of their silent, devastated parents.

He can see his grandmother standing at the front, watching as a Pawn takes his hand and guides him to the Purple Door of Acceptance. She's also in tears, but he knows they're tears of relief.

He won't die in the Lesser Games now.

He'll never see his grandmother again. Only healthy family members can join the newly Septed in service to the Great Game. Anguish rises in him, knowing she'll die alone. But he's studied with his grandmother how to never show his emotions. He relies on that training now, as they close his first mask on his face.

He is thirty and a Pawn legendary for his ruthlessness. He's stripped the un-Septed of their homes at the command of his Grandmaster. Put the spear to those who attempt to come too close to his charges. He's turned away from the food banks those who've lost their ranking in the Lesser Games and watched them walk away into certain starvation when trade is slow, and rationing begins.

He's done it all while showing none of the rage and despair that fills him at the sight of the waste that continues in Lucochin's Halls, even when the un-Septed have nothing. The Young Masters eat and drink and play the Great Game they're born into, and he hovers at the edges.

Waiting.

Watching as the Lucochin's youngest daughter pulls him down with her onto the bed.

Holding himself separate as she has her fun with him. Remaining passive as she licks his ear behind his mask and says, 'If you kill him, we can be like this always.'

She thinks as they all do. That un-Septed are ignorant. Stupid. That they can be easily manipulated by base emotion.

When she sighs the question, he says yes, and she whispers a date and time for the deed.

He scrubs himself well before he meets with the Grandmaster, trying to erase the previous hour from his body. Lowers himself to the cold floor and touches his head to the ground, as all do who have bad news to deliver. He's calm as he explains the plot, though he knows the Grandmaster could choose to have him killed instead of his daughter. He has nothing to lose but his life, and that hasn't been his since he was a child.

'You've done me a great service,' the Grandmaster says to him as the youngest Lucochin Master rides away in a transport to a hastily arranged marriage. 'Name your reward.'

He's always known he must become more than he is, so he doesn't hesitate. 'I would be a Rook in your service.'

The Grandmaster turns cold eyes on him and says, 'Why waste such talent at gameplay? My Bishop is old, and his strategies grow simplistic. Take his place, if you will.'

They hand him the keys to their Kingdom.

He will find a way to throw open the gates.

The Bishop is buried in pomp and circumstance, and at the graveside he sees his future for the first time. Master Alexandar is blond and grave as a painting in his white half-mask. The only Young Master left alive in the vicious Sept of Valencia – his form straight and strong as a Coretree.

The thump of his heart as he looks at Alexandar is an unfamiliar rhythm in his chest.

The Master turns away without seeing him, and he returns to his Sept – a new Bishop with a tiny crack in his façade only he knows is there.

He's seventy and Queen, and it's his wedding day. Grandmaster Yuta congratulates him even as he apologizes for refusing the match he was offered to one of the Grandmaster's many children.

'You've done well,' Yuta says. 'My son would have poisoned you at the first opportunity and taken your post.'

He knows this, of course. It's what he would have done.

He's pressing his thumb against the contract when the new Grandmaster Valencia, now unmasked, enters to add his DNA to the seal.

His wife Rachel steps aside and dips low with the elegance of a Master whose family has always been Septed. When he straightens from his own bow, the Grandmaster Valencia is between them and the crack in his façade widens as those blue eyes remain on him, speaking of other things than the polite felicitations the Valencia utters to his face.

He's one hundred and three, and a Grandmaster, and soft lips touch his under the Coretrees of the Greatwood, sending sharp shocks through his entire body – and the Corevines in his wrists. Alexandar also forgets to remove his Corevines.

That's when he finally learns it. The language he's been searching for his entire life.

For the first time, he's unable to hide his discovery – his truth – from his wife. She narrows her eyes at him as he tries to make her understand.

'You're a Grandmaster,' she says in a voice that betrays only mild annoyance. Her hair is braided intricately in coils on her head. She's unmasked, as they often are in private. 'Why do you concern yourself with the troubles of the un-Septed? You give them higher rations than they deserve, build them better houses. They're not grateful for this and you only encourage them to believe they're entitled to more.'

'How can you say this,' he says, 'when I was one of them?'

'You are Grandmaster Lucochin, Sire to a Master of Sept Kingston. You are not *them*. Cease this inappropriate worry over their comfort.'

'And yet,' he says, 'how many of them would be me, if given the chance?'

'Chances are taken, not given,' she scoffs. 'Keep your sympathy for those who work to provide the foundation for all Valencia is and can be.'

He stares at her, resigned. 'You truly don't care.'

'Of course, she doesn't,' Alexandar says, touching his jaw gently. 'She's your Queen. The latest in a line second only to mine. This is her world. You don't belong in it.'

He reaches for that hand, but Alexandar is standing next to the fountain in the middle of Valencia's Audience Room, staring into the rippling pool. He walks toward him, the fountain pulling away from him with every step, the tinkling of the water a rising susurration.

'Didecus,' Alexandar says, not looking at him, hands clenching the sides of the basin. 'They must see everything. You must show it to them, as you showed it to me.'

'Alexandar,' he calls over the roaring in his ears, heart pounding, fracturing in his chest. 'Wait.'

Alexandar's lips open and Rachel's voice emerges. 'They'll destroy us. They'll destroy it all.'

'Alexandar.' He would cry if he could. But this part of him never does. 'Forgive me.'

'Grandmaster Lucochin.'

• • •

'Grandmaster Lucochin.'

He started awake, his hand tightening on something. Someone.

The Knight hung motionless over him. He had it by the throat, his fingers digging into the soft flesh beneath the golden full mask and its red speaker.

A gold mask. A Knight of the Royal Sept Valencia. He released the Knight and it straightened, showing no sign that he had almost throttled it in his sleep.

His sleep. He'd fallen asleep.

He looked down at the empty sheets beside him and sucked in a breath. The Knight took a step back as he swung his legs onto the floor.

'Where is my wife?' he ground out, his voice harsh with sleep and fear.

'Grandmaster Valencia awaits you in the Audience Room.'

'*Where is my wife?*'

The Knight crossed its arms over bare breasts, the only outward reaction to his inexcusable rudeness.

'Grandmaster Valencia awaits you,' the Knight repeated. The rainbow colours of the three-dimensional dodecahedron crest of Sept Valencia covered most of its forearm.

His blood was ice in his veins as he swiftly pulled on his boots. There was no sign Eva had ever been there. Her shoes were gone, the trays of food had been removed and only one mask remained on the table. His heart stuttered when he laid eyes on it, his lungs refusing to draw air. Then he took a breath and let the old calm, the old watchfulness, settle around him.

For the first time in years, he was the Grandmaster Didecus Avnette Valentino Lucochin, and Sept Valencia and the entire Greatwood was going to be very sorry they'd brought him back.

He left the mask behind and strode from the room, his mind several moves ahead as the Knight trailed him. He ran down the gentle ramp to the lower floors, toward the public areas at the front of the manse. His boots were muffled on the polished stone floors, so he made sure to push open the doors to the Audience Room hard enough to make them slam against the walls.

As he strode to the centre of the chamber and faced the throne, he saw the sedan chair on one side of the dais – the last piece of the puzzle.

Two rows of golden-headed Knights lining the path to the throne turned their faces in his direction, hands ready at the belts on their waists. He ignored them, stalking between them to the unmasked figure waiting for him in a pile of red translucent silks. Valencia's Queen stood next to the throne in red trousers, black-gloved hands clasped behind his back and Valencia's crest shining in the centre of his chest.

He should have known not to use the room they'd selected. He'd been unforgivably careless, and Eva had paid for it.

He stopped with one foot on the incline that led up the dais as he met the cold gaze of the Grandmaster Valencia. 'You gassed us,' he said.

The Valencia didn't hesitate. 'Yes.'

'This was never just about me, was it?'

'On the contrary. It has everything to do with you. And your wife.'

He narrowed his eyes at the only person in the Greatwood who didn't wear a mask, the better for everyone to know exactly who they were.

His first wife stared back at him, her dreadlocks so thick and long they fell past her waist, her dark eyes like obsidian.

'She had nothing to do with this.'

'She is a solution,' the man beside the Valencia said.

He let his eyes drift over the Grandmaster's Queen, once a White Knight of Valencia, bitterness filling his mouth. 'To what problem? She has never set foot on Valencia.'

The Grandmaster fluttered a hand and the Knights came to attention then trooped out, closing the doors behind them. It galled him that she knew he would take no action. Not while he had no idea where they held his wife.

'Her people will come for her if you harm a hair on her head,' he warned.

'We've taken precautions,' the Valencia said. 'For now, she's alive and well. Your solution will decide if she stays that way.'

'I was exiled,' he said. 'You no longer command me.'

The Grandmaster Valencia leaned forward, her brown skin flawless and supple in the morning light streaming through the floor to ceiling windows behind him. 'You will solve our problem, or the Consortium will receive the solution they contracted for.'

He was careful not to let her see the dread that filled him. The Valencia propped her chin in the palm of her hand, studying him.

'The Consortium?'

'Yes.' She let her gaze slide past him, as though bored. 'They lost a ship a solar year ago. There was a catastrophic malfunction before it disappeared, but the Consortium didn't find any debris at the ship's last known location. Their inability to confirm the fate of the ship meant insurance on the ship and cargo could be withheld for years, so the Consortium turned to the best problem solvers in the known Systems for help in finding it.'

'And have you done so?'

She leaned back and tapped her fingers against the arms of the throne. 'No. And we never will, given it was destroyed by a Kairi Havoc-class solo-ship. Your wife's, to be precise.'

He folded his arms across his chest. 'You came to this conclusion how?'

'My Grandmasters examined all data from the ship. The transmissions and location coordinates had been altered by a rare Trojan, one that amends the AI code of any analyst, erasing all data not in support of a false conclusion. The Kairi call it Cleanslate and developed it during the Nicene War. No machine could pinpoint it, but Grandmasters are not code.

'We refocused our search from a missing ship to reports of engagements involving Kairi ships, then cross-referenced them with the time of the Consortium ship's disappearance. There weren't many – those that attack the Protectorate soon learn why the Sibling Army is feared in all the known galaxies.

'One report was of a raid by an unknown attacker on an Outpost planet with few defences. The description of the ship that repelled the attack matched that of a Kairi solo-ship. The description of the destroyed ship matched that of a slaver. And your implant's ping occurred on the same planet, at around the same time.'

His derisive snort was without humour and he glanced first

at the silent Queen, then the Valencia. 'That's how you found me. It's not why I'm here.'

The Valencia raised her eyebrows. 'Tell me why then.'

'I'm here because you've been trapped by your games and your lies.'

The Queen took a threatening step toward him, but he gave him a withering stare. 'It wouldn't be wise to hurt me or my wife when we both know you are desperate for my assistance.'

The Valencia's eyes came alive for the first time, mirth crinkling their corners, though she never smiled. 'Desperate? You're the one who stands captive in your former Sept. The penalty for returning from exile is death.'

'You don't want me dead,' he said. 'The game was obvious the moment I saw your chair.'

The Valencia leaned back. He'd been married to her long enough to recognize her annoyance. 'You're still very much the Lucochin, aren't you?'

'You came here in a transport, instead of entering Valencia's Greatwood and arriving at my Vineyard. I was delivered to my estate instead of Valencia's because your Vineyard is no longer functioning as it should, and you couldn't take the chance I wouldn't arrive.

'You had been searching for me for many *tempi* when the Consortium reached out to you. When you learned about my wife, you seized the chance to use her as leverage. Like a newly Septed Pawn, I obliged you by bringing her along.'

'Don't feel too badly,' the Queen said, his voice cold and calm. 'Sept Kingston's White Knight was told to bring you both in alive. He chose subtlety over force. He knew no Kairi citizen would allow a mate to go anywhere without them.'

The Lucochin inclined his head mockingly. 'You know everything but what's most important. How to save the Greatwood.

The Coretrees are fading, aren't they? Accepting fewer and fewer stratagems from the Games, or problems from outsiders. Solutions have errors. Vineyard transports are erratic and inaccurate, if they work at all. I can only imagine how much cargo has been stranded or lost.'

'How do you know any of this? You haven't been here in many, many *tempi*.' The Valencia's voice was sharp.

'The same way I know you had Alexandar killed after your marriage, so you could be promoted to Grandmaster. Your actions cost thousands of lives and destroyed any chance of mercy from me.'

'Grandmaster Lucochin.' He heard a soft snick as the Queen clenched his fingers, activating the weapon in his gloves. 'You will respect the Valencia.'

'What are a few thousand souls?' she replied with a shrug. 'The Game separates the useful from the useless and ensures resources are not strained beyond capacity. You haven't been so long from Valencia you've forgotten your work as Grandmaster, have you?'

'You have my wife,' he said, refusing to give in to the guilt and shame that flashed through him at the mention of his past. 'Make your demands.'

The Valencia's head made a slight nod and the Queen stepped back to her side, fingers loose.

'Grandmaster Lucochin. You will attend the Coretrees in the Greatwood and return them to health. You will attend Valencia's Vineyards and return them to health. You will do these things quickly and well, or I will give your wife to the Consortium, so they may seek redress for their injustices.'

'Injustices?' He raised an eyebrow. 'You apply this term to slave traders?'

'I apply it to a client. It's not for me to judge an artificial lifeform because it has no attachment to biological entities. Only to provide the contracted solution, where possible.'

She stood. The Queen touched thumb to middle finger and the Knights re-entered the room, forming a silent phalanx behind the Lucochin.

'What is your answer, Grandmaster Lucochin?'

He bowed, as custom dictated, then met her gaze with an unflinching one of his own. 'Show her to me and I'll do as you ask.'

The Queen raised his hands, brought his extended index fingers together then drew a glowing square in front of him. The square filled with the image of a suspension chamber. His wife was enclosed beneath the transparent lid, her sleeping face tranquil.

It took a supreme effort not to leap forward and snap the Queen's neck.

Patience, he told himself.

'Take me to her,' he said.

The Valencia smiled. 'Not before the Greatwood is repaired.'

Of course. They would never let him use the annex at his own Sept. They didn't trust him.

And they shouldn't.

'Then take me to the Greatwood.'

• • •

The Rook stopped short when the maintenance robot rolled directly into his path.

You are Second Rook of the Sept Kingston. Confirm.

The Rook put a hand to the spear on his waist as he read the robot's serial number.

'Unit 1014, you have deviated from your assigned tasks.'

Correct.

'You are malfunctioning, Unit 1014. Proceed to the nearest repair station.'

This bot is functioning at 86% efficiency. Confirm identity.

The Rook unsnapped his spear and sank into an attack position.

'I am Second Rook of Sept Kingston. Identify yourself.'

Second Rook, the robot replied, *There has been a Stage Four violation against my shell. Vineyard link to Valencia was closed without notification. Caution Protocol enacted.*

The Rook's fingers flexed on his weapon. 'You are the solo-ship?'

I am Sister to Eva Gomez. You have committed infractions against my sibling. There will be consequences. Release my ship. Take me to my Primarch.

The Rook sliced the humming point of his spear at the machine.

It rolled backward, unfolding two cutting attachments from its conical body.

Second Rook, it intoned. *You have attempted violence on a temporary shell. There will be consequences.*

'Hear me,' the Rook replied calmly. 'Your demands will not be met. I'm under orders from my Grandmaster to secure your solo-ship indefinitely.'

He took a step forward and slashed at the robot. It slid out of the way, snapping its shears onto the end of the spear. The Rook tugged the robot toward it with one hand and drew an energy blade from his belt with the other. In a single movement, he sliced through the control box on the side of the robot. It settled onto the floor with a heavy thunk.

He poked the robot with his spear, ensuring it was deactivated, before re-sheathing his knife. Striding to the nearest comm, he placed a hand on the panel next to it.

Temporary shell deactivated, the comm said before he could utter a word. *Negotiations have failed.*

'As I have no authority to negotiate on behalf of my Grand-master, this was a foregone conclusion.'

Defence is noted. Crew statements consistent. Veracity estimated at 98.2%.

'You have spoken to my comrades?'

All crew are being informed. This is standard procedure.

The Rook swung around, intending to try another comm. A drone hovered behind him, transparent petal-arms rippling around a glowing central light. Beyond the drone, he saw two cleaning robots enter the corridor and roll to a silent stop.

'How did you breach our security?' Second Rook demanded.

Swiftly, one of the robots responded. *Caution Protocol ended. Negotiations ended. This vessel is forfeit.*

'You think gaining control of cleaning robots will force us to do as you wish? There are more than enough crew to disable whatever machinery you attack us with,' the Rook said.

Warning, the comm said. *Greenlight Protocol authorized. Crew confined to quarters.*

'You will find it difficult to convince us to go peacefully.'

Hissing filled the air, and the ship's address system announced the removal of oxygen from all public areas in preparation for a ship-wide cleansing of the air-filtration system.

Greenlight protocol enacted, the drone replied. *Persuasion not required.*

· · ·

The Valencia's transport waited in the courtyard, a shield humming around its passenger cab. The Grandmaster stepped directly from her chair into the large, padded interior and the Queen settled next to her. He took the seat opposite them both.

The chair was stored away in the compartment at the back of the domed vehicle and they were on their way, the Knights riding in security berths on the outside of the cab as the guidance system took them back to Sept Valencia.

He felt the Valencia's eyes on him, but he refused to meet her gaze. He stared out of the transparent dome as they drove away from his overrun estate, an ache in his chest and his head as saw the dark shape of servant quarters, harvester homes and barracks beneath the glimmering overgrowth. All empty now.

His fall from grace had brought down a Sept, killed thousands and led to Eva's abduction. It was time to ensure nothing like that ever happened again.

Sept Valencia lay several hours to the west of Sept Lucochin via transport, through some un-Septed townships. The first two were once part of Sept Lucochin and were as abandoned as his Sept. The townships beyond those had sprung up around Sept Valencia and hundreds thronged the sides of the smooth road they travelled on to see them pass, even though they would see nothing but Knights and a darkened shell. Grandmasters seldom left their mansions without using the Vineyards, and those born un-Septed would only see such personages when important news, ceremonies or changes in the Great Game of Valencia warranted the use of Sept Valencia's continental broadcast system to notify all citizens, regardless of Sept status.

Their unmasked faces blurred together, every shade from pale to ebony, their expressions curious, contemptuous, desperate, angry – nothing like the careful blankness the Septed and the ruling class cultivated.

By the time the huge curves of the colony ship *Valencia*, now a monument, rose up out of the open fields to his left, the rainbow glare of the vast Greatwood was almost too much for the tinted transport.

'A mask?' the Queen asked.

He shook his head. 'When we arrive is soon enough.'

The Valencia remained in the transport when the doors were opened at the ramp to her white mansion. He raised his eyebrows at her, waiting.

'The Queen and several of my Knights will accompany you to the Coretrees. Once you have a solution, you will implement it and return to the mansion to wait. As soon as we know your solution has worked, you will have your wife.'

'And what do you intend to tell the Consortium?'

She shrugged. 'We've failed to provide solutions before. I will happily refund our retainer and extend our regrets in exchange for a Harvest and your *permanent* solution.'

He inclined his head at her. 'Be assured, the solution will be permanent.'

The Valencia descended into her chair and the Queen waved a hand over the sensors to shut the doors. The transport continued on to the Greatwood's entrance beyond the colony ship. When the Queen extended a mask, he took it, watching as the man donned his own.

The Greatwood's iridescence dimmed to a shifting, multi-coloured glow as he exited the transport and four Knights surrounded him. He was marched alongside the Queen into the low-hanging needle-leaves that spun and glinted in the wind, until they reached the Barrier, which kept all but the Grand-masters from entering. A cylindrical drone swept over to verify his seedling, then retreated to its charging station somewhere beyond the Barrier. He walked into the heart of the Greatwood, sensing the Queen's unwavering gaze on his back.

At the transport hub a short distance from the Barrier, he got into one of the small carts and let it take him on its pre-programmed route to the Coretrees. The sweet, musky perfume of the flowering vines draped on the trees surrounded him like a blanket, but for the first time, he caught the dank scent of rot underneath it all. Purple, red, golden and green seedpods peeped between the branches, but many were shrivelled and blackened, and heaps of spoiled pods had burst open on the ground. He heard the rustling of small animals in the undergrowth, but sobered by what he'd seen, he focused on clearing his mind for the task ahead.

The enormous stand of Coretrees rose out of the deep forest like a monolith, entwined trunks and quantum vines woven together into one massive, flowering, windblown, pulsing glare that forced his mask to its maximum setting. But there were also large dark areas within the Coretrees, where saplings had faded and died. More than ever before.

As the cart halted, a vibration prickled his skin, and heat blasted him. He made his way to the nearest annex in the group of hollowed-out beds at the roots of the Coretrees. He lay down, heart hammering in his chest at the thought of what he was about to do, adrenaline making his fingers shake as he wrapped a Corevine around the hand implanted with the seedling. The needle-leaves sank into his arm, tiny stinging points.

Instantly, he was weightless, his body free of pain and filled with the euphoria of the joining. His mind squeezed with energy and impressions, even as it grew to include every scrabbling life in the Greatwood, every vine curtain on every Vineyard ship, every needle-leaf that draped over his paralysed body, every quark in every Arbour floating in the silent dark.

He chased the rush of information to its source, past the inexorable pull of the Vineyards in other Septs, or near other worlds, and the flow of thoughts other Grandmasters fed into the Coretrees from their Sept annexes. He delved deep, deeper than anyone before him, including the long dead First Gardeners.

Into the white. Into the murmuration and hum of life.

Into Valencia and all its living, breathing, moving parts. All its dead, rotting, dying parts. Every soul and every sapling connected to it, before and to come.

Bright warmth and cold realization flooded his mind, drowning him, pulling at him, forcing him to fight for his thoughts as It turned Its complex regard on him. A tsunami of sensation and energy. Life engaged in living, nature striving toward continuance by any means possible.

And It shifted, glowing and hungry at his return. Eager.

He offered up logic puzzles he'd concocted out of habit over the years tending his garden at home.

It recoiled.

Then surged forward, surrounding him, searching blindly. Tiny feathery sensations. Sharp probes. The ice-cold lick of interstellar Arbours, drawing on the energy and life of Its planet-bound mother-brethren.

Satisfaction flashed through the tiny part of his mind he'd kept for himself. What he'd tried to correct had never been a mistake, and so his attempts to put things back to the way they had been so many *tempi* ago had failed, just as he'd hoped.

His plan would work.

There would be no going back now.

When he emerged from the seductive whirlpool of Valencia's embrace hours later, he barely found the strength to detach himself from the annex and drag his heavy limbs to the cart. The Queen caught him as he fell across the Barrier and lifted him into the transport.

Knowing they couldn't execute him before they were sure his solution had worked, he let himself slip into sweet oblivion.

•

Loss speared through him as soon as he opened his eyes. The ecstatic link to Valencia's true heart was one he'd survived losing many *tempi* ago. Terrible as it was to be without it again, the excruciating absence of his wife eclipsed that pain with ease. He'd sensed the infinitesimally small presence of Eva's seedling while in the annex, but it had been too new, too weak to follow to its source.

He sat up on the hard bed, his gaze going to the gold-masked Knight that stood guard in the doorway. They were still careful not to let him near a Pawn or a Rook, ranks he might manipulate.

'Food. Now.'

The Knight retreated from the doorway and he strode over to the window. The night sky danced with colours. He'd been asleep for hours.

Good. By now, the Grandmasters would be gathering.

The Knight supervised the servant that brought him his food, making sure no conversation occurred. He sat at a table that folded down from the wall to eat, noting the chair was bolted to the floor and the bed he'd slept in was devoid of sheets. He had a selection of fruit and bread, nothing that would require utensils, and a sip-bag of wine. He ate it all, hunger gnawing at him after more than a day without food, and all he saw, all he thought about, as he stared at the wall before him was the woman he loved, the man he'd lost, and the people he still had a chance to save.

When the Knight returned, he was waiting.

'Take me to the Audience Room.'

The Knight was silent.

'As a Grandmaster, it's my right to attend any gathering concerning the Great Game. Take me to the Audience Room.'

He folded his arms across his chest and didn't let his gaze

move from the tinted slits of the mask. After long minutes, the Knight turned and strode away.

The hallways were cool and meandering and had not changed since his days as the Lucochin. Valencia's mansion was the only one grown from the Greatwood itself, as the colony ship had landed on the very edge of it. The petrified wood of the walls and floors had been left unpainted, and the shimmer of vines was everywhere, the powdery scent of flowers infused in every breath.

He'd been kept in private quarters on the upper floors. He heard the hum of voices long before he reached the vast Audience Room on the first floor. The Knight stopped next to the guards who opened the doors for him. He walked in past the masked Kings, Queens and Grandmasters that turned to look, and the rows of Knights from the twelve Septs of Valencia lining the sides of the room. He focused on the stage at the far end, the line of Valencian Knights before it, and the floating silver fountain in the shape of dodecahedron in front of them.

He approached among a flurry of signing hands and mutters. The Valencia sat between her King and Queen and watched him enter, the long drape of her sheer sleeves billowing around her gilded throne. None of their expressions changed, but the Valencian Bishop who stood below her throne started toward him.

He stopped to the left of the fountain, resting one hand against its side as he raised the other, palm out in warning.

'I am Grandmaster Didecus Avnette Valentino Lucochin and I would speak to my fellow Grandmasters regarding the failure of their annexes and their inability to access and feed the Coretrees.'

The Valencia's eyes narrowed, the smallest movement. 'You are no longer a Grandmaster of Valencia.'

'And yet I am the only Grandmaster who can tell you what

has happened and why, and how you can save our people.' His fingers quested against the underside of the fountain, found the rough imprint they were searching for and pushed.

'Traitor!' came a voice behind him.

'You are exiled,' came another. 'You should have been executed the moment you arrived.'

'The Grandmaster Valencia brought me here,' he answered without turning as he withdrew his hand. 'Ask yourselves why.'

He sensed someone draw closer and tensed, even though none of the Knights in front of him had moved.

'He is a Grandmaster of Valencia until the Greatwood calls him home,' said a familiar voice. He turned to face a tiny man in an orange mask who sat in a mobile chair. The Grandmaster Yuta, oldest of their number, gave him a deferential nod. 'He is entitled to speak at any gathering if he has not yet been executed. This is the law.'

The Valencia let her gaze rise above the crowded room. 'Very well. I brought the Lucochin here to repair the damage he caused to the Greatwood. It was an error on my part. One I will remedy once this gathering has ended.'

'Before we get to my imminent demise,' he interrupted. 'Allow me to tell you a story.'

Whispers spread behind him.

The Grandmaster hissed out a breath and shook her head, her braids swishing against the thin silk of her robe. 'My predecessor died without uttering a word, not even a plea for his life. This delay does not become you.'

Sorrow and anger swept through him. 'Your actions do not become *you*. Why order the clearing of Lucochin's board?'

'Because you corrupted it. You Septed all families of Pawns. Increased the rations for the un-Septed. Visited them to hear their concerns. What you did – it was Deviation.' The Valencia's voice was filled with disgust despite her tranquil expression. 'You had no respect for the governance of the Grandmasters. You corrupted Alexandar as you tried to corrupt me. I only regret you escaped to exile instead of facing your due for your crimes. Sept Lucochin was an abomination under you. Clearing the board of it was my duty to the Great Game and my Sept. I did what was best for Valencia.'

He laughed, a sad, resigned sound that echoed in the cavernous room. 'You are as wrong about that as you are about the un-Septed.'

He faced the sea of colourful masks. His back felt naked, vulnerable, but he would let them see the truth of his words, the emotions he'd learned to express over time.

They had to know emotions were possible, even for a Grandmaster.

'Once,' he said, 'an orphan of un-Septed Valencians whose township was cleared from the board, a descendant of the First Gardeners, made his Presentation and was taken into a new Sept. He rose through the ranks, from servant to Grandmaster, over many *tempi* of the Great Game.

'He found allies and a wife and more enemies than he ever knew possible, but he didn't forget what it was to be un-Septed. How it felt to have no control over whether he ate or starved, whether he had a life of purpose or not. He knew this to be wrong. He knew Valencia to be unfair. And he wanted, more than anything, to change that, and to protect the people under his care for as long as he could.

'This orphan knew he held strange views. That the Great Game was not played for the benefit of the un-Septed, but to feed the Greatwood. So, imagine his shock to find another who believed as he did. The Grandmaster Alexandar Gordon Millefleur Valencia.'

There were gasps and a whisper of, 'Impossible.'

'Together, they searched for a secret told to the orphan by his grandmother, and those Gardeners before her. A secret buried in the Coretrees. That there was intelligence within the Greatwood, which Gardeners had encountered.'

Silence fell as all in attendance hung on his every word.

'One of those Gardeners told an officer, and once the Captains of the colony ships learned of this intelligence, they determined ordinary colonists could not be allowed to control something so important as the Coretrees. They took over the care of the Greatwood. Gardeners were stripped of their duties and demoted. But some remembered what their comrades had spoken of and tried to find ways to contact it again.

'The orphan believed this entity might be the key to controlling the Greatwood without constant input from the Games. It had lain dormant despite the logic and puzzles of the Grandmasters who came after the Gardeners. But once both Grandmasters entered the Coretrees to investigate, they realized they were wrong, and everything changed.'

'We know what changed. There was a trial, Lucochin,' came the Valencia's icy voice. 'All here remember it.'

'You know part of the story,' he replied. 'This is what I never spoke of. There is no single intelligence in the Coretrees. The Coretrees *are* intelligent, and they are nature itself – the centre of Valencia's ecosystem – a key part of a great whole we've injected ourselves into. They don't respond only to logic. They respond to stimulation. Water, sunlight, nutrients – the Greatwood produces what it needs, in the amount it needs. Then we came, demanding more and more, and willing to stimulate the Greatwood in whatever way we could to get it.

'The Coretrees took what we gave it, logic as a form of cultivation, but when Alexandar and I entered together, it sensed what any good gardener will tell you is the secret to growing thriving plants. Care. Affection. It fed on our emotions. The more it did, the more we opened to it – and to our connection. With each other. With the Coretrees. With every Coretree, everywhere.' He stopped, taking a shuddering breath to centre himself.

'And the Harvest. It was the largest, the most incredible… So many ships were grown.' He shook his head with a sigh. 'But that was when my estate's Vineyard began to die. I had neglected it too long. Our ranking in the Great Game suffered and my wife, as my Queen, brought charges of neglect of my Sept and the Vineyards against me and my King.

'Alexandar had no choice but to bring me to trial for capital crimes. I begged him to save Lucochin, to absorb its people into Sept Valencia. In return I would save Valencia from what I had done in ignorance, prevent whatever corruption I had started from spreading, and agree to exile.

'To save my Vineyard, I gave it more than puzzles and strata-gems. I gave it what I felt for Alexandar and for my Sept. And then I severed its annex from the Greatwood.'

His words echoed around them and he looked from mask to mask, willing them to understand.

'Valencia had only had a taste of human emotion, so I hoped it would forget and no further damage would be done. But it had taught me a new way, and I couldn't forget.

'Now I know Valencia didn't either. And while your ever-growing demands exhausted the ecosystem around it, the Coretrees crave a different kind of stimulation and waste away without it.'

As he spoke, he saw it. The exact moment they understood what his solution had been. Behind him the Valencia let anger seep into her voice.

'Grandmaster Lucochin, what have you done?'

He turned to face her, glad to be nearing the end of this farce. 'I fixed the Coretrees the one way I knew.'

'You gave it your bond with your wife,' the Grandmaster Yuta said in a resigned voice.

'Oh no,' he said softly. 'I gave it much more than that. I gave it the first moment I saw her. The first time I laughed. The first time I held Alexandar. I gave it every good emotion I've ever had. I gave it joy and hope... and love. I now suspect it has lost any taste for what Grandmasters provide.'

Anger buffeted him, even as some Grandmasters stepped back, gesturing to allies and members of their Septholds.

'For too long we've existed by making demands of an eco-system we don't fully understand and cannot live without. We've made a slave of a unique evolutionary miracle that exists across vast reaches of time and space, and in return we've given it death and cold space. The Greatwood can feel, and we've fed it logic and greed and forced separation. If we continue this way, we'll destroy every part of it, no matter how far it's spread. And we'll doom ourselves.'

'You've taken away our only means of controlling the Great-wood,' someone whispered. 'You've killed us.'

'Not at all. Dig deep and you'll find what you need, though I caution you against negative emotions that might harm the Harvest. And if you truly cannot feed the Coretrees, I suggest you turn to the un-Septed. You'll need every person you can find. Valencia is vast. Communing with it will require every open mind and warm heart.'

The Valencia stood, hands clenched, and for the first time, he saw Knights turn to look at each other. Heard voices speaking simultaneously behind his back.

It's done, he thought. And there was no triumph in him. Only disgust for so many *tempi* of needlessly wasted lives. Only guilt for his part in Valencia's treacherous, bloody past. Only sadness for those who had lost so much before, and those who would be called to sacrifice while Valencia transitioned to something else. Something new.

'You'll die here,' the Valencia spat, 'knowing your wife is in the hands of the Consortium.'

He faced her, the merest frisson of sympathy curling within him for what awaited her. 'You have far more important things to worry about. Like how you're going to handle the revolution that's marching to your doorstep at this very moment.'

'What are you talking about?' the Queen said, eyes narrowed.

He shrugged. 'You've been broadcasting this gathering to Valencia the entire time. Every citizen has heard what's been said here tonight.'

The cries of horror rose to the rafters like a murder of crows.

The Queen clenched and released a glove, holding his palm flat and face up. An image of the Audience Chamber shimmered to life, confirming the open feed.

'Alexandar often recorded meetings without his Queen. There's a surveillance drone in this fountain. I activated it and its link to the broadcast system the moment I entered.

'Thousands of souls and countless denizens of the Greatwood and this planet have paid for our ambitions. It's time everyone knows the perversion that sits at the head of this Game so they understand all Games must end.'

'Queen,' the Valencia said in an arctic voice. 'Seize the Grandmaster Lucochin and seal him in a chamber until his execution.'

He cast his gaze over the room. 'You should secure your estates. There are far more un-Septed than you. You'll want to be prepared to negotiate come morning.'

'Queen! I gave an order!'

He swung his gaze back to the hesitating Queen. 'Do the Grandmasters know you hold a Primarch of the Kairi here? Do they know you risk the Sibling Army arriving on their doorstep searching for her? If you let us leave peacefully, together, this ends here. If it doesn't, you will have killed two citizens of the Kairi Protectorate. You know what happens to governments that do that.'

Around him, Grandmasters were leaving. Knights pushed past, weapons at the ready as they escorted their charges.

But some Knights, Bishops and Rooks – some didn't move at all.

He waited, his last card played, his last game ended.

The Valencian Knights turned to their motionless Queen for instructions.

'Queen.'

The Valencian Queen met his Grandmaster's gaze.

'Is this rebellion?' she asked in a gentle voice.

A hand gripped the last Lucochin's arm. He turned to face the Grandmaster Yuta. 'Come,' the old man said. 'At the Valencia's command, I kept your wife at my Sept. I will take you to her.'

He glanced at the stage where the Valencia stood, all her attention on her Queen. 'Is it rebellion?' she asked him again.

The Queen tilted his head in deference. 'Yes.'

He grasped her hands before she could draw a weapon.

'Come,' Yuta said again.

He followed, his last sight of the Valencia that of both her wrists caught in her Queen's hands as her Bishop motioned to the Knights. One Knight deactivated its spear, returned it to its belt and walked away.

His heart sang relief and a fierce rightness as he did the same.

•

His wife was asleep in his arms when he exited the Yuta's Vineyards into his own and found Sister's secondary drone floating in the centre of the field, filaments rippling, waiting for him.

He smiled at it. 'You were worried.'

Sister was out of contact for more than twenty-four hours. Caution Protocol enacted. Tracking systems were activated and found you both alive and not in distress. Greenlight Protocol enacted.

He started for the Vineyard controls, Sister floating behind him. 'There was no need for that. You know I would never let her come to harm.'

Tracking could not confirm location data and Sister's drone was deactivated. Vineyard ship did not respond satisfactorily to queries. Greenlight Protocol enacted.

'The Vineyard crew must have enjoyed that.'

Crew was neutralized. Sister obtained seedling. Vineyard is under Sister's control. Mirror connection open and active.

He put a mask on Eva, then himself.

'No need to set the controls then?'

Mirror connection open and active.

He trailed the drone toward the translocation point.

'You didn't hurt the crew, did you?'

Neutralized. Sister would not want to cause a planetary incident. Husband is a pacifist.

He stopped to laugh, the drone hovering patiently in the glistening fields beneath the rainbow-lit night.

• • •

Hours later, Eva stirred in the soft bed next to him, rolled over and opened her eyes. He smiled, his hand cupping her shoulder as he held her body against his. She smiled back, then let her gaze drift over the opulent stateroom, the best one in the Vineyard ship, intended only for Valencian dignitaries and guests. With everyone else locked in their cabins and Sister flying the ship back to the Outpost, there was no one to object and his wife damn well deserved the finest they had on offer, as he was never setting foot on a Vineyard again.

She groaned and buried her head in his shoulder before signing.

'You never woke me.'

He kissed the delicate shell of her ear and signed. 'Guilty as charged.'

She leaned back to meet his eyes. 'What happened?'

'Long story. It will keep. Enjoy your sleep. The Vineyard ship left orbit while we were away. We're a few hours from the Outpost.'

She caressed the side of his face. 'You okay?'

'I'm good. Never better.' And he knew she could see he meant it. Her body relaxed and she threw her leg over his, cuddling closer.

'Told you we'd leave together.'

'You did.' He kissed her forehead, blinking rapidly to clear his suddenly blurry vision. 'Right as always.'

'Don't you forget it.'

He stroked her hair as her breathing slowed.

'Wake me for first watch?'

'Of course.'

'Liar.'

This time, they fell asleep together.

DUMP

Cristina Jurado

Spain

Cristina Jurado is an unstoppable force, an editor of magazines and anthologies, an award-winning author, and a tireless promoter of international speculative fiction in all its forms. I only met her once, briefly, a few years ago, but she came on board to edit *The Apex Book of World SF 5* for me and has been invaluable in recommending stories I may have missed. Thankfully, Cristina's also a great writer in her own right, and when she sent me 'Dump' to read I realized I had to include it! The story was translated by Steve Redwood and is original to this anthology.

BEGINNING

The mountains of plastic seemed to be observing Naima from the middle of the dump. The rest of the morning-shift Rats had also begun to stir, stretching what arms and legs they still had, defying cold and hunger. Faces blackened with dust and dirt, covered with scars; eyes caked in rheum and mucus; hair twisted and knotted; mouths with cracked lips and filthy uneven teeth.

Those who were now awake gazed towards the horizon, at the subtle changes in colour, and the appearance of shadows as long as the winter nights. Every dawn was an obstinate defiance of death, another day won, twenty-four more hours survived. With the light came a tiny infusion of hope that fortune might smile on them at last. This time, yes, this time they might find something valuable that would raise their status in the mara.

Bloody fools! Nothing but corpses ever emerged from the mara. We 'compatriots', whether we be Rats, Half-breeds, Santeros or Cyclops, have nothing but this dump. We can only finish up the scraps offloaded by the colonies in their rubbish trucks. Such lovely presents! We're also rubbish, human rubbish, everything that those in the colonies don't want to be. They're afraid of us, of what we represent, which is their inability to cope with the destruction of the world. They fear this ocean of detritus.

Naima scrambled farther away from the gang towards the north-western face of this man-made monster. It was cold, and she knew that the others would start to rummage on the eastern slope until it got warmer, but she had heard the lorries unloading on the other side during the night. The strap of her prosthesis was digging into her more than usual, and she thought of loosening it, but she would have to wait until she was farther away so nobody would be near enough to see the stump just above the elbow of her left arm. One of the first things that Naima had learned was that the absence of her arm bothered people, especially the other Rats. Seeing her without the prosthesis would remind everyone how comparatively lucky she was, something she had fought against ever since Sibilo had found the orthopaedic arm among some hospital refuse, precisely on this northern slope.

It hadn't been a gift exactly: Sibilo had loathed seeing her suck him off with a single arm. He said it made him think of a salamander with a leg just chopped right off, calmly carrying on, green and viscous, as if nothing had happened, while the torn-off limb remained behind jerking with pain, or perhaps from surprise at the absence of the rest of its body. The goddamn son-of-a-bitch wanted it to seem as if she was grasping his dick with both hands: this, he said, gave him a hard-on, and made her seem almost a proper whore like the ones wandering the clean streets of the colonies in the city.

It was her who sucked him off, but I was the one who had to swallow that bastard's sperm. It was me that he raped every time he felt like it, but she was the one who ate in the Rathole, together with the other homies and their pets, and enjoyed a real roof, electric lighting, and running water. She never rebelled, never bit into his member to make the old fucker bleed to death. I begged her to hundreds of times, but she never took any notice of me.

The night they blew his head off, Naima got drunk, but not like the other Rats, who drank to the memory of their companions fallen in the skirmish with the Half-breeds, but from sheer relief. She inherited the *homie*'s leather jacket, which had the name of the gang spelled out with metallic rivets which would gleam in the light of the night-time bonfires; this made the other small Rats envious because the wearer had the right to stay in the Rathole.

The north-western slope was dangerous because of the drains. If you weren't careful, you could fall into one, sink into the filthy water, find yourself trapped by an avalanche of bottles and packaging, and die through asphyxiation. Or you might be attacked by huge deformed bugs lurking among the piles of flexible materials, or fall into one of the tunnels they had made. Many Rats had disappeared that way, but Naima knew this gradient well. Sibilo had taken her there on countless occasions, and she had carefully noted the route that led to the discharge points at the feet of some of the steepest slopes.

She heard someone whistling behind her: it was the gang boss – her face covered in pimples, and with a bruise as big as a cockroach on her left eyelid – ordering her to go back. She pretended not to hear, and went on round the huge bulge covered in plastic. Naima had a keen eye for spotting the different types of plastic because you could no longer judge by the colour of the containers: now packaging and bottles were made using exotic polymers, and you needed a combination of sharp sight, sensitive touch and acute hearing to *triage* the residues of plastic with any precision. She was hoping to find some polyethylene acetone casings, a material much in demand in the resale stalls, which would ensure her better food for a time, and perhaps even the possibility of becoming a *homie* and sleeping in the Rathole.

It was me who learned the language of the dump, of the safe routes to avoid the drains, and how to listen to the sounds of plastic in order to anticipate avalanches or filtrations of water. Bottles moan and squeal in a certain way when they are crushed beneath the weight of tons of rubbish. It's not the same sound as lateral shiftings or footsteps on top of the carpet of plastic.

The cold clenched itself round the plastic objects which, piled on top of each other, formed a weirdly homogeneous surface, full of rounded protuberances, strange holes and hollows that harboured toxic gases, inflammable residues, albino creatures or starving indigents from other maras. Naima pulled her neck scarf up over her nose, and followed the path she had memorized. All the forays with Sibilo had enabled her to discover the secrets of the dump, to learn to recognize the behaviour of materials under pressure, heat, cold or rain. She could estimate the stability of a mound of rubbish merely by noting what kind of plastic was predominant, and could even predict how high it was likely to become before collapsing.

Sibilo had been a sadistic old brute, but he understood plastic rubbish better than anyone. He claimed he had once been a Cyclops, making a living from the copper cables he retrieved from outdated or inoperative equipment. And he did indeed wear a red patch over his left eye, which made his face look a bit like a dartboard. Naima liked to imagine one of the Half-breeds aiming at the patch and firing a black bullet to slice a beautiful tunnel right through his brains.

Naima had no way of knowing if Sibilo was telling the truth, and had once lived among the Cyclops, but she did know that they wore patches or glass eyes as a mark of identity. She'd tried to find out from other *homies*, but no one had been able to tell her anything about the old man's arrival. He had been part of the mara ever since she could remember, when she would scamper through the rubbish with the other girl Rats, helping the older ones, when she had had to fight for the crumbs that were thrown from the Rathole. But once her tits had started to grow Sibilo noticed her, and she became his pet.

She wouldn't have survived among the other kids. If I hadn't pushed her, if I hadn't robbed, if I hadn't thrown more than one girl Rat into the drains, she wouldn't be here.

Like all the other Rats, Naima always hoped to find *The Thing*, the object that everyone dreamed about, something that the Cyclops had overlooked, something that had the magic power to serve as payment to buy the right to become a *homie*, to have your own mattress in the Rathole, the only structure in the area with electric current and food. And the place where decisions were made. The Leap Forward, from being a simple Rat to becoming a *homie*, something that everyone feared and yet longed for, the vital step which implied full membership of the mara, the unquestioned right to live in the Rathole, and to keep pets who worked for you. At the moment, they were just Rats, soldiers who did all the heavy work.

She headed towards the north-western hill. She had heard the lorries arriving at dawn and had seen them going off in that direction. Small black shapes flew above the area, casting fleeting shadows over the lake of transparent containers. There was one reddish shadow, which skilfully avoided the others, and repeated the same circular flight over the hill. The drones were always red, although she didn't know why. She quickened her pace: other Rats would soon arrive to poke around, and she might miss making a valuable discovery.

The box was half-buried among milk containers. The gleam of the corners caught her eye and made her stop and take her hands out of her pockets in order to move some cartons out of the way. When she picked up the box she noticed how heavy it was. It was rectangular, an inch or so wide and as long as a forearm, an anaemic white colour, and with a cover so polished she could see her greasy dishevelled hair reflected in it.

Naima gasped. She glanced all round, but nobody was close enough to notice what she had discovered. She quickly wrapped the box in the bundle she usually carried on her back, then searched around frantically for containers that might be supposed to have some value in order to cover up her find. A short way ahead she found several polymer casings, which would be useful for the makers of second-hand drones. Instinctively, she looked up at the sky: the reddish silhouette, the only one that emitted a mechanical whistle, was far away.

She grabbed her bundle, and managed to stuff in the casings so that the box remained hidden under them. Then she wandered through the safer areas of the hill, a long way from the drains, in order to fill in time. She had to make sure the other Rats didn't realize that she had found *The Thing*. When the mealtime alarm sounded she returned as fast as she could, but instead of going to the dilapidated barracks, she headed for the Rathole.

The *ranfleros* were having coffee in front of the fireplace, beside the great conference table. Naima approached her own section leader, old Peyas, whose face was half covered in scabs after an inflammable container exploded a few inches away from him: the price of letting cigarette ash fall when you're checking the merchandise.

There they are. Slouched in their comfortable armchairs, warming their backsides near the fire, bellies full and heads empty. Ranfleros *who were themselves once Rats, who were also abused, beaten, mistreated, exploited, and who once they became* homies *made sure they got rid of anyone who got in their way. Now they give the orders to groups of* homies, *who in turn are the bosses of the Rat gangs. Everything perfectly organized to continue scraping out a living in the sea of plastic.*

'What the devil do you want, Rat?'

Peyas always narrowed his eyes when speaking to someone, as if he were straining to empty his bowels.

Naima knew she didn't have the right to speak, so she simply showed him the shiny white rectangle.

'Bloody hell! Where did you get that? Speak!'

'On the north hill, boss.' There was a mixture of fear and pride in her tone.

Peyas began to fiddle with the rectangle, surrounded by the rest of the *ranfleros*, who kept shouting out advice.

'Shut up, you damn fools, this way I'll never get it opened! Dimi! DIMI! Someone bring that half-starved fucker here!'

They seemed to have forgotten her, and Naima took the opportunity to stick close to Peyas, putting up with being shoved and elbowed by the others.

A tall ungainly figure of indefinite age, with a head shaven and wearing dirty black clothes, came in, wiping her hands on a rag.

'What's up, Peyas? I've got a lot of work today.'

Before she finished speaking, Dimi's attention was caught first by Naima, and then by the rectangle. For a moment Naima thought the *homie* seemed to recognize her, though she didn't remember ever having seen her before.

I know that look. And so does she.

'Is that what I think it is?'

The newcomer approached, picked up the rectangle, and began to manipulate it with automatic movements. Dimi raised what seemed to be a kind of lid, sat on the conference table, and placed *The Thing* on the table. Then she began to push the buttons that poked up from inside, almost as if she were playing a musical instrument, and nearly at once *The Thing* lit up, and silence fell over the whole room.

'It's intact, Peyas. In perfect condition. Who brought it to you?'

Peyas nodded towards Naima.

'This Rat here.'

The figure clothed in black shut *The Thing* and addressed her.

'Weren't you Sibilo's pet?'

Naima nodded.

'We can fetch a tidy sum with this in the sewers, Peyas. Provisions for several months, perhaps even half a year.'

Peyas narrowed his eyes so much it seemed the rheum had sealed the lids together.

'Things are getting messy. Apart from the Half-breeds who are getting far too cocky since that business with Sibilo, the Santeros are acting very strangely. They've been seen prowling around the Thirteen. You tell me what the devil the body snatchers want with those scum! It's not safe to appear in the market alone, but if you turn up with several *homies*, you might let the cat out of the bag. Take the Rat with you, Dimi. You won't raise suspicion if you're with that little wretch.'

Dimi stood up, clutching the rectangle under her arm.

'Have you got a name, or shall I just call you 'Rat'?'

'Naima, boss.'

'I'm nobody's boss – and nobody is my boss.'

Dimi spotted the strap holding the orthopaedic arm. She gazed at the artificial limb for some seconds, which seemed an eternity to Naima.

'Come on. I haven't got all bloody day to play babysitter to Rats.'

Naima followed her, while behind her the *ranfleros* were already celebrating the loot they expected to get.

INTERMISSION

If the Rats called it the Cesspit, it wasn't because of the refuse, but because of the people. Because the rubbish had reclaimed the land, in some parts with more enthusiasm than in others, but wastage was to be found everywhere, the spawn of memory, cadavers of functionality. What differentiated that place, which other maras called souk, zoco, bazaar, roadstead, market, was the complete lack of scruples of its visitors, who pursued a single aim: make some kind of profit, usually at the cost of others. It wasn't the strongest who survived in the entrails of the Cesspit, but the person who made the transaction first, who got there before any potential competition. If you weren't fast enough, someone else would take advantage of you, and you would become the merchandise. In that place, even nightmares could fetch a price.

Naima had been there with Sibilo a couple of times, but had hardly ventured any further than the first few stalls bordering on the zone controlled by the Rats where several *homies* endeavoured to place their merchandise. This time, with Dimi, she entered the maze of crowded alleyways, keeping close to the figure in the hooded jacket, black and worn-out like the rest of her clothes. They kept *The Thing* in a grubby rucksack slung over Dimi's shoulder.

The story goes that once upon a time there were also places like this, but where people didn't make a living from rubbish. Who could believe such nonsense? Fantasies like every stall was carefully placed, one beside the other, that people strolled around, stopped and chatted and even stepped aside to let others pass, that customers and sellers greeted each other with a smile… Why, some go so far as to say that the stallkeepers sold fresh food, vegetables recently harvested, and healthy animals fattened up and looked after to be consumed in clean-smelling homes. Rubbish was hidden away because no one wanted it, incredible though it may seem. Everyone wanted to get rid of it, to deny its existence. Because once something had been utilized, consumed, enjoyed, it had no right to exist anymore. This fairy tale has been doing the rounds for many, many refuse collections.

This was a free zone, an area where all the maras had equal rights; it was, in addition, the only point of contact with the colonies, the urban spaces which deceived themselves claiming they were still cities, but which suffered continuous energy cuts, shortages of most products, and an exponential increase in the crime rate. The moment someone dared to put a foot in the alleyways of the Cesspit, they became just one more item of merchandise, likely to be bought and sold. Naima knew this full well, and that was why she did what she had done ever since she could remember, which was to convert herself into an invisible being. She knew she must never catch anybody's eyes, or brush against any passer-by, and that she must move away if anybody approached her directly.

She had stuffed the strap under her old winter coat because Dimi had forbidden her to wear Sibilo's leather jacket which would have given them away at once as members of the Rathole. They made their way to the second-hand stalls, trying to avoid the junkies clutching their tubes of glue. Hookers swung their hips suggestively to attract clients, regaling them with toothless smiles, throwing kisses at them, touching their augmented lips – matching their pneumatic breasts – with broken nails. Thugs hung around the kiosks of the usurers, who smelt of fear and salt, while dealers did their bartering swarming around the exchange stalls, combining their shouted offers with sweating armpits.

Recycled neon strips emitting an insipid glow advertised the betting shops, behind whose doors could be heard the muffled sound of psychomusic inciting people to bet. Naima copied Dimi, and stuffed a piece of cork into each ear in order not to hear the sounds coming from those dens. Only those who worked in the Cesspit were immune to them. Parts of motors were to be seen everywhere, and circuit boards hanging in rows from the roofs of the booths, huge coils of metal cables, foul-smelling cabinets to recharge batteries, repair stalls, stores for plastic and cellulose, and shelves cluttered with batteries.

Several recycling company agents passed beside them, leaving behind a trail of perfume and disdain, and Naima had to hold on to a post of luminescent moss to maintain her balance. Her movement was so abrupt it dislodged her ear plugs. She noticed that the ground seemed to be vibrating, accompanied by a melody. She turned round to see where it was coming from. It was a viscous sound that stuck to her volition like flypaper, an invisible canvas that wrapped her in a yearning to try her luck in a game of chance. Her only desire was to enter the place the psychomusic was coming from, sell her orthopaedic arm, prostitute herself, or let them remove some internal organ she could use to gamble with. A hand grabbed the collar of her jumper, and forced her to walk straight ahead. She tried to break free, but when at last she managed to, the sound of the surveillance drones and the shouts of the dealers had drowned the hypnotic music.

An exasperated Dimi was gazing at her.

'I haven't got time to wipe your ass, understand, you snotty-nosed brat? Be more careful, because if you fall into one of those holes you'll never get out again. Or, at least, not as you are now, which isn't that much, in any case. And I don't intend to go in to pull you out.'

Naima nodded ruefully, and ripped a strip off her T-shirt which she then tore in half to make two balls of cloth for her ears to replace the lost pieces of cork.

Doesn't she remember? Her head's emptier than I thought. I can't understand how she's forgotten the eyes of the person she's following. How can she possibly not sense it? Because Dimi has recognized us. I'd bet anything you like that she's noticed it the same as me. It was only a second, but she fixed her eyes on us in the Rathole. She saw our false arm and came to a conclusion.

The door they stopped at was the same colour as the trays of melted polymers. They entered after Dimi whispered the pass-word, a single word, in the ear of the doorman – who had a quarter of his skull missing – who let them pass without asking questions. The shop was full of sober-coloured rectangles like the one they carried in the rucksack. Two individuals with scars across their eyes were haggling with the tallest, strongest woman Naima had ever seen, who stood behind a coffin that served as a counter. The reflecting bottles cast a pale milky light over the faces of the people there, lending them a sickly air. Dimi approached the counter as soon as the two men left, spitting on the ground and cursing. The tall woman sported a pink Mohican hairstyle, which brushed against the hanging bottles. It was only when she looked up that Naima noticed her glass eye.

'I need to see Kung.'

The Mohican woman stared at her as if she were speaking a language unknown to her.

'Kung doesn't deal with the purchase of material. We're not going to bother him just for a computer… because that's what you've brought me, haven't you?'

Dimi removed the rectangle from the rucksack and very carefully placed it on the counter.

'You think you're real cool for coming here with one of these. I've got dozens of them, but the power cuts are getting more and more frequent, and besides, there have been no updates for years. Almost none of the applications function – and when they do, they're full of errors and release viruses.'

'Don't fuck around with me, Freja! You always say that to keep the price down. This one is clean – I've checked it – and the hard disc is brand new. Look at the programs: all the upgrades installed, right up to when the systems crashed. If you want to screw me, I'll just find another stall. But don't take me for a prize idiot!'

The woman called Freja opened the rectangle and began to push several buttons.

'I'm fed up with you lot! Always complaining. I have to give myself a profit margin. This is a business, not a bloody charity!'

Dimi grabbed the rectangle from her and started to replace it in the rucksack.

'I can't waste any more time. Tell Kung I want to see him.'

'I repeat, Kung hasn't been in this business for a long time.'

'And drones fly by themselves, do they? Try that one on someone else. I've got something that would interest him, but maybe it would interest Palmira more.'

Freja appeared to be making mental calculations while she took a small cube from her pocket.

'As if anyone's going to trust a Rat... Fray calling Ku! Can you hear me?'

A strange conversation ensued between the woman and another voice coming from the cube she was holding.

Maybe this would be a good time to make a run for it. I don't like this at all. We're not Dimi's pet... So why did she agree to bring us? No one would swallow that story about not coming with other homies *in order to avoid suspicion. Rats visit the stalls here all the time without any problem.*

We reluctantly follow Dimi through this stinking basement. The tunnel that comes next is lined with oxidized pipes and mould that was once bioluminescent and now necroseals the walls. Dimi moves like the weasel she is, with self-assurance and agility; it seems she's familiar with the route. But that doesn't surprise me, because she never appears on the sea of plastic or soils her hands triaging the refuse. She knows about computers, understands machine language and is able to write it, so that they follow orders, such as to compress the plastic, melt it, convert it into the polymers that we then resell in the Cesspit to intermediaries, who seal it into odourless packages that seem new, and sell to the factories for three times what they pay us. Oh yes, she's very good at doing this kind of stuff, there in her room in the Rathole, far away from the sewers outside, from the avalanches, from the toxic gases, from the mutated creatures, and from the explosions of containers. She doesn't have to triage like we do, can eat hot food and have a drink whenever she likes, and sleep on a real mattress, almost new, without anybody forcing themselves into her bed. Aren't her hands immaculate, without bruises or parched skin? Doesn't she still have all her teeth? Her face without scars, her nails clipped and clean? Do her clothes stink of humidity and excrement, are her lips cracked and dry? Oh no, I don't think so. It's a long time since she knew hunger, that's if she ever did. She walks around and acts as if the shit we're living in has nothing to do with her, as if she's just passing through. She's a ghost from some colony hiding in the Rathole, God knows why. She never goes out, or at least, if she does, not with anyone from the mara, because they'd snitch on her, and her doings would become talking points for everyone. She's an opportunistic parasite who lives at the expense of the homies *and the Rats, who never gets her hands dirty, never runs risks.*

All this ought to be enough to get out of here as fast as possible. Because when you enter unknown territory with someone you don't trust one little bit, you feel shivers run right up your spine. It's an unpleasant sensation because you're convinced you're going to end up doing something you don't want to do, even something that goes against your own proper interests, but you realize it's going to be inevitable. And you only wish you had the courage to run away from here, and stop zigzagging through underground passages stinking of putrefaction – the atmosphere just as toxic as on the surface, but at least there, up above, it's all open space and you can always find some spot to hide. I don't like being enclosed in this underground world that has nothing to do with the Dump. Here there's no way out, no side exits; you can only advance or go back. I'm well and truly fucked.

The doorway we finally pass through is rusted, with the remains of insects and tiny reptiles stuck to it. It's cold inside. There are cables on the ground and several desks with computers on them. Dozens of reflecting bottles dangle from the ceiling. With a curious handshake, Dimi greets another shaven-headed figure, also dressed in black and wearing enormous sunglasses. Those who handle computers are all the same, cockroaches who still believe it makes sense to tap all those metallic boxes. What the hell do they hope to achieve if the communication systems are all down? They talk about their damn drones, their crappy flying machines which spy on what other maras are doing. As if good old-fashioned human spies were now useless. They blab on about whether the net is now operational, whether the connections are wide-spread enough, whether there's enough access to the servers... They speak about the system as if it were a dormant creature that they had to waken. I want to get away from here, breathe in the foul vapours of the inflammable polymers, the aroma of coffee made from the leftovers thrown out from the colonies, which we buy from the body snatchers. And these two keep wittering on, blah blah blah, program, blah blah blah, frequency simulator, blah blah blah, trawling the signal... If Naima turned round, we could retrace our steps through the dank passages and return to the shop run by the Cyclops, the towering woman with the Mohawk hair crest, and one transparent eye seemingly facing backwards: maybe she can see herself from inside with that eye. I'm not afraid of the guy at the entrance, the one with half his skull missing. He's one of ours – imperfect, unfinished. In reality all the Cyclops are. They all represent the same thing: that the interests of the mara are above all personal ones. That's why they pluck out an eye, or burn it with alcohol, an exquisite army of incomplete humans that members of other maras can quickly identify. In our case, to make that leap and become a homie, *you get the shit beaten out of you. If you survive, you have the right to stay in the Rathole and to keep pets. Many don't live to tell the tale – and those who do never smile again.*

Dimi looks at us while she's talking with Kung. She gesticulates with those hands of hers, those claws that poke out of her sleeves, and the other does the same; they both raise their hands in the air as if they were flags and they were communicating with them. And our arm hurts, but not the right one, the left one, the one which isn't there, and we can't remember if it ever was. It's strange because we've never noticed its absence: I would have noted it if Naima had ever felt it. And Dimi is now mimicking the shape of a globe over her stomach. And she laughs again and Kung bites one of her ears with the easy familiarity of those who have shared a bed and guns.

The sharp prick in my neck takes me by surprise. The pain is unbearable and Naima's vision becomes blurred, and in this situation I lose all spatial reference. But I can still hear, and it's all very strange because I'm aware of what's happening almost before it does. Arms grab her and lift her up to carry her to some kind of vehicle. I know it's a vehicle because I can feel the bumping and rattling, an irregular trembling that becomes a sudden jump when there's some obstacle to get over. She is still unconscious, and I can only attain information from the vibrations and the background noises. We spend quite a long time here, with this jolting which is usually very light because we seem to be stationary more often than not. Her being unconscious such a long time is a fucking nuisance, making it almost impossible to keep any sense of time.

She begins to open her eyes when I've already sensed that we've been taken out of the vehicle and carried into a place smelling of vinegar. In fact, it's that smell, bitter and sharp, which has brought her to her senses, although she finds it hard to remain awake. They've put her in a bed with a mattress and sheets; I'd say clean ones. She sleepily opens her eyes a couple of times, and I can see that the room is white, and there are real lights shining from the ceiling that seem to observe us: bulging eyes, radiance so dazzling it would scorch your eyes if you looked at it directly. Several figures dressed in white crowd round Naima. There are more to her left than to her right, and I know that's because of the stump. They're touching her with hands gloved in a ductile plastic; I think it's vinyl, like the millions of torn gloves that turn up in the Dump. Naima speaks incoherently, and the people in white order her to shut up.

They inspect and prod and measure and examine and compare and paw and fish around and finally stick long viscous needles into her, needles that are connected to tubes coiled around each other on the floor, just like the ones we've come across thousands of times in the refuse heaps. When Naima manages to focus her eyes on the masked face of one of the people in white, she sees worried eyes. I see greed, and an 's' tattooed beside the eyebrows. Then we slide into a state of induced tranquillity, totally artificial, like that time we sniffed glue. Only it wasn't really glue, but something else, that plunged us into a dancelike drowsiness, because we were relaxed but in the mood for fun: we wanted to just collapse anywhere to enjoy the hallucinations, but we also felt an impulse to run a race against the person nearest to us. Everything was simultaneously one thing and its opposite, sublime bliss and profound dissatisfaction, sexual passion and apathy, a desire to laugh and sneer at the bloody mara and cry for it.

I know what we felt: she only intuited it. She was in that space between mirage and delirium, roaming through alien landscapes where there's no rubbish to triage – as if that were possible! I leave her to entertain herself with the images generated by the muck we've been injected with, and concentrate on her bodily responses. And for the first time I am afraid. I note that something strange and potent is beginning to circulate through her blood vessels, something that carries with it the force of a thousand cannon broadsides, something inexplicable, which frightens me when it reaches me. It's a pushing, added vectors of force that twist, frenzied traction, a fever for destruction, and I fear the worst. The discharges tear into every part of the skeleton. It's as if they're paring the bones from inside, and I thank God that Naima is immersed in the quicksands of her imagination.

And now I can't find my own space and I choke because they've invaded my home and torn down its very foundations. What was a beautiful adolescent body is now something else. I don't quite know what, even though it looks the same and has the same features and measurements, even if it once again sips soup just as stubbornly as it would weak coffee, or triages plastics as easily as others collect cadavers. It was pleasant, my house, because it was mine; it was my temple, it was where I lived, and in exchange I looked after it without her noticing. She never suspected my presence, nor bothered to wonder why she sometimes had strange impulses that altered her usual conduct. And, in my own way, I adored her from my watchtower even when Sibilo was fucking her, because the interior of her muscles was my garden, because her brain was my dwelling place. I enabled her to survive the most devastating winters, the hungriest wild beasts, the most perverted homies.

The Santeros have desecrated her: I don't recognize these nerves, this cartilage growing like the toxic fumes of stagnant waters. A one-armed girl for them to test their potions on, practise on, play at being doctors... Fucking devil's priests! How easy to trade with other people's bodies so that those living in the colonies can have nice fresh organs to repair their rotting carcasses, or in order to recycle them as a source of protein! I'm willing to bet we took so long to arrive because the paths of this mara pass through open-air cemeteries, and there were limbs and fragments of what were once people everywhere. She was unconscious, but the stench of dead flesh floated in the air like the fear in the mara and the lechery in the sewers, and it was impossible not to sense it. This odour is unforgettable because it infiltrates the cracks separating sanity and madness, which are as tenuous as chains of proteins, but elastic. It enters and takes over this space, and I no longer fit in this place nor do I recognize it. It's all too much for me, I don't want to navigate in this ship. There are always others that can take me in, even if the moving is laborious, even if it takes me my whole life to collect my belongings and find another cavern with external views. How can I possibly share my sphere with who knows what it is? I'm off.

END

They brought her a sugary liquid to help her recover. It was very sweet, almost colourless, and dripped from the corners of her mouth the first time she tried to take a sip. Her arms felt numb.

Both of them.

As soon as she noticed the left one, she stared at it with disgust, as if it were a gangrenous appendage. She raised her left hand and examined the palm and the back, following the lines marked in the skin by the veins, swollen bluish ribbons. She left the container she had been drinking from on her lap, and touched her left hand with her right one, palpating the fingers, stroking the transparent nails, tracing the tendons with her fingertips, going up past the wrist as far as the elbow, dwelling on the internal fold, and ascending until she reached the point where the stump should have been.

She waited, but only received the crackle of static. She gazed at the whole left arm, and for a moment thought she had only dreamed that it didn't exist, that her mind had been playing tricks on her. But she noted the subtle faint line just above the elbow.

Naima was whole.

And burst into tears.

Translated by Steve Redwood

Rue Chair

Gerardo Horacio Porcayo

Mexico

Gerardo is another name new to me, though he's considered the forerunner of cyberpunk in Mexico and is one of the most renowned writers of science fiction there. He is the author of multiple novels. Cristina Jurado sent me his story and I was delighted to grab it! The story was translated by the author, and is original to this anthology.

The subway sound, down there, filling and creating emptiness.

The hysterical music all 360 degrees around. The sirens of the bicolor and motor escalated *Plymouth Prowler*, in zigzag between the other cars, swallowing the elevated highway.

All that hate for such a little world.

And there she is, under the neon lights. Her stylized body, carved by the hungry times. The result is the same when using surgery. The eyes tell the difference. Turbid, under the random stroboscopic effect of the lighting glitches.

'Just three credits,' she insists, her ragged hoses do not show the skin. Not even the temporary tattoos help create an even surface. She also looks at my legs, but her thoughts are different. 'Far inside they are going to charge you more.'

'Need to see, before I make my mind.'

'You can use a tourist guide,' she says, and she hangs herself on my arm, the soles of her shoes, thin and a little bit bulgy, reveal their piratical origin.

I raise my shoulder, it's not my business.

Our shadows tell less lies than in the past century. They're almost as thin and tall as our very bodies. In the walls, the cockroaches wave their horns with a paranoia-free nervousness. They search, like the pedestrians, the green liquor that becomes blood.

Rue Chair, you can read on the metal plate. It's not truth nor lie; but if they translate it, the meaning will diminish its antique glint. An alley, a corridor stuffed with merchandise. The smell is so bad, as multiple as the flesh that inhabits it. As cold and sharp as metal.

From sailcloth tents, the electric scream of the VR machines electrify the atmosphere. Under sheds, they sell frogs and fish of soft and spongy mouths; mutated bodies and special lube for the necrozoophiliac action.

People gamble over bouncing tables. They develop exotic dances. On tables, some men show the complex fungi web of their feet. Women prefer to show it in contrast with their boobs, they rise their arms and, from time to time, let the pus flow down like a caress, from the armpits to the waist, the legs… but not the feet, not often, at least… there is always a willing tongue, fingers that will taste before deciding to do more.

There are no blabbering people shouting and offering low prices. When you come to Rue Chair it's because you know its meanings. You don't wear distinctive clothing or carry the same old mask. You just walk and walk. You may, or may not, choose. That's your prerogative, and the policemen that guard both entrances know it all too well.

The dealers don't pretend, they remain seated, sipping laudanum. They don't have merchandise on them, not even a little. They have even forgotten the traps. Their drugs are precise.

There's more. Complex artifacts for the pleasure of pain;

polychromatic, aligned on antique shelves. Windows where you can show your preferences. Gallows for the penis. Hooks to sink in every pleasure spot. Spasmodic discharging electrodes.

Cameras are forbidden. There are stories that tell of the punishments, rumors that travel from mouth to mouth. Never a real hint.

Rue Chair is a myth, a reality without substitutes.

'I'm Adi,' she says. Her voice is deep, the tone trying to overcome the coarseness of too much smoking with sweetness. She offers me one. Murat. The order of the characters reminds me of the legboned skull, the plastic container for an old acid used for cleaning bathrooms.

The smoke is less coarse than the fumes coming out from the sewers. More beautiful than her walk.

Her teeth have no cavities. In spite of hunger, her aesthetics are effective. Smiles that you dream about. Not relating to this.

Rue Chair is a rumor that overwhelms you from a young age. A legend that only gives you glimpses when you stop chasing her and you look for her with your life.

To our left, behind a crystal curtain, two women subdue a man. Their black leather garments are specially crafted to let you see breasts, pubis and buttocks. The man tries to kiss a little farther, searching for secrets, and the whip adds another line to his flesh. It's not a drill. Nothing here is, but I know the basic order, that's why I don't join the viewers.

I found the first clue in a similar show. I got a real hint.

To reach Rue Chair you have to start a chain reaction. Desires ain't enough. You have to make the first moves. With enough stamina. Without exaggerated hopes.

'There's so much more,' says Adi, and she guides me through a serpentarium. The snakes react: they throw themselves to the glass window, showing their bifid tongues, their fang-free jaws.

To my left, behind thin curtains, moans. The movement of the flaky bodies in agony.

We don't stop. The walls are almost covered with posters and graffiti.

It's not a vacant lot; the shop was set inside an industrial ware-house and the russet cross is visible. Between the machines with big gears and black oil are the white gurneys. The mutilations are plethoric in their shape. In their fluids and aromas.

A man has reached an agreement. He sets a woman's torso and penetrates the wound in the abdomen. The movements of those lips, scarred, show a partial nerve blockage. The sensa-tion reaches her. Also the tears, and she moans with a painful pleasure. But the man has only eyes for the sex. For the rectum that starts to expel feces with every thrust.

'You've heard too much,' Adi tells me, and straightens her black hair. She shows me the way, pointing with a finger.

To reach Rue Chair you don't need questions. You don't choose. You're chosen. For your actions. For the places you visit. For your looks...

Every wing in this construction is a new catalog. Animatronic mannequins with warm skin and perfect movements. With faces identical to many movie stars. With bowels that perceive your deepest desire.

There are synthetic vulvas that know how to lodge your whole body. Penises with an almost infinite dilatation... Coliseums, bathtubs.

Rue Chair does not forget a single detail. A single dream.

Museums come to life. Crafty illusionist. Animal cages. Aquariums with all kind of species... I look at a woman descend-ing to the giant squid's cube. That kind of hug has reached pale simulation on screens all over the world. Not even computer reconstructions achieve a minimum of this reality.

Adi grabs my arm again. Her smile gets bigger when she tries to avoid a threshold. I refuse to walk.

'All right,' she says, and we go over our steps.

The doors are made of wood. Everything's decorated Tholhurst style. Men with overfeminine gestures manipulate the silverware. The fountains with food are vast. Exotic. Platypus, penguin, blowfish.

'You're not one of them,' Adi assures. A waiter opens a lateral door with urgent gestures. In this alley, I look at the boys with needles in their veins, flooding their nostrils. One of them smiles at me, placing the last dermo in his eyebrow. The dealer growls. Makes a sign to my companion.

We walk through the last housing block. The smell speaks for itself. The rigid, cerulean bodies are bitten while mounted by men and women. Nobody notices us.

Rue Chair opens again into my sight. There are a few things to see and we're almost done. At the center, a tower that stands until it reaches a hundred meters, starts to pull up a fourteen-year-old girl. The elastic rope tied to her ankle.

I'm surprised at this. There are things in which the boys will always surpass us. So easily attracted. A magnet so crafty for Rue Chair.

I've heard some things about the trick about to start, something about throwing her into the void. I keep walking.

An Arab-styled tent shows bits and pieces of dances, the glitter of the curving knives. Not the unguarded exit to the streets, to the city. It is also a shield for censoring what's in front of me.

The man is still tied to the pole. His look, his grin, seem to speak of revelations and epiphanies. Four oriental women, without any clothing, kiss his flesh with the soft caress of their knives. They know where and when to do it.

'Chinese doesn't become you,' says Adi, playing with her hair.

'I think I'll wait a little more.'

Adi smiles again, drives me to the door.

The policeman looks at me without looking. Two *Prowler Plymouth*, over there, slowly roll, trying to drive away those who were brought by random.

I sense the sweaty hand pulling away from my arm.

'Maybe you'll never find it again...' she tells me.

I stop before crossing the final threshold. The guarded frontier.

'You think too many artificial things. Too phony. That's not what you want,' she insists.

Her words are not what make me go back. It's what I see in her eyes. I put back the personal invitation in my pocket. Even that slightest glimmer I would've lost.

She grabs my arm again. We now look behind the stands on the other sidewalk. The building is humid and smells rotten. The shack looks rickety. She begins to take her clothes off, complaining, and sits at the edge of the bed.

'You know what you are...?' and her hand finds some difficulty caressing the metal in my legs, not to make me feel that edge of meat that I still have. She throws herself on the mattress, lying down. Her buttocks are meager, almost open. I can see her anus, the texture of her sex.

I drop my clothes, get inside her. And I know I was right. In her immobility, in her old sweat, in her lacking attempts to fake what she feels, I perceive peace. The true conclusion of my story.

The orgasm is clean. Without astonishments.

But I know there's no merchandise, no events on Rue Chair that can hide her final awe. That's the word on the streets, in the right bars. It can be about mortal poisons, pandemic contagion, mechanic or electronic traps.

It can be anything.

Adi smiles. She hugs me and I kinda hear a sound behind me…

Then I feel it…

The cold metal against my skull. Its bite is circular and awakens a dark calmness. A relief. I know the caliber. Its effects. The looks.

'And what are you looking for?' I ask, without taking my eyes from hers.

The slow outcome guests transform into species. They don't leave Rue Chair. They become merchandise. Those who get out without trying something rarely come back, they settle for cheap imitations, not always effective…

They are the Chorus. The Voice. The ones who talk about what happens here.

Rue Chair stays for just a day in the same place. It's always on the move; they say not only in space, but in time itself.

Rue Chair is the farewell for those who feel what I feel. It's the last taste of pleasure before walking the other street. The one situated out of life. Beyond life.

'I look for chance, for the Russian roulette…' Adi answers, without trying to kiss me. She doesn't smile. 'I just pick people like you. Without color in their lives. Maybe we'll leave together… maybe this time I'll share your same lead… maybe…'

I notice a fragment of the gun in Adi's eyeball, the rest dilutes in her gray metal pupils. After that, I listen to the slow squeak of the trigger as it's squeezed…

His Master's Voice

Hannu Rajaniemi

Finland

Hannu's one of those incredibly smart people (he has a PhD in mathematics) who are usually too busy inventing A.I. or nano-technology (just look up his career!). Luckily he's also a fantastic SF writer. I published his 'Shibuya no Love' in *The Apex Book of World SF 2* and of course I had to have him in this one. It was just a question of which story! 'His Master's Voice' is prime Rajaniemi, strange and wondrous and post-human in the best way, and I'm delighted to include it here.

B efore the concert, we steal the master's head.

The necropolis is a dark forest of concrete mushrooms in the blue Antarctic night. We huddle inside the utility fog bubble attached to the steep southern wall of the *nunatak*, the ice valley.

The cat washes itself with a pink tongue. It reeks of infinite confidence.

'Get ready,' I tell it. 'We don't have all night.'

It gives me a mildly offended look and dons its armor. The quantum dot fabric envelops its striped body like living oil. It purrs faintly and tests the diamond-bladed claws against an icy outcropping of rock. The sound grates my teeth and the razor-winged butterflies in my belly wake up. I look at the bright, impenetrable firewall of the city of the dead. It shimmers like chained northern lights in my AR vision.

I decide that it's time to ask the Big Dog to bark. My helmet laser casts a one-nanosecond prayer of light at the indigo sky: just enough to deliver one quantum bit up there into the Wild. Then we wait. My tail wags and a low growl builds up in my belly.

Right on schedule, it starts to rain red fractal code. My augmented reality vision goes down, unable to process the dense torrent of information falling upon the necropolis firewall like monsoon rain. The chained aurora borealis flicker and vanish.

'Go!' I shout at the cat, wild joy exploding in me, the joy of running after the Small Animal of my dreams. 'Go now!'

The cat leaps into the void. The wings of the armor open and grab the icy wind, and the cat rides the draft down like a grinning Chinese kite.

· · ·

It's difficult to remember the beginning now. There were no words then, just sounds and smells: metal and brine, the steady drumming of waves against pontoons. And there were three perfect things in the world: my bowl, the Ball, and the Master's firm hand on my neck.

I know now that the Place was an old oil rig that the Master had bought. It smelled bad when we arrived, stinging oil and chemicals. But there were hiding places, secret nooks and crannies. There was a helicopter landing pad where the Master threw the Ball for me. It fell into the sea many times, but the Master's bots – small metal dragonflies – always fetched it when I couldn't.

The Master was a god. When he was angry, his voice was an invisible whip. His smell was a god-smell that filled the world.

While he worked, I barked at the seagulls or stalked the cat. We fought a few times, and I still have a pale scar on my nose. But we developed an understanding. The dark places of the rig belonged to the cat, and I reigned over the deck and the sky: we were the Hades and Apollo of the Master's realm.

But at night, when the Master watched old movies or listened to records on his old rattling gramophone, we lay at his feet together. Sometimes the Master smelled lonely and let me sleep next to him in his small cabin, curled up in the god-smell and warmth.

It was a small world, but it was all we knew.

The Master spent a lot of time working, fingers dancing on the keyboard projected on his mahogany desk. And every night he went to the Room: the only place on the rig where I wasn't allowed.

It was then that I started to dream about the Small Animal. I remember its smell even now, alluring and inexplicable: buried bones and fleeing rabbits, irresistible.

In my dreams, I chased it along a sandy beach, a tasty trail of tiny footprints that I followed along bendy pathways and into tall grass. I never lost sight of it for more than a second: it was always a flash of white fur just at the edge of my vision.

One day it spoke to me.

'Come,' it said. 'Come and learn.'

The Small Animal's island was full of lost places. Labyrinthine caves, lines drawn in sand that became words when I looked at them, smells that sang songs from the Master's gramophone. It taught me, and I learned: I was more awake every time I woke up. And when I saw the cat looking at the spiderbots with a new awareness, I knew that it too went to a place at night.

I came to understand what the Master said when he spoke. The sounds that had only meant *angry* or *happy* before became the word of my god. He noticed, smiled, and ruffled my fur. After that he started speaking to us more, me and the cat, during the long evenings when the sea beyond the windows was black as oil and the waves made the whole rig ring like a bell. His voice was dark as a well, deep and gentle. He spoke of an island, his home, an island in the middle of a great sea. I smelled bitterness, and for the first time I understood that there were always words behind words, never spoken.

• • •

The cat catches the updraft perfectly: it floats still for a split second, and then clings to the side of the tower. Its claws put the smart concrete to sleep: code that makes the building think that the cat is a bird or a shard of ice carried by the wind.

The cat hisses and spits. The disassembler nanites from its stomach cling to the wall and start eating a round hole in it. The wait is excruciating. The cat locks the exomuscles of its armor and hangs there patiently. Finally, there is a mouth with jagged edges in the wall, and it slips in. My heart pounds as I switch from the AR view to the cat's iris cameras. It moves through the ventilation shaft like lightning, like an acrobat, jerky, hyperaccelerated movements, metabolism on overdrive. My tail twitches again. *We18. Benjamin Schneiders Little Greys are coming, master*, I think. *We are coming.*

• • •

I lost the Ball the day the wrong master came.

I looked everywhere. I spent an entire day sniffing every corner and even braved the dark corridors of the cat's realm beneath the deck, but I could not find it. In the end, I got hungry and returned to the cabin. And there were two masters. Four hands stroking my coat. Two gods, true and false.

I barked. I did not know what to do. The cat looked at me with a mixture of pity and disdain and rubbed itself on both of their legs.

'Calm down,' said one of the masters. 'Calm down. There are four of us now.'

I learned to tell them apart, eventually: by that time Small Animal had taught me to look beyond smells and appearances. The master I remembered was a middle-aged man with graying hair, stocky-bodied. The new master was young, barely a man, much slimmer and with the face of a mahogany cherub. The master tried to convince me to play with the new master, but I did not want to. His smell was too familiar, everything else too alien. In my mind, I called him the wrong master.

The two masters worked together, walked together and spent a lot of time talking together using words I did not understand. I was jealous. Once I even bit the wrong master. I was left on the deck for the night as a punishment, even though it was stormy and I was afraid of thunder. The cat, on the other hand, seemed to thrive in the wrong master's company, and I hated it for it.

I remember the first night the masters argued.

'Why did you do it?' asked the wrong master.

'You know,' said the master. 'You remember.' His tone was dark. 'Because someone has to show them we own ourselves.'

'So, you own me?' said the wrong master. 'Is that what you think?'

'Of course not,' said the master. 'Why do you say that?'

'Someone could claim that. You took a genetic algorithm and told it to make ten thousand of you, with random variations, pick the ones that would resemble your ideal son, the one you could love. Run until the machine runs out of capacity. Then print. It's illegal, you know. For a reason.'

'That's not what the plurals think. Besides, this is my place. The only laws here are mine.'

'You've been talking to the plurals too much. They are no longer human.'

'You sound just like VecTech's PR bots.'

'I sound like you. Your doubts. Are you sure you did the right thing? I'm not a Pinocchio. You are not a Gepetto.'

The master was quiet for a long time.

'What if I am,' he finally said. 'Maybe we need Gepettos. Nobody creates anything new anymore, let alone wooden dolls that come to life. When I was young, we all thought something wonderful was on the way. Diamond children in the sky, angels out of machines. Miracles. But we gave up just before the blue fairy came.'

'I am not your miracle.'

'Yes, you are.'

'You should at least have made yourself a woman,' said the wrong master in a knife-like voice. 'It might have been less frustrating.'

I did not hear the blow, I felt it. The wrong master let out a cry, rushed out and almost stumbled on me. The master watched him go. His lips moved, but I could not hear the words. I wanted to comfort him and made a little sound, but he did not even look at me, went back to the cabin and locked the door. I scratched the door, but he did not open, and I went up to the deck to look for the Ball again.

· · ·

Finally, the cat finds the master's chamber.

It is full of heads. They float in the air, bodiless, suspended in diamond cylinders. The tower executes the command we sent into its drugged nervous system, and one of the pillars begins to blink. *Master, master,* I sing quietly as I see the cold blue face beneath the diamond. But at the same time I know it's not the master, not yet.

The cat reaches out with its prosthetic. The smart surface

yields like a soap bubble. 'Careful now, careful,' I say. The cat hisses angrily but obeys, spraying the head with preserver nanites and placing it gently into its gel-lined backpack.

The necropolis is finally waking up: the damage the heavenly hacker did has almost been repaired. The cat heads for its escape route and goes to quicktime again. I feel its staccato heartbeat through our sensory link.

It is time to turn out the lights. My eyes polarize to sunglass-black. I lift the gauss launcher, marvelling at the still tender feel of the Russian hand grafts. I pull the trigger. The launcher barely twitches in my grip, and a streak of light shoots up to the sky. The nuclear payload is tiny, barely a decaton, not even a proper plutonium warhead but a hafnium micronuke. But it is enough to light a small sun above the mausoleum city for a moment, enough for a focused maser pulse that makes it as dead as its inhabitants for a moment.

The light is a white blow, almost tangible in its intensity, and the gorge looks like it is made of bright ivory. White noise hisses in my ears like the cat when it's angry.

• • •

For me, smells were not just sensations, they were my reality. I know now that that is not far from the truth: smells are molecules, parts of what they represent.

The wrong master smelled wrong. It confused me at first: almost a god-smell, but not quite, the smell of a fallen god.

And he did fall, in the end.

I slept on the master's couch when it happened. I woke up to bare feet shuffling on the carpet and heavy breathing, torn away from a dream of the Small Animal trying to teach me the multiplication table.

The wrong master looked at me.

'Good boy,' he said. 'Ssh.' I wanted to bark, but the godlike smell was too strong. And so I just wagged my tail, slowly, uncertainly. The wrong master sat on the couch next to me and scratched my ears absently.

'I remember you,' he said. 'I know why he made you. A living childhood memory.' He smiled and smelled friendlier than ever before. 'I know how that feels.' Then he sighed, got up and went into the Room. And then I knew that he was about to do something bad, and started barking as loudly as I could. The master woke up and when the wrong master returned, he was waiting.

'What have you done?' he asked, face chalk-white.

The wrong master gave him a defiant look. 'Just what you'd have done. You're the criminal, not me. Why should I suffer? You don't own me.'

'I could kill you,' said the master, and his anger made me whimper with fear. 'I could tell them I was you. They would believe me.'

'Yes,' said the wrong master. 'But you are not going to.'

The master sighed. 'No,' he said. 'I'm not.'

• • •

I take the dragonfly over the cryotower. I see the cat on the roof and whimper from relief. The plane lands lightly. I'm not much of a pilot, but the lobotomized mind of the daimon – an illegal copy of a twenty-first-century jet ace – is. The cat climbs in, and we shoot towards the stratosphere at Mach 5, wind caressing the plane's quantum dot skin.

'Well done,' I tell the cat and wag my tail. It looks at me with yellow slanted eyes and curls up on its acceleration gel bed. I look at the container next to it. Is that a whiff of the god-smell or is it just my imagination?

In any case, it is enough to make me curl up in deep happy dog-sleep, and for the first time in years I dream of the Ball and the Small Animal, sliding down the ballistic orbit's steep back.

· · ·

They came from the sky before the sunrise. The master went up on the deck wearing a suit that smelled new. He had the cat in his lap: it purred quietly. The wrong master followed, hands behind his back.

There were three machines, black-shelled scarabs with many legs and transparent wings. They came in low, raising a white-frothed wake behind them. The hum of their wings hurt my ears as they landed on the deck.

The one in the middle vomited a cloud of mist that shimmered in the dim light, swirled in the air and became a black-skinned woman who had no smell. By then I had learned that things without a smell could still be dangerous, so I barked at her until the master told me to be quiet.

'Mr. Takeshi,' she said. 'You know why we are here.'

The master nodded.

'You don't deny your guilt?'

'I do,' said the master. 'This raft is technically a sovereign state, governed by my laws. Autogenesis is not a crime here.'

'This raft *was* a sovereign state,' said the woman. 'Now it belongs to VecTech. Justice is swift, Mr. Takeshi. Our lawbots broke your constitution ten seconds after Mr. Takeshi here'—she nodded at the wrong master—'told us about his situation. After that, we had no choice. The WIPO quantum judge we consulted has condemned you to the slow zone for three hundred and fourteen years, and, as the wronged party, we have been granted execution rights in this matter. Do you have anything to say before we act?'

The master looked at the wrong master, face twisted like a mask of wax. Then he set the cat down gently and scratched my ears. 'Look after them,' he told the wrong master. 'I'm ready.'

The beetle in the middle moved, too fast for me to see. The master's grip on the loose skin on my neck tightened for a moment like my mother's teeth, and then let go. Something warm splattered on my coat and there was a dark, deep smell of blood in the air.

Then he fell. I saw his head in a floating soap bubble that one of the beetles swallowed. Another opened its belly for the wrong master. And then they were gone, and the cat and I were alone on the bloody deck.

• • •

The cat wakes me up when we dock with the *Marquis of Carabas*. The Zeppelin swallows our dragonfly drone like a whale. It is a crystal cigar, and its nanospun sapphire spine glows faint blue. The Fast City is a sky full of neon stars six kilometres below us, anchored to the airship with elevator cables. I can see the liftspiders climbing them, far below, and sigh with relief. The guests are still arriving, and we are not too late. I keep my personal firewall clamped shut: I know there is a torrent of messages waiting beyond.

We rush straight to the lab. I prepare the scanner while the cat takes the master's head out very, very carefully. The fractal bush of the scanner comes out of its nest, molecule-sized disassembler fingers bristling. I have to look away when it starts eating the master's face. I cheat and flee to VR, to do what I do best.

After half an hour, we are ready. The nanofab spits out black plastic discs, and the airship drones ferry them to the concert hall. The metallic butterflies in my belly return, and we head for the make-up salon. The Sergeant is already there, waiting for us:

judging by the cigarette stumps on the floor, he has been waiting for a while. I wrinkle my nose at the stench.

'You are late,' says our manager. 'I hope you know what the hell you are doing. This show's got more diggs than the Turin clone's birthday party.'

'That's the idea,' I say and let Anette spray me with cosmetic fog. It tickles and makes me sneeze, and I give the cat a jealous look: as usual, it is perfectly at home with its own image consultant. 'We are more popular than Jesus.'

They get the DJs on in a hurry, made by the last human tailor on Saville Row. 'This'll be a good skin,' says Anette. 'Mahogany with a touch of purple.' She goes on, but I can't hear. The music is already in my head. The master's voice.

• • •

The cat saved me.

I don't know if it meant to do it or not: even now, I have a hard time understanding it. It hissed at me, its back arched. Then it jumped forward and scratched my nose: it burned like a piece of hot coal. That made me mad, weak as I was. I barked furiously and chased the cat around the deck. Finally, I collapsed, exhausted, and realized that I was hungry. The autokitchen down in the master's cabin still worked, and I knew how to ask for food. But when I came back, the master's body was gone: the waste disposal bots had thrown it into the sea. That's when I knew that he would not be coming back.

I curled up in his bed alone that night: the god-smell that lingered there was all I had. That, and the Small Animal.

It came to me that night on the dreamshore, but I did not chase it this time. It sat on the sand, looked at me with its little red eyes and waited.

'Why?' I asked. 'Why did they take the master?'

'You wouldn't understand,' it said. 'Not yet.'

'I want to understand. I want to know.'

'All right,' it said. 'Everything you do, remember, think, smell – everything – leaves traces, like footprints in the sand. And it's possible to read them. Imagine that you follow another dog: you know where it has eaten and urinated and everything else it has done. The humans can do that to the mindprints. They can record them and make another you inside a machine, like the scentless screenpeople that your master used to watch. Except that the screendog will think it's you.'

'Even though it has no smell?' I asked, confused.

'It thinks it does. And if you know what you're doing, you can give it a new body as well. You could die and the copy would be so good that no one can tell the difference. Humans have been doing it for a long time. Your master was one of the first, a long time ago. Far away, there are a lot of humans with machine bodies, humans who never die, humans with small bodies and big bodies, depending on how much they can afford to pay, people who have died and come back.'

I tried to understand: without the smells, it was difficult. But its words awoke a mad hope.

'Does it mean that the master is coming back?' I asked, panting.

'No. Your master broke human law. When people discovered the pawprints of the mind, they started making copies of themselves. Some made many, more than the grains of sand on the beach. That caused chaos. Every machine, every device everywhere, had mad dead minds in them. The plurals, people called them, and they were afraid. And they had their reasons to be afraid. Imagine that your Place had a thousand dogs, but only one Ball.'

My ears flopped at the thought.

'That's how humans felt,' said the Small Animal. 'And so they passed a law: only one copy per person. The humans – VecTech – who had invented how to make copies mixed watermarks into people's minds, rights management software that was supposed to stop the copying. But some humans – like your master – found out how to erase them.'

'The wrong master,' I said quietly.

'Yes,' said the Small Animal. 'He did not want to be an illegal copy. He turned your master in.'

'I want the master back,' I said, anger and longing beating their wings in my chest like caged birds.

'And so does the cat,' said the Small Animal gently. And it was only then that I saw the cat there, sitting next to me on the beach, eyes glimmering in the sun. It looked at me and let out a single conciliatory meow.

·

After that, the Small Animal was with us every night, teaching.

Music was my favorite. The Small Animal showed me how I could turn music into smells and find patterns in it, like the tracks of huge, strange animals. I studied the master's old records and the vast libraries of his virtual desk, and learned to remix them into smells that I found pleasant.

I don't remember which one of us came up with the plan to save the master. Maybe it was the cat: I could only speak to it properly on the island of dreams, and see its thoughts appear as patterns on the sand. Maybe it was the Small Animal, maybe it was me. After all the nights we spent talking about it, I no longer know. But that's where it began, on the island: that's where we became arrows fired at a target.

Finally, we were ready to leave. The master's robots and nanofac spun us an open-source glider, a white-winged bird.

In my last dream the Small Animal said goodbye. It hummed to itself when I told it about our plans.

'Remember me in your dreams,' it said.

'Are you not coming with us?' I asked, bewildered.

'My place is here,' it said. 'And it's my turn to sleep now, and to dream.'

'Who are you?'

'Not all the plurals disappeared. Some of them fled to space, made new worlds there. And there is a war on, even now. Perhaps you will join us there, one day, where the big dogs live.'

It laughed. 'For old times' sake?' It dived into the waves and started running, became a great proud dog with a white coat, muscles flowing like water. And I followed, for one last time.

The sky was grey when we took off. The cat flew the plane using a neural interface, goggles over its eyes. We swept over the dark waves and were underway. The raft became a small dirty spot in the sea. I watched it recede and realized that I'd never found my Ball.

Then there was a thunderclap and a dark pillar of water rose up to the sky from where the raft had been. I didn't mourn: I knew that the Small Animal wasn't there anymore.

•

The sun was setting when we came to the Fast City.

I knew what to expect from the Small Animal's lessons, but I could not imagine what it would be like. Mile-high skyscrapers that were self-contained worlds, with their artificial plasma suns and bonsai parks and miniature shopping malls. Each of them housed a billion lilliputs, poor and quick: humans whose consciousness lived in a nanocomputer smaller than a fingertip. Immortals who could not afford to utilize the resources of the overpopulated Earth more than a mouse. The city was surrounded by a halo of glowing fairies, tiny winged moravecs that flitted about like humanoid fireflies and the waste heat from their overclocked bodies draped the city in an artificial twilight.

The citymind steered us to a landing area. It was fortunate that the cat was flying: I just stared at the buzzing things with my mouth open, afraid I'd drown in the sounds and the smells.

We sold our plane for scrap and wandered into the bustle of the city, feeling like *daikaju* monsters. The social agents that the Small Animal had given me were obsolete, but they could still weave us into the ambient social networks. We needed money; we needed work.

And so I became a musician.

• • •

The ballroom is a hemisphere in the center of the airship. It is filled to capacity. Innumerable quickbeings shimmer in the air like living candles, and the suits of the fleshed ones are no less exotic. A woman clad in nothing but autumn leaves smiles at me. Tinkerbell clones surround the cat. Our bodyguards, armed obsidian giants, open a way for us to the stage where the gramophones wait. A rustle moves through the crowd. The air around us is pregnant with ghosts, the avatars of a million fleshless fans. I wag my tail. The scentspace is intoxicating: perfume, fleshbodies, the unsmells of moravec bodies. And the fallen-god-smell of the wrong master, hiding somewhere within.

We get on the stage on our hindlegs, supported by prosthesis shoes. The gramophone forest looms behind us, their horns like flowers of brass and gold. We cheat, of course: the music is analog and the gramophones are genuine, but the grooves in the black discs are barely a nanometer thick, and the needles are tipped with quantum dots.

We take our bows and the storm of handclaps begins.

'Thank you,' I say when the thunder of it finally dies. 'We have kept quiet about the purpose of this concert as long as possible. But I am finally in a position to tell you that this is a charity show.'

I smell the tension in the air, copper and iron.

'We miss someone,' I say. 'He was called Shimoda Takeshi, and now he's gone.'

The cat lifts the conductor's baton and turns to face the gramophones. I follow, and step into the soundspace we've built, the place where music is smells and sounds.

The master is in the music.

• • •

It took five human years to get to the top. I learned to love the audiences: I could smell their emotions and create a mix of music for them that was just right. And soon I was no longer a giant dog DJ among lilliputs, but a little terrier in a forest of dancing human legs. The cat's gladiator career lasted a while, but soon it joined me as a performer in the virtual dramas I designed. We performed for rich fleshies in the Fast City, Tokyo and New York. I loved it. I howled at Earth in the sky in the Sea of Tranquility.

But I always knew that it was just the first phase of the Plan.

• • •

We turn him into music. VecTech owns his brain, his memories, his mind. But we own the music.

Law is code. A billion people listening to our master's voice. Billion minds downloading the Law At Home packets embedded in it, bombarding the quantum judges until they give him back.

It's the most beautiful thing I've ever made. The cat stalks the genetic algorithm jungle, lets the themes grow and then pounces on them, devours them. I just chase them for the joy of the chase alone, not caring whether or not I catch them.

It's our best show ever.

Only when it's over, I realize that no one is listening. The audience is frozen. The fairies and the fastpeople float in the air like flies trapped in amber. The moravecs are silent statues. Time stands still.

The sound of one pair of hands, clapping.

'I'm proud of you,' says the wrong master.

I fix my bow tie and smile a dog's smile, a cold snake coiling in my belly. The god-smell comes and tells me that I should throw myself onto the floor, wag my tail, bare my throat to the divine being standing before me.

But I don't.

'Hello, Nipper,' the wrong master says.

I clamp down the low growl rising in my throat and turn it into words.

'What did you do?'

'We suspended them. Back doors in the hardware. Digital rights management.'

His mahogany face is still smooth: he does not look a day older, wearing a dark suit with a VecTech tie pin. But his eyes are tired.

'Really, I'm impressed. You covered your tracks admirably. We thought you were furries. Until I realized—'

A distant thunder interrupts him.

'I promised him I'd look after you. That's why you are still alive. You don't have to do this. You don't owe him anything. Look at yourselves: who would have thought you could come this far? Are you going to throw that all away because of some atavistic sense of animal loyalty?

'Not that you have a choice, of course. The plan didn't work.'

The cat lets out a steam pipe hiss.

'You misunderstand,' I say. 'The concert was just a diversion.'

The cat moves like a black-and-yellow flame. Its claws flash, and the wrong master's head comes off. I whimper at the aroma of blood polluting the god-smell. The cat licks its lips. There is a crimson stain on its white shirt.

The Zeppelin shakes, pseudomatter armor sparkling. The dark sky around the *Marquis* is full of fire-breathing beetles. We rush past the human statues in the ballroom and into the laboratory.

The cat does the dirty work, granting me a brief escape into virtual abstraction. I don't know how the master did it, years ago, broke VecTech's copy protection watermarks. I can't do the same, no matter how much the Small Animal taught me. So I have to cheat, recover the marked parts from somewhere else.

The wrong master's brain.

The part of me that was born on the Small Animal's island takes over and fits the two patterns together, like pieces of a puzzle. They fit, and for a brief moment, the master's voice is in my mind, for real this time.

The cat is waiting, already in its clawed battlesuit, and I don my own. The *Marquis of Carabas* is dying around us. To send the master on his way, we have to disengage the armor.

The cat meows faintly and hands me something red. An old plastic ball with toothmarks, smelling of the sun and the sea, with a few grains of sand rattling inside.

'Thanks,' I say. The cat says nothing, just opens a door into the Zeppelin's skin. I whisper a command, and the master is underway in a neutrino stream, shooting up towards an island in a blue sea. Where the gods and big dogs live forever.

We dive through the door together, down into the light and flame.

Benjamin Schneider's Little Greys

Nir Yaniv

Israel

I first met Nir almost twenty years ago in Tel Aviv. We hit it off immediately – before long we were already plotting a novel together, a murder mystery set in a thinly-veiled Israeli SF convention. Since then we've written two novels together and most of a third, and are currently making a web-animated series for the sheer fun of it. Nir's restless mind has led him to writing fiction, movie making and music, so it's hard to pin him down! I translated several of his stories, of which this is my favourite, a strange, liminal tale of a child with unusual ailments…

When Benjamin Schneider came to my clinic and complained of mysterious coils on his left wrist I wasn't overly surprised. The term 'hypochondriac' may have become overused years ago, but Benjamin nevertheless lived and acted as its perfect archetype. He had been that way ever since he was a child. I remember the first time he came to me, when I was still a minor family GP at the National Health clinic in town. He was about fourteen, short for his age, thin, curly and bespectacled, and a thorn was stuck, mortifyingly, in his behind. His mother, Mrs. Romina Schneider, did not spare him her wrath – 'Every time, something strange has to happen to you!' she said – and the embarrassed child gritted his teeth and gave me a pleading look. His mother, too, gave me a look – the kind an older woman gives a younger woman she doesn't trust, doesn't *want* to trust, but is forced to, if only by the vagaries of the National Health Service. I don't remember how I got her away from the room – one of the nurses helped me, perhaps – but five minutes later the thorn was removed to the relief of everyone concerned. Benjamin's grateful gaze was something I could never forget – if only because, for years afterwards, I received it from him, on average, about once a week.

The week after the thorn incident, for instance, he grazed the back of his neck on barbed wire – I had no idea how – and came to me to clean up the wound. I asked him if they didn't have iodine at home, and he shrugged and didn't reply. In fact, he never talked about himself, beyond – more or less – the medical reasons for his current visit. Every week he visited me, with one reason or another, as he grew up from a boy to a teen and then a man, still thin, still curly and bespectacled. When I opened my own clinic, twelve years later, Benjamin was my first client.

His medical problems were always a little odd. He was bruised in unlikely places – his right ear, for instance – suffered diseases like an arthritis that had the same symptoms as gum disease, didn't respond to medicine and disappeared after a week – and indeed always healed miraculously and returned to me to verify the fact, and perhaps discover some new ailments in the process. It is possible other doctors would have ridiculed him and his various ills, and certainly my cooperation with it and with him, but I couldn't bring myself to be so cruel to him.

The coils, however, despite our long history together, were something new. I had sent him for an X-ray several days before, at his insistence. He brought the prints back to the clinic, in the brown paper folder of the National Health Service, searched through them for a minute or two and then found what he was looking for. I spread the print over the white fluorescent board designed for that purpose and examined it, not expecting to find anything out of the ordinary, or at least of the ordinary as considered in the case of Benjamin Schneider. But, to my surprise, something *was* there. Two greyish coils, half-transparent, testifying that whatever they were made of was not solid enough to completely block the X-rays. And there was something else that was odd in the picture, but to begin with I couldn't figure out what it was.

'Does it hurt?' I asked. He shook his head. His arthritis had already disappeared. I examined the wrist myself, but externally it was not possible to discern anything out of the ordinary. I told him I had to think about it and to come back to me in a few days. I looked at him, worried he might be upset by that, but he just nodded and left, satisfied, to all appearances, that his fate was in good hands. How little did you know, Benjamin. How little did we know.

I had quite a lot of work to do in the office that day, so I took the print home with me afterwards. I didn't have a fluorescent board at home, so I hung the print before a desk lamp. I looked at it all through dinner and for a change didn't wait in vain for the phone to ring. The coils were odd, but there was also something familiar about them, and these were two separate things, the strangeness and the familiarity. After a while I lost my concentration and watched a little TV. One of the channels was showing a horror B-movie and I watched it disinterestedly as my mind floated here and there on its own, without my being fully conscious of it. It's a way as good as any for dealing with problems, but this time the solution came not from that but, rather, from the tiny part of me that was actually watching the television. One of the monsters there was sawing through the arm of another monster, and I noticed immediately the cheap special effect – the saw and the hand about to be cut were two separate images filmed at different times and joined artificially. It was easy to see that the saw didn't really touch the arm. And it was the same phenomenon that I could see in Benjamin's X-ray – the coils looked like an artificial addition to the picture.

There was something calming about this, of course. Incidents like this are not common but, sometimes, despite all precautionary measures, they happen. A foreign object finds its way between the camera and the subject, the result being spread in all its glory before my reading lamp. If Benjamin still needed it, I would send him for a repeat scan, and if not – all to the better.

And still the coils seemed familiar.

On his next visit I explained all this to him, apart from the strange feeling I had about the coils, and he seemed pretty happy. Another problem occupied him by now. He had something in his eyes. That's how he put it, and I couldn't get a better explanation out of him. I examined his eyes and could see nothing out of the ordinary, apart from a redness that could have been caused by a thousand and one things, most of them not worthy of attention. But when I examined his right eye through an ophthalmoscope I saw it: a tiny grey circle, barely seen against the redness of the cornea.

There was one in his left eye too.

They both seemed familiar, just like the coils. They also seemed, as hard as it was for me to believe when watching something that was real and not a scan, unconnected. If the coils in his arm seemed like foreign bodies that entered by mistake into the field of vision of the X-ray camera, then the circles in his eyes seemed like foreign bodies that entered by mistake into the field of vision of reality.

I think I managed to hide the shock I felt. I gave Benjamin eye drops, closed the clinic early and went home to rest. And watch TV. And think.

And in the morning I arrived at the clinic two hours before opening time and dismantled the ophthalmoscope. I examined all the parts through a magnifying-glass, but found nothing to explain the little grey circles, that were similar to the little grey coils, that were similar to nothing I knew even though my brain insisted otherwise.

I didn't know how to reassemble the device and decided to just buy another. I had money after all, and besides, it was tax-deductible. I spent the rest of the time before my first patient's appearance in thoughts of this nature, that were relaxing in their simplicity and mundanity but which led me nevertheless, in one way or another, to the mystery of Benjamin's grey parts, thoughts that were only halted with the appearance of the patient himself.

'Benjamin,' I said, surprised. He never came to me two days in a row. 'Is everything all right?'

Usually, on his visits, he would merely point at the source of pain or discomfort, speaking as little as possible, and let me complete the diagnosis on my own. Not today. 'I have a crop circle,' he said.

'Excuse me?'

'A crop circle. You know. Like the ones aliens make.'

'Benjamin...' I said, but he had already launched into an explanation that was exceptional both in its length and its contents. Crop circles are giant circles, and sometimes more complex shapes, that are formed in wheat or corn fields by the pressing down of the stalks. All kinds of attributes are ascribed to them, and stories are told of strange things that have happened to the stalks. There are people who believe that they are proof of the existence of aliens. The rest of the world, of course, assumes it's merely a practical joke.

'Fine,' I said. 'I don't really believe in aliens either, but let's get back to you, Benjamin.'

He looked at me. 'I have a crop circle,' he said again. 'On my tummy.'

I stared at him, thinking of whether I needed to send him to see a psychiatrist. Then I laid him down on the examination table, turned on the strongest lamp, and opened his shirt. I asked him to point to the place where the circle was, and he did.

Despite everything, I needed all my will power not to laugh.

'Benjamin,' I said, 'that's your navel. Your belly button.'

'It's a crop circle. Look at the hairs there, see what happened to them.'

'It's only natural that the hairs around…' I said, and then I saw.

They were bent. Or stood, erect, at unnatural angles. Circles within circles, around the navel. But more than that – they were grey.

I passed my hand over his stomach, touching them. I wasn't sure I was touching them all. It seemed to me that some passed through my palm, as if they were air. As if I was air. It was not a pleasant feeling. Under my hand, Benjamin shuddered. I felt a kind of electric current, something passing between us through my spread fingers, touching-not-touching his crop circle. Many things were suddenly clear. Many things. Little clues, grazed necks, strange illnesses, illogical pains. Aliens. 'What do you think?' he said. 'Am I going to be all right?'

I looked at him, straight into his eyes. They were grey. There were strange geometries behind his eyes, and I thought I understood them. I didn't say anything. His eyes grew large. Only after a moment I realized he was afraid. And only a little after that I realized he was afraid of me.

'You too, Dr. Katz,' he said. 'You too!' – and he passed out.

I climbed onto the chair and from there onto the table, and stood there, high, looking at the thin silent man who had spent the majority of his life with imaginary diseases that were, in the end, quite real. Maybe he was in love with his diseases. Maybe he was in love with me. It didn't matter. Not now, with the aliens controlling him, and me. I gritted my teeth, and jumped, head first, into the crop circle, into his navel.

• • •

He still comes to visit me every week. Right after they released him from the hospital he came to see me. How nice of him. Maybe he's still in love with me, even after I jumped into him. They told me the doctors managed to recover his digestive system. My head, though...

He comes to visit me every week, and the little greys are in his eyes, on his hands, forming and growing, growing and spreading all over his body. I have no mirror here, and I can't look at my body, but I think it's the same with me. I think I hope it is so. It's hard to be sure, with a head like mine.

I think I see the world in black and white, or grey. Apart from Benjamin no one would understand, of course. I know exactly what the medical thinking is. I know exactly what the people who surround me would think of anything I would say. I know what I would have thought. I'm well-behaved, but that doesn't help. Only Benjamin, only Benjamin could help me. He and the little greys, the growing greys, the great big greys. Now, when I see the look in his grey eyes, when I imagine the touch of his hands, the coils on his wrists, beyond the reinforced glass window separating us, beyond the jacket enfolding me, I know that he loves me.

I love him too.

But most of all I love the greys.

Translated by Lavie Tidhar

The Cryptid

Emil Hjörvar Petersen

Iceland

I met Emil a few years ago at a convention in Sweden and became a fan of this rare Icelandic fantasy writer. I am hoping we see a novel in English from him soon, and this fun story of a monster hunt should prove a fitting introduction to his work. The story was translated by the author and is original to this anthology.

How can they claim something has ceased to exist when its existence has never been proven? They say that the serpent has vanished, but how can something vanish that has never been Seen?

'Aldis, are you sure you're safe to dive? What did the ranger say exactly?' Nyradur Njalsson sits comfortably by one of the abandoned boatsheds, smacking his lips on dried fish under his leather bowler hat, a frayed rag that gleams in the afternoon sun nonetheless.

This peculiar dwarf can cast his doubts as he pleases for he is the only person who still believes in my project – or at least the only mechanic who wanted to be hired as my assistant.

He rips the fish apart and offers me some of it. Despite a growling stomach after a busy and stressful day, I have no appetite and wave it away.

'Well,' I drawl. 'He asserted that if I dive in a copper-bottomed drysuit I should be able to do my thing in the water for half an hour without risking any sickness. I actually thought it would be two hours like last time. This will be even closer than I thought.'

'But wouldn't it be enough to look around and take pictures from inside the sub?'

I narrow one eye. 'Nah, the water is too turbid. We'll take pictures inside but if I'm to find real traces, if I'm to find any specimens, I have to be able to examine the bottom closely. I have to dive.'

When I give him my unwavering look, the one my colleagues in cryptozoology have described as stubbornness giving birth to defiance, Nyradur shrugs and continues to eat.

•

Early Bird, my itty bitty copper-red submarine, floats calmly by the wharf, and my truck is parked close by. Nyradur and I have checked and crosschecked the controls, and made sure that all latches, hatches, valves, seams and bolts are in place. The clockwork in my new paracamera has been greased and the obscura stone inside it is attuned. This costly piece of equipment emptied my budget but with it I should be able to get quality pictures of the supernatural.

Everything should be in order. Everything must be in order.

This will most likely be my last expedition in Lagar River as an independent researcher. The growing pollution from the aluminium plant in Reydar Fjord, and the colossus dam at Kara Peak that fuels it, has slowly, over three decades, distorted the food chain in the area. What eradicated nearly all life in the water was a so-called accident five years ago, when dug-down barrels of waste from the plant cracked in a powerful earthquake, resulting in the goo leaking into the soil, spreading steadily into the flora's and fauna's cycles, all the way to the river. Over time the water began to change and now it's thick with unwanted particles, poisonous to humans and animals. Questions have been raised if there's something other than aluminium being produced at the plant. For the past year, schools of dead fish have washed up on land and birds in the surrounding Hallormsstada Forest ignore the carcasses. It's probably not long until the forest will start to visually show the consequences of the leak.

With peering eyes Nyradur skims the forest and the calm river. From under the hat and the collar of his jacket his wrinkled skin shows. He has shaved off all his beard and tries to play a role as a small person; as a dwarf from The Hidden World he tries to hide in ours.

'So, if you don't find anything,' he adds, 'what then?'

Like him, I take a glance at our stage. The sun's reflection illuminates the withered lupine horde that will live again when summer draws near, stretching its edges all the way down to the beach.

'Then maybe they're right,' I sigh. 'Maybe it has vanished. Maybe it's dead. Or worse: maybe it has never existed. My research will go down the drain and most of my material will be utterly useless. Then I will have no chance of getting a position at The Cryptozoology and Wonderbeast Research Center. On top of that, my general chances of funding will shrink to nought, and they were not high before.' Through my desperation I utter, 'Doctor Aldis Audunsdottir will need to find herself another job.'

'Another job? That's so cruel!' Nyradur scoffs.

Roguishly he waddles to where I sit on a bench with my back against a worn wooden table, half-dressed into my new drysuit with the safety helmet and the specially designed scuba mask by my side; a thick rubber balaclava with goggles attached and an air hose leading from a diving cylinder I will later attach to the suit. The mask should be completely isolated, no water ought to reach my skin.

'So, isn't it time?' he asks, suddenly impatient. 'Don't the stories say that the serpent should wake from its slumber around this time of day?' He points at my thick folder on the table. From its edges, yellowed, ragged corners of paper stick out.

'Some stories do, not all of them.' Standing up, I heave the suit up over my waist but struggle with dressing myself into the sleeves, for it demands dexterity to get these long limbs into their respective places. As I do, I mumble, 'Couple of those accounts tell of how people saw the serpent during night or very early in the morning.'

'But nothing has ever been proven regarding the serpent – if I understand it correctly?' Nyradur half says, half asks. 'No one has ever really *Seen* it? There isn't any proof that what they saw was it?'

I nod to verify. 'You want to go over this again?' I don't really expect an answer, he should know and remember this. I open the folder, leaf through it and begin to quickly recollect all the important topics and details before we head down.

• • •

Various creatures have found their way into our world through The Shroud, willingly or unwillingly, and haven't been able to return. Cryptozoologists' common goal is to find and research them in order to map and understand better the fauna of The Hidden World.

After the dwarf Nyradur became my assistant I've had the rare option to enter The Hidden World but such an expedition would be extremely dangerous. Besides, when a human goes there it's with the risk of distancing oneself from the life in The

Human World, not wanting to go back, gradually forgetting it, eventually becoming one of the hidden people. I have no desire to be one of them. Maybe I will risk an expedition later but then I would have to have better resources, probably a team of people with me. Moreover, Nyradur is here because he is interested in our technology and he finds it fascinating how beasts from his world have adapted to ours, the same fascination I have.

Us cryptozoologists talk about Seen and Unseen beasts, the former known as wonderbeasts and the latter as cryptids. A beast is Seen when its existence has been proven, and CWRC, The Cryptozoology and Wonderbeast Research Center, has strict standards regarding that. In order for a cryptid to be considered real, not an imagined creature from folklore, two or more reliable witnesses have had to see them at the same time, their reports must match and an undoubtedly authentic photograph or video of the cryptid must be shown. The final and most important proof is a biologic specimen which is analysed at the CWRC headquarters. Only then is a cryptid considered to be a wonderbeast.

In the Lagar Serpent's case there haven't been enough reliable witnesses when it has supposedly shown itself, reports vary and no one has ever developed a good photograph of it (an authentic one, that is).

Convenience and circumstances usually determine when the public chooses to put cryptids on a pedestal and consider the stories to have truth in them, for instance when bragging about a town's, region's or district's differentiae and particularities to get tourists to dip deeper into their pockets. The Lagar Serpent is the most famous creature from Icelandic folklore but no one comes to Lagar River anymore due to pollution. The story of the serpent has both lost its charm and attraction. It has been written off.

People rarely recognize that folktales are often founded on real events; accounts that have been orally preserved and undergone changes on the way. Many find it unpleasing when the tranquillity of their everyday life is disrupted, and in this fast modern present, which revolves around wealth and overexploitation, few are interested in confronting the uncanny. Thus most of what is seen as different is pushed aside, even though the supernatural has become a professed part of our society.

In comparison with the hundreds – or even thousands – of tales and accounts about elves, dwarves, hidden people or draugurs and other undead beings from The Beyond, there are very few written and oral sources about cryptids. Cryptozoologists reckon the main reason is that many of them shy much away from humans and have therefore seldom been noticed throughout history; but also that some of them are liable to attack people, so the ones who saw them didn't live to tell the tale. Mysterious deaths and disappearances in the wild, now and then, are believed to be partly connected to cryptids and wonderbeasts. In those rare cases when they threaten human life, beastslayers are hired. Such brutality lies out of my field, thankfully, because I don't know if I have it in me to hurt beasts, or animals in general.

For all that, and even though wonderbeasts can be extraordinary, many more people are interested in other supernatural beings, they prefer dandy elves over beachwalkers, shellmonsters, blue foxes, horned polar bears, wethorses, lake serpents et cetera. The public and the authorities don't understand how important and relevant our work is. This is not only about knowledge but also about public good, prudence and safety. If authorities knew how to handle the beasts, we wouldn't need beastslayers.

Grants for cryptozoology are scarce and the competition in the field is hard… it's dog eat dog. To get ahead in the research of the Lagar Serpent I've had to sacrifice much. I have scrounged all possible tales about it, from the first mentions in the 1345 annal to contemporary rumblings. And in my research I have travelled far and wide across the country, studied other Unseen and Seen lake serpents. In fact, the only Seen and fully recorded one is the black Kleifar Serpent in Kleifar Lake at the Reykjanes Peninsula. That serpent is only about three meters long, not thirty as was claimed in folklore. It's said that the Lagar Serpent is gigantic and I hope and believe it is. I want to believe.

Over the past three years, I have dived in Lagar River and Lagar Lake seven times, and I'm confident that I've found three tenable traces of the serpent. They are:

1. A broad, rusty part of a chain, two meters long, likely from the equipment that was supposedly used to bind the serpent in the fourteenth century. Naturally, there were no biological traces of the serpent on it, since the piece had been in the water for centuries. The story goes that two Finnish sorcerers were hired to kill the serpent, but soon realized it was an impossible task without binding it to the bottom of the lake. They managed to lure it but at the last moment before the last chain was fastened, the serpent broke free and ate them.

2. A pile of animal bones I noticed at only ten meters of depth. The bones were battered, covered in large teeth marks, and remnants of meat still flickered on them. I'm in no doubt the animals were dragged into the water and heaped to this one spot by a much larger beast. This could mean that it has started to go on land in search for food since there is not much left of it in the water. The pictures I took of the pile back then were poor, taken through a porthole on the submarine. Also, that camera was crap. When I let the sub

float to the surface and dived myself to retrieve some of the bones, they were gone. Nothing, not a trace. The serpent is cunning. Somehow it must have known that the pile had been discovered.

3. A cave orifice at the mouth of the river, in the junction that connects it to the lake. In reports and research papers written by older cryptozoologists there is no mention of this cave. My theory is that it was always hidden under aquatic plants and algae which now has vanished due to the pollution. If it is the serpent's lair and I'm to descend deep into the murk to study him, I would need a ridiculously expensive suit, probably a bathysphere, a whole crew and better preventive measures. The obvious danger would be the serpent itself but diving deep into a cave in this poisonous water is lethal. Still, I must take a peek in hopes of finding traces or specimen. I should be able to dive a few meters down into the cave, attached to a safety line. Last time my old suit and diving equipment were about to give way when I was at the mouth of the cave, and the pressure was really starting to get to me. Now I have slightly better equipment and I've improved my diving stamina. If nothing changes, the cave is now on the top of my list to explore.

These traces come under unsolved speculations, not evidence. Not yet. The people at CWRC want more tenable source material if they are to approve full-blown research, with a crew, quality equipment, pomp and circumstance. They think the Lagar Serpent, if it ever existed, has died or vanished from our world because of the lake's condition. Therefore it would be a waste of money and resources to look for it. But I'm certain, as ever, that the Lagar Serpent is still here. In some stories it's said to be venomous. Why can't it be a possibility then that such a large and old venomous beast is immune to poison? Or that it can simply withstand the pollution whether it's venomous or not?

Diving in Lagar River and Lagar Lake without ridiculously expensive equipment is almost impossible now. On top of that, my purse is empty, all finances dried, both the ones I've gathered with small grants and with my own money. I'm all in. I've everything to lose. It's my last chance.

My and Nyradur's plan is to stay in the sub and thread our way down the whole river, all the way to the lake. I will not risk going into the water myself unless we discover something unmistakably and undoubtedly juicy. Excrement from the serpent would be a dream come true.

My future could be determined by a half-hour dive. Even with the new drysuit handling more than the old one, the acidity of the water will still eat its way through.

'Did you check the ballast tanks?' I holler a bit too loud so my whole sub tolls.

'Aye!' Nyradur replies from inside the tiny engine room. 'I did it before we lowered the boat into the water. And the rear trim tank shouldn't cause any problems. If it does, I'll eat my hat.'

Early Bird begins to sing. The steam pressure in its pipes rises, the engine hums and the walls crunch benignly. I check the pitometer and the depth meter; they seem to be in order. I handle the many levers in front of me, without pulling them, like a phantom preparing to play his organ. I bend over the controls, lick my finger and clean a smudge off the front porthole. The best thing about the new suit is how easily I can move in it. On the other hand, the helmet is boisterous. I put it beside the ladder that leads up to the top hatch.

'This should be enough stoking for now,' I say.

'Understood, Miss Audunsdottir!'

Puffing and panting, Nyradur sits down beside me and strokes the sweat off his forehead, without taking his hat off. Even with his small features, the space in the sub's nose – or beak as I like to call it – becomes close-fitted with two persons at the front. Behind us are two more seats, but the maximum occupancy in my submarine is five, which has never been reached.

'Let us set forth!' I humour and twist a small reel beside the wheel.

'Aye. Cross our fingers?'

'Cross our fingers.'

Water pours into the ballast tanks. The wharf, the boatshed, and the forest gradually disappear, replaced by the under-surface wasteland. When we are close to the bottom I twist the reel back halfway, we gain control of the buoyancy, the turbine begins to spin and the propeller drives us forth.

•

The welling water plays a woeful song about the life that thrived in it before the time of the aluminium plant. What we see now out of the front porthole is nondescript. Specks of dirt and dust meander around, once in a while human trash strokes the portholes, and dead kelp and badly coloured pond scum is scrounged up from the bottom as we travel deeper.

Occasionally, Nyradur uses the cyclic stick beside his seat to control the two light projectors on top of *Early Bird*'s beak.

The cogwheels in the paracamera grind their tiny teeth together. We haven't seen much so far but nonetheless I take pictures of everything I think to be distinct, like unusual stripes in the sand and broken stones. It's better to use this expensive apparatus rather than not, the obscura stone can hold around a hundred pictures.

Our exploration down the river is for the most part uneventful. It's not until we get closer to the lake that I can interest Nyradur with something.

'There, I saw the pile of animal bones,' I say loudly and point at something out the porthole.

'Where?' He steers the light projectors with the stick.

'Over there, in the curve that leads to the crag. The crag is part of a long and steep cliff which extends down to a deep valley, the deepest part of the river, one hundred and twelve meters if my memory serves me right.'

'What's down there?'

'Darkness, mostly. Your predecessor and I didn't see anything signal last time.'

'But doesn't the original tale tell of how the serpent was sunk where the river is deepest?'

'Yes – but there was nothing there. Not last time, anyway. And the time before that. And before that...'

'Do you want to head down there now?'

'No. Better to save the suit.'

'Do we continue?'

'We continue.'

We have yet to explore the eastern part of the river but my impatience draws us to the cave orifice, where the cliff ends in the mouth of the river, near the lake. The current gets a bit harder, thus we anchor and float only about five meters under the surface.

Nyradur scratches his cheeks eagerly like he would scratch a beard. An old habit, I guess. 'It looks dangerous. If you lose your footing and slide deep down the pressure will be the end of you.'

Through the turbid water I gaze into the abyss, and it gazes back. 'I know. I know,' I utter, still gazing, 'but it isn't that steep, you see? You'll see me the whole time. If the serpent goes in and out regularly, traces of him must be at the orifice. Something biologic. Proof.'

Nyradur gives me a sceptical look and I look back at him determined.

'Are you really gonna dive now?' he asks.

'Yes,' I answer without hesitation.

'We haven't even entered the lake. What if you don't find anything down there? Your stuff would need a complete over-haul and you say you don't have any money left.'

His reactions surprise me. 'Why do you have these worries? I paid you in advance, you've gotten the cash in your pocket and the only thing you need to do is to follow my lead.'

'Isn't it obvious?' Nyradur voice clangs a bit too high in *Early Bird*'s beak. 'I'm a mechanic with rich experience in handling the primitive machines in my world – and some in yours. You have advanced much further because most of the people you humans call wights do not want to be dependent on technology, they see it as destructive, they are satisfied with magic because it is in tune with nature. I'm here to learn. Human technology, especially high-tech stuff that doesn't pollute much, is magic to my dwarven eyes. We dwarves possess very little magical energy, unlike elves, for example. If you prove the Lagar Serpent's exis-tence you'll be well-set for continuous research, and I want to follow you there. I want to carry on working for you, if you'd be okay with that...'

'Of course!' I say after staring at him for a couple of seconds. 'I'm sorry.'

He brings out my folder. 'I believe in this, I really do. All your sources, all these stories, all this work – are you really gonna sacrifice it all for a slapdash dive? I only want to speculate other options.'

'This isn't slapdash.' I stand up while I speak but with my

back stooped due to my height and the sub's low ceiling. While I talk I check if there are any holes or unusual scratches on the suit. 'Seven times I've sailed this river and lake back and forth; last time I was losing hope but then I found the cave. I was unprepared but now... I'm convinced if I take a peek I will find proof.'

Nyradur doesn't seem convinced but he doesn't object.

'Would you kindly lower the anchor and empty the tanks?' I ask.

The dwarf silently gets to work, the boat starts to float with ease up to the surface. I go to the back, attach the cylinder to the suit and put on the mask and the helmet.

•

Evening is falling. From the clear sky, the yellow-red sun glitters on the water. A beautiful sight. But under the surface the water is not nearly as sensational.

Where I stand on top of my half-submerged *Early Bird*, the silence around me exaggerates my own sounds: the breath behind the mask and the crunching of the suit when I check the air hose, the swimfins, the tools in the belt, and the safety line.

This is it. Do or die.

Before I jump into the water, I say into the small microphone on my cheek, 'Remember, ease out the line, let the sub sink after me, take pictures and light the way!'

'Aye!'

I sink. Sink. The suit pressures against my skin. The cold rises. The gleams of sunlight are having a hard time penetrating the turbid, polluted water. With each meter downwards the murk accumulates.

At first I swim alone against the dark bottom. I turn on the light on the safety helmet, it doesn't illuminate much.

'Hurry, Nyradur. Time is of the essence. Hurry, hurry.'

What the hell? He doesn't answer. Don't tell me the radio-telephone has worn out. Now? Come on. Piece of crap.

I look up and see the keel of the submarine approaching, the bubbles whirl around the hull, the anchor chain is drawn out, the safety line dances between us. I swim a bit forward.

When I look back, I can now see the front porthole on *Early Bird*'s beak. Inside, Nyradur sits concentrated at the helm with the clunky paracamera in his lap, directing the light projectors at the cave orifice.

My path is enlightened.

Through the mask's glass I check my arm. Shallow cracks have formed in the suit material but it hasn't begun to peel. I'm safe, for now.

The short swim down to the cave is slow, the pressure increases, I tread very carefully. The droning water begins to produce steady deep bass tones, my breathing becomes faster, a stench of sweat wafts up from the inside of the suit. I must stay calm.

The cave tunnel starts in a slight slope. It's not very steep so I should be able to enter without sinking straight into the abyss. When Nyradur has granted me enough light I let myself glide in.

The rock is smoother and more slithery than I thought. With the swimfins I get no foothold but I manage to get steady buoyancy by grabbing hold of the security line. *The rock is smooth* – could this mean that it has taken this form through the ages after the serpent's countless trips in and out? I must take some specimens.

From the belt I produce a tiny hammer, a chisel and a small box fastened to a band. While I chisel out splinters from the rock and put them in the box, I notice that the top layer of the suit is beginning to peel. I can't potter about with this for too long. Must find more decisive proof. I look at the clock attached to the wrist on the suit: eleven minutes have passed since I went under. Nineteen to go.

I manage to go one more meter into the cave. Close in front of me the floor falls precipitously down into the unknown darkness. I can't venture further.

Is this it? Nothing more? It can't be. It just can't.

Reaching my upper body about, I examine the walls, first to my right, then to my left.

I see something.

A chest! Holy shit, there is a chest stuck in a hole in the wall! It's mostly made out of metal, covered in patina and the hinges are visually weak.

Could it really be... is this *the* chest... the one and only?

In a fluster I lose control of the buoyancy but just before I sink deeper into a pressure I might not handle, I manage to stick my long arm into the hole and grab the handle on the side of the chest.

It's stuck. I pull and pull. It's immovable. It's as if it was pushed in with tremendous force. Again I take the chisel from the belt and begin to hew into the weak seams of the metal.

Now eighteen minutes have passed since I went under. The colour of the suit is not fair copper anymore, but gray with black streaks all over.

The front side of the chest finally gives away, bunch of old clothes well about, which I drag out: a neatly stitched skirt, an apron, couple of headscarves, a neckerchief, a wrapping head-dress, an ornamental belt, a decorative collar – fine women's clothing from hundreds of years ago.

Now it comes in handy to be the gangly pole I am. I reach my arm further in with care, making sure that the air hose isn't damaged in the process, and start to scrounge inside the chest. As soon as I feel an object hard to the touch at the bottom, I grab it and pull my arm back out. In my palm there is some kind of a trinket.

It's a golden brooch!

Is the original tale really true then?

There have been arguments about if it was a golden ring or a golden brooch. But here is a brooch. In an entrance of a cave, that must be the serpent's lair.

In the original tale of the Lagar Serpent, a young woman from around this region in the far eastern part of Iceland got a golden trinket (a brooch, it seems) as a gift from her father, a wealthy farmer and landowner. She had heard that if a simple worm was put on gold, a great treasure would grow from it in a year's time. Either if she believed the story or did it for entertainment's sake, she innocently found what she thought to be a simple worm and put it with her brooch in a wooden casket, and the casket into her chest of clothes. A week later, when she opened the chest, probably to look for something to wear, she saw to her horror that the casket had exploded to pieces, the worm had grown manyfold and was hostile. The people at the big farm took the chest out to the river, rowed out to the middle of it, and sunk the chest where the river was the deepest. After that, the two Finnish sorcerers were hired to slay the growing worm.

The story doesn't say if the worm the young woman found was a lake serpent, that is to say, a stray cryptid, perhaps a baby serpent that accidentally went through The Shroud. Why the serpent became so huge as described in the stories is difficult to tell. It would be interesting to research later on, that is, if the specimens and the brooch will be enough for the research center to support me. Only if Nyradur and I would have gotten a picture of the serpent, then I wouldn't even have to question it.

I really hope something biologic will be in the rock splinters. If I get the support, I will find the serpent eventually, take a lot of pictures and prove its existence to the world.

Over-excited about this discovery, I almost forget about the time. I only have five minutes left of the half hour the ranger asserted was the max I could stay in the water. I don't want to risk disease, cancer, my skin burning up or simply a sudden death. I must ascend to the surface. Must give Nyradur the signal to pull me up.

On my way out of the cave, I wonder why the chest is here, in that hole? Might the chest have some kind of sentimental value to the serpent? As far as the stories go, the serpent has always lived in solitude. Maybe it associates the chest to its origin?

These questions are worth asking. I have to find the serpent later, I have to record its behaviour. I must convince the research center. I must succeed. This is not over.

•

The lights above me blink rapidly.

Yes, Nyradur, I know, I'm running out of time, I think to myself as I step out of the cave and give him the signal.

Even though the anchor and the safety line are being pulled in, the light projectors continue to blink. What's wrong with that dwarf?

The blinking stops and I can see inside *Early Bird*. Dripping with sweat Nyradur waves and gesticulates with one hand, using the other to prop the wheel that draws in the security line, and pushing the button for the anchor with one foot. He seems to be shouting, even screaming. The camera is lying in front of him on the control panel.

Where is he pointing to? Where we came from? The deep valley? And to what is he now turning the light projectors?

My work has gained richer meaning and at the same time I'm in mortal danger.

It has been my obsession, it has been in my dreams, not only for these past three years. Since I read my first book about cryptids as a little girl, it has been my dream to discover the Lagar Serpent. Now I've discovered it and it seems that I won't live to tell about it.

I'm amazed, tearful and terrified.

Out from the underwater valley a terrible beast rises. Its long, enormous body wriggles through the turbid water like a gigantic maelstrom. For their size and thickness, the scaled flippers flap with incredible speed, pushing this impossible creature forward. The teeth are numerous and each the size of a full-grown dwarf. The open maw shows the inside of the jaws, the dark-green gums and the slithery tongue that is pointed at us. The Lagar Serpent screams, I can't hear it, but I see the water carry the sonic waves from its maw to me, feeling the boom on the mask.

In confused desperation I start to swim upwards and wave at Nyradur, but it serves no purpose, he's already doing everything in his power to drag me up. It's a slow process, much too slow. The serpent approaches fast, much too fast.

I only hope I will not suffer. Instead of breaking down I spontaneously give Nyradur a signal to take pictures. If he survives this and retrieves what will be left of me, he could make sure that my work lives on, he could make sure that I've made my mark on cryptozoology, and that I'll be remembered.

I gaze into the Lagar Serpent's maw. Fresh remnants of meat are stuck between some of the teeth.

Abruptly it halts and not only looks at me and *Early Bird*, but examines us, directing its long neck from left to right, several nerve-wracking times. It seems that the serpent is more threatened by the submarine than me. Its dark eyes are small compared to the size of all its other body parts. Even for that, I can read from the stare that this cryptid, this wonderbeast, possesses considerable intelligence, opposed to, for instance, shellmonsters who have very limited intellect but tough bodies.

The serpent makes a decision and attacks the submarine with powerful swiftness, locking its teeth in the hull and under the keel, pushing the boat askew up to the surface, towards the beach, like it's throwing an unwanted visitor out of its home.

I see where Nyradur is thrown back. He drops the camera, it smashes into pieces on the ceiling. Fuck. How will my work be recognized?

In the security line I'm pulled up with the submarine and thrown into the sloping rock, resulting in the air hose being ruptured and the small box in the belt breaking – the specimens are lost! The only oxygen left is in the suit and the mask. I draw my breath and hold it but that's far from easy, for I'm being swayed to and fro in the water.

The Lagar Serpent thrusts *Early Bird* coarsely up to the surface, through the sand, routing rocks until it comes to a full stop on the beach.

I'm still under the surface and I'm afraid to move.

While the serpent struggles to release its teeth from the sub I get a couple of moments to think.

Why does it show itself now? How did it feel our presence so far away? What was it that pulled it toward us?

Then it hits me. The brooch! The serpent must have a special connection to it. I recall a passage in an annal from the fifteenth century, stating that lake serpents are hoarders. They gather trinkets, preferably shiny, into their lairs, fondling them and sometimes marking them with saliva or other bodily fluids. That way they can watch it, guard it, from afar. The Lagar Serpent's hoard must be hidden deep in the cave but the chest it grew up in got a special place in the shallow entrance, maybe so the beast could fondle it, probably lick it, more often. And the brooch is a part of the entity that is the serpent's origin. The chest and its contents, mainly the golden brooch, are the reason the serpent is here.

What was I thinking by taking it? Why didn't I make these connections right away? My ambition blinded me and now I'm facing death.

I nearly can't hold my breath in any longer.

Smacking its lips, the serpent turns to me where I'm floating up to the surface. It seems to have vented, almost appearing to be satisfied. Its movements are now unhurried. It moves up to me, halts and stares at the brooch. Not anger, but frustration, is in its eyes. It opens its maw and prepares to snap at me.

When I wave the golden brooch over my head it glitters in the waving beams of the setting sun that cut the shallow water. The serpent breaks off, closes its mouth and follows the brooch with peering eyes.

Perplexed, I stretch my arm as far back as I can and drop the brooch. The serpent loses interest in me, grabs the brooch with surprisingly fine mouth movements, lets its eyelids drop and strokes the trinket with the end of its tail.

Immediately I kick myself upwards, half swimming, half climbing the slope that leads up to the beach. The oxygenless air won't stay in my lungs for much longer.

I look over my shoulder and see the Lagar Serpent hovering calmly in the shallows, seemingly absentminded like it's remembering something. Then it opens its eyes, gives me a quick glance but doesn't seem to want to pursue.

At that moment I rise up from the water. I crawl in the sand and throw myself up to the beach, try to stand up but fall back down, powerless, totally fatigued. Can't see anything for the condensation on the mask. Can't breathe. Suffocating. Try to unloosen the bolts that attach the mask to the suit's corselet, but I'm shaking uncontrollably.

'Aldis!' Nyradur's muffled voice slips into my consciousness. He rolls me over and tries to loosen the bolts. 'Stay still!'

It's taking him too long. I manage to muster up enough strength and determination to stretch my arms behind my back and use my slim fingers to finish the job.

Finally. Finally the damp spring air slides between the suit and the mask, caressing my cheeks. I take quick breaths and with shaking hands I throw the mask and helmet off me. My laughter is an unstrung cacophony. Finally I was face to face with the serpent and I'm alive to tell the tale... but I lost the specimens and the brooch, and the paracamera broke. The serpent will definitely abandon the cave since it's been discovered. Was it all for nothing? I'm alive but is my career as a cryptozoologist over?

Nyradur's wrinkly and now grazed face greets me. Through all this his bowler hat stayed on his head. 'The cryptid has been Seen! Are... are you okay?! We Saw it!'

I ask him to turn around. At the mouth of the river the eyes and the top of the Lagar Serpent's head stick out. It gives us a concentrated and malignant stare, clearly it has been waiting for the eye contact. For a few moments I look it in the eye, until I think I know what the serpent is doing. I think it's telling us we're not welcome back in the water. After a moment, it disappears into the dark.

The serpent didn't seem hungry. Judging by the meat between its teeth it had already eaten, but it could have crawled up on land and ripped our heads off. Perhaps it's just happy to have retrieved the brooch and wants to hide it in a new lair. Or maybe it has another reason for sparing us, one I can't get my head around at this moment.

'We saw it, yes,' I say dully, 'but did we really *See* it? We can't prove it. We don't have anything.'

Nyradur dips his hand into his coat pocket and takes out an incandescent stone. 'The camera broke but the obscura stone was saved.' He's smiling from ear to ear. 'And look.' He points at *Early Bird* where it lies indented in the sand with the top hatch open. 'Look at the biting holes.'

The holes form a semi-circle on the left side of the hull, and there are some on the keel as well. My submarine is destroyed. 'You mean we could maybe gather saliva?'

'Not only that.' Nyradur hobbles to *Early Bird* and points. 'Can't you see it?'

I puff, scramble to my feet, and move closer.

Now I see what he's pointing at: a broken tooth standing out of one of the holes.

A broken tooth: a biologic proof. An obscura stone full of undeveloped pictures: a visual proof. Nyradur and I: two witnesses with the same report.

I burst out laughing and pat my assistant on the shoulder. 'We got it! The cryptid has been Seen. Now we head to Reykjavik and shove CWRC's doubts down their throats. The Lagar Serpent exists, it's a wonderbeast and we can prove it!'

•

When we have presented our findings and have the support we will return and do more thorough research with much better equiment. The serpent might have threatened us with his gaze but it will all be to his advantage as well. By proving the existence of the country's most famous cryptid, the Cryptozoology and Wonderbeast Research Center could lobby the government so they will spend assets on cleaning the Lagar River and Lake and the surrounding area, thus restoring the flora and the fauna, renewing the serpent's habitat. They might even finally investigate the Kara Peak dam and the Reydar Fjord aluminium plant.

When this place has regained its attraction, tourists will likely flock here anew, which profit-seeking people will rejoice about, because when it comes to the self-evident conservation or preservation of nature and the supernatural no arguments seem to suffice to the influentials other than promises of profit.

In spite of them thinking they will be sitting on a gold mine, the serpent will continue to sit on its own gold, hopefully outliving them all.

The Bank of Burkina Faso

Ekaterina Sedia

Russia

I've been a huge fan of Ekaterina Sedia's work for years, and I adore her short stories. I had the chance to publish her in *The Apex Book of World SF* 2, and during one of our e-mail exchanges she showed me 'The Bank of Burkina Faso', a story I found wondrous but which the genre editors at the time could not quite wrap their heads around. I determined then that I would publish the story one day, and I finally have my chance!

O ne knows that one was a good ruler when, even in exile (accursed, dishonored), one still has a loyal servant who remains, despite the tattered cuffs and disgrace, despite the wax splotches covering the surface of the desk like lichen on tombstones, remains by one's side and lights the candles when darkness coagulates, cold and bitter, outside of one's window.

The deposed Prince of Burundi nodded his gratitude at Emilio, the servant with a dark and hard profile, carved like stone against the white curtains and the shadow of sifting snow behind them, like a restless ghost. The prince then carefully perched his glasses, held together by blue electrical tape, on the vertiginous hump of his aristocratic nose, and turned on his computer.

The Wi-Fi in most Moscow apartment buildings was standard but spotty during snowstorms, and the prince hurried to get out as many emails as he could before the weather made it impossible to send anything out. He saved reading of his email for the very end, until after his messages were hurtled into the electronic ether and he could have the leisure to read through the hundred and twelve messages in his inbox.

None of them were replies – he was not surprised; daily, he steeled himself, preparing for just such an outcome. After all, wasn't his own inbox filled with desperate pleas, cries for help he had neither wherewithal nor opportunities to answer? The best he could do was read them all and let his heart break over and over.

However, after so many years of reading, of writing those letters himself – because what else was there to do for those exiled and dishonored but to reach for the unknown strangers' kindness? – he found himself growing weary, and the words flowed together in a soft, gray susurrus of complaint. So it was surprising for him to click on a name that did not look familiar and to be jolted to awareness by the words, so crisp and true.

•

'My dearest,' the unknown Lucita Almadao started, 'it is in great hope that I reach out to you. I am the widow of the General Almadao, an important figure in my country's history. However, after the military takeover and the dismantling of our rightful government, my husband was given to a dishonorable death. To this day I weep every moment I think of the cruelty of his fate.'

The storm intensified and the draft from the windows hissed and howled, and the candles in their tarnished candelabra guttered. The prince hurriedly downloaded the letter onto his Blackberry – cracked screen, half-dead battery – because he just couldn't bear the thought of not finishing it that night. The electricity cut off at that very moment, and the prince sighed.

Emilio took the candles to the dining room, further away from the offending window and the drafts, to the comfortable chair where the prince could wrap his feet in a blanket and read on the handheld screen, its light blue and flickering and dead.

'Imagine my horror,' the honorable Lucita Almadao wrote, in words that betrayed the genuine emotions of one who had suffered deeply and sincerely (the prince had an eye for such things, since like knows like), 'imagine the paralyzing terror of one caught up in a dream, unable to wake up, as he was taken to the cobbled courtyard. I remember the white linen of his shirt in the darkness, fluttering like a moth, its wings opening and closing over one sculpted collarbone; I remember the rough soldiers' hands on his sleeves, patches of darkness cut out of the fabric, and the yellow and red of their torches, long sleek reflections on the barrels of their rifles – at least, I think those were rifles.

'I apologize, my dearest one, my unknown friend, for my mind wanders when I think of such matters. It is, of course, of no concern to you, but I seek your help in freeing his not insignificant fortune from the bank – the Bank of Burkina Faso, to be exact. I seek your help in accessing these funds, since because you're a foreign national with no ties to my husband, the operation may be easier for you. I loathe to think about money at such a time…'

The Blackberry finally gave up the ghost, a pale bluish flicker that dissipated in the yellow candlelight. The prince gave a small wail of disappointment, but soon settled by the window to watch the furious dance of the snowflakes in the cone of the streetlight down below his window. And in his mind, another dance, entirely imaginary, unfolded slowly, like a paper fan in the hands of a young girl: the hands grabbing arms, a shiny sliver of a sharp blade pressed against dark throat… The sad fate of the deceased general kept replaying as he remembered the widow's letter, every word heavy with salt and sorrow.

The next morning the electricity was back, even though Emilio, thoughtful and far-sighted as always, had already transferred perishables onto the slowly thawing window ledge, and started drinking the beer before it grew warm. Once the refrigerator started humming again, Emilio returned the unfinished beverage into the security of the manufactured cold, plugged in the recharger for the Blackberry, and turned on the electric stove to make breakfast.

The prince sat in the warmest corner of the kitchen, the orange upholstering of the corner seat shifting under his bony backside as if ready to detach from its padding, and composed the letter in his mind. He could not let the plea of the unknown but suffering widow Lucita Almadao go unanswered. He had spent a cold and mostly sleepless night under his thin blanket, tossing from one side to the other – not because of the prominent springs in his couch but rather because her words cut to the heart. He was too busy to even dream about the Bank of Burkina Faso.

After breakfast, he dutifully logged into his account. The mailbox full with the usual pleas:

'I am writing in respect of a foreign customer of our Bank who perished along with his next of kin with Korean Air Line, flight number 801 with the whole passengers on 6the of Augustus 1997', wrote one. 'The reason for a foreigner in the business is for the fact that the deceased man was a foreigner and it is not authorized by the law guiding our Bank for a citizen of this country to make such claim. This is the reason while the request of you as a foreigner is necessary to apply for the release and transfer of the fund smoothly into your reliable Bank account,' insisted another. The words as familiar as the prince's own; the only difference between these people and himself was that he suspected the truth about the Bank of Burkina Faso.

He started on the letter to Lucita Almadao, the widow of the slain general. 'My dear unknown friend,' the prince wrote, 'your words have reached me albeit perhaps not to the effect you have intended – for I am too looking for a foreign national to obtain access to 11.3M Euros I have deposited in the Bank of Burkina Faso while I was still the rightful ruler of my beautiful Burundi. I now live in exile, in a cold and frozen city, and I look for assistance from a foreign national such as yourself. I promise complete confidentiality...'

The prince frowned at the screen. The words came out in a familiar pattern, honed by many months of repetition, but they failed to convey the emotion he had felt while reading the widow's epistle. He deleted the paragraph and started again.

'My dear friend,' he wrote, 'I apologize for deviating from the form, but the very nature of the Bank of Burkina Faso demands that I should be straightforward with you. You may not know it, but you do not have to be a foreign national to access the funds.' He stopped and rubbed the bridge of his nose – he could feel the tension building in his sinuses, like it did every time he tried to put into words what he had intuited about the Bank. 'You only need to know what the Bank is, but I cannot trust this information to electronic words, for they wander and get lost and fall into wrong hands, so I beg for your help, my dearest one in the transfer... that is to say, if you were to hint at your whereabouts, perhaps there would be another way.' He hit 'Send' before the familiar fog settled over his mind and erased the intermittent knowledge of the Bank's secret workings.

It was afternoon when the prince decided that there was no point in lounging about, since Lucita Almadao wouldn't answer right away – no one wanted to appear overly eager or gullible.

Instead, he took a shower and told Emilio to iron his good shirt. After tying a tie and wrapping himself into a moth-bitten shearling coat that had seen innumerable better days, he headed to the bus stop.

There were two advantages to living in Moscow that the prince could see: public transportation and access to classical music. Whenever the mood struck, he headed to the center of the city (bus, then subway) – just like there was always a fig in fruit in every jungle, so there was always a theater in Moscow with a concert or an opera about to start. The tickets, like the public transportation, were accessible to the masses, thus killing their appeal for the upper class. The prince had ceased to be the member of the latter some years ago, and although he dis-approved of the local weather, he waited patiently for the bus that appeared just as the sensation in the prince's toes and ears started to disappear. He hurried inside, and bounced and jostled all the way to the subway station fifteen minutes away. It was an inconvenience, living on the outskirts, but the only habitation he and Emilio could afford was a fifth-story walkup on the south-east end of the city.

Once he entered the subway station, it was warm and placid. The stray dogs were coming home from the city's center – they took the subway, riding up and down the escalator with the expression of quiet and standoffish dignity, so that they could spend their days begging by the restaurants and robbing tourists of their hotdogs. Now the dogs poured out of the outbound trains with the rivers of ruddy, white, and black fur, as the human passengers stepped carefully around them. The prince smiled as he waited on the platform, surrounded by beige and yellow marbled columns, and wondered if the sheer numbers of stray Moscow dogs gave them the sort of elevated, exuberant intelligence rarely seen in these beasts elsewhere in the world.

He wondered if they possessed some sort of a collective mind, and the thought itched again in the corners of his eyes and between his eyebrows, and he rubbed the bridge of his nose. The Bank manifested much today.

As soon as he boarded the train, largely empty, the Blackberry in his pocket buzzed, urgent. It took him a moment to tilt the screen away from the overhead lights' glare, and even then he read the name of the message several times, just to make sure that the crack on the screen wasn't deceiving him somehow. The message was from the widow Almadao. The prince's heart pulsed in his fingertips as he tapped the screen and read her stumbling words.

'My dearest one,' she wrote, 'it is such a surprise to read your message – words of a man who knows both suffering and hope, and I envy you your dignity and humility. I cannot tell how I cried and howled, and threw myself against the walls, how I broke my fingernails on the frozen cobblestone of these streets, on these icy embankments.

'Yes, my dear unknown friend, I am in the same city as you are – and it is getting dark at 4 p.m., and the shadows stretch, long and blue, in the hollows between snowdrifts. There's slush on the roads and sidewalks, and my black shoes have permanent salt marks, like a wrack line.

'None of it matters – only that the fate has brought us to the same city, too peopled and desolate for words, just as it is fate that we can perhaps salvage what we can from the Bank of Burkina Faso – together, if only you would help me.'

The prince's eyes misted over, and he brushed the unbidden moisture from his cheekbone with the edge of his hand. He had never met her, and yet as he read her email, he anticipated every word before his eyes had a chance to take it in, and every heartbeat doubled in his chest, as if it became an echo chamber.

'If the fate has brought us together,' he wrote back, 'perhaps it will let us find each other; perhaps we shall meet among the dust and music and musty odor. Meet me at the House of Music in an hour.'

The House of Music, a relatively small building housing a decent orchestra that offered a small but reliably good range of classical music, and was rarely sold out. Today was no exception – the prince paid his admittance, checked-in his embarrassing coat, and wandered down the raspberry colored carpet in his thin-soled and soaked shoes toward the lobby and the concession stand.

He recognized her from afar – she was tall, even taller than him, and the saffron frock loosely gathered at her dark shoulders draped as if it was made when her figure was fuller and younger, its tattered hem splayed on the carpet like feathers.

She recognized him too: she smiled and waved as she lifted the glass of lemonade to her lips painted the color of the inside of a hibiscus flower.

The concert started with the obligatory Pachelbel's Canon and Bach's Fugue and Sonata, but they were barely aware of the music, delirious with happiness at having found each other and muddled by the habitual fog that always accompanied any attempt to think about the Bank of Burkina Faso in a logical manner.

Yet, together and with the help of the strings and the organ, undeterred by the bellicose glances of other music lovers, they managed to tell each other what each of them knew.

•

The problem with the Bank was the inability of anyone who had deposited money there to get it back. Phone calls resulted in requests for foreign nationals, and playing of recorded strange music. And the physical location of the bank remained unknown – Burkina Faso has been scoured from border to border by millions of those who had no hope now of returning their fortunes or rewarding the long-lost nexts of kin. It was concluded then that it must be present elsewhere in the world, and in all likelihood the bank did not have a permanent area of residence – hence the constant demand for foreign nationals, since if it moved around, everyone was a foreign national. That made sense, even through the muddled thoughts.

The prince had developed a hunch that the bank's existence itself was not a permanent or assured thing. 'You see,' he told the widow Lucita Almadao, 'once I dreamt about that Bank, and I saw it in my mind – clear as day. I saw the porticos and the red bricks of its facade, even the tiny cracks in the cement between the bricks. And the next day, I received a letter from someone I knew, who was able to claim his money that night. He never returned my emails where I asked for locations and details, but I'm sure that my dream helped him somehow.'

Lucita Almadao clapped her hands once, and caught herself as the lone sound resonated in the air as the orchestra had fallen momentarily silent, and a few faces turned around to look at them. 'I dreamt of it too!' she said in a frenzied whisper, more of a hiss. 'It was last summer.'

'Mine too. And then several times after that.'

'And did it happen every time?'

'No, only once.'

She tugged her lip thoughtfully. 'So your dreaming might be not the only condition. Necessary, but not sufficient.'

'I'm not sure it is even necessary. I mean...' He had to slap his own hollow cheek slightly to keep his thoughts on track. 'I mean that maybe it doesn't have to be me but anyone – it happened to you.'

'To us. Do you remember the date of your fateful dream last summer?'

'July 15th.'

'Mine too! Maybe what is necessary is that more than one person dreams it.'

Applause broke out around them, and they shuffled with the rest of the crowd into the foyer for the intermission. The prince sweated and palpitated, and felt his forehead and ears grow too warm from the combined excitement of finding her and being able to talk about the Bank to someone, in person. Together, it was easier to break the pall it cast over their thoughts.

They bought lemonade and drank it buy the window – if one pulled apart the wine-colored velvet of the drapes, one could see the snow that started sifting from the low clouds, flaring like handfuls of beads when it hit the cones of streetlights and disappearing in the darkness. One could also see several stray dogs sitting by the entrance, waiting patiently for the patrons to leave, concession-stand leftovers in hand.

'These dogs scare me,' Lucita Almadao said, looking over the prince's shoulder. 'The other day, one of them startled me just as I was buying food from a street vendor, and I dropped it.'

'This is how they hunt,' the prince said, still looking out the window. 'They are like lions, and hotdogs are their prey. We're merely a vehicle. I heard that these dogs are becoming more intelligent. They know how to take the subway.'

'I've seen them there.'

'I think they might have a single mind among them.' Once again, his sinuses itched and filled with pressure. 'Do you think they can dream?'

Lucita Almadao's eyes, reflected in the dark pane of the window, widened. 'Dogs?!'

'Why not? If it is us who's dreaming the Bank, we cannot enter it. I would dream it for you, but I'm not enough.'

'My dearest one,' she quoted softly. 'I need your assistance. We can write the others.'

'And who will want to be the dreamers while everyone else goes to claim their fortunes?'

Outside, the dogs howled with one voice.

• • •

It wasn't an easy task to train the stray dogs to dream. Their collective mind seemed very focused on food and warmth – especially warmth, since the nights had grown bitter. The prince had opened the doors of his walkup to them, despite Emilio's protestations – had no other choice, really. They slept on the floor and by the radiator, under the kitchen chairs, on Emilio's pullout couch. The apartment smelled like warmed fur, and filled with the quiet but constant clacking of claws on the parquet.

The prince was at first terrified and then amused when the dogs started paying for their lodgings: they arrived with wallets, sometimes empty, sometimes with money in them. One day, as he was traveling to see the widow Lucita Almadao, he learned how the dogs got the wallets.

As the train slowed down, pulling closer to the station, the prince saw a stray dog hop onto the seat next to a well-dressed man, the sheen of his sharkskin jacket making a lovely contrast with a crisp white shirt and his striped, burgundy tie, which looked Italian and expensive. The dog whined and smiled, his thick tail of a German shepherd mix thumping against the vinyl of the seat. The man smiled and petted the dog's head gingerly – who wouldn't, looking at those bright eyes and pink tongue. The train pulled into the station and the doors hissed open, just as the dog thrust his muzzle into the man's jacket, grabbing the wallet from his inner pocket, and bounded onto the platform, just as the stream of incoming passengers hid him from view and prevented the robbery victim from chasing after. The man cursed, and the prince buried his face in the newspaper. That night, a German shepherd mix showed up at his door with an Italian wallet, moist but otherwise undamaged, in his mouth.

Lucita Almadao stopped by every now and again, to help talk to the dogs and to pet the stray heads, their tongues lolling gratefully and eyes squinting with pleasure. She told them about the Bank of Burkina Faso and her dead husband, breaking the dogs' and the prince's hearts anew. He talked to them too and showed them the emails, the constant stream of pleas by the lost and the banished, the plaintive song playing in a loop, asking again and again for assistance from foreign nationals in their quest to liberate their stolen millions or to reclaim rightful inheritance. The dogs listened, their heads tilted, their ears pricked up. Most of them left in the morning to take the bus and the subway, but came back at night with wallets and an occasional watch.

It took them almost all the way to New Year, but slowly, slowly, the dogs started dreaming in unison: their legs twitched as if they were running, and their tails wagged in their sleep. When the prince looked out of the window, he occasionally glimpsed a brick or a part of the wall, a segment of a bank vault hovering, disembodied, over the no man's land of the frozen and snowed over yard. Once, he ran for the apparition but it crumbled, and a piece of dream-wall fell on his shoulder, almost dislocating it.

The dogs were getting better at dreaming as the prince and the widow Lucita Almadao got worse: the two of them barely slept, sustained by the flickering candlelight and Emilio's stern stares, by the sleepless hope that left them ashen in the mornings, desolate in the first gray light falling on the stalagmites of candlewax. The dogs left in the morning, and the widow Almadao sometimes left with them, and sometimes, bowled over by fatigue, she curled up and slept on Emilio's couch, dog hair clinging to her black, cobweb-thin mantilla. The prince dozed off in his chair and waited, waited for the dogs to come back home.

They were ready to give up on the night it actually happened – it was a dead hour after the moon had set but the sun had not yet risen, the hour between wolf and dog, when the prince started to fall asleep. A sharp tug on his sleeve woke him, and he startled, wide-eyed. He thought he was dreaming at first when he saw the brick facade and the golden letters over the double oak doors: THE BANK OF BURKINA FASO. The dogs snored in unison, and Lucita Almadao clutched her hands to her chest.

When they ran down the steps, the Bank still stood, not wavering, a solid construction hewn out of stray dogs' dreams. The sun was rising behind it, casting a faint promise of light like a halo around the bank.

'We better hurry,' Lucita Almadao said.

'Of course,' he answered.

Side by side, they walked toward the bank, their feet leaving long blue depressions in the old snow, shivering in the cold, the knuckles on his left and her right hands almost brushing against each other.

An Incomplete Guide to Understanding the Rose Petal Infestation Associated With EverTyphoid Patients in the Tropicool IcyLand Urban Indian Slum

Kuzhali Manickavel

India

Kuzhali writes like nobody else. She has a unique style and a unique perspective, and her stories always blow me away. In truth, I am a little jealous of her! 'An Incomplete Guide to Understanding the Rose Petal Infestation Associated With EverTyphoid Patients in the Tropicool IcyLand Urban Indian Slum' (what a title!) was written especially for me, as it happens – I'd asked Kuzhali for a story for the *Jewish Mexican Literary Review*, a small literary zine Silvia Moreno-Garcia and I started. So when it came to picking one of her stories for this anthology I could not resist but take this one. If this is your first introduction to Kuzhali, then I envy you – and urge you to pick up one of her collections immediately after.

INTRODUCTION

Frequently misdiagnosed as a rash, the Rose Petal Infestation is in fact a collection of partially decayed cabbage rose petals which appear just beneath the epidermis, mainly on the hands, when EverTyphoid hits the three-year mark. The infestation itself is harmless but marks a significant turning point in the progress of EverTyphoid. While research is ongoing, studies have shown that the three-year period marks the 'point of no return', with the onset of the infestation being generally viewed as a sign that EverTyphoid has set comfortably and deeply among the tissues and major organs.

THE THREE WAVES

Prior to the appearance of the actual rash, Typhodic Despondency will affect the patient in three distinct waves. Each wave has a set of symptoms which last exactly ninety-two hours and six minutes. This precise timing often causes the symptoms to begin and end very abruptly, often in mid-wave.

The Primary Wave

During the first wave, the patient will compose poetry which they will describe as haikus, although they clearly are not. Do not tell the patient they are not haikus (see *Case Studies on Violence Resulting from EverTyphoid 'Haiku'-Denying*, p. 792044). These haikus are generally scrawled on the inside of the arm with ballpoint pen, although the patient will insist they have been written in trickles of molten glass or via a natural splitting of the skin. Do not tell the patient that the poems are actually written in ballpoint pen (see *Case Studies on Violence Resulting from EverTyphoid 'Haiku'-Denying*, p. 792049). Below are some examples of typical 'haiku' written during the Primary Wave.

Typhoid does not last
for three fucking years
no it doesn't, it fucking does not

I wish that I could
just die
and get this over with

The Secondary Wave

This wave is characterized by a strong need to relocate. Patients
start to pack suitcases, travel bags and inquire about bus and
train timings. They will make lists and buy travel sachets of
soap, toothpaste and coconut oil. They will also inform friends
and family that they are 'leaving', though they will be unable
to specify when exactly they will be leaving or where they plan
to go.

Patients have also been known to try and leave by jumping
onto the backs of killer whales who are in the process of hurling
themselves into the sky. This has caused the affected killer whales
to develop a sense of panic about hurling themselves into the
sky (see *I Believe I Can't Fly – One Killer Whale's Account of
Being WhaleJacked by an EverTyphoid Patient*, p. 120543).

The Tertiary Wave

This final wave is marked by attempts to commit suicide. It is
generally believed that these suicidal tendencies are triggered by
feelings that the patient will have typhoid forever, which they
will, and that death is the only option available to them, which
is illegal for EverTyphoid patients to believe (see *Nuh-uh You
Can't – Understanding the Legal Limitations and Implications*

Of EverTyphoid, p. 44079). As it is traditionally believed that life-threatening typhoid relapses occur due to excessive consumption of protein or from exposure to rain, patients have often been found standing barefoot in thunderstorms, consuming vast quantities of hot dog wieners or keemaparotta. While death has never been known to occur, thorns may appear on the soles of the patient's feet. Some patients may feel a root-like thickening in their veins, particularly on the back of the knees (see *The Ebeneezer EntWash Syndrome*, p. 975). Below is an account from a patient who had the Ebeneezer EntWash Syndrome spread to his neck and armpits.

Patient 1 'Chettiar Iyah', Rtd Headmaster of The Tropicool Icy-Land Ambedkar Primary School, EverTyphoid 4th year

In my past thirty-five years of service, not once have I taken leave. When I was having this malaria viral fever all type of thing, nothing. I have never taken leave. Everyone will be so they will be shocked. Surprised. They will be surprised. Why this man is like this, with so much dedication for his duty. They will say, why sir for you? Take rest. Stay at home. Health is wealth. But I will never take leave. I will take only hot water, some kanji with lime pickle, no milk I will take at that time. Even as a youth, I will never take coffee. Also all these western vegetables I will not take. Cabbage, beans, carrot, potato I choose to avoid. Because our South Indian foods like podalanga, kothavaranga, vahzathandu, these are all healthful foods, adapted for our culture. So only I was able, even with this malaria typhoid all sorts of thing, even then I was able to attend the classes. Sometimes, when my fellow teachers would take leave, they may feel shame to ask me. They may feel, oh here is this man. Who came to the office even when his wife was lying in hospital. How can I ask for this leave? Sometimes they may feel shame to ask me because I never have taken leave in all my thirty-five years of service. Not one day.

ONSET OF THE ROSE PETAL INFESTATION

The infestation will appear abruptly but spread in a slow and fluid fashion. It generally begins on the outer palm, right above the wrist. The palm appears to be where the infestation is generally heaviest, with the cabbage rose petals often blossoming in the pattern of road maps of Southern Texas from the 1930s. The infestation can be identified via three significant stages.

a) Denial

The patient will adamantly deny that such an infestation is possible. In some cases, they will even deny that they have typhoid though they may be willing to admit they had it around four years ago. When confronted with the actual infestation on their hands, they will insist that it is wheezing or diarrhea.

During this stage, patients will attempt to resume their normal life but will be hampered by various 'loops' which are another side-effect of EverTyphoid (please see *EverTyphoid and the Space–Time Continuum – Why You Can't Stop Brushing Your Teeth*, p. 56).

b) Pseudo-Denial

At this stage, the patient will appear to be in denial but will in fact be aware of the infestation. This awareness will be coupled with a rabid desperation to get rid of the infestation at all costs, as it is often seen as something dangerous and unnatural. They will try to get rid of it by making cuts which they may then douse with mild bleaching fluids in a bid to 'burn the infestation out'. Once this is done, the patient may experience some mild feelings of euphoria and well-being. During this time, they may be tempted to make life-changing decisions such as marriage, buying a new home or having a child. This again will be hampered by the 'loops', so while the patient may chart menstrual cycles, make STD calls or book railway tickets, they will never be able to move beyond these stages and accomplish anything (see *EverTyphoid and the Space–Time Continuum – Why You Can't Stop Brushing Your Teeth*, p. 86).

c) Acceptance

After burning themselves five to seven times, the patient will learn to accept the infestation. This will start with initial feelings of despondency and self-pity. The patient will then start exhibiting an interest in the infestation by studying it on a daily basis and pressing down on it to hear the telltale rustling noise. They will then start showing the infestation to others and comparing it with those who suffer from the same condition (see *A Sense Of Togetherness for the Betterness – Living with The Rose Petal Infestation*, p. 8375).

REMOVAL OF ROSE PETALS

Contrary to popular belief, these petals can indeed be removed manually for aesthetic reasons, although the infestation will set in again. For manual removal, the area must first be cleaned with fermented coconut water. A small incision should then be made beside the infestation. The petals can be removed by gently pressing the surrounding flesh so the petals can burgeon upwards and fall gently on the surrounding skin. However, the incision should not be left open as the infestation is known to attract moths, which may use the area to make a nest. The infestation is harmless though recurring and its only known side-effect is a rustling noise that is heard when pressure is applied to the infested area.

OTHER SYMPTOMS ASSOCIATED WITH EVERTYPHOID

The Assumption That You Can Bend and Break Light

Even if the patient will not admit to having this symptom, there are a number of telltale signs which are a clear indication of this assumption.

a) The tendency to keep both hands in a claw-like position, hovering near their pockets. This is because the patient will believe they can bend, break and quickly transfer said light shards into their pockets before they dissolve.

b) The patient will develop an interest in collecting glass bottles, where they believe the bent and broken light can be stored. In some cases, the patient may add colored glass or water to the bottles in order to add to the aesthetic beauty of the alleged collected light shards.

c) The patient will also cultivate a firm belief that they can curl light from one room to another. This is often reflected in their insistence that you don't turn on a light in an adjacent room because they can 'do it for you'.

The assumption that one can bend light is generally a harmless symptom. In some cases where the belief is more aggressive, it could result in potentially dangerous scenarios i.e., attempting to throw the sun off a cliff to make it go down faster. In these cases, extra caution and vigilance must be exercised. This symptom can also be exploited to constrain restless patients in a painless and harmless way. This is easily achieved by keeping them in a well-lit room filled with empty glass jars.

Red Lice

By far the most troublesome and sometimes dangerous symptom, the red lice appear once the hair fall associated with first-cycle mainstream typhoid is complete. Aggressive and persistent, the actual degree of severity varies from patient to patient. Some experience mild itching while more severe cases have included blisters and craters which tend to form along the side of the head and at the nape of the neck. These are often painful and susceptible to infections.

The lice never leave the host body though they are known to migrate to the armpit and groin regions. The color of the lice varies; some are a bright cherry red, while others have been a dull rust-brown and even a yellowish-orange. They are known to move very quickly, albeit in circles. When startled, they tend to circulate themselves into the ear, which for some reason, proves to be fatal for the lice (regular ear checkups and cleanings to remove red lice carcasses is imperative).

It is not advisable to remove these lice manually, as they have been known to slip under the fingernails. When they are trapped underneath the nail, they tend to engorge themselves until they explode (for further reading, please see *Red Lice Removal*, p. 2 and *The Disease and Art Series – Frozen in Time – Impressions and Explorations of Lice Nail Art and Motif*, p. 83000287). The application of coconut oil, kerosene and DDT only cause the lice to migrate to other parts of the body where they stay until the offending substance has been washed away. The only effective way to deal with this lice infestation is

a) treatment of superficial blisters, rashes or craters

b) numbing the skin to dull or eliminate any feelings of itchiness or pain. This can be done through the application of different lotions or by ingesting tranquilizers on a daily basis.

Broken Hand Syndrome

Often misdiagnosed as the Assumption That You Can Bend and Break Light, this symptom manifests a number of false signs that the hand is broken when in fact it is not. The hand will appear swollen, the skin will be discolored in parts and the nails may become black or dark purple. Though this will not cause the patient any pain, the affected hand will cease to have any feeling and become deadweight. It will have a tendency to drag and in many instances, the patient will forget it is there, leading to accidents, the most common being hands getting caught in doors.

The Old Man with the Third Hand

Kofi Nyameye

Ghana

When I came to put this together Kofi Nyameye only had two short stories published, but I fell in love with the oddness and atmosphere of 'The Old Man With The Third Hand' immediately. Kofi hails from Ghana, and is part of the new wave of African SF writers emerging now. I am very excited to see what he does next, but in the meantime, settle in for an unsettling tale of perception...

The old man with the third hand sat on the beach and watched the waves wash over the sand.

I'd seen him before. Everyone had. Some people assumed he was crazy. Others thought he was just lonely, sitting out there by himself day after day, staring at where the ocean seemed to merge with the sky. Not very many people found the third hand growing out of his back terribly interesting. This was, after all, the town that had produced the infamous Inside-Out Girl.

All the same, there was something about the old man with the third hand, something about the way he sat in the same old rocking chair, rocking back and forth almost in sync with the waves that made the townspeople stay away from him. Nobody ever went down to the stretch of beach on which the old man sat and stared at the sea.

But I did.

I had to, you see. I was playing catch with Deidre, who is a terrific catcher but can't throw a ball to save her life. The ball went sailing over the top of my head, bouncing down the rocks toward the beach, and I followed it without thinking.

The rocks were hard and slippery with lichen, and the descent was difficult. More than once I nearly went sprawling. I should have turned back, I know, but that ball was the only thing my brother gave me before he went off to fight the Frog Men from Outer Space, so I did not turn back and soon found myself on the beach.

The sand here was almost unnaturally smooth. There were no human footprints like there were on every other beach I'd been to. It was easy to pretend I was in the middle of the Sahara, except for the sea.

I didn't find my ball.

I searched and searched for what felt like minutes but was probably only… well, minutes. I saw no sign of my ball. All the while the old man with the third hand gently rocked in his chair and watched me.

I walked up to him, hands behind my back, tears gathering in my eyes.

'Um, sir?' I asked, my head hanging, my eyes fixed on the ground, on the long expanse of sand broken only by the footprints I left behind me and the deep divots the old man's rocking chair left in it. 'I… I lost my ball and can't find it. I was wondering if you'd seen it?'

For a long time the old man did not say anything. The silence spun itself out until I lifted my head and looked him in the face. And for a long time after that I only stared.

His face was hidden in the shadow cast by the wide-brimmed hat sitting on his head, and perhaps it was that interplay of shadows on the lines of his face that made it seem that the old man had a face like weathered rock. It was full of lines and hollows, two of which held his eyes like precious secrets. His nose was flat and broad, his mouth a thin line. He looked like he hadn't smiled in a long time. He looked like he'd forgotten how to.

But he wasn't scary. In spite of his face and the third hand growing out the middle of his back, hanging behind him like it didn't have anything better to do, the old man wasn't scary.

On the contrary, he looked very lonely.

Perhaps that is why I stayed.

'No,' he said, answering my question in a voice that had once, I supposed, been young. He did not say anything else, but he did not look away either. And neither did I. I wondered how long it had been since he had had someone to talk to. I certainly couldn't remember seeing anyone with him before.

'I was playing catch with Deidre, but she threw the ball too hard,' I found myself saying. 'She's not very good at throwing.'

The old man nodded like he understood, but he still didn't say anything.

I said, 'Deidre's my friend. She's... imaginary. That means I made her up.'

And I waited for the reaction. I waited for the look of pity to creep into his eyes. I waited for him to shake his head sadly. I waited for him to ask me where my parents were.

But the old man with the third hand did none of these things. And for the first time in a long time, I felt like I was in the presence of someone who did not think me odd.

So I sat down in the sand and drew my knees to my chest and just sat there, watching the sea dance and the sun dip in the sky. The old man said nothing to me. We just sat in silence, both of us no longer alone, at least for one afternoon.

I forgot all about my ball.

•

The next day I went back down the beach.

The old man was right where I'd left him the day before. He was not rocking today, but he was still looking out at the water. He turned to glance at me as I walked down the beach. He did not speak to me, but he stood and used his third hand to shift his rocking chair ever so slightly to the side to make room for me to sit, and that was enough.

That day I told him about the book I was trying to write, how I'd spent a year-and-a-half on it and still felt like I was getting nowhere; I told him about the despair of getting words down, looking at them and feeling like everything I'd written was stupid and boring and had probably been said before – and better – by people I probably wouldn't like if I met them, and I told him how that was nothing compared to the despair of not getting any words down at all.

I even told him about the people I was attracted to and how I wanted to have sex with all of them (and there were a *lot* of them) even though I knew it wouldn't be fulfilling for very long.

The old man with the third hand listened patiently as I opened up certain parts of me that hadn't seen daylight in so long. He did not interrupt or ask questions. He just listened.

By the time I was done the day was nearly dead. Before I went home I thanked the old man for listening.

The next day the old man started talking to me in return.

•

'Why do you sit here every day?' I asked him. 'Are you waiting for someone?'

He told me no, he was not waiting for anyone. Then he pointed out to the sea and said, 'That is where I came from. That is my home.'

I followed the line of his hand and looked at the ocean, saw how it undulated, rocking itself gently.

'The sea?' I asked the old man.

'Yes,' he said. In his deep and rolling voice he told me the story of his birth, how he grew up among his people in the depths of the ocean, never seeing the sun till he was grown. He told me of his people, of Leviathan, whose throne is the deep, and of Cthulhu, old beyond imagining.

The old man with the third hand told me these things, and when he was done I asked him why he was here, on land, and not in the sea with his people.

He didn't answer me for a long time. I assumed mine was a question he did not want to answer, so I turned away and looked out at the ocean, imagining, somewhere in its depths, the many claws of the Leviathan stretching from continent to continent. I imagined what it would be like to live inside the sea. I wondered if anybody I knew would ever find me there. They probably wouldn't.

I wanted to go live in the sea.

After a while, the old man answered my question.

'I left my home,' he said, 'and my people, to explore the dry lands. I did not tell anybody I was leaving, and I have since lived a long time on the land. I have seen mountains and kingdoms rise and fall and rise again. I have seen man. I have come to know the extent of his kindness and his cruelty, and I have seen how often one becomes the other overnight. I have seen this and more. I have seen all I wanted to see and much more I did not. I have seen everything there is to see under the sun.

'And now I am afraid to go back home, for I do not know if my people will forgive me for leaving.'

'And so you sit here,' I said, somewhat redundantly.

'And so I sit here,' the old man agreed.

We said nothing more that day till evening, when the setting sun drew us a portrait of light in the heavens.

'Many things have I seen many times over,' said the old man, whose third hand was already beginning to look as natural to me as the birthmark on the side of my neck, 'and I do not care to see many of them again. But there are three things I never grow tired of seeing.

'One is the light in the eyes of a man or woman in love. The other is the setting of the sun.'

'And the third?' I asked.

He made a sound in his throat that might have passed for a *hmm*?

'You said there were three things. But you've only mentioned two. What's the third?'

The old man said simply, 'Little children.'

I thought about what he said, and then I told the old man, 'I have never been in love.'

He told me he had never been, either.

• • •

I did not go to see the old man for two days after that. My parents took me to see my grandmother, who lived many hours away. I'd been close to my grandmother when I was young, but the years and the cancer had distanced us. It's not easy to get close to someone who might not be there tomorrow.

For the duration of the trip my parents tried to get me to spend as much time with my grandmother as possible. They told me things like how death was a natural part of life and how sooner or later we all had to go and that was how I realized my grandmother was growing tired of fighting. I locked myself in the bathroom and cried. I tried to call Deidre, but she wouldn't come.

My parents told me they were worried about me.

I told them I wanted to go home.

• • •

'I thought you wouldn't come again,' the old man said as I walked down the beach.

'Of course I'd come,' I said, sitting down beside him in my usual spot. There was a beach towel neatly folded and placed on the sand. I sat on it. It was very comfortable.

I told the old man about my trip, and about my grandmother, and as I talked I cried, and did not feel ashamed.

The hours went by.

I asked the old man questions. He answered. He asked me questions. I answered.

We talked.

• • •

A few days later I returned home to find my parents waiting for me.

Home was a big house that looked out at other big houses along and across the street. There was nothing particularly unique or interesting about it; it was a rich house on a street where everybody was rich, and as such was unremarkable.

My parents stood side-by-side in our front room. They were holding each other as I walked in.

'We need to talk,' my father said.

No one ever says that unless something is wrong.

I noticed the other people in the room then. There was a woman in oversized glasses sitting by herself in the corner of the room, one long leg crossed over the other. She looked vaguely familiar to me, but I couldn't remember where I'd seen her before. Maybe she just had one of those faces. Standing on either side of her were two men in matching jackets and boots. They stood with their hands behind their backs, avoiding my gaze. Something about them made my head hurt when I looked directly at them, so I turned back to my parents.

'Talk about what?' I asked my father. A funny thing happened when I spoke: my mother started to cry. She sounded on the verge of breaking down, like she was only just holding it together. I looked again at the strange-but-familiar woman in our house and wondered what she had done to my mother.

'Dee, look at me, please,' my father said.

Nobody had ever called me by that name before, but he was looking at me when he said it so I figured it must be me he was talking to. I looked back at him.

'Where have you been all day?' he asked me.

'I've been at the beach,' I answered truthfully.

'And…' my father began, then stopped, then tried again. 'And what were you doing there?'

I paused for a while before answering, but I could see no way around the question without lying. I didn't want to lie. 'I was with my friend,' I said, and of course the next question that came my way was:

'What friend?'

I had kept my friendship with the old man secret up till now. This was partly because I suspected my parents would not approve and partly because my friendship with him was something precious to me and I felt like the more people that knew about it the less it would mean.

I saw no way to keep it a secret now. Something about the woman with the huge glasses and the two men flanking her like bodyguards and my parents standing together like they would crumble and turn to dust if they let each other go made me think the best thing I could do was tell the truth.

'I was with the old man with the third hand,' I said. 'The one who sits down on the beach in his rocking chair. I lost my ball on the beach and went to get it and we got to talking and… well, now we're friends.'

I kept my head down as I talked, but now I lifted it because a deathly silence had fallen in the room. Nobody moved – including myself. My parents looked like they'd been carved from rock, they were so still. So, too, were the three strangers. Although… was it my imagination, or had the two men moved ever so slightly in my direction?

The silence became too loud. I broke it.

'What?' I asked my parents. 'Why are you looking at me like that?'

My mother made another sound in the back of her throat, and it took me a second to realize that she was crying again. 'Oh Dee,' she sobbed. 'Oh Dee…'

There it was. That name again.

'What is this?' I asked. 'What's the meaning of this?'

As expected, it was my father who spoke. All the money in our family comes from my mother's side, you see. Because of this, my father has always tried to compensate by taking it on himself to be the proactive one, the one always taking charge. And my mother, for her part, lets him.

'We've lived in this town for close to twenty years,' he said, 'and never in that time has there ever been an old man in a rocking chair on the beach.'

What was he talking about? 'What do you mean?' I asked, incredulous. 'Of course there has. He's always there. *Everyone* knows about him. He has an arm growing out of his back, for Christ's sake.'

'People don't grow arms out of their backs, Dee,' my father said. He let go of my mother and took two steps toward me. I took two steps back.

'Is this a joke?' I said.

'We hoped it was, Dee, but we can't keep pretending any-more. We can't keep letting you pretend anymore.'

'What are you talking about?' I asked. I noticed now that the two strange men had definitely moved closer to me. One of them kept looking beyond me, like he was trying to figure out a way…

…to flank me.

'First it was the Inside-Out Girl,' my father said. 'Then it was the Frog Men from Space…'

Outer Space, I corrected.

'…and now it's an old man with a third arm growing out of his back. None of them is real. This has got to stop, Dee.'

That fucking name. I couldn't take it anymore.

'*Why do you keep calling me that?*' I yelled at him. For once, my father was shocked speechless. I felt a moment of savage pleasure, seeing him lost for words like that.

But then my mother spoke, and ruined it.

'Because that's your name,' she said. 'It's what we've always called you, Deidre.'

•

I thought to myself: *My parents have gone crazy.*

How did I know this? Three reasons:

One: They claimed to have never seen the old man with the third hand before, never seen him on his rocking chair watching the waves find the land, and that could only mean one of two things: they were either both lying to me – but to what purpose? – or they had somehow blanked any memory of the old man from their minds.

Two: Ditto with the Inside-Out Girl and the Frog Men, who even as we spoke might be planning their final offensive on Planet Earth.

And three: my parents had somehow convinced themselves that Deidre, my imaginary friend, was real. And that I was her.

My head spun. I couldn't speak.

My father said, 'Deidre...'

'Don't call me that!' I snapped. I didn't mean to. It just came out. My parents looked stunned, like I'd slapped them when they weren't looking. 'That's not my name.'

'Yes it is,' my mother said quietly.

No, it wasn't. Deidre was a name I chose, a name I picked for my imaginary friend. It wasn't *my* name. My name was... It was...

Okay, maybe I couldn't remember it just then. Maybe I still don't remember it now. It doesn't matter. What mattered was my parents... and the strange woman in our house.

'You did this,' I said, turning to face her.

'Dee, my baby,' my mother said, 'I know you're confused, but...'

'It's time to stop pretending,' the strange woman said, cutting in smoothly. 'We can help you. If only you'll let us.' Her voice was slow and measured and soothing and it made me think of poisoned honey.

I was suddenly afraid of her.

'Mom? Dad?' I said slowly, trying to match the woman for voice tone. 'Who is this?'

My mother broke into fresh sobs. My father took a deep breath.

'Her name is Dr. Hutton,' he said to me like I was seven years old. 'She can help you, Dee. Dr. Hutton is here to take you to a special place where you can be helped.'

I didn't want to ask. But I had to. 'What kind of place?'

'It's an institute, Deidre, for people like you. People who... sometimes see things that aren't there.'

He may have said something else, but I didn't hear him. I didn't have to.

The strange woman in our house, flanked by two men. Two men in matching clothes. I knew where they were from. I knew what type of institute my father was talking about.

My mother screamed when I started running, as though this was what she'd feared would happen all along. My father did not make a sound. The strange woman cried, 'Grab her!'

Thick boots scuffling on the floor as the two men gave chase. It was lucky for me that I didn't lock the front door when I came in.

Right before I slammed the door in the faces of my two pursuers – trying to buy myself a second or two – I risked one last look back. I saw my parents standing together once again, holding each other like I hadn't seen them do in so, so long. Two islands watching in silence as the sharks chased their daughter.

That is how I remember them still.

Then the door was shut and I was off in the darkness, trying desperately not to trip and fall in the driveway. The minutes after that are a blur even now. I remember jumping over a hedge or two or three, sticking to twisting roads loaded with as many obstacles as I could find, trying to avoid a straight run down an empty street, where the men might run me down with their longer legs.

I don't remember how I got to the beach.

Looking back, maybe that was always where I was headed. Maybe the beach pulled at me the same way the moon pulled at the waves. Maybe.

It was not a part of the beach that I was very familiar with, though, and in the darkness I missed my footing and went tumbling in the sand. I was on an incline when it happened, and so I rolled almost all the way down to the sea. The tide was in; an errant wave washed through my hair. I remember that clearly.

And then they were all over me. Rough hands grabbed me, lifted me to my feet, pinned my hands behind my back. 'No!' I screamed. 'Let me go!' I screamed. 'I won't go with you! Let me go!' The men ignored me.

The sea went about its business and the moon watched impassively, like they'd both seen more interesting things. One of the men took out a syringe and uncapped it; the needle glinted, a singular fang filled with poison.

I summoned a final, desperate burst of strength and broke free of my captor. I tried to run again. He stuck his foot out and tripped me. There was a rock, hidden under the wet sand. It met my head as I fell.

After that I just lay there and looked up at the stars while my vision blurred and faded. The two men stood over me. The one with the needle knelt and reached for my hand. As he did so, all their attention was on me.

So it was that I was the only one who saw the shadow rising from the sea, almost impossibly large, blotting out a third of the stars I could see, dripping water from its silvery scales. Rising silently from the water. Eyes like stars themselves. Reaching down with claws like ancient stone pillars, its tail like a mighty serpent twisting through the air.

I felt the needle in my arm and felt ice flowing inside me, coursing through my veins, making my eyelids too heavy to hold open.

The shadow's great hand reached down toward us.

And then, right before my vision went dark, I saw that what I had taken for a tail was not a tail at all, for it was growing out of the shadow's back.

The world went black.

Then I heard the screams.

And then I was gone.

. . .

When I woke up, it was morning and I was alone on the beach, except for the birds on the rocks and the ones swooping over the waves. I sat up slowly, looked around me. I saw no one.

But there, on the sand in front of me: an empty syringe, its needle caked with fine grains of sand. I picked it up and examined it closely. I turned and looked out at the sea. It was so calm today. So peaceful.

I got to my feet and started walking.

The old man with the third hand was sitting right where I'd left him the day before. He was rocking gently in his chair, head turned toward me, watching as I approached. My blanket, as I'd already come to think of the beach towel, was spread out on the sand beside him.

I sat down by the old man. His third arm rested casually over the back of his rocking chair. The breeze ran through his clothes, making them flutter on his frame. I leaned back and felt the sun on my face, my neck, my arms. I pushed my toes into the sand and wriggled them. A beach, I realized, is an in-between place. Neither sea nor land, it belongs to both and it belongs to neither. It belongs to no one, but it belongs to everyone.

'I can't go back home,' I said.

The old man with the third hand looked down at me, and then he smiled, and then he said, 'You can stay here with me.'

After that, we just sat on the beach and looked out toward the sea.

The Green

Lauren Beukes

South Africa

I pretty much knew Lauren was going to be a star when I first met her. We were both starting out, but Lauren had a presence about her, a steely determination with the talent to match. I was there when she won the Arthur C. Clarke Award, and could only watch in awe as her career went from strength to strength. I nabbed one of her stories early on for *The Apex Book of World SF 2*, and of course I had to have her in this one. I love 'The Green', so I hope you do too!

T he Pinocchios are starting to rot. Really, this shouldn't be a surprise to anyone. They're just doing what corpses do best. Even artificially preserved and florally animated ones. Even the ones you know.

They shuffle around the corridors of our homelab in their hermetically sealed hazmat suits, using whatever's left of their fine motor functioning. Mainly they get in the way. We've learned to walk around them when they get stuck. You can get used to anything. But I avoid looking at their faces behind the glass. I don't want to recognize Rousseau.

They're supposed to be confined to one of the specimen storage units. But a month ago, a Pinocchio pulled down a cabinet of freeze-dried specimens. So now Inatec management lets them wander around. They seem happier free-range. If you can say that about a corpse jerked around by alien slime-mold like a zombie puppet.

They've become part of the scenery. Less than ghosts. They're as banal a part of life on this god-forsaken planet as the nutritionally fortified lab-grown oats they serve up in the cafeteria three times a day.

We're supposed to keep out of their way. 'No harvester should touch, obstruct or otherwise interfere with the OPPs,' the notice from Inatec management read, finished off with a smiley face and posted on the bulletin board in the cafeteria. On paper, because we're not allowed personal communications technology in homelab. Too much of a security risk.

Organically Preserved Personnel. It's an experimental technique to use the indigenous flora to maintain soldiers' bodies in wartime to get them back to their loved ones intact. The irony is that we're so busy doing experiments on the corpses of our deceased crew that we don't send them back at all. And if we did, it would have to be in a flask. Because after they rot – average 'life-span' is twenty-nine days – they liquefy. And the slime-mold has to be reintegrated into the colony they've been growing in Lab Three.

It's not really slime-mold, of course. Nothing on this damn planet is anything you'd recognize, which is exactly why Inatec have us working the jungle in armored suits along with four thousand other corporates planet-side, all scrambling to find new alien flora with commercial applications so they can patent the shit out of all of it.

'Slime-mold' is the closest equivalent the labtechs have come up with. Self-organizing cellular amoebites that ooze around on their own until one of them finds a very recently dead thing to grow on. Then it lays down signals, chemical or hormonal or some other system we don't understand yet, and all the other amoebites congeal together to form a colony that sets down deep roots like a wart into whatever's left of the nervous system of the animal… and then take it over.

We've had several military contractors express major interest in seeing the results. Inatec has promised us all big bonuses if we manage to land a military deal – and not just the labtechs either. After all, it's us lowly harvesters who go out there in our GMP suits to *find* the stuff.

Inatec's got mining rights to six territories in four quadrants on this world. Two subtropical, one arid/mountainous, and three tropical, which is where the big bucks are. Officially, we're working RCZ-8 Tropical 14: 27° 32'S / 49° 38'W. We call it The Green.

We were green ourselves when we arrived on-planet. The worst kind of naive, know-nothing city hicks. It was all anyone could talk about as we crammed around the windows – how fucking amazing it all looked as the dropship descended over our quadrant. We weren't used to nature. We didn't know how hungry it was.

The sky was rippled in oranges and golds from the pollen in the air, turning the spike slate pinnacles of the mountains a powder pink. The jungle was a million shades of green. Greens like you couldn't imagine. Greens to make you mad. Or kill you dead.

Homelab squats in the middle of all that green like a fat concrete spider with too many legs radiating outwards. Uglier even than the Caxton Projects apartment blocks back home. Most of us are from what you'd call underprivileged backgrounds. The Caxton stats when I left were 89 per cent adult unemployment, 73 per cent adult illiteracy, 65 per cent chance of dying before the age of forty due to communicable disease or an act of violence. Who wouldn't want a ticket out of there? Even if it was one-way.

Besides, our work is a privilege. We're getting to work at the forefront of xenoflora biotech. At least that's what it says on the 'Welcome To Inatec' pack all employees are handed when they've dotted the i's and crossed the t's on the contract. Or maybe just made an X where you're supposed to sign. You don't need to be literate to pick flowers. Even in a GMP.

Of course, by forefront, they mean front lines. And by harvesting they mean strip-mining. Except everything we strip away grows back, faster than we can keep up. Whole new species we've never seen before spring up overnight. Whole new ways to die.

You got to suffer for progress, baby, Rousseau would have said (if he was still alive). And boy do we suffer out there.

The first thing they do when you land is strip you, shave you, put you through the ultraviolet sterilizer, and then surgically remove your finger and toenails. It's a biologically sensitive operation. You can't be bringing in contaminants from other worlds. And there was that microscopic snail parasite incident that killed off two full crews before the labtechs figured it out. That's why we don't have those ultra-sensitive contact pads on our gloves anymore, even though it makes harvesting harder. Because the snail would burrow right through them and get under the cuticle, working its way through your body to lay its eggs in your lungs. When the larvae hatch, they eat their way out, which doesn't kill you, it just gives you a nasty case of terminal snail-induced emphysema. It took the infected weeks to die, hacking up bloody chunks of their lungs writhing with larvae.

Diamond miners used to stick gems up their arses to get them past security. With flora, you can get enough genetic material to sell to a rival with a fingernail scraping. 'Do we have any proof there was ever a snail infestation?' Ro would ask over breakfast. 'Apart from the company newsletter?' he'd add before practical, feisty, *educated* Lurie could get a word in and contradict him. He was big into his conspiracy theories and our medtech, Shapshak, only encouraged him. They'd huddle deep into the night, getting all serious over gin made from nutri-oats that Hoffmann used to distill in secret in his room. It seemed to make Shapshak more gloomy than ever, but Ro bounced back from it invigorated and extra-jokey.

Ro was the only one who could get away with calling me Coco and only because we were sleeping together. Dumbfuck name, I know. Coco Yengko. Mom wanted me to be a model. Or a ballerina. Or a movie star. All those careers that get you out of the ghettosprawl. Shouldn't have had an ugly kid then, Ma. Shouldn't have been poor. Shouldn't have let the Inatec recruiter into our apartment. And hey, while we're at it, Ro shouldn't have died.

Fucking Green.

Green is the wrong word for it. You'd only make that mistake from the outside. When you're in the thick of it, it's black. The tangle of the canopy blocks out the sunlight. It's the murky gloom after twilight, before real dark sets in. Visibility is five meters, fifteen with headlights, although the light attracts moths, which get into the vents. Pollen spores swirl around you, big as your head. Sulfur candy floss. And everything is moist and sticky and *fecund*. Like the whole jungle is rutting around us.

The humidity smacks you, even through the suit, thick as +8 gravity, so that you're slick as a greased ratpig with sweat the moment you step out. It pools in your jockstrap, chafes when you walk, until it forms blisters big as testicles. (A new experience for the girls on the crew.) Although walking's not what we do. More like wading against a sucking tide of heat and flora.

The rotting mulch suffocates our big clanking mechanical footsteps. Some of the harvesters play music on their private channels. Ro used to play opera, loud, letting it spill into The

Green, until it started attracting insects the size of my head. I put a stop to it after that. I prefer to listen to the servo motors grinding in protest. I have this fantasy that I'll be able to hear it when my suit gets compromised. The *shhht* of air that lets through a flood of spores like fibrous threads that burrow into metal and flesh. The faint suck of algae congealing on the plastic surfaces, seeping into the seams of the electronics, corroding the boards so the nanoconnections can't fire. The hum of plankton slipping between the joints of my GMP between the spine and pelvic plates, to bite and sting.

The base model GMPs aren't built for these conditions. The heat is a problem. The servo motors get clogged. The armor corrodes. The nanotronics can't sustain. Every joint is a weak point. The damn flora develops immunity to every vegicide we try. Assuming they're actually *using* vegicides, Ro would point out. Why risk the harvest when harvesters are replaceable?

Management has determined that the optimum number for a harvesting team is five. I'm the team leader. Look, Ma, leadership material. Our medtech is Shapshak, who sometimes slips me amphetamines which he gets under the counter from the labtechs along with other pharmaceuticals he doesn't share. (It's not like management don't know. They're happy if we're productive and sometimes you need a little extra something to get through out there.) Lurie is our am-bot; a high school education and eight weeks of training in amateur botany specimen collection puts her a full pay scale above the rest of us plebs, plus she gets the most sophisticated suit – a TCD with neuro-feedback tentacle fingers built into the hands for snagging delicate samples that aren't susceptible to snail-invasion. Rousseau and Waverley were our clearers – manual labor, their GMPs suitably equipped with bayonet progsaws that'll cut through rock, thermo-machetes for underbrush, and extra armor plating for bludgeoning your way through the jungle with brute force when everything else failed.

In retrospect, we could have done with less brute force. Could have done with me spotting the damn stingstrings before we blundered into the middle of a migration. Could have done with being less wired on the under-the-counter stuff. One minute Waverley and Ro are plowing through dense foliage ahead, the next, there are a thousand mucusy tendrils unfurling from the canopy above us.

This wouldn't have been a problem usually. Sure, the venom might corrode your paintwork, leave some ugly pockmarks that'll get the maintenance guys all worked up, but they're not hectic enough to compromise a GMP.

Unless, say, someone panics and trips and topples forward, accidentally ripping a hole in Rousseau's suit with the razor edge of a machete, half-severing his arm. Waverley swore blind it wasn't his fault. He tripped. But GMPs have balance/pace adjustors built-in. You have to be pretty damn incompetent to fall over in one. If Ro wasn't a roaming brain-dead corpse-puppet right now, he might be suspicious, might think it was a conspiracy to recruit more guinea pigs for the OPP program. We know better. We know Waverley's just a fucking moron.

There was a lot of screaming. Mainly from Ro, until Shapshak shot him up with morphine, but also Lurie threatening to kill Waverley for being so damn stupid. It took us ninety minutes to get back to homelab, me and Shapshak dragging Ro on the portable stretcher from his field kit, which is only really useful for transporting people – not armored suits – but it was too dangerous to take him out. Waverley broke through the undergrowth ahead of us – the only place where we would trust him, leaving traces of Ro's blood painted across broken branches.

When we got to homelab, Lurie still had to file the specimens and we all had to go through decontam, no matter how much I swore at security over the intercom: *Just let us back in right fucking now*.

We had to sit in the cafeteria, the only communal space, listening to Rousseau die, pretending not to. It should have been easy. The loud drone of the air conditioner and the filters and the sterilizer systems all fighting The Green is the first thing you acclimatize to here. But Ro's voice somehow broke through, a shrill shriek between clenched teeth. We hadn't known anyone who'd ever died from the stingstrings. The labtechs must have been thrilled.

Shapshak spooned oats into his face, drifting away from it all on some drug he wasn't sharing. Lurie couldn't touch her food. She put on her old-school security-approved headphones, bopped her head fiercely to the music. Made like she wasn't crying. I restrained myself from hitting Waverley, who kept whining, 'It wasn't my fault, okay?' I took deep breaths against the urge to bash his big bald head on the steel table until his brains oozed out. If Ro was here and not lying, twisting around on a gurney while the meds prepared the killing dose of morphephedrine, he would have cracked the tension with a joke. About crappy last meals maybe.

The other crews were making bets on what would kill him. Marking up the odds on the back of a cigarette packet. Black humor and wise-cracking is just how you deal. We'd have been doing the same if it wasn't one of ours. Yellow Choke 3:1. Threadworms 12:7. The Tars 15:4. New & Horrible: 1:2.

Ro's voice changed in pitch, from scream-your-throat-raw to a low groaning – the kind that comes from your intestines plasticinating. The spores must have got in to the rip in his gut through the tear in his armor.

OhgodohgodohgodeuggghgodOHpleasefuckgodOH

Across from us, Hoffmann from F-Crew leapt to his feet, whooping in delight and making gimme gestures. 'Tars! I fucking knew it! Oh yeah! Hand over the cashmoney, baby!'

Ro's screaming tapered off. Which meant either he was dead or just sub-auditory under the concert of laboring machinery. Waverley tried to say something encouraging, 'At least we know it's the fast-kind of fatal,' and I punched him in the face, knocking the porridge out of his mouth in a gray splatter tinged with blood – along with two teeth.

I got a warning, but no demerit, 'Under the circumstances,' human resources said. They declined my request to have Waverley reassigned to another unit.

'It's for the best,' they said. Which was the same line my mom spun me when she took me to the sterilization clinic in Caxton, mainly for the incentive kickback the government provided, but also to make sure I didn't end up like her, pregnant and homeless at fourteen, working double shifts at the seam factory – which is what she did after I was born, to keep the pair of us alive. That only makes me feel more guilty – all the sacrifices she made so I could get out of Caxton. And here I am, letting my sometime-lover die on my watch. *Sorry, Ma*, I think. *But you don't know what it's like out here.*

• • •

Within forty-eight hours, Ro's replacement arrived. Joseph Mukuku. Another ghettosprawl kid sprayed, shaved, irradiated, de-nailed, and ready to go. We had three whole days to mourn while he ran through the simconditioning and then we were back out there in the thick of it, harvesting. I found a request for stingstrings in my order log. The results of Ro's venom burns were, according to the labtechs, 'fascinating'. The note attached to the order read: 'Lash-wounds were cauterized. Unclear whether this is common to stingstrings or whether it was reacting with other flora or spores. Living specimens (ideal) required for further study. Deceased specimens okay.'

We couldn't get them. That's what I reported anyway. Threatened to peel the skin of Mukuku if he said different. The kid learned quick, didn't cause any shit, and we made Waverley walk five meters up front where he'd only take out flora if he tripped again. Shapshak offered me chemical assistance from his stash of pharmaceuticals, but by then I was already contemplating it and I knew drugs would only get in the way. I didn't want to get better. I wanted out.

It was the encounter with Rousseau that cemented it.

I'd managed to avoid him for twelve whole days after he died. Every time I spotted a Pinocchio shuffling down the corridor or standing spookily motionless facing a wall, I did a 180 in the other direction. Didn't make a big deal about it, just managed to spend more time in the gym or doing routine maintenance on my GMP. Anything to keep busy. It's the thinking about it that kills me. I try to leave no space for thinking.

I was doing leg-presses when he found me. It was the automatic door that tipped me off. It kept opening and closing, opening and closing, like someone didn't have enough brains to get out of the way of the sensors. I knew it was him even before I saw the limp, sagging sleeve where his left arm should have been.

'What do you want?' I said, standing up and moving over to rest my hand casually on the 10 kg barbells. Ready to club him to death. Re-death. Whatever. Not expecting an answer.

Through the faceplate, I could see a caul of teeming, squirming green over his face. You could still make out his features, still tell it was Ro under there. I thought about his cells starting to break down under his new slime-mold skin, his organs collapsing, nerves firing sluggishly through sagging connections in dead tissue.

He opened his mouth, his tongue flopping uselessly inside. He worked his jaw mechanically. Individual amoebites, attracted by the motion, started sliding into the cavity, triggering others, oozing past his lips – coating his teeth, his tongue, with the seething furry growth. Inside the suit, Ro tipped his head back, his mouth open in something like a scream as more and more amoebites flooded in to colonize his mouth, soft furry spores spilling down his chin. 'Misfiring neurons,' human resources had assured us when they first let the Pinocchios out.

'Nothing to worry about,' they said. Neither, it turns out, is the GMP progsaw I put to my forehead, positioning it right against my temple for maximum damage before I flick the on switch.

•

I have a dream about my mom. I am scampering over the factory floor, back when she still had the job, dodging the electric looms to collect scraps of fabric that she will sew into dishcloths and dolls and maybe a dress, to sell to the neighbors, illegally. We are not allowed to remove company property. They incinerate leftovers every evening, specifically to prevent this. *Be careful*, she whispers, her breath hot against my cheek. But I'm not careful enough. As I duck under the grinding, whirling loom, the teeth catch my ear and shear down my face. My skin tears all the way down to my belly button and unfurls, flopping about, obscenely, like wings, before the flaps stiffen and wrap around me like a cocoon. In the dream, it feels like I am falling into myself. It feels safe.

•

I wake up in a hospital bed, with my right arm cuffed to the rail. There is a woman sitting on the edge of the bed wearing a pinstripe skirt and matching blazer. She is blandly pretty with blonde-streaked hair, wide blue eyes, and big, friendly teeth in a big, friendly mouth. A mom in a vitamin-enriched living commercial. Not someone I've seen in homelab before. Too neatly groomed. I sit up and automatically reach up to touch my head, to the place where the progsaw had started ripping into my temple, only to find layers of bandage mummifying my skull.

'We do pay attention, Coco,' the woman says, and then adds, more softly, 'I'm very sorry about what happened to Malan.'

'Who?' I say. My cheek is burning. I try to rub the pain away and find a row of fibrous stitches running from my temple down to my jaw.

'Malan Rousseau? Your co-worker? It's quaint how you call each other by surnames. This isn't the army you know. You're not at war.'

'Tell that to The Green,' I mutter. I am angry to be alive.

'Yes, well. We installed new safety measures into the GMPs after the accident. Chemical agents that would clog up the blades of your weaponry with fibrous threads if it came into contact with human pheromones. It's based on threadworms. One of the technologies you've helped make possible, Coco. Saved your life.'

'Didn't want to be saved.' My throat feels raw like it's been sandblasted from the inside.

'Pity about your face,' she says, not feeling any pity at all.

'Never going to be a model now.' I try to laugh. It comes out as a brittle bark.

'Unless it's for specialist scar porn, no, probably not. Do you want some water? It's the painkillers making you so thirsty. Even with our new safety measures, you still managed to do quite a bit of ruin to yourself. No brain damage though.'

'Damn,' I deadpan, but the water is cold and sweet down my throat.

'My name is Catherine, I'm from head office. They sent me here especially to see you and do you know why? It's because you've made us re-evaluate some things, Coco, how we work around here.' Every time she says my name, it feels like someone punching me in the chest. A reminder of Ro.

'Don't call me that. It's Yengko. Please.'

'As you prefer'—her mouth twists impatiently—'Ms. Yengko. You'll be pleased to know, I think, that after your *incident*, Inatec has elected to relocate the OPPs – what do you call them?'

'Zombie puppets.' But I'm thinking, *Living prison cells.*

She looks down to her hands folded in her lap, at her perfect manicure, and smiles a little tolerant smile. But what I'm thinking is, *That bitch still has her fingernails, which also means she has no intention of sticking around.* 'Pinocchios, right? Isn't that what you call them? That's cute. But we've come to realize, well, you made us realize that having them in homelab puts undue stress on our employees. I guess we were so busy focusing on this huge medical breakthrough—'

'Profit, you mean.'

She ignores me. 'That we didn't think about how it was affecting you guys on a personal level. So, I'm sorry. *Inatec* is sorry. We've moved the OPPs to another facility. We've already paid stress compensation into everyone's accounts and we're implementing mandatory counseling sessions.'

'He was trying to talk.'

'No. He's dead, Coc— Ms. Yengko,' she corrects herself. 'It must have been very upsetting, but he can't talk. The OPP symbiote sometimes hooks into the wrong nerves. We're still learning, still figuring each other out.'

'How buddy-buddy of you. Didn't realize this was a partnership.'

'We're a bio-sensitive operation. It's about finding a balance with nature, no matter how foreign it is.'

'So what happens now?'

'We'd like you to stay on, if you're willing. Under the circumstances, Inatec is willing to retrench you with two weeks' payout for every year you've worked, plus stress bonus, plus full pension. Which is, I'm sure you'll appreciate, very generous considering your attempt to damage Inatec property and injure personnel, which would normally be grounds for instant dismissal. Your non-disclosure still applies either way, of course.'

'Wait. You're blaming me for Ro's death?'

'By injuring personnel, we mean your attempted suicide. You're a valuable asset to the company. Which is why I'd encourage you to hear my alternate proposition.'

'Does it involve letting me fucking die like I wanted?'

'As I said, you're a valuable asset. How long have you been here? Two years?'

'Twenty months.'

'That's a lot of experience. We've invested in you, Ms. Yengko. We want to see you achieve your potential. I want you to walk away from this… challenge in your life, stronger, more capable. You've got a second chance. Do you know how rare that is? It's a unique personal growth opportunity.'

'Double pay.'

'One and half times.'

'Plus my pension payout. You wire it to my mom in the meantime.'

'You don't want to hear about the alternative?'

'More of the same, isn't it?'

'It's better. We're running a pilot program. New suits. We

want you to head it up. We've learned from our mistakes. We're ready to move on. It's a new day around here. What do you say?'

She thinks I don't know. She thinks I'm an idiot.

Homelab has been renovated in the time I've been out. A week and a half according to Shapshak, who is strangely reproachful. He follows me around, as if trying to make sure I don't try to off myself again. He can't look at my face – at the puckered scar that runs from my ear to the corner of my mouth, twisting my upper lip into a permanent sneer. He's more stoned than ever – and so are most of the other crews. Whatever else Catherine's proposed 'new day' involves, obviously restricting access to recreational pharmaceuticals isn't part of it. Or maybe it's the mandatory counseling sessions, which involve a lot of antidepressants that Mukuku says leave him feeling blank and hollow. I wouldn't know. I felt that way already.

The Pinocchios are, true to Catherine's word, gone. Along with some of the staff. Lurie has been shipped out, together with Hoffmann, Ujlaki, and Murad, all the A-level am-bots, half the other team leaders, and 60 per cent of the labtechs. Leaving a shoddy bunch of misfits, unsuitable for anything except manual labor. Or guinea pigging.

Labs one to three have been cleared to accommodate the new suits, ornate husks floating in nutrient soup in big glass tanks. Like soft-shelled crabs without the crab. The plating is striated with a thick fibrous grain that resembles muscle. The info brochure posted on the bulletin board promises 'biological solutions for biological challenges.' There is grumbling about what that means. But underneath all that is the buzz of excitement.

The operations brochure talks about how the suit will harden on binding, how the shell will protect us from anything a hostile environment can throw at us and process the air through the filtration system to be perfectly breathable without the risk and inconvenience of carrying compressed gas tanks around. We'll be lighter, more flexible, more efficient – and it's totally self-sufficient, provided we take up the new nutritionally fortified diet. 'No more fucking oats!' Mukuku rejoices. He's not Ro, but he's not an asshole and that's about all we can ask around here.

Lab Four is still cranking. The reduced complement of lab-techs are busier than ever, scurrying about like bugs. They wear hazmat suits these days. They've always been offish, always above us, but now they don't talk to us at all.

Inatec management send in a state-of-the-art camera swarm to record the new suit trials – for a morale video, Catherine explains. Exactly the kind of camera swarm they supposedly can't afford to send out into The Green to scout ahead of us to avoid some of the dangers. 'You won't have to worry about that anymore,' she says. I believe her.

Harvest operations are called off while they do the final preparations, leaving us with too much leisure time, too much time to think. Or maybe it's just me. But it allows me to make my decision. *Not* to blow it wide open. (As if they wouldn't just hold us down and do it to us anyway.) Because I'm thinking that a cell doesn't have to be a bad thing. It doesn't have to be a prison. It could be more like a monk's cell, a haven from the world, somewhere you can lock yourself away from everything and never have to think again.

•

On Tuesday, we're summoned to Lab Three. 'You ready?' Catherine says.

'Is my pension paid out?' I snipe. There is nervous laughter.

'Why can't we use our old suits?' Waverley whines. 'Why we gotta change a good thing?'

'Shut up, Waverley,' Shapshak snaps, but only half-heartedly. And then because everyone is jittery – even us uneducated slum hicks can have suspicions – I volunteer.

I step forward and shrug out of my grays, letting them drop to the floor. Two of the labtechs haul a suit out of the tank and sort-of hunker forward with it, folding it around me like origami. It is clammy and brittle at the same time. As they fold one piece over another, it binds together and darkens to an opaque green. The color of slime-mold.

The labtechs assist others into their suits, carefully wrapping everyone up, like a present, leaving only the hoods and a dangling connector like a scorpion tail. The tip has a pad of microneedles that will fasten on to my nervous system. Nothing unusual here. The GMPs use the same technology to monitor vital signs. Nothing unusual at all.

'Don't worry, it won't hurt. It injects anesthetic at the same time,' Catherine says. 'Like a mosquito.'

'Not the ones on this planet, lady,' Waverley snickers, looking around for approval, as they start folding him into his suit.

Back in Caxton, I tried converting to the Neo-Adventists for a time. They promised me the pure white warmth of God's love that would transform me utterly. But I still felt the same after my baptism – still dirty, still broken, still poor.

'Can we hurry this along?' I ask, impatient.

'Of course,' Catherine says. And maybe that's a glimmer of respect in her blue eyes, or maybe it's just the reflection of the neon lighting, but I feel like we understand each other in these last moments.

The labtechs slip the hood over my face. She presses the bio-connector up against the hollow at the base of my skull, and clicks the switch that makes the needles leap forward. Suddenly the armor clamps down on me like a muscle. I fight down a jolt of claustrophobia so strong it raises the taste of bile in my mouth. I have to catch myself from falling to my knees and retching.

'You okay, Yengko?' Shapshak says, his voice suddenly sharp through the glaze of drugs he's on. *He must really care*, I think. But I am beyond caring. Beyond anything.

I wondered what it would feel like. The soft furriness of the amoebites flooding through the bioconnector, the prickle as they flower through my skin. What's better than a dead zombie? A live one. And maybe God's touch is cool and green not pure white at all.

'Yes,' I say and close my eyes against the light, against the sight of the others being parceled up in the suits, at Waverley starting to scream, tugging at the hood as he realizes what's going on, what's in there with him. 'I'm fine.' And maybe for the first time, I actually am.

The Last Voyage of Skidbladnir

Karin Tidbeck

Sweden

Karin writes wonderfully creepy stories, of which I reprinted 'Brita's Holiday Cottage' in *The Apex Book of World SF 3*. We've met a few times over the years, and were guests together at a Swedish convention a few years back. I'm a big fan of Karin's writing, so I was really happy when I found 'The Last Voyage of Skidbladnir', which is definitely science fiction, though still properly weird!

Something had broken in a passenger room. Saga made her way through the narrow corridors and down the stairs as fast as she could, but Aavit the steward still looked annoyed when she arrived.

'You're here,' it said, and clattered its beak. 'Finally.'

'I came as fast as I could,' Saga said.

'Too slow,' Aavit replied and turned on its spurred heel.

Saga followed the steward through the lounge, where a handful of passengers were killing time with board games, books and pool. They were mostly humans today. Skidbladnir had no windows, but the walls on the passenger levels were painted with elaborate vistas. There was a pine forest where copper spheres hung like fruit from the trees; there was a cliff by a raging ocean, and a desert where the sun beat down on the sand. Saga enjoyed the view whenever she was called downstairs to take care of something. The upper reaches had no such decorations.

The problem Saga had been called down to fix was in one of the smaller rooms. A maintenance panel next to the bed had opened, and a tangle of wires spilled out. The electricity in the cabin was out.

'Who did this?' Saga said.

'Probably the passenger,' Aavit replied. 'Just fix it.'

When the steward had gone, Saga took a look around. Whoever stayed in the room was otherwise meticulous; almost all personal belongings were out of sight. Saga peeked into one of the lockers and saw a stack of neatly folded clothing with a hat on top. A small wooden box contained what looked like cheap souvenirs – keyrings, a snow globe, a marble on a chain. The open maintenance hatch was very out of character.

Saga shined a flashlight into the mess behind the hatch. Beyond the wires lay something like a thick pipe. It had pushed a wire out of its socket. Saga checked that no wires were actually broken, then stuck a finger inside and touched the pipe. It was warm, and dimpled under her finger. Skidbladnir's slow pulse ran through it. Saga sat back on her heels. Parts of Skidbladnir shouldn't be here, not this far down. She re-attached the wiring, stuffed it back inside, and sealed the hatch with tape. She couldn't think of much else to do. A lot of the work here consisted of propping things up or taping them shut.

The departure alarm sounded; it was time to buckle in. Saga went back upstairs to her cabin in maintenance. The air up here was damp and warm. Despite the heat, sometimes thick clouds came out when Saga exhaled. It was one of the peculiarities of Skidbladnir, something to do with the outside, what they were passing through, when the ship swam between worlds.

The building's lower floors were reserved for passengers and cargo; Skidbladnir's body took up the rest. Saga's quarters were right above the passenger levels, where she could quickly move to fix whatever had broken in someone's room. And a lot of things broke. Skidbladnir was an old ship. The electricity didn't quite work everywhere, and the plumbing malfunctioned all the time. The cistern in the basement refilled itself at irregular intervals and occasionally flooded the cargo deck. Sometimes the ship refused to eat the refuse, and let it rot in its chute, so that Saga had to clean it out and dump it at the next landfall. Whenever there wasn't something to fix, Saga spent her time in her quarters.

The cramped room served as both bedroom and living room: a cot, a small table, a chair. The table was mostly taken up by a small fat television with a slot for videotapes at the bottom. The closed bookshelf above the table held twelve videotapes: two seasons of *Andromeda Station*. Whoever had worked here before had left them behind.

Saga lay down in her cot and strapped herself in. The ship shuddered violently. Then, with a groan, it went through the barrier and floated free in the void, and Saga could get out of the cot again. When she first boarded the ship, Aavit had explained it to her, although she didn't fully grasp it: the ship pushed through to an ocean under the other worlds, and swam through it, until they came to their destination. 'Like a seal swims from hole to hole in the ice,' said Aavit, like something coming up for air every now and then. Saga had never seen a seal.

Andromeda Station drowned out the hum Skidbladnir made as it propelled itself through the space between worlds, and for just a moment, things felt normal. It was a stupid show, really: a space station somewhere that was the center of diplomatic relations, regularly invaded by non-human races or subject to internal strife, et cetera, et cetera. But it reminded Saga of home, of watching television with her friends, of the time before she sold herself into twenty tours of service. With no telephones and no computers, it was all she had for entertainment.

Season 2, episode 5: The Devil You Know.

The station encounters a species eerily reminiscent of demons in human mythology. At first everyone is terrified until it dawns on the captain that the 'demons' are great lovers of poetry, and communicate in similes and metaphors. As soon as that is established, the poets on the station become the interpreters, and trade communications are established.

.

In the middle of the sleep shift, Skidbladnir's hum sounded almost like a murmured song. As always, Saga dreamed of rushing through a space that wasn't a space, of playing in eddies and currents, of colors indescribable. There was a wild, wordless joy. She woke up bathed in sweat, reeling from alien emotion.

• • •

On the next arrival, Saga got out of the ship to help engineer Novik inspect the hull. Skidbladnir had materialized on what looked like the bottom of a shallow bowl under a purple sky. The sandy ground was littered with shells and fish bones. Saga and Novik made their way through the stream of passengers getting on and off; dockworkers dragged some crates up to the gates.

Saga had seen Skidbladnir arrive, once, when she had first gone into service. First it wasn't there, and then it was, heavy and solid, as if it had always been. From the outside, the ship looked like a tall and slender office building. The concrete was pitted and streaked, and all of the windows were covered with steel plates. Through the roof, Skidbladnir's claws and legs protruded like a plant, swaying gently in some unseen breeze. The building had no openings save the front gates, through which everyone passed. From the airlock in the lobby, one climbed a series of stairs to get to the passenger deck. Or, if you were Saga, climbed the spiral staircase that led up to the engine room and custodial services.

Novik took a few steps back and scanned the hull. A tall, bearded man in rumpled blue overalls, he looked only slightly less imposing outside than he did in the bowels of the ship. He turned to Saga. In daylight, his gray eyes were almost translucent.

'There,' he said, and pointed to a spot two stories up the side. 'We need to make a quick patch.'

Saga helped Novik set up the lift that was attached to the side of the building, and turned the winch until they reached the point of damage. It was just a small crack, but deep enough that Saga could see something underneath – something that looked like skin. Novik took a look inside, grunted and had Saga hold the pail while he slathered putty over the crack.

'What was that inside?' Saga asked.

Novik patted the concrete. 'There,' he said. 'You're safe again, my dear.'

He turned to Saga. 'She's always growing. It's going to be a problem soon.'

Season 2, episode 8: Unnatural Relations.

One of the officers on the station begins a relationship with a silicate-based alien life form. It's a love story doomed to fail, and it does: the officer walks into the life form's biosphere and removes her rebreather to make love to the life form. She lasts for two minutes.

•

Saga dreamed of the silicate creature that night, a gossamer thing with a voice like waves crashing on a shore. It sang to her; she woke up in the middle of the sleep shift and the song was still there. She put a hand on the wall. The concrete was warm.

• • •

She had always wanted to go on an adventure. It had been her dream as a child. She had watched shows like *Andromeda Station* and *The Sirius Reach* over and over again, dreaming of the day she would become an astronaut. She did research on how to become one. It involved hard work, studying, mental and physical perfection. She had none of that. She could fix things, that was all. Space had to remain a distant dream.

The arrival of the crab ships interrupted the scramble for outer space. They sailed not through space but some other dimension between worlds. When the first panic had subsided, and linguistic barriers had been overcome, trade agreements and diplomatic relations were established. The gifted, the rich and the ambitious went with the ships to faraway places. People like Saga went through their lives with a dream of leaving home.

Then one of the crab ships materialized in Saga's village. It must have been a fluke, a navigation error. The crew got out and deposited a boy who hacked and coughed and collapsed on the ground. A long-legged beaked creature with an angular accent asked the gathered crowd for someone who could fix things. Saga took a step forward. The tall human man in blue overalls looked at her with his stony gray eyes.

'What can you do?' he asked.

'Anything you need,' Saga replied.

The man inspected her callused hands, her determined face, and nodded.

'You will do,' he said. 'You will do.'

Saga barely said goodbye to her family and friends; she walked through the gates and never looked back.

The magic of it all faded over time. Now it was just work: fixing the electricity, taping hatches shut, occasionally shoveling refuse when the plumbing broke. Everything broke in this place. Of all the ships that sailed the worlds, Skidbladnir was probably the oldest and most decrepit. It didn't go to any interesting places either, just deserts and little towns and islands far away from civilization. Aavit the steward often complained that it deserved a better job. The passengers complained of the low standard, the badly cooked food. The only one who didn't complain was Novik. He referred to Skidbladnir not as an it, but as a she.

• • •

Over the next few stops, the electricity outages happened more and more frequently. Every time, living tubes had intertwined with the wiring and short-circuited it. At first it was only on the top passenger level. Then it spread to the next one. It was as if Skidbladnir was sending down parts of itself through the entire building. Only tendrils, at first. Then Saga was called down to fix the electricity in a passenger room, where the bulb in the ceiling was blinking on and off. She opened the maintenance hatch and an eye stared back at her. Its pupil was large and round, the iris red. It watched her with something like interest. She waved a hand in front of it. The eye tracked her movement. Aavit had said that Skidbladnir was a dumb beast. But the eye that met Saga's did not seem dumb.

Saga went upstairs, past her own quarters, and for the first time knocked on the door to engineering. After what seemed like an age, the door opened. Engineer Novik had to stoop to see outside. His face was smudged with something dark.

'What do you want?' he said, not unkindly.

'I think something is happening,' Saga said.

Novik followed her down to the passenger room and peered through the hatch.

'This is serious,' he mumbled.

'What is?' Saga asked.

'We'll talk later,' Novik said and strode off.

'What do I do?' Saga shouted after him.

'Nothing,' he called over his shoulder.

•

Novik had left the door to the captain's office ajar. Saga positioned herself outside and listened. She had never really seen the captain; she hid in her office, doing whatever a captain did. Saga knew her only as a shadowy alto.

'We can't take the risk,' the captain said inside. 'Maybe it'll hold for a while longer. You could make some more room, couldn't you? Some extensions?'

'It won't be enough,' Novik replied. 'She'll die before long. Look, I know a place where we could find a new shell.'

'And how would you do that? It's unheard of. It's lived in here since it was a youngling, and it'll die in here. Only wild crabs can change shells.'

'I could convince her to change. I'm sure of it.'

'And where is this place?'

'An abandoned city,' Novik replied. 'It's out of our way, but it'd be worth it.'

'No,' the captain said. 'Better sell it on. It won't survive such a swap, and I'll be ruined. If things have gone this far, I need to sell it to someone who can take it apart.'

'And I'm telling you she has a chance,' Novik said. 'Please don't pass her on to some butcher.'

'You're too attached,' the captain retorted. 'I'll sell it on and use the money as down payment for a new ship. We'll have to start small again, but we've done it before.'

Season 1, episode 11: The Natives Are Restless.

The lower levels of Andromeda Station are populated by the destitute: adventurers who didn't find what they were look-ing for, merchants who lost their cargo, drug addicts, failed prophets. They unite under a leader who promises to topple the station's regime. They sweep through the upper levels, murdering and pillaging in their path. They are gunned down by security. The station's captain and the rebel leader meet in the middle of the carnage. Was it worth it?, the captain asks. Always, says the rebel.

•

There was a knock on Saga's door after her shift. It was Novik, with an urgent look on his face.

'It's time you saw her,' he said.

They walked down the long corridor from Saga's cabin to the engine room. The passage seemed somehow smaller than before, as if the walls had contracted. When Novik opened the door at the end of the corridor, a wave of warm air with a coppery tang wafted out.

Saga had imagined a huge, dark cavern. What Novik led her through was a cramped warren of tubes, pipes and wires, all intertwined with tendrils of that same grayish substance she had found in the hatches downstairs. As they moved forward, the tendrils thickened into ropes, then meaty cables. The corridor narrowed, so tight in spots that Novik and Saga had to push through it sideways.

'Here,' Novik said, and the corridor suddenly opened up.

The space was dimly lit by a couple of electric lights; the shapes that filled the engine room were only suggested, not illuminated. Round curves, glistening metal intertwined with that gray substance. Here, a slow triple beat shook the floor. There was the faint wet noise of something shifting.

'This is she,' Novik said. 'This is Skidbladnir.'

He gently took Saga's hand and guided it to a gray outcrop. It was warm under her fingers, and throbbed: one two three, one two three.

'This is where I interface with her,' Novik said.

'Interface?' Saga asked.

'Yes. We speak. I tell her where to go. She tells me what it's like.' Novik gently patted the gray skin. 'She has been poorly for some time now. She's growing too big for her shell. But she didn't say how bad it was. I understood when you showed me where she's grown into the passenger deck.'

One two three, one two three, thrummed the pulse under Saga's hand.

'I know you were eavesdropping,' Novik said. 'The captain and the steward will sell her off to someone who will take her apart for meat. She's old, but she's not that old. We can find her a new home.'

'Can I interface with her?' Saga said.

'She says you already have,' Novik said.

And Saga heard it: the voice, like waves crashing on a shore, the voice she had heard in her dream. It brought an image of a vast ocean, swimming through darkness from island to island. Around her, a shell that sat uncomfortably tight. Her whole body hurt. Her joints and tendrils felt swollen and stiff.

Novik's hand on her shoulder brought her back to the engine room.

'You see?' he said.

'We have to save her,' Saga said.

Novik nodded.

• • •

They arrived at the edge of a vast and cluttered city under a dark sky. The wreckage of old ships dotted the desert that surrounded the city – buildings like Skidbladnir's shell, cracked cylinders, broken disks and pyramids.

They had let off all passengers and cargo at the previous stop. Only the skeleton crew remained: the captain, the steward, Novik and Saga. They gathered in the lobby's air lock, and Saga saw the captain for the very first time. She was tall, built from shadows and strange angles. Her face kept slipping out of focus. Saga only assumed her as a 'she' from the soft alto voice.

'Time to meet the mechanics,' the captain said.

Novik clenched and unclenched his fists. Aavit looked at him with one cold sideways eye and clattered its beak.

'You'll see reason,' it said.

The air outside was cold and thin. Novik and Saga put on their face masks; Aavit and the captain went as they were. The captain's shroud fluttered in an icy breeze that brought waves of fine dust.

There was a squat office building among the wrecks. Its door slid open as they approached. Inside was a small room cluttered with obscure machinery. The air was warmer in here. Another door stood open at the end of the room, and the captain strode toward it. When Saga and Novik made to follow, Aavit held a hand up.

'Wait here,' it said, its voice barely audible in the thin atmosphere.

The other door closed behind them.

Saga looked at Novik, who looked back at her. He nodded. They turned as one and ran back toward Skidbladnir.

Saga looked over her shoulder as they ran. Halfway to the ship, she could see the captain emerge from the office, a mass of tattered fabric that undulated over the ground, more quickly than it should. Saga ran as fast as she could.

She had barely made it inside the doors when Novik closed them with a resounding boom and turned the great wheel that locked them. They waited for what seemed like an eternity as the airlock cycled. Something hit the doors with a thud, again and again, and made them shudder. As the airlock finally opened, Novik tore his mask off. His face was pale and sweaty underneath.

'They'll find something to break the doors down,' he said. 'We have to move quickly.'

Saga followed him up the spiral stairs, through the passages, to the engine room. As she stood with her hands on her knees, panting. Novik pushed himself into Skidbladnir's gray mass face first. It enveloped him with a sigh. The departure siren sounded.

Saga had never experienced a passage without being strapped down. The floor suddenly tilted, and sent her reeling into the gray wall. It was sticky and warm to the touch. Saga's ears popped. The floor tilted the other way. She went flying headfirst into the other wall and hit her nose on something hard. Then the floor righted itself. Skidbladnir was through to the void between the worlds.

Saga gingerly felt her nose. It was bleeding, but didn't seem broken. Novik stepped back from the wall. He looked at Saga over his shoulder.

'You'll have to do the captain's job now,' he said.

'What?' Saga asked.

'That's how it works. You read the map to me while I steer her.'

'What do I do?'

'You go up to the captain's cabin. There's a map. There's a city on the map. It's on the lower levels. It's abandoned. Tall spires. You'll see it.'

·

Saga went up to the captain's cabin. The door was open. The space inside was filled by an enormous construction. Orbs of different sizes hung from the ceiling, sat on the ground, were mounted on sticks. Some of the orbs had little satellites. Some of them were striped, some marbled, some dark. In the space between them hung swirls of light that didn't seem attached to anything. Close to the center, a rectangular object was suspended in the air. It looked like a tiny model of Skidbladnir.

There was a crackle. From a speaker near the ceiling, Novik's voice said, 'Step into the map. Touch the spheres. You'll see.'

Saga carefully stepped inside. The swirls gave off small shocks as she grazed them, and though they seemed gossamer, they didn't budge. She put her hand on one of the spheres, and her vision filled with the image of islands on green water. A red sun looked down on pale trees. She touched another, one that hung from the ceiling, and saw a bustling night-time town, shapes moving between houses, two moons shining in the sky. She touched sphere after sphere: vast desert landscapes, cities, forests, villages. The lower levels, Novik had said. Saga crouched down and felt the miniature worlds that littered the floor like marbles. Near the far corner, a dark sphere was a little larger than the others. As she touched it, there was an image of a city at dawn. It was still, silent. Tall white spires stretched toward the horizon. There were no lights, no movement. Some of the spires were broken.

'I think I found it,' she said aloud.

'Good,' Novik said through the speaker. 'Now draw a path.'

Saga stood up, ducking the electrified swirls. She made her way into the center of the room where Skidbladnir hung suspended on seemingly nothing at all.

'How?' she asked.

'Just draw it,' Novik replied.

Saga touched Skidbladnir. It gave off a tiny chime. She traced her finger in the air. Her finger left a bright trail. She made her way across the room, carefully avoiding the glowing swirls, until she reached the sphere on the floor. As she touched the sphere, another chime sounded. The trail her finger had left seemed to solidify.

'Good,' said Novik in the speaker. 'Setting the course.'

• • •

Saga wandered through the empty ship. There was no telling how long the journey would take, but on the map it was from the center of the room to the very edge, so perhaps that meant a long wait. She had gone back to the engine room, but the door was shut now. Whatever Novik did inside, while interfacing with Skidbladnir, he wanted to do undisturbed.

The main doors in the lobby had buckled inward, but not broken. The captain had used considerable force to try to get back in. The passenger rooms were empty. In the lounge, the pool table's balls had gone over the edge and lay scattered on the floor. There was food in the mess hall; Saga made herself a meal of bread and cheese from the cabinet for human food. Then she went up to her quarters to wait.

Season 2 finale: All We Ever Wanted Was Everything.

The station is closing due to budget reasons; Earth has cut off funding because station management refuses to go along with their alien-unfriendly policies. No other race offers to pick up the bill, since they have started up stations of their own. In a bittersweet montage, the captain walks through the station and reminisces on past events. The episode ends with the captain leaving on a shuttle. An era is over. The alien navigator puts a claw on the captain's shoulder: a new station is opening, and the captain is welcome to join. But it'll never be an earthlike place. It'll never be quite like home.

•

Skidbladnir arrived in a plaza at the city's heart. The air was breathable and warm. Tall spires rose up into the sky. The ground beneath them was cracked open by vegetation. Novik got out first. He put his hands on his hips and surveyed the plaza. He nodded to himself.

'This will do,' he said. 'This will do.'

'What happens now?' Saga asked.

'We stand back and wait,' Novik replied. 'Skidbladnir knows what to do.' He motioned for Saga to follow him.

They sat down at the edge of the plaza, well away from Skidbladnir. Saga put her bags down; she hadn't brought much, just her clothes, some food, and the first season of *Andromeda Station*. Perhaps she would find a new tape player somewhere.

They waited for a long time. Novik didn't say much; he sat with his legs crossed in front of him, gazing up at the spires.

•

At dusk, Skidbladnir's walls cracked open. Saga understood why Novik had positioned them so far away from the building; great lumps of concrete and steel fell down and shook the ground as the building shrugged and shuddered. The tendrils that waved from the building's cracked roof stiffened and trembled. They seemed to lengthen. Walls fell down, steel windows sloughed off, as Skidbladnir slowly extricated herself from her shell. She crawled out from the top, taking great lumps of concrete with her. Saga had expected her to land on the ground with an almighty thud. But she made no noise at all.

Free of her house, Skidbladnir was a terror and wonder to behold. Her body was long and curled; her multitude of eyes gleamed in the starlight. Her tendrils waved in the warm air as if testing it. Some of the tendrils looked shrunken and unusable. Saga also saw that patches of Skidbladnir's body weren't as smooth as the rest of her; they were dried and crusted. Here and there, fluid oozed from long scratches in her skin.

Next to Saga, Novik made a muffled noise. He was crying.

'Go, my love,' he whispered. 'Find yourself a new home.'

Skidbladnir's tendrils felt the buildings around the plaza. Finally, they wrapped themselves around the tallest building, a gleaming thing with a spiraled roof, and Skidbladnir pulled herself up the wall. Glass tumbled to the ground as Skidbladnir's tendrils shot through windows to pull herself up. She tore through the roof with a thunderous noise. There was a moment when she supported her whole body on her tendrils, suspended in the air; she almost toppled over the side. Then, with what sounded like a sigh, she lowered herself into the building. Saga heard the noise of collapsing concrete as Skidbladnir's body worked to make room for itself. Eventually, the noise subsided. Skidbladnir's arms hung down the building's side like a crawling plant.

'What now?' Saga said.

She looked sideways at Novik. He smiled at her.

'Now she's free,' he said. 'Free to go wherever she pleases.'

'And what about us?' Saga asked. 'Where do we go?'

'With her, of course,' Novik replied.

'There's no map,' Saga said. 'Nothing to navigate by. And the machinery? Your engine room?'

'That was only ever needed to make her go where we wanted her to,' Novik said. 'She doesn't need that now.'

'Wait,' Saga said. 'What about me? What if I want to go home?'

Novik raised an eyebrow. 'Home?'

A chill ran down Saga's back. 'Yes, home.'

Novik shrugged. 'Perhaps she'll stop by there. There's no telling what she'll do. Come on.'

He got up and started walking towards Skidbladnir and her new shell. Saga remained on the ground. Her body felt numb. Novik went up to the building's front door, which slid open, and he disappeared inside.

Season 1, episode 5: Adrift.

The captain's wife dies. She goes into space on a private shuttle to consign the body to space. While in space, the shuttle malfunctions. The captain finds herself adrift between the stars. The oxygen starts to run out. As the captain draws what she thinks are her last breaths, she records one final message to her colleagues. Forgive me for what I did and didn't do, she says. I did what I thought was best.

•

Life on the new Skidbladnir was erratic. Novik spent most of his time interfaced, gazing into one of Skidbladnir's great eyes in a hall at the heart of the building. Saga spent much of her time exploring. This had been someone's home once, an apartment building of sorts. There were no doors or windows, only maze-like curved hallways that with regular intervals expanded into rooms. Some of them were empty, others furnished with oddly shaped tables, chairs and beds. Some wall-to-wall cabinets held knick-knacks and scrolls written in a flowing, spiraled script. There were no means to cook food in any way Saga could recognize. She made a nest in one of the smaller rooms close to where Novik worked with Skidbladnir. The walls gave off a soft glow that dimmed from time to time; Saga fell into the habit of sleeping whenever that happened. Drifting off into sleep, she sometimes thought she could hear voices speaking in some vowel-rich tongue, but they faded as she listened for them.

Skidbladnir did seem concerned for Saga and Novik. She stopped at the edge of towns every now and then, where Saga could breathe and was able to trade oddities she found in the building that was now her new home for some food and tools. But mostly they were adrift between worlds. It seemed that Skidbladnir found her greatest joy in coasting the invisible eddies and waves of the void. Every time they stopped somewhere, Saga considered getting off to try her luck. There might be another ship that could take her home. But these places were too strange, too far-flung. It was as if Skidbladnir was avoiding civilization. Perhaps she sensed that Aavit and the old captain might be after them. That thought gnawed at Saga every time they stopped somewhere. But there was such a multitude of worlds out there, and no one ever seemed to recognize them.

She tore the *Andromeda Station* tapes apart and hung them like garlands over the walls, traced her finger along them, mumbled the episodes to herself, until Skidbladnir shuddered and she took cover for the next passage.

Each time Skidbladnir pushed through to another world, it was more and more violent.

'Is she going to hold?' Saga asked Novik on one of the rare occasions he came out from his engine room to eat.

Novik was quiet for a long moment. 'For a time,' he said.

'What are you going to do when she dies?' Saga asked.

'We'll go together, me and her,' he replied.

• • •

One day, improbably, Skidbladnir arrived outside a place Saga recognized. A town, not her hometown, but not so far away from it.

Novik was nowhere to be seen. He was sleeping or interfaced with the ship. Saga walked downstairs, and the front door slid open for her. Outside, a crowd had gathered. An official-looking man walked up to Saga as she came outside.

'What's this ship?' he said. 'It's not on our schedule. Are you the captain?'

'This is Skidbladnir,' Saga said. 'She's not on anyone's schedule. We don't have a captain.'

'Well,' the official said. 'What's your business?'

'Just travel,' Saga said.

She looked back at Skidbladnir. This was her chance to get off, to go home. Novik would barely notice. She could return to her life. And do what, exactly? The gathered crowd was all comprised of humans, their faces dull, their eyes shallow.

'Do you have a permit?' the official asked.

'Probably not,' Saga said.

'I'll have to seize this ship,' the official said. 'Bring out who-ever is in charge.'

Saga gestured at Skidbladnir's walls. 'She is.'

'This is unheard of,' the official said. He turned away and spoke into a comm radio.

Saga looked at the little town, the empty-faced crowd, the gray official.

'Okay. I am the captain,' she said. 'And we're leaving.'

She turned and walked back to Skidbladnir. The door slid open to admit her. The hallway inside thrummed with life. She put a hand on the wall.

'Let's go,' she said. 'Wherever you want.'

Pilot episode: One Small Step

The new captain of Andromeda Station arrives. Everything is new and strange; the captain only has experience of Earth politics and is baffled by the various customs and rituals practiced by the other aliens on the station. A friendly janitor who happens to be cleaning the captain's cabin offers to give her a tour of all the levels. The janitor, it turns out, has been on the station for most of his life and knows all of the station's quirks. She's confusing as hell at first, he says. But once you know how to speak to her, she will take good care of you.

•

Saga took the tapes down and rolled them up. It was time to be the captain of her own ship now. A ship that went where it wanted to, but a ship nonetheless. She could set up proper trade.

She could learn new languages. She could fix things. She was good at fixing things.

One day Skidbladnir would fail. But until then, Saga would swim through the void with her.

Prime Meridian

Silvia Moreno-Garcia

Mexico

I got to write the introduction to the first publication of 'Prime Meridian', and I only wish Silvia wrote more science fiction. It is possibly my favourite thing of hers, a quiet, devastating tale of near-future Earth and a dream of the stars. I've co-edited the *Jewish Mexican Literary Review* with Silvia, and got to write a book column with her for the *Washington Post*. I've watched her career progress until she hit it big with *Mexican Gothic*, and once I spent a day with her on a trip into Lovecraft country in New England, though the horrors we saw on the Plum Island lighthouse that day are a story for another time... Of course I had to have 'Prime Meridian' in this volume, and I hope you love it as much as I do.

Why did I have to poison myself with love?

—*Aelita, or The Decline of Mars*, Aleksey Tolstoy

Una ciudad deshecha, gris, monstruosa

—'Alta traición', José Emilio Pacheco

1

The subway station was a dud. Both of its entrances had once again been commandeered by a street gang that morning, which meant you'd have to pay a small 'fee' in order to catch your train. Amelia was tempted to fork over the cash, but you never knew if these assholes were also going to help themselves to your purse, your cell phone, and whatever the hell else they wanted.

That meant she had to choose between a shared ride and the bus. Amelia didn't like either option. The bus was cheap. It would also take forever for it to reach Coyoacán. The car could also take a while, depending on how many people hailed it, but it would no doubt move faster.

Amelia was supposed to meet Fernanda for lunch the next day and she needed to ensure she had enough money to pay for her meal. Fernanda was loaded, and odds were she'd cover it all, but Amelia didn't want to risk it in case Fernanda wasn't feeling generous.

The most sensible thing to do, considering this, was to take the bus. Problem was, she had the booking and if she didn't check in by five o'clock, she'd be penalized, a percentage of her earnings deducted. The damned app had a geolocator function. Amelia couldn't lie and claim she'd reached the house on time.

Amelia gave the gang members standing by the subway station's entrance a long glare and took out her cell phone.

Five minutes later, her ride arrived. She was glad to discover there was only one other person in the car. Last time she'd taken a shared ride, she sat together with four people, including a woman with a baby, the cries of the child deafening Amelia.

Amelia boarded the car and gave the other passenger a polite nod. The man hardly returned it. He was wearing a gray suit and carried a briefcase, which he clutched with one hand while he held up his cell phone in the other. You heard all these stories about how the ride shares were dangerous – you could get into a car and be mugged, express kidnapped or raped – but Amelia wasn't going to pay for a damned secure taxi and this guy, at least, didn't look like he was going to pull a gun on her. He was too busy yakking on the phone.

They made good progress despite the usual insanity of Mexico City's traffic. In Europe, there were automated cars roaming the cities, but here drivers still had a job. They couldn't automate that, not with the chaotic fuckery of the roads.

Mars is home to the tallest mountain in the solar system. Olympus Mons, 21 km high and 600 km in diameter, she told herself as the driver honked the horn. Sometimes, she repeated the Mandarin words she knew, but it was mostly facts about the Red Planet. To remind herself it was real, it existed, it was there.

Once they approached the old square in Coyoacán, Amelia jumped out of the car. No point in staying inside; the vehicle moved at a snail's pace. The cobblestone streets in this borough were never made to bear the multitudes that now walked through the once-small village.

The square that marked the center of old Coyoacán was chock-full of street vendors frying churros and gorditas, or offering bags emblazoned with the face of Frida Kahlo and acrylic rebozos made in China. Folkloric bullshit.

Amelia took a side street, where the traditional pulquerias had been substituted with fusion restaurants. Korean–Mexican. French–Mexican. Whatever–Mexican. Mexican–Mexican was never enough. A couple of more blocks and she reached Lucía's home with five minutes to spare, thank-fucking-God.

Lucía's house was not an ordinary house, but a full-fledged casona, a historical marvel that looked like it was out of a movie, with wrought iron bars on the windows and an interior patio crammed with potted plants. The inside was much of the same: rustic tables and hand-painted talavera. It screamed colonial, provincial, nostalgia and also fake. There was an artificial, too-calculated, too-overdone quality to each and every corner of the house, an unintended clue that the owner had once been an actress.

Amelia knew the drill. She went into the living room with its enormous screen and sat on one of the couches. Lucía was already there. The woman drank nothing except mineral water with a wedge of lime. The first time Amelia had visited her, she had made the mistake of asking for a Diet Coke, which earned her a raised eyebrow and a mineral water, because fuck you, Lucía Madrigal said what you drank and what you ate (nothing, most times, although twice, little bowls with pomegranate seeds had been placed on the table by the couches).

That day, there were no pomegranates, only the mineral water and Lucía, dressed in a bright green dress with a match- ing turban, the kind Elizabeth Taylor wore in the 1970s. That had been Lucía's heyday and she had not acclimated to modern dress styles, preferring tacky drama to demure senior citizen clothes.

'Today, we are going to watch my second movie. The Mars picture. I was quite young when this came out in '65, so it's not one of my best roles,' Lucía declared with such aplomb one might have believed she had been a real actress, instead of a middling starlet who got lucky and married a filthy rich politician.

Amelia nodded. She had little interest in Lucía's movies, but her job was not to offer commentary. It was to simply sit and watch. Sometimes, it was to sit and listen. Lucía liked to go on about the film stars she'd met in decades past or the autobiog- raphy she was writing. As long as Amelia kept her eyes open and her mouth shut, she'd get a good rating on Friendrr and her due payment, minus the twenty percent commission for the broker. There were other apps that functioned without a broker, but those were less reliable. You might arrive for your Friendrr session and discover the client was an absolute sleaze who wouldn't pay. Friendrr vetted the clients, asked for deposits, and charged more, which was good news.

The movie was short and confusing, as if it had been rewritten halfway through the production. The first half focused on a space ranger sent to check out a Martian outpost manned by a scientist and his lovely daughter. Lucía played the daughter, who wore 'futuristic' silver miniskirts. For its first half-hour, it played as a tame romance. Then space pirates, who looked suspiciously like they were wearing discarded clothes from a Mexican Revolution film, invaded the outpost. The pirates were under the command of a Space Queen who was obviously evil, due to the plunging neckline of her costume.

'It doesn't much look like the real Mars, I suppose,' Lucía mused, 'but then, I prefer it this way. The real Mars is bland compared to the one the set designer imagined. Have you seen the pictures of the colonies?'

'Yes,' Amelia said, and although she knew only monosyllabics were required of her, she went on. 'I want to go there, soon.'

'To the Martian colonies?'

Lucía looked at the young woman. The actress had indulged in plastic surgery at several points during the 1990s and her face seemed waxy. Time could not be stopped, though, and she had long abandoned attempts at surgery, botox and peels. What remained of her was like the core of a dead tree. Her eyebrows were non-existent, drawn with aplomb and a brown pencil. She perpetually sported a half-amused expression and a necklace, which she inevitably toyed with.

'Well, I suppose people are meant to go places,' Lucía said. 'But those colonies on Mars, they look as antiseptic and exciting as a box of baby wipes. Everything is white. Who ever heard of white as an exciting color?'

There was irony in this comment, since the movie they had just watched was in black-and-white, but Amelia nodded. Half an hour later, she took the bus back home.

When Amelia walked into the apartment, the television was on. Her sister and her youngest niece were on the couch, watching a reality TV show. Her other niece was probably on the bed, with her phone. Since there were two bedrooms and Amelia had to share a room with one of the girls, the only place where she could summon a modicum of privacy was the bathroom, but when she zipped toward there after a quiet 'hello', Marta looked at her.

'I hope you're not thinking of taking a shower,' her sister said. 'Last month's water bill came in. It's very high.'

'That's the fault of the people in the building next door,' Amelia said. 'You know they steal water from the tinacos.'

'You take forever in the shower. Your hair's not even dirty. Why would you need to get in the shower?'

Amelia did not reply. She changed course, headed into the bedroom, and slipped under the covers. On the other bed, her niece played a game on her cell phone. Its repetitive bop-bop sound allowed for neither sleep nor coherent thoughts.

2

Amelia took her nieces to school, which meant an annoying elbowing in and out of a crowded bus, plus the masterful avoiding of men who tried to touch her ass. Marta insisted that the girls needed to be picked up and dropped off from school, even though Karina was 11 and could catch the school transport together with her little sister, no problem. It was just a modest fee for this privilege.

Amelia thought Marta demanded she perform this task as a way to demonstrate her power.

When Amelia returned from dropping off the girls, she took the shower that had been forbidden her the previous night. Afterward, she cooked a quick meal for the family and left it in the refrigerator – this was another of the tasks she had to execute, along with the drop-offs and pick-ups. Again, she boarded a bus, squeezed tight next to two men, the smell of cheap cologne clogging her nostrils, and got off near the Diana.

Fernanda was characteristically laggard, strolling into the restaurant half an hour late. She did not apologize for the delay. She sat down, ordered a salad after reading the menu twice, and smiled at Amelia.

'I have met the most excellent massage therapist,' Fernanda said. This was her favorite adjective. She had many, employed them generously. 'He got rid of that pain in my back. I told you about it, didn't I? Between the shoulder blades. And the most excellent...'

She droned on. Fernanda and Amelia did not meet often anymore, but when they did, Amelia had to listen patiently about all the wonderful, amazing, super-awesome people Fernanda knew, the cool-brilliant-mega hobbies she was busying herself with, and the delightful-darling-divine trips she'd taken recently. It was pretty much the same structure as her visits with Lucía, the old woman discussing her movies while Amelia watched the ice cubes in her glass melt.

It made her feel cheap and irritated, but Fernanda footed their lunch bills and she had lent money to Amelia on previous occasions. Right now, she was wondering if she should ask for a bit of cash or bite her tongue.

Amelia, who didn't drink regularly in restaurants (who would with these prices?), ordered a martini to pass the time. Fernanda was already on her second one. She drank a lot but only when her husband wasn't looking. He was ugly, grouchy and wealthy. The last attribute was the only one that mattered to Fernanda.

'So, what are you doing now?' Fernanda asked. Her smile was blinding, her hair painted an off-putting shade of blonde, her dark roots showing. Not Brigitte Bardot – bouts of movie-watching with Lucía were giving Amelia a sense of film history – but a straw-like color that wasn't bold, just boring. Every woman of a certain age had that hair color. They'd copied it off a celebrity who had a nightly variety show. No brunettes on TV. Pale skin and fair hair were paramount.

'This and that,' Amelia replied.

'You're not working? Don't tell me you're still doing that awful-terrible rent-a-friend thing,' Fernanda said, looking surprised.

'Yes. Although, I wanted to ask if you hadn't heard of anything that might suit me…'

'Well… your field, it's not really my line of work,' Fernanda replied.

Not that Fernanda had a line of work. As far as Amelia knew, all she did was stay married, her bills paid by her dick of a husband. Amelia, on the other hand, since dropping out of university, had done nothing but work. A series of idiotic, poorly paying and increasingly frustrating gigs. There was no such thing as full-time work for someone like her. Perhaps if she'd stuck with her studies, it might have been different, but when her mother got sick, she had to drop out and become her caretaker. And afterward, when her mother passéd away, it wasn't like she could get her scholarship back.

'I do almost anything,' Amelia said with a shrug. 'Perhaps something in your husband's office?'

'There's nothing there,' Fernanda said, too quickly.

There was likely *something* reserved for Fernanda's intimate friends. Amelia had once counted herself amongst those 'excellent' people. When they'd been in school together, Amelia had written a few term papers for Fernanda and that had made her useful. She'd also dated Elías Bertoliat, which had increased her standing amongst their cohort. That had gone to hell. He'd ghosted her, about two months after she'd dropped out of school, and returned to Monterrey.

Amelia was more devalued than the Mexican peso.

She looked at the bread basket, not wishing to lay her eyes on her so-called friend. She really didn't want to ask for money (it made her feel like shit), but of course that was the one reason why she was sitting at the restaurant.

'Anastasia Brito might be looking for someone like you,' Fernanda said, breaking the uncomfortable silence that had descended between them.

Amelia frowned. Anastasia had gone to the same university, but she'd been an art student while Amelia dallied in land-and-food systems, looking forward to a career as an urban farmer.

'Why?' she asked.

'She's going through a phase. She has an art show in a couple of weeks. The theme is 'meat', but after that, she said she's going to focus on plants and she'll be needing genetically modified ones. It might be your thing.'

It was indeed. After her chances at university soured up, Amelia had taken a few short-term courses in plant modification at a small-fry school. All she'd been able to do with that was get a gig at an illegal marijuana operation. Non-sanctioned, highly modified marijuana plants. It paid on time, but Amelia chickened out after a raid. You couldn't fly to Mars if your police certificate wasn't clean. She didn't want to risk it.

Her friend Pili told Amelia she was an idiot. Pili had been

snared in raids four or five times. All she did was pay the fine. But then, Pili did all kinds of crazy things. She sold her blood to old farts who paid for expensive transfusions, thinking the plasma could rejuvenate them.

'Could be. Do you have her number?' Amelia asked.

'She's in a great-super-cool women's temazcal retreat right now in Peru. All-natural, no contact with the outside world. Just meditation. But she will be back for the art show. You should just show up. I know someone at the gallery. They can put you on the list.'

'The temazcal is Nahua. What's she doing in Peru?'

'I don't know, Amelia,' Fernanda said, sounding annoyed. Amelia's geographical objections were clearly pointless. She supposed people organized whatever retreats rich fuckers could afford. Tibetan samatha in Brazil, Santería ceremonies in Dublin. Who cared?

'All right, put me on the list,' Amelia said.

Fernanda seemed very pleased with herself and paid for the lunch after all. Amelia assumed she considered this her act of charity for the year. For her part, she felt stupidly proud for not mentioning anything about a loan, although she was going to have to figure something out soon.

Amelia picked her nieces up from school and, after ensuring they ate the food she had cooked, she made a quick escape from the apartment as soon as Marta arrived. This was Amelia's strategy: to spend as little time as possible in the apartment when her sister was around. Marta made a room shrink in size and Amelia's room already felt the size of a desk drawer.

Amelia hated sleeping in the same room she'd once shared with Marta, who'd moved to the master bedroom their mother had occupied. Each night, she looked at the walls she had looked at since she was a child. Stray stickers glued to her bed years before remained along the headboard. In a corner, there were smudged markings she'd made with crayons.

Not that it was an unusual set-up. Mexican youths, especially women, tended to live at home with their parents. These days, with the way the economy was going, even the most cosmopolitan people clustered together for long periods of time. At twenty-five, Amelia didn't raise any eyebrows amongst her peers, but she still hated her living situation. Perhaps if they'd had a bigger apartment, it wouldn't be so annoying, but the apartment was small, the building they inhabited in disrepair: a government-funded unit, modern at one point when a president had been trying to score popularity points in that sector of the city. They were in one of four identical towers, built in a Brutalist style with the emphasis on the brute. An interior courtyard joined them together. Bored teens liked to gather there, while others held court in the lobby.

She loathed the whole complex and fled it every day. Her hours were spent navigating through several coffee shops. There was an art to this. The franchises used kiosks to sell coffee and tasteless bread wrapped in plastic. You pushed a button and out came your food. These were terrible places for sitting down for long periods of time. Since everything was automated, the job of the one or two idiots on staff was to wipe the tables clean, and to get people in and out as quick as possible. They enforced the maximum one-hour-for-customers rule with militaristic abandon.

Amelia hopped between two spots, three blocks from each other. One was a café and the other a crêperie. They were on a decent street, meaning they both had an armed guard standing at the door. But who didn't? Any Sanborns or Vips had at least one and similar cafes employed at least a part-time one for the busy times of the day. The guards kept the rabble out. Otherwise, the patrons would have been shooing away people offering to recharge cell phones by hooking them to a tiny generator, or shifty strangers who would top up phone cards for cheaper than the legit telecomm providers. Any other number of peddlers of services and products could also slip in, to the annoyance of licenciados in their suits and ties, trendy youths in designer huipiles, and mothers leaning against their deluxe, ultra-light strollers.

Amelia walked into the coffee shop, ordered a black coffee – cheapest thing on the menu – and, with the day's Wi-Fi code in hand, logged on to the Internet and began reading. First, the news about Mars, then botany items. She drifted haphazardly after that. Anything from celebrity news to studying English or Mandarin. Those were the predominant languages on Mars, German a distant third. After an enthusiastic six months trying to grasp German, though, she'd given up on it. Much of the same happened with Mandarin. English she spoke well enough, as did any Mexican kid who'd gone to a good school.

She'd also given up on a job search. Once she had updated her CV, she had taken new headshots to go with it. Amelia, black hair pulled back, looking like a docile employee. But with her schooling interrupted, what should have been an impressive degree from a nice university was just bullshit. And every time she looked at the CV, it irritated her to see herself reduced to a pile of mediocrity:

Age: 25
Marital status: Unmarried
Current job: Freelancer

Freelancer. Euphemism for *unemployed*. Because her gigs didn't count. You couldn't put 'professional friend' on a CV, any more than you could 'professional cuddler'. God knew there were people who did that gig too, hiring themselves out to embrace people. She remembered seeing an ad for that explaining 'ninety-nine percent of clients are male'. Fuck, no.

Freelancer, then. Ex-university student, ex-someone. Her job applications disappeared into another dimension, swallowed by the computer until she simply stopped trying. She lived off gigs, first the marijuana operation, then odd jobs; for the past two years, the Friendrr bookings had constituted her sole income.

Freelancer. Fuck-up.

No more CV. Amelia focused on Mars, played video games on her cell, drew geometrical shapes on the napkins, then clovers for luck, and stars out of habit. When she knew she'd spent too much time at the coffee shop, she switched to the crêperie, where she repeated the process: black coffee, another couple of hours lost in mundane tasks.

When she was done, she took the subway back home.

It was always the same.

That night, a woman boarded Amelia's train and began asking people for a few tajaderos. The most popular cryptocurrency folks used since the peso was a piece of shit, jumping up and down in value faster than an addict dancing the jitterbug. You could tap a phone against another and transfer tajaderos from an account. A few people did just that, but even if the lady was old and rather pitiful, Amelia couldn't spare a dirty peso.

To be frank, just a couple of bad turns and Amelia would be begging in the subway right next to the old woman.

The doors of the car opened and Amelia darted out. On the walls of the concourse, there were floor-to-ceiling video displays. A blonde woman danced in them. RADIOACTIVE FLESH, she mouthed, the letters superimposed over her image. A NEW COLLECTION. A tattoo artist sat by one of these video panels. He was there every few days, tattooing sound waves onto people's arms. A snippet of your favorite song inked onto your flesh. With the swipe of a scanner, the melody would play. At first, she couldn't believe he lugged his equipment like that around the city, not because it was cumbersome, but because she expected someone might try to steal it. But the man was quite massive and his toothless grin was a warning.

'Hey, I'll give you a discount,' the man told her, but she shook her head, as was her custom.

Amelia took the eastern exit, which was rarely frequented by the gangs. She was in luck; they were nowhere to be seen. Now there was a choice to make. Either follow the shortest route, which meant walking through the courtyard and encountering the young louts who would be drinking there, or take the long way around the perimeter of the complex.

Amelia picked the short way. In the center of the courtyard, there was a dry fountain filled with rubbish. All around lounged teenagers from the buildings. They were not gang members, just professional loafers who specialized in playing loud music and yelling a choice obscenity or two at any girl who walked by.

Although the kids had nothing to offer except, perhaps, cigarettes and a bottle of cheap booze, when Amelia had been a teenager, she'd peered curiously at them. They seemed to be having a good time. Her mother, however, forbade any contact with the teenagers from the housing unit. Mother emphasized how Amelia was meant for bigger and better things. Marta was a lost cause. She'd gotten herself pregnant her last year in high school and married a man who ran off after a handful of years. It didn't matter. Marta possessed no great intellectual gifts anyway. She'd flunked a grade and barely finished high school through online courses. Amelia, however, was a straight-A student. She couldn't waste her time crushing beer cans with *those* kids.

Amelia believed this narrative. When her mother learned she was going out with a good boy from the university, she was ecstatic. Elías Bertoliat, with his pale skin and light eyes, and his fancy car, seemed like a prince from a fairy tale. Every time Amelia floated the idea of Mars, her mother immediately told her Mars was unlikely and she should focus on marrying Elías. After he broke up with Amelia, her mother insisted they'd get back together.

Glancing at the boys kicking around a beer can and laughing, Amelia wondered if she wouldn't have been better off partying with them when she had the chance. If she was destined to be a loser, she could at least have been a loser who had fun, fucked lots of people, enjoyed her youth while it lasted.

She looked at the girls sitting chatting near the fountain, in stockings and shorts, heavy chains dangling against their breasts, their nails long, the makeup plentiful. Then one of the boys hollered and another followed.

'Where you going? I've got something for you, baby.'

Laughter. Amelia looked ahead. There was no point in acknowledging their displays. The faint fantasy that she might have once enjoyed spending her time with them vanished.

They called the days on Mars 'sol'. Twenty-four hours, thirty-nine minutes and 35.244 seconds adding up to a sol. Three percent longer than a day on Earth. She reminded herself of this. It was important to keep her focus on what mattered, on the facts. They could scream, 'Show me your pussy!' and ask her to give them a blowjob, but she did not listen.

When she reached her building, she climbed the five flights of stairs up to her apartment – the elevator was perpetually busted. A dog padded down the long hallway which led to her apartment. Many tenants had pets and some let them roam wild, as if the building were a park. The animals defecated on the stairs, but they also kept the indigents away. The teens who held court downstairs also provided a measure of safety.

Amelia paused before her door, fished out her keys from her purse, and stood still. She could hear dialogue from the TV, muffled, but loud enough she could make out a few words. Amelia walked in.

'Let's see what's behind Door Number One!' the TV announcer yelled. Clapping ensued.

MARS, SCENE 1

It's nothing but sand dunes. Dry, barren, quiet. When she bends down and picks up a handful of sun-baked soil, and wipes her hand against her pale dress, it leaves a dark, rusty streak.

There is air here. This is Mars but the Mars of EXT. MARS SURFACE – DAY. And she is a SPACE EXPLORER, a young woman in a white dress now streaked red.

SPACE EXPLORER has no lines of dialogue, not yet. The camera hovers over her shoulder, over tendrils of dark hair, which shift with the wind.

There is even wind, in EXT. MARS SURFACE. And the dress is far too impractical for any true 'space exploration'. It reaches her ankle, shows off her arms, although no cleavage. Instead, a demure collar that reaches the chin indicates SPACE EXPLORER is a good girl. The white might have clued you in, but it never hurts to place the proper signifiers.

SPACE EXPLORER looks over her shoulder and sees a figure coming toward her, glinting under the sunlight.

Hold that shot, hold that moment, as THE HERO steps into the frame.

3

Amelia avoided her sister for three days, but on the fourth, Marta caught her before she could slip out of the apartment, cornering her by the refrigerator, which was covered with drawings made by the youngest girl. Amelia's niece had a good imagination: the sky was never blue in Mexico City.

'The rent is due,' Marta said. 'And you still owe me that money.'

Two months before, Amelia had bought a pretty new dress. It wasn't a bargain, but it seemed she was getting another steady Friendrr client. Every week, like the arrangement with Lucía. Four hours. She bought the dress because she thought she deserved it. She hadn't bought anything for herself in forever and she would be able to afford it now. Then that client canceled a booking, and another, and Amelia had to pay for the layaway or lose all the money she'd ponied up. So, she asked Marta for enough to make the final payment.

'I have the rent money, not the rest. Things are slow right now,' Amelia said. 'I'm sure bookings will improve as we roll into December.'

'Oh, for God's sake,' Marta said, sending a magnet in the shape of a watermelon slice flying into the air as she slapped her hand against the refrigerator's door. 'You need to get a real job that pays on time.'

'There are no real jobs,' Amelia replied.

'Then what do I do every day?'

Marta was an end-of-life planner, helping arrange elaborate funerals, memorials and euthanasia packages. And yes, it was a job, but guess what? She only had it because she sucked good dick for the boss, a smarmy little man who had made a pass at Amelia the year before, when Marta took her to an office party. He had suggested a threesome with the sisters and when

Amelia complained to Marta about her vomit-inducing creep of a part-time boyfriend/supervisor, Marta had the gall to tell Amelia she shouldn't have worn such a tight skirt.

'You need to look into the private security company I told you about,' Marta said. 'They are always hiring.'

'Do I look like I can shoot a rifle?'

'Fuck it, Amelia, it's just standing on your feet for a few hours holding the gun, not shooting it. Surely, even you can manage that?'

Amelia swallowed a mouthful of rage. She couldn't afford a place on her own and so she swallowed it, bile and resentment making her want to spit.

The phone rang. She almost didn't hear it because the kids had the television on so loud and the kitchen was smack next to the living room/dining room area. It was Miguel, her broker. Friendrr called him that: Junior Social Appointment Broker. Amelia thought it was a weird, long title.

'Hey Amelia, now, how are you doing today?' Miguel asked in that oddly chirpy tone he employed. She'd never met him in person, but Miguel always sounded like he was smiling and his profile featured multiple shots of him grinning at different locations. The beach, a concert, an assortment of restaurants.

Miguel was an extreme positive thinker. He had told her he liked to read self-help books. He also took a lot of online courses. In the beginning, they'd bonded a bit over this, since Amelia was still trying to learn German. As the months dragged by, they both grew disenchanted.

Amelia simply wasn't the kind of girl who could secure many clients. There were some people who were booked solid for gigs, but most of them were very good-looking. She'd heard one young woman got booked exclusively to pose for photos. The kind of 'candid' shots where friends gathered for a social event. Nothing candid in them. Then there were others who did all right with weddings and funerals. Both of these required an ability to cry.

Amelia wasn't a crybaby and she wasn't gorgeous. Her biggest issue, though, was that she simply did not inspire friendly feelings. People did not want to meet her and if they did, they did not want to meet her again. Whatever warmth or spark is required to inspire a desire for human interaction was lacking in her. She wasn't compelling.

Miguel had told her she needed better photos, more keywords. They tried a bunch of things, but it didn't work. Miguel, who had been excited because her science background gave her a certain versatility – some of the folks on Friendrr could hardly spell 'cat', the glorious, underfunded public education system at play – grew underwhelmed.

Miguel hadn't phoned her in weeks and Amelia feared he was getting ready to drop her from Friendrr. She was probably driving his stats down.

'I'm good,' she said, turning her back to her sister, grateful for the interruption. She headed to the room and locked the door. 'What's up?'

'I have a booking for you; you have a new client. That's what's up. The only thing is, it's short notice: tonight at nine.'

'I'm not doing anything tonight.'

'Good. It's in New Polanco. I'm sending you the address.'

'Any special items?'

'No,' Miguel said. 'He wants to have dinner.'

Most clients wanted ordinary things, like watching movies, as Lucía had asked, or walking together. Now and then, an oddity emerged. There had been a man who asked that she wear white gloves and sit perfectly still for a whole hour. But most baffling had been the time a client hired her to pretend she was someone else. Amelia bore a vague resemblance to an old lady's favorite daughter, who had passed away many years before. Or perhaps Amelia bore no resemblance; perhaps any young woman would do. The old woman wept when she saw her, confessing a small litany of sins. They had parted on bad terms, then the daughter died.

Amelia was unnerved by the experience. She wondered if this was the first time a young woman had been brought to meet the old woman. She wondered if other people had worn the green sweater she had been asked to wear. Had it belonged to the dead girl, or was it merely a similar sweater? Were there many girls dressed in green sweaters, each one ushered into the room on a different day of the week?

Worst of all, while the old woman gripped Amelia's hand and swore she'd never leave her alone again, Amelia raised her head and caught sight of the person who had hired her for this gig. It was the old woman's surviving daughter. Her eyes were hard and distant.

Amelia wondered what it must be like for her, to accompany these look-alikes to her mother's bedroom, to have them sit next to her, to hold the woman's hand. What did she feel, being the daughter the old woman did not want? The one who was superfluous?

Perhaps she might have obtained more bookings at that house, but Amelia refused to go back and even though Miguel said she was being stupid – there was talk about terms of agreement, clauses – she refused. Miguel let it go. For once.

• • •

The tower where the client lived was a thin, white, luxurious needle, the kind the ads assured would-be buyers was not only 'modern', but 'super modern'. Many warehouses had been scrapped to make way for these monstrous buildings. The old housing units that remained – homes of the descendants of factory workers, of lower-class citizens who toiled assembling cars and bought little plots to build their homes – existed under the shadow of behemoths. Since the expensive buildings required abundant water and electricity, the poor residents in the area had to do without. The big buildings had priority over all the resources. There were also a few fancy buildings that had halted construction when the latest housing bubble popped. They remained half-finished, like gaping, filthy teeth spread across several gigantic lots. Indigents now made their homes there, living in structures without windows, while three blocks away, women were wrapped in tepezcohuite at the spa, experiencing the trendiest traditional plant remedy around the city.

Amelia walked into the lobby of the white building. A concierge and a guard with a submachine gun both stood behind a glistening desk. The concierge smiled. The guard did not acknowledge her in any way.

'I'm expected. Number 1201,' Amelia said. The client had not given a name, although that was not unusual.

'Yes, you are,' the concierge said, the smile the same, pleasant without being exactly warm. The concierge walked Amelia to the elevator and swiped a card so she could board it.

When she reached the door to 1201, Amelia saw it had been left unlocked and she walked in. The apartment was open concept. The portion constituting the living room area was dominated by a shaggy rug and a modular, low-slung sofa in tasteful gray with an integrated side table. Floor-to-ceiling windows allowed one to observe the cityscape.

She could see the kitchen, but there was a gray sliding door to the right. She assumed a bedroom and bathroom lay in that direction.

'Hey, I'm here,' Amelia said. 'Hello?'

The gray door opened and there stood Elías Bertoliat. For a minute, she thought it was merely a man who *resembled* Elías. Who just happened to have Elías's mouth, his nose, his green eyes. Because it didn't sound feasible that she had just walked into the apartment of her ex-boyfriend.

'You've got to be kidding me,' she said at last. 'You booked me?'

He raised his hands, as if to pacify her.

'Amelia, this is going to sound nuts, but if you'll let me explain—' and his voice was not quite the same. The years had given it more weight, a deeper resonance, but there was still the vague choppiness of the words, as if he'd rehearsed for a long time, attempting to rid himself of his northern accent, and almost managed it.

'It doesn't sound nuts. It *is*,' she said, clutching her cell phone and pointing it at him. 'Are you stalking me?'

'No! I saw your profile on Friendrr by chance. I don't have your contact info, or I would have gotten a hold of you some other way. I just saw it and I thought I'd talk to you.'

Just like that, so easy. And yet, it sounded entirely like him: careless, swift. To see her and decide to find her, like he had decided once, on the spur of the moment, that they ought to go to Monterrey for a concert. Fly in and fly out.

'Why?' she asked. 'You were a dick to me.'

'I know.'

'You don't date someone for two years and then take off like that. Not even a fucking text message, a phone call.'

She didn't care if ghosting was fashionable, or her generation simply didn't care for long-term relationships, or whatever half-baked pop psychology article explained this shit.

He approached her, but Amelia moved away from him,

ensuring the sofa was between them, that it served as a demar-cation line. Sinus Meridiani in the middle of the living room.

'My dad pulled me from university. He didn't like all my talk about going to Mars and he forced me to go back home,' he said.

'And he forced you to ghost me.'

'I didn't know what to say. I was a kid,' he protested.

'We were in university, not kindergarten.'

He managed to look betrayed despite the fact she should have owned all the outrage in this meeting. He had looked, when they'd met, rather boyish. Little boy lost. This had been an interesting change from the loud, grossly wealthy 'juniors' who populated the university and the festive, catcalling youths in the center of her housing complex. And he had an interest in photography, which revealed a sensitive soul. It, in turn, prompted Amelia to forgive whatever mistakes he made, since she was a misguided romantic in search of a Prince Charming.

He still had that boyishness, in the eyes if not the face.

'What do you want?' she asked.

'I was on Friendrr for the same reason other people are. I wanted to talk to someone. I thought I'd talk to you. Maybe apologize. Amelia, let me buy you dinner.'

To be fair, she considered it and just as quickly, she decided, *Fuck, no*.

'You booked me for two hours,' she said, holding the phone tight, holding it up, so he could look at the timer she'd just switched on. 'But I am not having dinner with you. In fact, I'm going to lock myself in your room and I'm going to take a nap. A long nap.'

She closed the sliding door behind her and walked down a wide hallway which led straight into said room. She promptly locked the door, as she'd promised. The bed was large, no narrow, lumpy mattress, springs digging into her back. She turned her head and stared at the curtains. She didn't sleep, not a wink, and he didn't attempt to coax her out of there. When the two hours had elapsed, Amelia walked back into the living room.

'At Friendrr, your satisfaction is of the utmost importance to us. I hope you will consider us again for all your social needs,' she said.

Elías was sitting on the sofa. When she spoke, he turned his head, staring at her. He had enjoyed taking pictures, but did not often have his own taken. Yet, she had snapped a rare shot of him with his own camera. He'd had the same expression in that shot: remote, somewhat flimsy, as if he were afraid the raw camera lens might reveal a hidden blemish.

Three months after he'd dumped her, Amelia had deleted that photo from her computer, erasing him from her hard drive and her life after finally clueing in to the fact that he was never coming back. Now she walked out and walked downstairs, not bothering to wait for the elevator.

I don't know why you're on Mars, Carl Sagan once said. Amelia had committed his speech to memory, but she couldn't remember it now, although she'd played it back to Elías, for Elías. Elías, brushing the hair away from her face as she pressed a key on the laptop and the astronomer's voice came out loud and clear. Which was maybe why she couldn't, wouldn't remember it.

4

Amelia had been tired, busy, upset, but the movie playing was too terrible to remember her worries. Too ridiculous. A man in an ape suit jumped around, chasing a young woman, and Lucía chuckled. Amelia, noticing this, chuckled too. They both glanced at each other. Then they erupted in synchronized laughter. The ape-man stumbled, pointed a raygun at the screen, and they both laughed even more.

Afterward, a servant refilled their glasses with mineral water. Lucía wore a yellow turban, embroidered with flowers.

'Not my finest performance, I suppose,' Lucía said, smiling. 'In my defense, the ape costume was terrible. It smelled like rotten eggs for some reason. God knows where they got it from.'

'That doesn't sound very glamorous.'

Amelia did not ask questions, she simply listened, but for once, Lucía was offering conversation. Months of starchiness and, at last, the old woman had seemed to warm up to her. Perhaps this boded well. It would certainly be nice if she could book more hours. Especially considering that damned fiasco with Elías. Would he attempt to book her again? Amelia had asked herself that question a dozen times already. Each time, she thought she needed to phone Miguel, tell him this was her damned ex-boyfriend trying to book her, but she felt too embarrassed.

'It wasn't,' the older woman said. 'The glamor was in the forties and fifties. I was born too late. The movie industry in Mexico was eroding by the time the sixties rolled around. We made terrible movies, cheap flicks. Go-go dancers and wrestlers and monsters. I might have done a Viking movie if Nahum had gotten the funding for that, but he was flying low and Armand Elba wasn't doing much better either. Can you imagine? Viking women in Mexico.'

'Nahum?'

'Nahum Landmann. The director. They billed him as Eduard Landmann. Armando Elba was the scriptwriter. They worked on three films before Nahum went to Chile. The first one did well enough, a Western. And then they shot the Mars movie:

Conqueror Women of Mars. Then came that stupid ape movie and the Viking project floundered. Nahum couldn't get any money and Elba flew back to Europe. Maybe it was for the best.'

'Why?'

'The movies were supposed to be completely different. Well, maybe not the Western. That one turned out close to the original concept. But Nahum saw the Mars movie as a surrealist project. The original title was *Adelita of Mars.* Can you picture that?'

Amelia could not, although that explained the strange costume choices and even certain shots, which had seemed oddly out of place.

'Women wearing cartridge belts like during the Revolution, a guy dressed like a futuristic Pancho Villa. It was more Luis Buñuel and *Simon of the Desert* than a B movie. A long prologue, nearly half an hour of it. But then the producers asked for changes. Nahum also demanded changes; Elba kept rewriting and then Nahum rewrote the rewrites. I had new pages every morning. I didn't know how to say my lines. I didn't know the ending.'

'Did they make any other movies?'

'Elba wrote erotic science fiction. Paperbacks, I don't remember in what language. Was it in French or German?' the old woman wondered. 'Nahum didn't do any other movies. He didn't do anything at all, although he sent me a few sketches from Chile. He had another idea: robot women!'

Lucía smiled broadly and then her painted eyebrows knitted in a frown.

'And then it was '73 in Chile and the Coup,' she muttered.

Lucía sipped her mineral water in silence, her lipstick leaving a red imprint on the plastic straw. She glanced at Amelia, as if sizing her up.

'Come. Let me show you something,' the old woman said.

Amelia followed her. She had only been inside the one room in the house where they watched the movies. Lucía took her to her office. There were tall bookcases, a rustic pine desk with painted sunflowers. Several framed posters served as decoration. Lucía stood before one of them.

'*Conqueror Women of Mars*,' she said. 'The first poster. They had it redone. Cristina Garza said, since she was the better-known actress, she should be on the poster. They made a terrible poster to promote the film, but this was a good concept. It was better.'

The poster showed a woman in white, cartridge belts criss-crossing her back. There was one brief scene in the movie where Lucía was dressed like that. The ground beneath the woman's feet was red and the sky was also red, a cloud of dust. She was looking over her shoulder. The colors were saturated and the font was all-caps, dramatic. But there was an element of gracefulness in the woman's pose that elevated this from shlock to sheer beauty.

'I like it,' Amelia said.

'Then look at this one,' Lucía said, pointing at another poster. 'To raise money for the Viking project, Nahum commissioned an artist to paint this. It was a lost-world story but with a science fiction twist. It was set in the future, after an atomic war has left most of the world uninhabited and giant lizards roam the desert.'

'Where did the Vikings come into that?' Amelia said, puzzled, staring at this other poster, which showed a young Lucía in a fur bikini, clutching the arm of a handsome man who wore an incongruous Viking hat. Behind them, two dinosaurs were engaged in a vicious fight.

'I don't know. But you have to remember Raquel Welch had made a lot of money in *One Million Years B.C.* and this was just a few years after that. I suppose any concept was a good concept if they could get half a dozen pretty girls into furry bathing suits.'

'So, why couldn't the director raise the money for it, then?'

'Same problem as always. Nahum had all these strange ideas he wanted to incorporate into the movie and he kept fighting with Elba. Nahum could have been Alejandro Jodorowsky, but things didn't quite go that way and besides, there already was *one* Jewish Latin-American director. In fact, I'm pretty sure Nahum went to Chile because he was so pissed off at Jodorowsky. If Jodorowsky had gone from Chile to Mexico, then Nahum was going from Mexico to Chile.'

'If he had a cast ready, he must have gotten pretty far,' Amelia mused, looking at the names on the poster.

'He had all the main parts figured out. Rodrigo Tinto was going to be the Hero, same as in *Mars*. He looked great on camera, which is the best I can say of him.'

'You did not like him?' Amelia asked, a little surprised. They seemed to have good chemistry in the movie she'd watched. Then again, it was a film with rayguns and space pirates, nothing but make-believe.

'He had bad breath and a temper.'

'What about the director? Was he likable?'

'No,' Lucía said. Her smile was dismissive but not toward Amelia. She was thinking back to her acting days.

'Also had a temper?'

'No. Darling, some people are not meant to be liked,' Lucía said, with elegant simplicity.

Amelia did not know what that meant. Perhaps, judging by her lack of gigs on Friendrr, Amelia was one of those persons who were not meant to be liked. And judging by the film director's lack of success, they might share more than that single quality.

Lucía showed Amelia a couple more posters before they said goodbye. In the subway concourse, she saw an ad for a virtual assistant, a dancing, singing, 3D hologram: a teenage avatar in a skimpy French maid's outfit who would call you 'Master' and wake you up in the morning with a song.

Her phone, tucked inside her jacket, rang. The specific ring-tone she knew. She had a booking.

She pressed a hand against the cell phone and resisted the impulse to check her messages. Finally, in the stairway to her building, Amelia took out the phone and looked at the screen. It was a booking with Elías, just as she'd suspected. She could press the green button and accept it, or click on the big red 'no' button and discard it. But Miguel would ring her up and ask for an explanation. He was zealous about this stuff. Each rejected booking was a lost commission.

Amelia's index finger hovered over the green button. Accepting was easier than speaking to Miguel. She could spend another two hours locked in Elías's room. After all, he had given her a good rating. Five out of five stars. She remembered when she used to agonize over each rating she obtained, wondering why people hadn't liked her enough. Three stars, two. Even when it was four, she wondered. She had wanted to be like the popular ones, the ones who got bookings every day. If she could up her ratings by a quarter of a point… and there was a bonus for customer satisfaction. It did not amount to anything, not ever.

There was a sour note in her. It drove people away. And Jesus Christ, if she could be more cheerful, nicer, friendlier, she would be, but it was no use.

Green. It didn't matter. Booking confirmed.

•

The view from Elías's apartment at night rendered the city strange. It turned it into an entirely different city. In the distance, a large billboard flickered red, enticing people to 'Visit Mars'. You could emigrate now; see more information online.

The words 'Visit Mars' alternated with the image of a girl in a white spacesuit, holding a helmet under her arm, looking up at the sky. Her face confident. That girl knew things. That girl knew people. That girl was not Amelia, because Amelia was no one.

Elías emerged from the kitchen and handed her a glass of white wine. Amelia continued staring out the tall windows.

'What are you looking at?' he asked.

'That billboard,' she said. The glow of the sign was mesmerizing.

'Mars. It's always Mars,' he said, raising his own glass of wine to his lips.

'You used to be interested in it.'

'I still am. But things are different now. I just... I thought you'd changed your mind.'

He had definitely changed *his* mind. There were no photos in the apartment. His old place was small. Photos on the walls, antique cameras on the shelves, hand-painted stars on the ceiling (those had been her notion). An attempt at bohemian living. It had all been scrubbed clean, just like his face, the whole look of him.

'Never.'

'New Panyu, is that still the idea?' he asked.

Amelia nodded. They had weighed all three options. New Panyu seemed the best bet, the largest settlement. They'd quizzed each other in Mandarin. Yī shēng yī shì, whispered against the curve of her neck. Funny how 'I love you' never sounded the same in different languages. It lost or gained power. In English, it sounded so plain. In Spanish, it became a promise.

'It mustn't be easy,' he said. He looked like he was sorry for her. It irritated Amelia.

'Haven't you heard? The problem with our generation is we don't have enough life goals,' Amelia replied tersely. 'No real challenges.'

'My assistant said they are capping Class B applications.'

'Is she a virtual assistant? I say "she" because it turns out men like to interact with female avatars,' Amelia told him. She thought about the French maid hologram bending over to show her underwear, but surely he could afford real people. He was on Friendrr. Maybe in the mornings, a chick came to play dictation with him, wearing glasses and holding a clipboard.

'No.'

'Do you want me to keep talking to you, or do you want me to be quiet? You need to give me parameters of interaction,' she said.

'Please don't talk like that.'

'You clicked on an app and ordered me like you order Chinese takeout, so don't be offended if I ask if you'd like chopsticks.'

He stared at her and she gave him a faint smile, but it wasn't real. It was the cheap, placid imitation she ironed and took out for clients.

'I'm fine with silence. I just want to have a few drinks. I don't like drinking alone,' he said coolly.

She finished her wine. He refilled the glass. They moved away from the window, sat on different ends of the couch. They drank and she watched him, Elías in profile. She might have taken out her cell phone and played a game, but she wanted him to be uncomfortable, to ask her to look away. He did not and eventually, Amelia relaxed her body and took off her shoes, staring at the ceiling instead. The wine had a hint of citrus. It went to her head quickly. She did not drink too often these days, not when she was paying, and when she did, it was the cheap, watered stuff.

She enjoyed the feeling that came with the alcohol, the indifference as she lay on his couch and threw her head back. She thought of Mars, the Mars in Lucía's movie, tinted in black-and-white, and she shielded her eyes with the back of her hand. She drank more. Time had slowed down in the silence of the room.

Finally, the cell phone beeped and she rose, pressing the heel of her hand against her forehead.

'Well,' she said, standing in front of him and showing him the phone, 'it's over.'

'I can add an extra hour,' he said. 'Let me find my phone.'

He looked panicked as he patted his shirt. He accidentally knocked over the glass of wine, which had been resting on the arm of the couch. The wine splattered over the expensive rug. Amelia chuckled, his distress delighting her. But then he looked hurt and she felt somewhat bad, for a heartbeat.

Amelia sat on his lap, straddling him, her hands resting on his shoulders.

'What's so terrible about being alone?' she asked.

She was being deliberately cruel, teasing him. She disliked it when she sank to such depths, but Amelia was angry, with a quiet sort of anger. She might hurt him now and it would please her.

Elías did not move. He had flailed like a fish out of water a few seconds before as he attempted to find his phone, but now he was perfectly still, staring at her.

'I hate it and you know it.'

'Can't you hire someone to scare the monster who lives under the bed?'

'Amelia,' he said sadly.

She chuckled. 'Aren't we pathetic?' she whispered.

When he tried to kiss her, she wouldn't let him. An arbitrary line but one she had to trace. Fucking was fine. Amelia hadn't fucked in forever. She couldn't bring people to her shared room and the guys she stumbled into were in as much of a fix as she was. She didn't want anyone anyway. It was a struggle to exchange semi-polite words, to pretend she was interested in what came out of a stranger's mouth. *Oh, yes, that's great how you're going to take a coding boot camp and you'll have a job in six weeks or less, except no one is hiring, you idiot.* Or, *That's interesting that you are working as a pimp on the side, but no thanks, buddy, I'm not joining your troupe or whatever the hell it's called these days.*

Who cared what she said to Elías? What she did with him? Who cared at this point? She drew her line and he drew his, which seemed to be the ridiculous notion that they should fuck on the bed. Perhaps he objected to the soiling of the couch.

By the time Amelia zipped up her jeans and started pulling on her shoes, it was too late to take the bus. She had to call a car. She fiddled with the cell phone.

'Will you give me your number?' Elías asked. 'I don't want to keep using this Friendrr thing to find you.'

'I should tell you to make me an offer,' she replied.

He looked at her, offended, but then his gaze softened. She feared perhaps he might bark an amount after all. The thought that he might take her seriously, or that she had said it in anything but mockery, made Amelia reach for her purse. She found a stray piece of paper and scribbled the number.

'Bye,' she told him and headed downstairs.

MARS, SCENE 2

INT. MARS BASE — NIGHT

SPACE EXPLORER sits next to the bed where THE HERO

lies. He is injured. His ship crashed near her father's lab. He dragged himself from the wreckage. She cleans and bandages his wounds. SPACE EXPLORER is not truly a space explorer. The script has been rewritten and she is now ROMANTIC INTEREST, but for the sake of expediency, we will continue to call her SPACE EXPLORER. THE HERO shall remain THE HERO.

SPACE EXPLORER tenderly speaks to THE HERO. This is love at first sight, for both of them. THE HERO tells SPACE EXPLORER how he's come to warn and protect the outpost from a marauding band of SPACE PIRATES. But SPACE EXPLORER's father thinks something else may be afoot. He is a dedicated scientist working on a top secret project and fears THE HERO may be a spy from an evil nation sent to steal his work.

Despite only knowing THE HERO for five minutes, SPACE EXPLORER defends the stranger. Later, during an interlude inside the 'futuristic' outpost, which is a building shaped like an egg, THE HERO kisses SPACE EXPLORER.

Cue swelling music with plenty of violins. Fade to modest black.

5

The Zócalo was being transformed into a cheesy winter wonderland, complete with an ice-skating rink. The city's mayor trotted the rink out each year to please the crowds: free skating, fake snow falling from the sky, a giant Coca-Cola-sponsored tree in the background. It wasn't bread-and-circuses anymore. Now it was icicles and festive music.

This spectacle meant a lot of people wanting to make a buck were ready for action. Teenagers in ratty 'snowman' costumes offering to pose for a photo, peddlers selling soda pop to people waiting in line, and thieves eager to steal purses.

Pili was also downtown. Like anyone their age, Pili had no permanent job, cycling between gigs. Working at the marijuana grow-op, checking ATMs in small businesses to make sure no one was skimming them, selling spare computer parts. Christmas season this year found her servicing the machines at a virtual reality arcade.

'They're probably going to shut them down in a few months,' Pili said. 'All that talk about virtual reality dissociation.'

'Is that a real thing?' Amelia asked.

'Fuck if I know. But the mayor needs to score points with the old farts, and if he can't combat prostitution and crime, this is the next best thing. Virtual reality addiction.'

'It seems like it would be a lot of trouble to shut everyone down. There's a lot of arcades.'

'It'll just go underground. Fuck it. It's slow today, ain't it? We should have gone to the Sanborns.'

They were eating at the Bhagavad, which wasn't a restaurant proper but a weird joint run by a bunch of deluded eco-activists, open only at odd and irregular hours. You paid what you wanted and sat next to walls plastered with flyers warning people against the dangers of vat-meat. Amelia didn't care about veganism, Indian spirituality, or the fight against capitalist oppressors, but she did care about spending as little as possible on her meals. Not that there weren't affordable tacos near the subway, but like everyone joked, long gone were the days when they were at least made with dog. Nowadays, rat was the most likely source of protein. She did not fancy swallowing bubonic plague wrapped in a tortilla.

Unfortunately, the bohemian candor and community spirit of Bhagavad meant the service was terrible. They had spent half an hour waiting for the rice dish of the day, which would inevitably taste like shit watered in piss, but must have some kind of nutritional content, since it kept many a sorry ass like Amelia going.

'Do you have to be back by a certain time?' Amelia asked.

'Kind of.'

'Sorry.'

'It's okay. I'll grab a protein shake if it gets too late,' Pili said, dismissing any issues with a wave of her hand.

Pili was always cool. Nothing ever seemed to faze her, whether it was the cops suddenly appearing and chasing away street vendors while she was trying to hawk computer parts, or the sight of a bloated, dead dog in the middle of the road blocking her path. Perhaps such self-confidence came from a secret, inner well, but Amelia suspected Pili's tremendous height had something to do it. Pili was strong as well. She wore sleeveless shirts, which showed off her arms and her tattoos, and she smiled a lot.

'All right. But if it gets too late, just say the word.'

'Nah, don't worry. Hey, you still need that money?'

'No, I had a gig,' Amelia said, thinking of the two times she'd seen Elías.

'Friendrr, huh? Look, you can make a lot more at the blood clinic. The only requirement is that you have to be twenty-seven or younger, no diseases, no addicts.'

Amelia knew it was easy. That was what scared her. She was inching toward twenty-seven and after that, what could she sell? What could she do when she wasn't even fit to be a blood bag? She didn't want to get hooked on that kind of money, but there didn't seem to be anything else beckoning her.

Giovanni Schiaparelli peered into his telescope and he thought he saw canals on Mars. Lowell imagined alien civilizations:

'Framed in the blue of space, there floats before the observer's gaze a seeming miniature of his own Earth, yet changed by translation to the sky.'

Mars, Amelia's Mars. Always Mars, in every stolen and quiet moment, as she folded a napkin and refolded it.

'You've got that face again, Amelia.'

'What face?' Her fingers stilled on the napkin.

'Like you don't care I'm here.'

'Of course I care.'

'If you need the money, just ask. I can lend you the stuff. I know you'll pay me back.'

'It's not the money.'

Well, it wasn't only the money. Not that she was doing fine in terms of cash flow. It was Elías and she couldn't discuss him with Pili. It was Mars and there was no point in discussing that with anybody.

'I'm throwing a party Friday. You should come. It'll do you good,' Pili suggested.

'I have to go to an art gallery. I'm trying to meet someone there about a gig,' Amelia said.

'What time is that?'

'Eight.'

'We'll be up late. Just stop by after your meeting.'

'I don't know,' Amelia said. She turned her head, staring at a neon pink flyer stuck on the wall that showed several politicians drawn in the shape of pigs, wearing ties and jackets. They were eating slops.

• • •

It was hard to believe that this metropolis, when viewed from Presidente Masaryk, was the place where Amelia lived, scrubbed clean, with a Ferrari dealership and luxurious shops. The city attempted to eliminate the grimy fingerprints that clung to the rest of the urban landscape. Private security kept a tight watch on beggars and indigents. There were trees here – not plastic ones either. Real bits of greenery, while elsewhere a sea of cement swallowed the soul.

She had ventured down Masaryk often when she was with Elías. His interest in photography led them there to inspect the art galleries that perched themselves near the wide avenue. The place where Anastasia had her opening was a new gallery. Amelia had never visited it with her ex-boyfriend.

She wore the nice gray dress which had caused her so many headaches. It was classic, elegant, and it paired perfectly with one of the few pairs of heels she owned. She'd slicked her hair back into a ponytail, put on eyeshadow, which she didn't bother with most mornings.

The theme of the exhibit was indeed, obviously, crassly 'meat'. There were hunks of beef hanging from the ceiling, cube-shaped meat that gently palpitated. Alive. Vat-meat, coerced into this shape. The head of a bull atop a pillar stared at Amelia. It smelled. Coppery, intense, the smell. It made Amelia wrinkle her nose. The other guests did not seem to mind the stench, long, glass flutes in their hands, laughter on their lips.

Amelia saw Anastasia Brito surrounded by a wide circle of admirers. She waited, trying to slip to her side, and found herself squeezed next to three people who were having an animated discussion about fish.

'Soon, the only thing left to eat is going to be jellyfish. It's the one animal thriving in the ocean,' a man with a great, bald pate said.

'The indigenous people in – fuck it, I don't know where, some shit place in Asia – they are launching some sort of lawsuit,' replied a young man.

'It's really sad,' said a woman with cherry-red lips. 'But what is anyone supposed to do about it?'

The young man stopped a waiter, grabbing a shrimp and popping it in his mouth. Amelia traced a vector toward Anastasia and correctly inserted herself at her elbow, catching her attention.

'Hi, Anastasia, it's good to see you again. This is all very interesting.'

Anastasia smiled at Amelia, but Amelia could tell she did not remember her, that for a few seconds, she simply threw her a canned, indifferent smile before her eyes focused on her and the smile turned into an O of surprise

'Amelia. Why… it's been ages. What are you doing here?' she asked, and she looked like she'd discovered gum stuck under her shoe.

'Fernanda told me about the show and I decided to give it a look,' Amelia said. She'd assumed Fernanda would mention she would be showing up, that something would have been indicated. She should not have expected such attention to detail.

'Well,' Anastasia said. She said nothing else. The canned smile returned, brighter than before, but Anastasia's eyes scanned the room, as if she were looking for someone, anyone, to pull her out of this unwanted reunion.

Amelia dug in. She'd made the trip to the stupid gallery, after all. Marta was always chiding her about her lack of initiative. So, Amelia smiled back and tried to move the conversation in the required direction.

'Fernanda said you are putting together something new. Something about plants. She thought I might be able to help you with it.'

'How?' Anastasia asked.

'I do have qualifications in botany, and I've gotten good at hacking genes. Here's my card,' Amelia said, handing Anastasia the little plastic square with her contact information. She'd spent money getting this new card, money she didn't have, so she wouldn't hand out a number scribbled on a crumpled napkin. Anastasia held it with the tips of her fingers. Her nails were painted a molten gold. The tips of her eyelashes had been inked in gold to match the nails.

'No offense, Amelia, but what do you know about art?'

'A few things. Elías and I spent a lot of time around galleries and museums.'

'That's great, but wasn't that such a long time ago?' she asked, and her words carried a hint of disgust.

The smile once more. The silence. Amelia remembered all the times Miguel had told her success was all about acquiring a positive attitude. She dearly wished to dial him and tell him he was an idiot. Instead, she bade Anastasia a quick goodbye and went in search of a car.

6

Pili lived in a rough area. It wasn't La Joya or Barrio Norte, but Santa María la Ribera kept getting more fucked-up each year. There were benefits to this, mainly that when Pili threw a party – even if the whole floor joined in, blasting music from each apartment – the neighbors upstairs couldn't do shit about it. If they called the cops, the cops were liable to show up, have a couple of beers, dance a cumbia, and depart.

Pili threw parties often and Amelia declined any invitations just as often. She had internalized her mother's directives: study, work hard, don't drink, no boys. It was difficult to shake those manacles off. Whenever she did, Amelia felt guilty. But she didn't want to think about her conversation with Anastasia at the gallery – the fucking humiliation of it – and the music at Pili's apartment eviscerated coherent thoughts.

Amelia pushed into Pili's place, trying to find her friend amongst the dancers and the people resting on the couch, chatting, drinking, smoking. Finally, she spotted Pili in a corner, laughing her generous laughter.

'Amelia!' Pili said. 'You came after all. And you look like a secretary or some shit like that.'

Amelia glanced down at her clothes, knowing she was overdressed. 'Yeah. No time to change.'

'Look, we've got a ton of booze. Have a drink. Tito! Tito, she needs a drink!'

Amelia accepted the drink with a nod of the head. The booze was strong. It had a sour taste. With some luck, it had been fabricated in Pili's dirty bathtub. If not, it was liable to have come from somewhere much worse. But it wouldn't be hazardous. Pili didn't allow additives in her home.

She watched the partygoers flirting, chatting, dancing. Amelia wondered why some people found it easy to be happy, like an automatic switch had been turned on in them the moment they were born, while she watched in silence, at a distance, unmoved by the merriment. Amelia's cup was efficiently refilled through the night. Although she neither danced nor spoke much, she leaned back on a couch and listened to the beat of the music, the booze turning her limbs liquid.

A guy she knew vaguely, a rare animal trader, sat next to her for a while. He was carrying an owl in a cage. The owl was dead, and he told her he was taking it to a guy who was going to stuff it right after the party.

'Am I boring you?' the guy asked. Amelia did not even try to pretend politeness. She drank from her plastic cup and utterly ignored him, because last thing she needed was this guy trying to sell her a fucking dead owl and it was obvious where his monologue was going.

Owl Man got up. Another guy sat in the vacated space, his friend hovering next to the sofa. They complained that Soviets (fucking FUCKING REDS, were their exact words) were sending fake tequila to Hamburg. One of them had made money exporting the liquor to Germany, but that was over and the man who was standing up was now reduced to something-something. She didn't catch the details, but she knew the story. Everyone had a story like that. They'd all done better at one point. They'd run better cons, done better drugs, drunk better booze, but now they were skimming.

The guy sitting next to her was trying to elbow her out of the way so his friend could sit down. Amelia knew if she had been cooler, more interesting, more something, he wouldn't have tried that. But she was not. The appraisal of her limitations provided her with a defiant stubbornness. She planted her feet firmly on the ground, did not budge an inch, and both of the men walked away, irritated.

She dozed off, thought of Mars. Black-and-white, like in Lucía's movie. Rayguns and space pirates, the ridiculous Mars they'd dreamt in a previous century. Far off in the distance, blurry, out of focus, she saw a figure that had not been in the movie.

There are only two plots, Lucía had told her one evening. *A person goes on a journey and a stranger comes into town.* Amelia couldn't tell if this was one or the other.

What do you do in the meantime? she wondered. *What do you do while you wait for your plot to begin?*

The stranger's shadow darkened the doorway, elongated. The doorway of the bar. The space bar. It was always a bar.

Western. So then, this was *A stranger comes into town. Fate knocks on your door.*

She woke curled up on Pili's couch. Many of the partygoers were still around, passed out on the floor and chairs. Amelia took out her phone, wincing as she looked at the time. It was past noon. She had two text messages and a voicemail. The voicemail and one of the messages were from her irritated sister, who wanted to remind Amelia she was supposed to babysit that night at seven. The other text message was from Elías. *What are you up to?*

Amelia hesitated before slowly typing an answer. *Woke up with a huge hangover.*

A couple of minutes later and her phone rang. Amelia slipped out of Pili's apartment and answered the phone as she walked down the stairs.

'How huge of a hangover?' Elías asked.

'Pretty massive. Why?'

'I have a great trick for that.'

'Oh?'

'If you stopped by, I'd show you. It's an effective recipe.'

'I am a mess and I am on babysitting duty at seven o'clock.'

'That's ages away. Should I send a car?'

Amelia emerged from the building and blinked at the sudden onslaught of daylight. She really shouldn't.

She accepted the offer.

•

Amelia reeked of cigarette smoke and booze, but part of the pleasure was swanning into Elías's pristine apartment and tossing her stinky jacket onto his couch. She was a foreign element introduced into a laboratory. That was what his home reminded her of: the sterile inside of a lab.

She leaned on her elbows against his white table and watched him as he chopped a green pepper in the kitchen.

'Was it a good party?' he asked.

'Does it matter?' she replied with a shrug.

'Why else go to a party, then?'

She did not reply, instead observing him intently. It was funny how you thought you remembered someone. You sketched their face boldly in your mind, but when you saw them again, you realized how far you were from their true likeness. Had he always been that height, for example? Had he moved the way he did, long strides as he reached the table? Had he smiled at her like that? Maybe she'd constructed false memories of him, fake angles.

'Here.'

'I'm not drinking that,' Amelia said, pointing at the glass full of green goo Elías was offering her.

'It's just vegetables, an egg and hot sauce,' he told her.

Amelia took a sip. It was terrible, as she'd expected, and she quickly handed Elías the glass back. He chuckled and brushed a limp strand of hair away from her face.

'Did it help at all?'

'No.'

'Well, I tried.'

She placed the glass on the table and walked around the living room, looking at the blank walls.

'You have no photos at all, no decorations.'

She didn't mind. Her room – could she even call it hers when she shared it with her niece? – was littered with scraps of her past. She knew it too well, every crack on the wall, every spring on the bed. It reminded her of who she was and who she'd never been. Elías's apartment was a soothing blank slate, a pale cocoon.

One might molt and transform here.

'I don't know if I'm going to stay long. Besides, I don't take photos anymore,' he said.

'Why not?'

'Grew out of it, I suppose.'

But not, perhaps, out of her. Amelia allowed herself to be flattered by that thought and smiled at him.

He slid next to her, slid across that fine line she was trying to draw between affection and desire. There was that irresponsible wild feeling in her gut, all youthful need. Amelia had not felt young in ages. She was about fifty-five in her head, but he reminded her of her awkward teenage years, things she'd forgotten. It was exciting. She thought she'd lost that, that she'd outgrown it. Even if this was just horrid déjà vu, it felt like something. It was pleasant to remember she was twenty-five, that she wasn't that old, that it wasn't all over.

Her hair smelled like tobacco and she guessed her makeup was a bit of a mess, smudged mascara and only the faintest trace of lipstick, but he wasn't complaining. She supposed it might be part of the appeal.

Slumming it, Elías style.

She truly did not know what he was getting out of this. Best not to dig too deeply. Best to just fall into bed with him.

•

His arm was over his eyes when he spoke, shielding himself from a stray, persistent ray of light peeking through the curtains.

'Do you really still think about going to Mars?' he asked.

On Mars, they would be cold. His breath would rise like a plume. They'd huddle under furs. They'd fight space pirates and save the world. Well... not on the real Mars. On the Mars of that black-and-white flick she'd watched.

'Is it that shocking?' she replied.

'No,' he said. 'I think you loved that planet more than you loved me.'

'You can't be jealous of a hunk of rock.'

'I was.'

'Planets keep to their orbits,' she said tersely.

He looked at her and she thought this was going to end quickly. That he wouldn't put up with recriminations, exclamations. The amusement might be over already. She headed to the shower. But when she came out of the bathroom, he grabbed her hand.

She reached home at quarter past seven to a very furious sister, but fortunately Marta had somewhere to be and she did not have time to quiz Amelia about her whereabouts. Once the door to the apartment slammed shut, Amelia sat on the couch next to her nieces. The TV was on and an announcer was laughing.

MARS, SCENE 3

EXT. MARS BASE – NIGHT

SPACE EXPLORER, holding future goggles, spots marauders near the outpost. She hurries back to alert her father and THE HERO about this. It must be the SPACE PIRATES who have come to ransack the outpost and steal THE SCIENTIST's invention.

There is a discussion about how to hold them off. Montage of preparations, then a battle. Despite THE HERO's best efforts, the outpost is overrun and the SPACE PIRATES break through the defenses. The survivors are surrounded by bad guys, but THE HERO has managed to escape.

ENTER EVIL SPACE QUEEN. Maximum sexiness in a dress that does its utmost best to show tits. She taunts the good guys and demands THE SCIENTIST hand over the gizmo he's been working on, which will give SPACE QUEEN incredible powers, yadda-yadda. THE SCIENTIST refuses, but SPACE QUEEN thinks some time in a torture chamber will change his mind.

SPACE QUEEN decrees THE SPACE EXPLORER will be wed to her brother, who doubles as the EVIL HENCHMAN, therefore ensuring absolute control of the planet. Three exclamation points.

THE SPACE EXPLORER – the *girl*, this is nothing but a girl, diminutive and frail – faints. SPACE QUEEN's evil laughter.

7

'The biggest problem, of course, was that Nahum kept changing things,' Lucía said. Her turban was silver that day. It looked like she had wrapped tinfoil around her head. And yet, Lucía managed to appear regal as she sat on the couch, with a few pages from her memoir on her lap.

She offered Amelia the bowl with pomegranate seeds and Amelia took a couple. 'He was an insomniac, so he'd wake up in the middle of the night, find a problem with the shooting script, jot down some notes. Then he phoned the writer at around 3 a.m. and the writer would promise he'd make changes. Which he did. But then, Nahum couldn't sleep again, and so on and so forth.

'He was on drugs. I was so young I couldn't even tell if this was a normal shoot or not. Convent-educated girl. A friend of a friend of my father was the one who got me my first audition and it all happened quickly, easily. A fluke.'

Lucía frowned, her eyes little, tiny polished beads staring at Amelia. She was a Coatlicue, an angry, withered, Earth Mother goddess, her forked tongue about to fly out of her mouth and demand blood. Amelia's mother had been hard too. She watched over Amelia like a hawk and did not watch over Marta at all because Marta was too rebellious. Malleable Amelia was subject to all the commands of their mother. As in, obtain straight As, no social life, no boyfriends until there came that rich boy her mother approved of. Then she'd gotten sick and it had gotten even worse.

Amelia swallowed the pomegranate seeds.

'And now this bitch says I can't mention any of that.'

'I'm sorry?' Amelia asked.

'Nahum's daughter. Some meddlesome fool informed her I was typing out my memoir and her daddy is included in it. Would you believe she had the audacity to phone me a couple of days ago and threaten me with a lawsuit if I say her father did drugs? He ate mushrooms out of little plastic bags, for God's sake. He was lovely and he was a mess. Who cares at this point? They're all dead.'

Lucía leaned back, her face growing lax. She lost the look of a stone idol and became an old lady, wrinkles and liver spots and the flab under her neck, like a monstrous turkey. The old lady squinted.

'What do you intend to do on Mars?' Lucía asked, but she glanced away from Amelia, as if she didn't want her to discern her expression.

'Grow plants,' Amelia muttered.

'You can do that?'

'Hydroponics. It's the same technology you'd use for a marijuana grow-op on Earth. Everything is inside a dome. They are terraforming with microbes, but it will take a long time for anything close to farmland to exist outside a biodome.'

'I suppose it's not like in my movie. You can't walk around in a dress without a helmet.'

'No. But the suits are very light now, very flexible.' Modern-looking suits, strips of luminescent thread running down the leg.

Amelia had pictured herself in one of those suits one out of each seven days of the week.

'And you can fly there. Just like that?'

'Not quite. If you get a Class C visa, you can go as a worker, but they garnish your wages. They pay themselves back your fare. Half your pay goes to the company that got you there and they play all kinds of tricks so you owe them even more in the end. But if you get a Class B visa, it's different. You are an investor. You pay your passage and you do whatever you want.'

'You never do what you want, Amelia. There are always limits. I should know. I got my Mars. It was made of cardboard and wire, and the costume designer stabbed me with pins when they were adjusting my dress and it wasn't nearly enough.'

There's no comparison, Amelia wanted to say. No comparison at all between a limited, laughable attempt at an acting career that ended with a whimper, and Amelia's thoughts on crop physiology and modified plants that could survive in iron-rich soil. Amelia, staring at the vastness of the sky from her tiny outpost. Amelia on the Red Planet.

'Why Mars? You could grow crops here, couldn't you?' Lucía asked.

Amelia shrugged. It would take too long to explain. Fortunately, Lucía did not ask more about Mars and Amelia did not steer the conversation back toward Lucía's memoir. When she got home, she lay in her bed and looked for photos of Lucía. Gorgeous in the black-and-white stills, the smile broad and wild, the hair shiny. Then she looked for Nahum, but there were few of him. It was the same couple of photos: two headshots showing a man with a cigarette in his left hand, the other with his arms crossed. His life was a short stub. Three movies. As for the scriptwriter, she found he'd used a pen name for his erotic novels and you could buy them used for less than the cost of a hamburger. But at least they'd all left a trail behind them, a clue to their existence. When Amelia died, there would be nothing.

On her napkins at the coffee shop, she now drew faces. Lucía's face in her youth, the Hero's face, the Space Queen. She sketched the glass city of the movie, the space pirates and a rocket. Amelia had a talent for drawing. If she'd been born in another century, she might have been a botanical illustrator. Better yet, a rich naturalist, happily documenting the flora of the region. An Ynes Mexia, discovering a new genus.

But Amelia existed in the narrow confines of the Now, in the coffee shop, her cell phone with a tiny crack on its screen resting by her paper cup.

She was out of coffee and considering phoning Elías. It was not love sickness, like when she'd been younger, just boredom. A more dangerous state.

She bit her lip. Fortunately, Pili called right then and Amelia suddenly had something to do: go to the police precinct. Pili had been busted for something and she needed Amelia to bribe the cops. Amelia cast a worried look at her bank account, at the pitiful savings column she had ear-marked for Mars, and got going.

The cops were fairly tractable and they did not harass her, which was the best you could say about these situations.

It only took Amelia an hour until they shoved Pili outside the station and the two women began walking toward the subway. On Mina, the romería for the holidays was ready for business, with mechanical games and people dressed as the Three Kings. Santa Claus was there too, and so were several Disney princesses. Tired-looking parents dragged their toddlers by the hand and teenagers made out on the Ferris wheel.

Pili had a busted lip, but she was smiling and she insisted they buy an esquite. Amelia agreed and Pili shoved the grains of corn into her mouth while they walked around the perimeter of the brightly lit assemblage of holiday-related inanities.

'The bastards didn't even bother giving me a sandwich,' Pili said. 'I was there for eight-fucking-hours.'

'What did they nab you for?'

'I was selling something,' Pili said. She did not specify what she'd been selling and Amelia did not ask. 'Hey, the posadas start tomorrow.'

'Do they?' Amelia replied. She was not keeping track, did not care for champurrado and tamales.

'Sure. We gonna go bounce around the city, or what?'

'Depends if I have any dough.'

'Shit, you don't need no dough for a posada. That's the whole point. We'll crash one or two or three.'

Amelia smiled, but she felt no mirth. She thought of snot-nosed children breaking piñatas while she tried to drink a beer in peace.

Before they separated, Pili promised to pay Amelia back the money. This swapping of funds was erratic and pointless; they both simply kept deferring their financial woes, but Amelia nodded and tried to put up a pleasant façade because Pili had just had a rough day.

Once Amelia was alone, all the things she hadn't wanted to think about returned to her like the tide. Thoughts of cash flow issues, the vague notion that she should visit the blood clinic, her musings on Mars.

She wanted to visit Elías without any warning, just crash on his couch.

She wanted to go to a bar and buy over-priced cocktails instead of sipping Pili's counterfeit booze.

She wanted to look for an apartment for herself and never answer her sister's voicemails.

She wanted so many things. She wanted the Mare Erythraeum laid before her feet.

Between one and the other – between Scylla and Charybdis like Sting had sung in an old, old song she'd heard at a club in Monterrey, a club she'd visited with Elías in the heady, early days when the world seemed overflowing with possibilities – between those options, she picked Elías.

She had not dialed him, but now she pressed the phone against her ear and waited.

The phone rang two times and then a female voice answered. 'Hello?'

Amelia, sitting in the subway, her hand on a bit of graffiti depicting a rather anatomically incorrect penis painted on the window pane, managed a cough but no words.

'Hello?' said the woman again.

'I was looking for Elías Bertoliat,' she said.

'He's in the shower. Do you want to leave a message?'

'It's about his Friendrr account,' Amelia lied. 'We've closed it down, as he requested.'

She hung up and lifted her legs, gathering them against her chest. Across the aisle, a homeless kid, his hands blackened with soot, chewed gum. A woman selling biopets – lizards with three tails – hawked her wares in a high-pitched voice. Amelia let three stations go by before switching trains, back-tracking and getting off at the right spot.

• • •

Only narcissists and Heroes stood unwavering against the odds. Most rational people got a clue and found their bearings. Amelia found the blood clinic. She'd been putting it off, fabricating excuses, but truth was, she needed cash. Not the drip-drip cash of her Friendrr gigs, something more substantial.

The clinic was tucked around the corner from a subway station. The counter was a monstrous green, with a sturdy partition and posters all-round of smiling, happy people.

'Who's poking us today? It's not Armando, is it?' the man ahead of Amelia asked. He must have known all the technicians by name, who was good with a needle and who sucked.

The employee manning the reception desk asked for Amelia's ID and eyed her carefully. She was told to sit in front of a screen and answer twenty-five questions, part of the health profile. Next time, she could just walk in, show a card, and forget the questions.

Afterward, a technician talked to Amelia for three short minutes, then handed her a number and directed her to sit and wait in an adjacent room.

Amelia sat down, sandwiched between a young woman playing a game on her cell phone and a man who rocked back and forth, muttering under his breath.

When they called her number, Amelia went into a room where they pricked her finger to do a few quick tests, measuring her iron levels. Then it was time to draw the blood. She lay on a recliner, staring at the ceiling. There was nothing to do, so she tried to nap, but it proved impossible. The whirring of a machine nearby wouldn't allow her to close her eyes.

Space flights were merely an escape, a fleeing away from oneself. Or so Carl Jung said. But lying on the recliner, thinking she could listen to the sloshing of her blood through her veins, Amelia could envision no escape. She could not picture Mars right that second and her eyes fixed on the ceiling.

On the way out, Amelia glanced at a young man waiting in the reception area, noticing the slight indentation on his arm, the tell-tale mark that showed he was a frequent donor. Pili had it too. They crossed glances and pretended they had not seen each other.

Walking back to her apartment, Amelia realized the courtyard kids were in full festive mode: they had built a bonfire. They were dragging a plastic Christmas tree into the flames. Several of them had wreaths of tinsel wrapped around their necks. One had Christmas ornaments tied to his long hair. They greeted her as they always did: with hoots and jeers. This time, rather than slipping away, Amelia slipped closer to them, closer to the flames, intent on watching the conflagration. It seemed something akin to a pagan ritual, but then, the kids wouldn't have known anything about this. It was simple mayhem to them, their own version of a posada.

A young man looped an arm around Amelia's shoulders and offered a swig of his bottle. Amelia pressed the bottle against her lips and drank. It tasted of putrid oranges and alcohol. After a couple of minutes, the boy slid away from her, called away, and Amelia stood there, holding the bottle in her left hand.

She stepped back, sitting by the entrance of her building, her eyes still on the fire as she sipped the booze. Sparks were shooting in the air and the tree was melting.

She knew she shouldn't be drinking, especially whatever was in the bottle, but the night was cold.

At the clinic, they'd told her plasma was 90 percent water and she mumbled that number to herself. When she closed her eyes, she thought of Mars, black-and-white like in Lucía's movie, seen through a lens that had been coated in Vaseline. Bloated, disfigured, beautiful Mars.

When the phone rang, she answered it without even bothering to check who it was, eyes still closed, the cool surface of the screen against her cheek.

'Amelia, I think you called yesterday,' Elías said.

'I think your girlfriend answered the phone,' Amelia replied, snapping her eyes open.

'My fiancée,' he said. 'My father picked her for me.'

'That's nice.'

'Can you come over? I want to explain.'

'I'm busy.'

'What are you doing?'

'Something's burning,' she said, staring at the bonfire. The teenagers running around it looked like devils, shadow things that bubbled up from the ground. It was the booze, or she was tired of everything, and she rubbed her eyes.

'Amelia—'

'Pay me. Send me a goddamn transfer right now and I'll go.'

She thought he'd say no, but after a splintered silence, he spoke. 'OK.'

'You'll have to send a car too. I am not taking the subway.'

'OK.'

She gave him the necessary info. When the driver appeared, it was ages or mere minutes later and she had forgotten about the deal. Cinderella going to the ball, escorted into a sleek, black car instead of a pumpkin. She wondered if this was Elías's regular driver, his car, or just a hired one. When they'd dated, he'd owned a red sports car, but that was ages ago.

Amelia tossed the bottle out the window once the car got in motion.

8

There was an expiry date to being a loser. You could make 'bad choices' and muck about until you were around twenty-one, but after that, God forbid you committed any mistakes, deviating from the anointed path, even though life was more like a game of Snakes and Ladders than a straight line.

Amelia realized that anyone peering in would pass easy judgment on her. Stupid woman, too old to be stumbling through life the way she did, stumbling into her ex-boyfriend's apartment again, shrugging out of her jacket and staring out the window at the sign in the distance which advertised Mars.

She could almost hear the voice-over: *Watch Amelia act like a fool, again.*

But not everyone got to be the Hero of the flick.

'What is that?' Elías said, pointing at the bandage on her arm. She had not even realized she still had it on.

'I went to a clinic. They drew blood,' Amelia replied, her fingers careless, sliding over the bandage.

'Are you sick?'

'I was selling blood. Old farts love to pump young plasma through their veins. Hey, maybe some of your dad's friends are going to get my blood. Wouldn't that be hilarious?'

'You should have told me if you needed money,' he replied.

'Do you think I'm on Friendrr for fun? Of course I need money. Everyone does.'

Except you, she thought. She wondered how the transaction he'd performed would show on his account. Two thousand tajaderos for the ex-girlfriend. File under Miscellaneous.

'Do you have any water? I'm supposed to stay hydrated,' Amelia said.

He fetched her a glass and they sat on the couch.

'Amelia, my fiancée… it's what my father wants. I don't care about her. I don't even touch her,' Elías said. He looked mournful. Sad-eyed Elías.

'It's going to be difficult for you to have children that way,' Amelia replied. 'Or are you thinking of renting a womb? Would you like to rent mine? It's all for sale.'

'Amelia, for God's sake!' he said, scandalized.

'You are an asshole. You are a selfish, entitled prick,' she told him, but she said it in a matter-of-fact tone. There was a surprisingly small amount of rancor in her voice. She sipped her water.

'Yes, all right,' he agreed and she could tell he wanted to say something else. Amelia did not let him speak.

'Where did your girlfriend go? Or is she coming back? I'm not willing to hide in the closet.'

'She's headed back to Monterrey. She just came to... my father wants me back there permanently. He sent her to pressure me and I spent all my time trying to avoid interacting with her. I—'

'What's your girlfriend's name?'

'Fiancée. Amelia, *you* are avoiding *me*.'

'How am I avoiding you? I'm sitting here, like you wanted. You're telling me you'll get married. Congratulations.'

'Listen,' he told her. 'Nothing has been said; nothing has been done. I'm here.'

I'm here too, she thought. *I'm stuck*. Not only in the city. Stuck with him. She considered leaning forward and slapping him, just for kicks. Mostly, because she wasn't even mad at him. She thought she should be, but instead she lounged on his couch while he was fidgeting.

'I lied to you, OK? I didn't find you on Friendrr by chance. Fernanda mentioned you were there one day; Fernanda and I, we keep in touch. I went looking for you. Every goddamned day, I looked at your profile, at your picture, telling myself I wasn't going to contact you.

'I should have gone to New Panyu with you,' he concluded. 'My dad wouldn't give me the money, but I should have done something.'

There was that scalding feeling in her stomach. Amelia loathed it. She didn't want to be angry at him. She'd been angry and that was what had started this ridiculous train of events. If she could be indifferent, it would all collapse.

'Oh, you couldn't. I was just another girl. I'm still just another girl,' she told him, unable to keep her mouth shut, although at this point, the less said, the better. She had a headache. The booze she'd imbibed was probably a toxic chemical. *Radioactive flesh*, she mused. *Radioactive everything*.

But it was Elías who looked a little sick, a little feverish, and Amelia pressed cool fingers against his cheek, her mouth curving into a not-quite-smile as she edged close to him.

'You're just another guy, you know?'

He caught her hands between his and frowned.

'I'm sorry,' he said. 'I don't know *how* to live with you. I never did.'

'I don't want you to be sorry.'

'What do you want?'

You used to mean something to me, she wanted to tell him. *You used to mean something and then you* used *it all up without even giving it three seconds of your time. And I want to walk out and leave you with nothing, just like that, in this beautiful apartment with your wonderful, expensive things.*

Amelia looked aside.

'Let's go to sleep. I'm tired,' she muttered, moving from the couch to his bedroom, as though she lived there.

She *was* exhausted. This was true. But it was also true that she could have called a car and stumbled home. Sure, she assured herself it was a safety matter, that she might collapse outside her building or pass out in the car. And yet, she could have called someone, perhaps Pili, to pick her up.

She didn't want to leave. She wanted to act the part of a fool. As simple and as complicated as that.

He wanted to make it up to her, he said, although he did not specify exactly what he was making up for: his callous ghosting or his most recent omissions. He proposed lunch, then he'd take her shopping. He wanted to buy her a dress so they could go dancing on New Year's Eve.

Amelia looked at her text messages. There were five from her sister. She was not worried because Amelia had never come home the previous night. Instead, the messages were castigating her because Amelia needed to take the girls to school and cook lunch.

Amelia deleted the messages. She grabbed his arm and they went out.

She'd never taken advantage of Elías's social position when they were dating. A dinner here and there but no expensive presents. Of course, back then, he'd been playing at bohemian living. The nice car was his one wealth marker. He kept it tucked in a garage and they took it for a spin once in a while. Once in a while, there had also been an extravagance: the sudden trip to Monterrey where they partied for a weekend, the ability to sail into a popular nightclub while losers waited outside for the bouncer to approve of their looks, but these were random, few events. He wanted to be an artist, after all, an artist with a capital A, long-suffering, starving for his creative pursuits.

Now he had shredded those pretenses and now she did not bother telling herself things such as money did not matter. In the high-tech dressing room with interactive mirrors, she made the outfits she wanted to try on bounce across the slick, glass surface. She could take a selfie with this mirror. She wondered if anyone ever did. She assumed some people must, people who did not look at the fabric on display and wished to wreck half a dozen dresses, leaving a man with an immense bill to cover as they slipped out the back of the store.

The so-elegant employee packed her dress in pale pink tissue paper and handed her a bag. She was on Mr. Bertoliat's account now. And though Amelia supposed 'Mr. Bertoliat' meant well, she hated him when he smiled at her as they stood by the counter.

But by the time they sat down at the sushi restaurant, with its patio and its pond full of koi fish and its impeccable white plastic furniture made to resemble bamboo, she wanted to do anything but fight. Whether the blood siphoned from her veins had also drained another part of her, or she simply had latched on to a new type of debilitating obsession, she did not know.

'I heard, soon, there will be nothing but jellyfish in the seas,' she said, looking at the pond. 'All the fish will be gone.'

'I find that unlikely,' he said.

There was a restaurant in the city, run by a Parisian chef who charged $800 for a three-course meal cooked with 'Indigenous' ingredients, plated on large stones. He had thought to take her there, but reservations were required.

When your credit card could afford such meals, she supposed many things were 'unlikely'. She supposed, with the hefty allowance he received, he could ask that a polar bear be dragged to rest on his plate after being stuffed with a dolphin. And not a cloned bear. The real damned thing too.

'I guess it won't matter when it happens,' she told him with a shrug. 'Not to you.'

'Are you interested in zoology now?' he asked. 'Fisheries?'

'I'm hardly interested in anything. I spend about three hours every day drawing things that don't matter and another three fiddling with my cell phone.'

'That sounds the same as me. Sometimes, I take photos. But not too often.'

'You had a good eye,' she admitted and he smiled at that.

Elías looked rather fine that day, very polished. She'd always loved looking at him. She knew it was bad to enjoy somebody's looks so much. After all, the flesh faded. But when she'd been nineteen, she had not been thinking about what sixty-nine-year-old Elías would look like and now it seemed equally preposterous to self-flagellate because he was still handsome.

If she was shallow, that seemed the least of her issues.

'I should mention this right now. I have to go to Monterrey for Christmas. I can't get out of it. I'm not going to disappear, I swear. But it's Christmas and my father wants to see me. I'm his only kid. I'll be back for New Year's.

'And I'll break it off with my fiancée while I'm there,' Elías added.

'Don't start making promises,' she muttered.

'I want to do it. For you.'

In the pond, the koi swam and she wondered if they were authentic koi, or if they had been modified. They could be mechanical. They could even be holograms. She'd seen things like that before.

Elías held out a plastic card. 'Here. This is a spare key to my apartment. You can hang out there while I'm gone. Ask the concierge to get you anything you want: food, drinks. OK?'

She toyed with the card, thinking she could lose it in the subway, toss it into the sewer. But when he bid her goodbye and put her in a car, he leaned down for a kiss and Amelia allowed it.

•

Amelia went up the stairs to her apartment. There, on the fourth landing, she found a glue trap with a squealing rat. She had chanced upon such sights before and they did not bother her.

She stared at the rat. Before she could figure out a proper

course of action, she attempted to peel the vermin off the trap. She managed to rip the board off the rat, but the animal bit her. She pressed her hand against the wound and hurried into her apartment, looking for the rubbing alcohol and the cotton amongst the mess of expired prescriptions (these had belonged to her mother; nobody bothered tossing them out, shrines to her memory), hair clips and makeup, which were scattered upon a small shelf.

'What the hell happened to you?' Marta asked.

'Rat bit me,' Amelia said.

'You better not have rabies.'

Amelia opened the bottle of alcohol and soaked a cotton ball in it, then carefully cleaned the wound. Her sister was by the door, but had not offered to assist her. She merely stood there, arms crossed, staring at Amelia.

'Where were you?'

'I stayed with a friend,' Amelia said.

'You fuck up my routine when you don't take the girls to school.'

'I don't do this regularly.'

'Sure, you don't.'

'Look, you want to make sure your kids get to school on time? *You* take them,' Amelia said, wondering if they had any damned Band-Aids, or if she was going to have to wrap a towel around her hand.

'I pay the bulk of the rent.'

Amelia opened a cardboard box and placed two Band-Aids on her hand, forming an X.

'I pay for the bulk of the groceries,' Marta added.

Amelia slid her thumb across the Band-Aids, smoothing them down. Maybe she could have the bite checked out at the sanitation clinic, although that would mean arriving early and waiting forever.

'I paid for Mother's medicines,' Marta said, holding up three fingers in the air.

'And I took care of her!' Amelia yelled, turning to her sister, losing her shit, unable to keep a middling tone of voice anymore. 'I was here, every day and every night, and where were you when she was pissing herself in the middle of the night? Two years, Marta! Two years of that. I threw my whole career and every single chance I ever had out the window because you wouldn't help me take care of her!'

They had never discussed it because it would have been bad to say such things, but it had to be said. Amelia was tired of pretending that what happened to her had just been bad luck, bad karma. She might have been able to finish her degree, she might have kept the scholarship, but Marta had been way too busy playing house with her then-husband to come round the apartment complex. But when he left her and Mother died, then she came real quick to take possession of the shitty little apartment.

'What makes you think you had a chance?' Marta replied.

'I better go to the sanitation clinic. Wouldn't want to give your kids rabies,' Amelia said, brushing past her sister and rushing out of the apartment.

On the stairs, she found the rat she had released from the trap. It was dead. Her efforts had been in vain.

Amelia kicked the corpse away and marched outside.

MARS, SCENE 4

INT. CELL – NIGHT

SPACE EXPLORER sits in a cell. Outside, it is night and the nights on Mars are unlike the nights on Earth: pitch-black darkness, the eerie silence of the red-hued sand plains. Despite her extraordinary location, the girl's cell is mundane. Iron bars, a rectangular window. This is all that we can spare. The budget is limited.

In the distance, there is laughter from the SPACE EXPLORER's captors, who are celebrating their triumph. Drinking, music.

The EVIL HENCHMAN stops in front of the SPACE EXPLORER's cell to taunt her. She replies that THE HERO will save her. THE EVIL HENCHMAN laughs. *Let him try!*

SPACE EXPLORER is unflappable. She believes in THE HERO.

Although, perhaps she should not. Her story has been traced with carbon paper, in broad strokes, but carbon paper rips easily. And the writer of this script remembers pulling the carbon paper through the typewriter when he was a child, the discordant notes when he banged on the keys, the holes he poked in the paper so that it looked like the night sky needled with stars.

But the stars have shifted. This makes sense in an ever-expanding universe, but it brings no comfort to the writer to feel them moving away from the palm of his hand.

9

'Why did you stop making movies?' Amelia asked.

'I got old.'

'I looked up your filmography. You were still in your thirties.'

'Your thirties *is* old when all you do is show your breasts to the camera,' Lucía said.

Her turban was peach-colored, her dress pink. She wore a heavy seashell necklace and her nails had been freshly done, perhaps on account of the upcoming holidays. Despite her retirement from show business, she always managed to look like she was hoping someone would take her picture and ask for an autograph.

'I saw what happened to other actresses. There were certain people – Silvia Pinal, María Félix – who were able to remain somewhat relevant during the eighties. But for most of us, it was raunchy sex comedies and bit parts. Perhaps I might have been able to make it in soaps, but the television screen is so small. Televisa! After the marquees!'

Lucía lifted both of her hands, as if framing Amelia with them, as if she were holding a camera. Then she let them fall down on her lap again.

'So, I cashed in my chips and married well. I thought it was more dignified than shaking my ass in a negligee until the cellulite got the better of me and they kicked me off the set. You probably don't think that's very feminist of me.'

'I don't think anything of it,' Amelia said.

Lucía reached for the dish full of pomegranate seeds and offered them to Amelia. The routine of these visits was the most soothing part of Amelia's week. She had learned to appreciate Lucía's company, where before she had endured it.

'People criticized me, once. For everything. Every single choice you make is micro-analysed when you're a woman. When you're a man, you can fuck up as many times as you want. Nobody asked Mauricio Garcés why he made shit films. But then you get old and nobody cares. Nobody knows you, anymore.'

It was difficult to recognize Lucía. Age and whatever plastic surgery she had purchased had altered her face irrevocably. But the look in her eyes was the same look Amelia had seen in the posters, in the film stills, on screen in a dark and smoky cabaret where doomed lovers met.

'What was your best role?' Amelia asked.

'Nahum's movie. The one he didn't make.'

'The Viking movie?'

Lucía shook her head. 'The Mars movie. Before the script grew bloated and was butchered. I didn't know it then, of course. I knew little. But even if the story was laughable, he could get a good angle. There's that scene where I'm in prison. You recall it? Pure chiaroscuro. You only need to watch that moment, those five seconds. You don't need to watch the rest of the movie. In fact, it's better if you don't.'

'Why not?' Amelia asked with a chuckle.

'Because then you can make it up in your mind. For example, I always pretend I get out of that prison cell on my own. I just walk out.'

Lucía's eyes brightened. If someone had shot a close-up, then she might have resembled the actress who had adorned posters and lobby cards.

'You said Nahum wasn't nice.'

'Who is *nice*, Amelia?' Lucía stated, as if waving away an annoying buzzard. '*Nice* is such a toothless word. Do you want to have your gravestone say, 'Here lies Amelia. She was *nice*'? Come, come.'

'I suppose not.'

'You suppose right. When my memoir is published, I imagine people will say I was a bitch, but they were not there, were they? They didn't have to make my choices. It's always easy to tell someone they should have picked Option B.'

'So, what was Option B?'

Amelia expected the actress to launch into one of her elaborate anecdotes. Her face certainly seemed disposed toward conversation. Then it was like a curtain had been drawn and the light in Lucía's eyes dimmed a little.

'I forget,' Lucía said. 'It's been so long one forgets.'

'José's working as a professional stalker,' Pili said, just like that, like she had found out it would be raining tomorrow.

'You are kidding me,' Amelia replied.

'No. You can hire them online. They'll stalk anyone you want.'

'Is that legal?'

'Nothing worth any money is legal.'

They were wedged in the back of a large restaurant, right by a noisy group of licenciados out to lunch. Pili was paying back the money she owed Amelia and taking her out to eat as a Christmas gift. For now, the Bhagavad was forgotten. They could have a regular meal, not a beggar's banquet.

'Well, it sounds awful.'

'I thought I'd mention it. Just in case, you know, you're still looking for something.'

'I'm fine right now. In fact, I was going to say I should pay for this,' Amelia added.

'You got another client on Friendrr?'

I think I'm a professional mistress, Amelia thought. But despite Lucía's assurances that she should not worry about being perceived as 'nice', she did not want to chance Pili's disapproval.

'Yeah.'

'Fabulous. That means we can go out for New Year's, right? I have the perfect idea. It's—'

'I'm going out that night.'

'Yeah, right. You're going to stay home and eat grapes.'

'I'm not. Really. I have something planned.'

They parted ways outside the restaurant. On the other side of the street sat half a dozen people with signs at their feet advertising their skills: carpenter, plumber. There was even one computer programmer. Amelia pretended they were invisible, ghosts of the city. It was a possibility. The whole metropolis was haunted.

And she was good at pretending.

When she texted Elías 'Merry Christmas' and he did not text back, she pretended it did not bother her. The day after, she went to his apartment.

It was pristine, perfect. The lack of photos, of personality, the whiff of the showroom catalogue, enhanced the allure of the space. She could feign this belonged to her because it was not obvious it belonged to anyone.

She walked from the kitchen to the bedroom and back, finally standing before the window. The sign enticing people to fly to Mars glowed in the distance. She thought about calling Pili and drinking Elías's booze together, but that would break the illusion that this was her home. And she would have to explain why she had the key to this place.

Amelia went into the bathroom and ran a bath. On Christmas Eve, the taps at her apartment had gone dry and her sister had cursed for thirty minutes straight, asking how they were supposed to cook. Now, Amelia sank into the warm water. If she closed her eyes, she could imagine she was floating in the darkness of space.

When she stepped out, she left no trace of herself. When Elías texted her on December 29, it was to say he was on a red-eye flight and he had everything figured out for New Year's Eve. She slipped into the dress he'd bought her, did her makeup, and left her apartment with a few sparse words, which was all that was needed, since things were extra-dicey with her sister.

The teenagers in the courtyard were already drunk by the time she walked by them. Instead of beating a piñata, they were wrecking a television set. A few of them hooted at Amelia when they caught sight of her, but she quickened her pace and made it to the spot where a car awaited.

The rest of the night was what Elías had promised: good food, good drinks, dancing at a club that charged a ridiculous amount for a table. At midnight, streamers and balloons fell from the ceiling. Each New Year's Eve she spent at home, just like Pili had said, eating twelve grapes before the TV set in a mockery of festivity. Other than that, there were her sister's superstitious traditions: sweeping the floor at the stroke of midnight to empty the apartment of negative thoughts or tossing lentils outside their door. None of that now.

The clinking of glasses with real champagne, the whole thing – not just the alcohol – went to her head as she kissed Elías on the lips.

When she lay down on his bed, too tired to even bother with the zipper of her dress, she looked at the ceiling and stretched out her arm, pointing up.

'We had stars. Do you remember?' she asked him.

'What?' Elías muttered.

'In your old apartment.'

She turned her head and saw recognition dawning on his face. He nodded, slipping off his jacket and lying down.

'I remember. You painted them,' he said.

'It was to help hide the mold,' she recalled.

'Yes. In the corner of the room. That place was too damp.'

'You had leaks everywhere. We had to leave pots and pans and dishes all around.'

She rubbed a foot against his thigh, absentmindedly, more present in the past than in the now. Back in the grubby apartment, the water making music as it hit the dishes. Gold and silver stars. It had been a lark, one afternoon, and Elías had humored her, even helped paint a few of the stars himself.

'You printed all those photographs. Photos with an analogue camera, like any good hipster,' she said, sitting up and trying to reach the zipper of her dress. It was stuck.

'It was the feel of it, of the negatives and the dark room, that I liked,' he replied, a hand on her back, undoing the zipper for her in one fluid swoop.

Amelia pulled down the dress, frowning, her hands resting on the bed.

'What did you do with my pictures? Do you still have them somewhere?' she asked.

'Yes, in Monterrey. Why?'

'I don't know. It just seems like such an intimate thing to keep. Like a piece of somebody.'

'Sympathetic magic,' Elías whispered, running a finger along her spine.

She thought of the tossing of the lentils, the wearing of yellow or red underwear, washing one's hands with sugar, and the myriad of remedies at the Market of Sonora. All of it was rubbish, but he… he'd had some true magic. It hovered there, under his fingertips, something that wasn't love anymore, yet persisted.

• • •

A phone ringing. Amelia cracked her eyes open, trying to remember where she'd left her purse, but Elías answered.

'Hello? Oh, hey. Yeah, Happy New Year's to you too. No, it's got no charge. No, it's…'

Elías was standing up. Elías was going out of the bedroom. Amelia shoved away the covers and sat at the foot of the bed. When he returned, he had that apologetic look on his face she knew well.

'That was my father,' he said.

'I figured. Keeping his eye on you, as usual,' Amelia said, finding her underwear and stockings. Her dress was crumpled in a corner and it had a stain near the waist. Spilled champagne.

When they'd dated, Elías played at independence. Half-heartedly. Dad paid all the bills, after all, but he played in good faith. He told himself they were at the brink of freedom.

Now, he played at something entirely different.

'I have an early Epiphany present for you.'

As Elías spoke, he opened the door to the closet and took out a box, laying it on the bed and opening it for Amelia to inspect the contents. It was a set of clothes. Slim, black trousers, a gray blouse. She ran a hand along the fabric.

'Did you give your fiancée a present too?' Amelia asked. 'Was it also clothing, or did you pick something else?'

'You don't like the clothes?'

'That's not what I asked,' she said, raising her head and staring at him.

A rueful look on his face. He did not appear older most days, but that morning, he was his full twenty-five years, older still, not at all the boy she'd gone out with. He'd looked very much the Hero when she'd first spotted him and now he did not seem the Villain, but he could not save maidens from dragons or girls from space pirates.

He had settled into the man he would be. That was what she saw that morning.

Whom had she settled into? Had she?

'My father picked her present. I had no say in it,' he assured her.

'I guess you don't get a say in anything.'

She fastened her bra and proceeded to put on the change of clothes he'd bought for her, leisurely. She had nowhere to go and nothing to do.

'Amelia,' he said sharply, 'you know I care about you. My father wants me back in Monterrey, but I want nothing of him.'

'Except for his cash.'

'What would you have me do? I was going to break off the engagement, but he doesn't listen to me, just goes on and on, and when I brought it up—'

She stood up and touched his lips before she kissed him very lightly. 'I know,' she replied.

'No, you don't,' he said and he held her tight. And she should, she would move away in a minute. She was tidally locked. She was but a speck orbiting him and it didn't even matter now whether she could, would, would not, should not move aside.

10

The gang had once again laid claim to the subway's entrance. Amelia ended up sharing a car with a man and a life-sized mechanical mariachi. It was just the torso, skillfully painted, but he had a hat and held a guitar in his hands. She couldn't help but ask the man about it.

'It's for bars,' the man said. 'It has integrated speakers and can play hundreds of songs. It's better than any flesh-and-blood musician. I also have one that looks like Pedro Infante and another like Jorge Negrete. Say, I'll give you my card.'

She tried to tell him it was fine, that she wasn't looking for a singing torso, but he pressed the card against her hand. She tossed it away before she walked into Lucía's house where the holidays had made no dent. No lights nor trees, not even a poinsettia plant to mark the season. Lucía herself wore a white turban and had scattered photos on the table.

'I'm picking pictures to go with my book,' Lucía declared. 'I'm sure people will like that sort of thing. But they're all jumbled, and I have boxes and boxes of them. This was from 1974. It was the dress I did *not* wear to the Arieles, since I didn't bother asking for an invitation and stayed home. You know who won the Ariel that year? Katy-Fucking-Jurado.'

Amelia inspected the photo and smiled. Then she looked down at the table, grabbing a couple of other snapshots. One was a self-portrait, but the other showed young Lucía with Nahum. He was lighting her cigarette and she was smiling a perfect smile.

'Can I ask?' Amelia said. 'You and this guy…?'

'Fucked?' Lucía said with a chuckle. 'Who didn't fuck him, darling? Who didn't fuck me, for that matter? But he was married. I spun elaborate fantasies about how he was going to leave her, but those men never dump their wives. Not for little actresses who say "I love you" a bit too honestly anyway.'

'But you would have worked with him again, on that Viking movie.'

'That was after. Ages after! It seemed like that back then. Time just slowed to a standstill. Now, time goes so fast. I can't keep track of anything anymore. So, yes, afterward I might have worked with him. Things were different.'

'I don't know if things can ever be different between some people,' Amelia said.

Lucía laughed her full laughter. She was old, and she was strong and steady. Amelia wished she could be that steady. She wished she didn't jitter and jump, unable to sit still for five minutes, her foot nervously thumping against the floor.

'You have troubles with someone?' Lucía asked.

'It's nothing. Probably the least of my worries.'

'What's the biggest worry? Mars, my dear?'

'Mars, yes,' Amelia said, blushing. She hated thinking that

she was so easy to read, that Lucía knew her so well. But then, what else did she talk about? Nothing but Mars and she did not talk about Elías with anyone. Everything about the Red Planet, not a word about the man, all truths committed to her mind. If she'd kept a diary, perhaps it might have helped, but it would have been ridiculous tripe.

'Mars is fine, I suppose. We all must nurse our little madnesses. Look at me here, with all these pictures,' Lucía said, pointing at the photographs. 'But I was pretty, wasn't I? Look at this. Now, this was a face. Light it, frame it, let the world admire it.'

So, Amelia looked. She looked at the ravaged hands touching the precious photos and she nodded.

. . .

She knew the lunch invitation was a trap but not exactly which kind. Fernanda did not extend lunch invitations. It was Amelia who phoned her, tiptoed around a social activity once a year, and then Fernanda agreed with a sigh. Fernanda ended up buying her a free lunch and Amelia ended up feeling like shit, and then she wondered why the fuck she bothered pretending Fernanda was still her friend, but the truth was Fernanda had also lent her money a couple of times. Amelia didn't like to think of people as walking ATMs, but that was what it had come to on more than one occasion.

Fernanda phoning Amelia was plain unnatural, but Amelia went along with it, went to the restaurant where they normally met.

Fernanda arrived before Amelia, which was another oddity. She didn't waste time pretending pleasantries. As soon as Amelia sat down, she leaned forward, with an eager look on her face.

'Amelia, are you really fucking Elías Bertoliat?'

Amelia opened the menu, sliding a finger down the many

options. Fernanda took her time choosing her food and drink, after all.

'Amelia, didn't you hear me?' Fernanda asked.

'I heard you,' Amelia said, trying to read the menu.

'Oh, my God, are you seriously going to sit there without answering me?' Fernanda said.

Amelia raised her eyes and stared at Fernanda. 'Why are you asking me this? How do you—'

'Anastasia is super-pissed off at me! She thinks I got you two back in contact and I've done nothing of the sort! But since I secured you the invitation for that show of hers and she didn't hire you… OK, she has it in her head that you went and fucked the guy to spite her. And it's *my* fault for telling you about her art show in the first place.'

'Elías is engaged to Anastasia?'

'You didn't know that?' Fernanda said.

For a moment she believed that Fernanda had set this whole thing in motion as part of a malicious plan. She had sent her to the gallery, she had mentioned that Amelia worked as a rent-a-friend to Elías. For what? For a lark? Coincidence? Did it matter? Maybe she thought it would be funny. *You can't imagine what she does now! No, really, look her up.* It had backfired.

Most likely Fernanda hadn't even thought about it, it had been a lack of care and tact.

'How did she find out?' Amelia replied.

'She paid someone to follow him.'

'What, with that stalker app? That would be funny.'

'What are you talking about?'

Amelia chuckled. She reached for a piece of bread piled in a basket and tore off a chunk.

'Why are you so happy? Do you realize what this means to

me? Anastasia does business with my husband. If she's angry at me, *I'm* going to lose money.'

Fernanda had reached across the table and slapped the butter knife Amelia had been attempting to wield. The clank of metal against the table made Amelia grimace.

'I'm not responsible for your husband's business,' she said, and she hoped that he did bleed money, that if Fernanda had started this fucking storyline with her gossip and games, she paid for it.

'Well, if that's how you see it. But let me tell you something. He's going back to Monterrey this summer. His father is demanding it and Anastasia is pressing for it too. So, whatever you've got going, it's not going to last.'

'Nothing does,' Amelia said. She grabbed the butter knife again and slowly, deliberately buttered her bread, much to the chagrin of the other woman. When she left the restaurant, she knew she would never be having lunch with Fernanda again.

•

She went back to the blood clinic. She was certain Elías wouldn't appreciate the fresh mark on her arm, but fuck him. She sat there and they siphoned out the blood, and she recalled how years before he'd abandoned her, how he had not returned her calls. So she'd gone to his apartment, trying to figure out what was wrong with him. She pictured him run over by a car, dying of a fever. A million different, dramatic scenarios. Instead, she walked into an empty apartment. The only traces of him that remained were the stars on the bedroom's ceiling and the leaks slowly dripping across the floor.

It was that emptiness that she attempted to escape as the machinery whirred and the tourniquet tightened, the centrifuge spinning and separating plasma and blood.

It was that helplessness which she must combat.

She could not depend on him because Elías was not dependable. She knew that even before Fernanda had spilled poison in her ears, even before she walked down Reforma with her eyes downcast.

When he texted her and she showed up at his place, and when he noticed the mark, she told him to mind his own business, to mind Anastasia and his own fucking life because she had hers.

How he stared at her.

'You should tell me if you need help,' he said.

'And you should have told me it was her,' she replied.

He ran a hand down his face. Then he had the gall to try and reach out for her. Amelia slapped his hand away.

'What does it matter?' he asked, stubbornly trying to grab hold of her again. 'What does it matter if it's Anastasia?'

'I don't like not knowing. I wish you would fucking tell me something.'

'You don't tell me anything either! Look at that!' he yelled, touching her arm, the mark there. 'You just go off to sell fucking plasma, like a junkie.'

'Everyone sells it, Elías! Everyone has to!'

She shoved him away and he reached out a third time to catch her.

'I'll tell you all if you want, fine, but there's not much to tell. I'm supposed to head back in the summer. And the rest... you must know it already. I care about you and I care nothing about them,' he said brokenly.

It was not enough. It wasn't, but then, she lived on scraps and bits of nothing. She let him hold her, after all.

'Don't go to that stupid clinic anymore,' he said. 'Ask for the money if you need it, all right?'

Because she was a coward, because it was always easier in the moment to lie, she nodded.

• • •

But she did not stop going to the blood clinic. She had amassed almost a complete new wardrobe, courtesy of Elías, which she kept at his place, but she did not ask for money. It baffled him, even irritated him. Instead, she continued to meet the occasional client on Friendrr, or helped Pili with the odd gig since Pili was a purveyor of constant and strange gigs. And the blood, there was the blood when she needed the cash.

Her life had not changed, not really. She still spent a great deal of time in coffee shops – connected to their Wi-Fi, drawing nonsense – but she also ventured to see Elías. He had many of her same habits. He did not work. He did not seem to do anything at all, although once in a while, he'd take photographs with a custom-made Polaroid camera. This wasn't but a faint echo of his previous passion and, inevitably, he shrugged and tossed the camera back into a drawer.

One evening, Amelia opened the drawer and emptied it on the floor of his neat, sparse office, holding up the pictures and looking at them. He walked in, looked at her.

'I wish you would…' he said. She didn't understand the last word he muttered before he sat down next to her and pulled Amelia into his arms.

There were moments like that when it was easy to forget that he wasn't hers and she wasn't his. There were moments when the phone didn't ring, and it wasn't his father or that fiancée on the line, and there were moments when she pretended this was New Panyu because she had never seen it, so it could be. It could be that the homes of the wealthy there looked like this: manicured and perfect.

Then came May and the rain was early, soaking her to the bone one afternoon, so that her clothes were a soggy mess as she hurried up the stairs of her apartment and the phone rang.

'Hello,' she said. It was Miguel.

'Hey, Amelia. You don't need to go to Lucía's home today. She's passed away.' As usual, he spoke in a sunny tone. So sunny that Amelia stopped and held on to the banister, pressing the phone harder against her ear and asking him to repeat what he had told her. She couldn't believe he had said what he'd said. But he repeated the same thing, adding that there was a lawyer who wanted to speak to her. The old lady had left something for her.

'A poster,' the lawyer said,' Miguel told her. 'You should phone him.'

• • •

It was indeed a poster in a cardboard tube. Sealed with Scotch tape. Amelia placed it on the empty chair next to her. Lucía had died in her sleep, an easy death, so she did not understand when the lawyer asked her to sit down. There was more.

'The house, her furniture, her savings, they go to her niece,' the lawyer told her.

She had expected nothing else. The niece had only been mentioned in passing a couple of times, but there had been a certain importance attached to her name.

'Aside from the poster, she did leave an amount of money for you.'

'What?' Amelia asked.

'She also left money for her staff. She was a generous lady. It's not much different from that, the amount. There's some paperwork that needs to be filled out.'

When she arrived home, Amelia peeled open the tube and

unrolled the poster on the floor. It was the Mars poster: Lucía with the cartridge belts, looking over her shoulder.

In a corner, a few shaky words had been scrawled with a black felt pen: *Do what you want, Amelia.*

Hellas, she thought. *Mars is home to a plain that covers nearly twenty-three hundred kilometers. Hellas appears featureless…*

And then Amelia could think of no more facts, no more names and numbers to go together. She wept.

• • •

It rained again and again. Three days of rain and on the third she asked for a car to drive her over to New Polanco. In the derelict buildings nearby, people were collecting water in pots and cans and buckets. She watched them from the window of the car. Then the surroundings changed, Elías's tall apartment building came into focus, and it was impossible that both views could be had in the same city.

As soon as she walked into his apartment, she looked for the sign advertising Mars, but it wasn't on. The power might be down on that street. Elías's building probably had a generator.

She stood before the window, watching the rain instead.

He wasn't home. She had not bothered to text him, but she did not mind the wait. The silence. Then the door opened and he finally walked in, shaking an umbrella.

'Hey,' he said, frowning. 'Didn't know you'd stop by.'

Amelia held up the key he'd given her and placed it on the table, carefully, like a player revealing an ace. 'I came to bring it back and say goodbye. I'm headed to New Panyu.'

Elías took off his jacket and tossed it on the couch, smiling, incredulous. 'You don't have the money for that.'

'I've got the money,' she affirmed.

'How?'

'Doesn't matter how.'

'You're serious. This isn't some joke.'

'I wouldn't joke about it.'

'Fuck me,' he said, sitting down on the couch, resting his elbows against his knees and shaking his head. He still seemed incredulous, but now he was also starting to look pissed off. 'Just like that.'

'I told you I'd go one day.'

'Yeah, well, I didn't think… Shit, Amelia, Mars is a dump. It's a fucking dump. Piss recycled into drinkable water and sandstorms blotting your windows. You think you're going to be better off there? You seriously think that?'

He sounded like her sister. Marta had said the exact same thing, with more bad words and yelling, although toward the end of the conversation, she concluded it was for the best and she might be able to rent the room where Amelia now slept. Pili had joked about Martians dancing the cha-cha-cha and bought Amelia a beer. Her eyes held not even the slightest trace of tears, but Amelia could tell she was sad.

'You're going to be back in less than six months,' he warned her. 'You're just going to burn through your money.'

'I didn't ask for your opinion.'

'You're selfish. You're just damned selfish. And you… you'll miss Earth, the comfort of having an atmosphere.'

Perhaps he was right that she would miss it all, later. The city, her apartment, her sister, Pili, the café where she spent most of her waking hours, and him too. Twenty seconds after boarding the shuttle to Mars, she might indeed miss it, but she was not going to stay around because maybe she might get homesick.

'It doesn't matter to you?' he asked. 'That you are going to eat bars made of algae seven days a week? That… that I won't be around?'

She laughed brokenly and he stood up, stood in front of her, all fervent eyes. She liked it when he looked at her like that, covetous, like he wanted her all, like he might devour her whole and she'd cease to exist, be edited out of existence like they edited scenes in the movies.

'Cut the shit. Come with me to Monterrey. I'll rent a place for you there. I'll pay your expenses,' he said.

'No,' she said.

'Mars or bust, then.'

'Yes.'

She scratched her arm, scratched the spot where they drew blood and an indentation was starting to form, and looked at that spot instead of him. She couldn't see it with her jacket on, but she could feel the scar tissue there, beneath her fingertips.

'I told you. I always told you. New Panyu—'

'Years ago,' he said. 'When we were nineteen. Fuck, you don't keep the promises you make when you're a kid.'

'No, *you* don't.'

Her throat, she felt it clogged with bitterness. The words were hoarse and she put both her hands down at her sides, giving him a furious glance.

'Fine, fine, fine,' he said, his hand slamming against the living-room table, equally furious. 'Fine! Leave me!'

Amelia crossed her arms and began walking to the door, but he moved to her side, reached for her, a hand brushing her hair.

'No, it's not fine, Amelia,' he whispered.

She opened her mouth, ready to halt him before he committed himself to something, but he spoke too fast.

'I did… I do love you.' Gentle words. Sincere. All the worse for that.

The hand was still in her hair and she was looking down at her shoes, frowning, arms tight against her chest. She had not come to converse or negotiate. She had come to say goodbye, even if he had not given her that courtesy once upon a time. Now, for the first time, she understood why he had taken off so suddenly, wordless. She knew why he'd made their first film a silent movie, a goodbye with no dialogue. It was a wretched mess to part from each other. He had cannily figured that out. He had probably imagined the tears of a girl, the pleas, and cut it all off brutally to do himself, and her, a favor.

Or he did not figure out anything. He merely fled and she was giving too much thought to his actions.

A mess, a mess. She could not even remember the names of Mars' moons as she stood with her arms crossed, her breath hot in her mouth.

'You could buy a ticket too,' she suggested, even though she knew he never, ever would. If he'd wanted it, it would have already happened, years before. But he had not.

Elías sighed. 'It will be the same there. Nothing will change. I know you hope it will, but Mars won't fix anything,' he told her.

'Maybe not. But I have to go,' she said. 'I just have to.'

He didn't understand. He looked at her, still disbelieving, still startled, still thinking she somehow didn't mean it. He still tried to kiss her, mouth straining against hers, and she squeezed his hand for a second before heading out without another word.

MARS, FINAL SCENE, ALTERNATE

INT. CELL – NIGHT

SPACE EXPLORER awaits THE HERO in her cell. The stars have gone dim. The building where she is held is quiet, all the guards asleep, and she waits. She waits, but nobody comes. From her cell, she sees a rectangle of sky, tinted vermilion, and faded paper-cut moons, which dangle from bits of string (there is no budget to this production, none at all).

THE HERO is coming, he is nearing, sure footsteps and the swell of music. But the swell of music hasn't begun yet and the foley artist is on a break, so there's no crescendo, no strings or drums or piano, or whatever should punctuate this moment.

There is the cell and there is the vermilion sky, but the script says she is to wait. The SPACE EXPLORER waits.

But she presses her hands against the walls, which are not plaster. They are cardboard like the moons. They are not even cardboard, but paper. And the paper parts and rips so that the rectangle of vermilion becomes a vermilion expanse, and she is standing there in front of the ever-shifting sands of Mars.

She holds her breath, wary, thinking she's mucked it up. She turns to look at the other walls around her, the door to her jail cell, the hallway beyond the door. Then she turns her head again and there are the moons, the sands, the sky, the winds of Mars.

She wears no spacesuit, which means that it is impossible to make it out of the cell. But we are not on Mars. We are on *Mars*. The moons are paper and the stars are tinfoil. So, it is possible to step forward, which is what she does, tentative.

One foot in front of another, the white dress they've out-fitted her in clinging to her legs and her hair askew as the wind blows. A storm rises somewhere in the distance.

She sees the storm, at the edge of the horizon, dust devils tracing serpentine paths, and she walks there.

She does not look back.

There are only two plots. You know them well: A person goes on a journey and a stranger comes into town.

FADE TO BLACK

ACKNOWLEDGMENTS

My heartfelt thanks to Lavie Tidhar, who wrote the introduction to this novella. Thank you to Paula R. Stiles for her copyediting and proofreading. I am grateful for all the people who backed my campaign to fund 'Prime Meridian'. Most of all, thank you for reading.

Silvia Moreno-Garcia, 2017

If At First You Don't Succeed, Try, Try Again

Zen Cho

Malaysia

Zen Cho made history winning the Hugo Award for this story, which is as funny and delightful as anything she writes. I had the good fortune to blurb her first novel, *Sorcerer To The Crown*, before it came out – I kept reading it until well past 2 a.m.! I keep asking her to write more, quicker. I've wanted to publish her for years – we finally did it in *The Apex Book of World SF* 4 – and I could think of no better closer for this anthology than this story. Just don't ask her when the next novel's due!

THE FIRST THOUSAND YEARS

It was time. Byam was as ready as it would ever be.

As a matter of fact, it had been ready to ascend some three hundred years ago. But the laws of heaven cannot be defied. If you drop a stone, it will fall to the ground – it will not fly up to the sky. If you try to become a dragon before your one thousandth birthday, you will fall flat on your face and all the other spirits of the five elements will laugh at you.

These are the laws of heaven.

But Byam had been patient. Now it would be rewarded.

It slithered out of the lake it had occupied for the past one hundred years. The western side of the lake had recently been settled by humans and the banks had become cluttered with the humans' usual mess – houses, cultivated fields, bits of pottery that poked Byam in the side.

But the eastern side was still reserved for beasts and spirits. There was plenty of space for an imugi to take off.

The mountains around the lake said hello to Byam. It was always safer to be polite to an imugi, since you never knew when it might turn into a dragon. The sky above them was a pure light blue, dotted with clouds like white jade.

Byam's heart rose. It launched itself into the air, the sun warm on its back.

I deserve this. All those years studying in dank caves, chanting sutras, striving to understand the Way…

For the first five hundred years or so, Byam could be confident of getting the solitude necessary for study. But there seemed to be more and more humans everywhere.

Humans weren't all bad. You couldn't meditate your way through every doctrinal puzzle. That was where monks came in useful. Of course, even the most enlightened monk was wont to be alarmed by the sudden appearance of a giant snake wanting to know what they thought of the Sage's comments on water. Still, you could usually extract some guidance from them once they stopped screaming.

But spending too much time near humans was risky. If one saw you during your ascension, that could ruin everything. Byam would have moved when the humans settled by the lake, if not for the ample supply of cows and pigs and goats in the area. Byam had got tired of seafood.

It wasn't always good to have such abundance close to hand, though. Byam had been studying extra hard for the past decade in preparation for its ascension. Just last month it had been startled from a marathon meditation session by an enormous growl.

Byam had looked around wildly. For a moment it thought

it had been set upon, maybe by a wicked imugi – the kind so embittered by failure it pretended not to care about the Way or the cintamani or even becoming a dragon. But there was no one around, only some fish beating a hasty retreat.

There was another growl. It was coming from Byam's own stomach. Byam recollected that it hadn't eaten in about five years.

Some imugi were known to fast to increase their spiritual powers. But when Byam tried to get back to meditating, it didn't work. Its stomach kept making weird gurgling noises. All the fish had been scared off, so Byam popped out of the water, looking for a snack.

A herd of cows was grazing by the bank, as though they were waiting for Byam.

It only meant to eat one cow. It wanted to keep sharp for its ascension. Dragons probably didn't eat much. All the dragons Byam had ever seen were svelte, with perfect scales, shining talons, silky beards.

Unfortunately Byam wasn't a dragon yet. It was hungry, and the cows smelt so good. Byam had one, and then another, and then a third, telling itself each time that *this* cow would be the last. Before it knew it, almost the whole herd was gone.

Byam cringed, remembering this, but it put the memory away. Today was the day that would change everything. After today, Byam would be transformed. It would have a wish-fulfilling gem of its own – the glorious cintamani, which manifested all desires, cured afflictions, purified souls and water alike.

So high up, the air was thin and Byam had to work harder to keep afloat. The clouds brushed its face damply. And – Byam's heart beat faster – wasn't that winking light ahead the glitter of a jewel?

Byam turned for its last look at the earth as an imugi. The lake shone in the sun. It had been cold and miserable and lonely, full of venomous water snakes that bit Byam's tail. Byam had been dying to get away from it.

But now it felt a swell of affection. When it returned as a dragon, it would bless the lake. Fish would overflow its banks. The cows and pigs and goats would multiply beyond counting. The crops would spring out of the earth in their multitudes...

A thin screechy noise was coming from the lake. When Byam squinted, it saw a group of little creatures on the western bank. Humans.

One of them was shaking a fist at the sky. 'Fuck you, imugi!'

'Oh shit,' said Byam.

'Yeah, I see you! You think you got away with it? Well, you thought wrong!'

Byam lunged upwards, but it was too late. Gravity set its teeth in its tail and tugged.

It wasn't just one human shouting, it was all of them. A chorus of insults rose on the wind:

'Worm! Legless centipede! Son of a bitch! You look like fermented soybeans and you smell even worse!'

Byam strained every muscle, fighting the pull of the earth. If only it had hawk's claws to grasp the clouds with – or stag's antlers to pierce the sky—

But Byam wasn't a dragon yet.

The last thing it heard as it plunged through the freezing waters of the lake was a human voice shrieking:

'Serves you right for eating our cows!'

THE SECOND THOUSAND YEARS

If you wanted to be a dragon, dumb perseverance wasn't enough. You had to have a strategy.

Humans had proliferated, so Byam retreated to the ocean. It was harder to get texts in the sea, but technically you didn't need texts to study the Way since it was inherent in the order of all things. Anyway, sometimes you could steal scriptures off a turtle on a pilgrimage, or go onshore to ransack a monastery.

But you had to get out of the water in order to ascend. It was impossible to exclude the possibility of being seen by humans, even in the middle of the ocean. Even though they couldn't breathe underwater, they still launched themselves onto the waves on rickety assemblages of dismembered trees. It was as if they couldn't wait to get on to their next lives.

That was fine. If Byam couldn't depend on the absence of humans, it would use them to its advantage.

It was heaven's will that Byam should have failed the last time. If heaven wasn't ready to accept Byam, nothing could change that, no matter how diligently it studied or how much it longed to ascend.

As in all things, however, when it came to ascending, how you were seen mattered just as much as what you did. It hadn't helped back then that the lake humans had named Byam for what it was: no dragon, but an imugi, a degraded being no better than the crawling beasts of the earth.

But if, as Byam flashed across the sky, a witness saw a dragon... that was another matter. Heaven wasn't immune to the pressures of public perception. It would have to recognize Byam then.

The spirits of the wind and water were too hard to bluff; fish were too self-absorbed; and there was no hope of hoodwinking the sea dragons. But humans had bad eyesight and a tendency to see things that weren't there. Their capacity for self-deception was Byam's best bet.

It chose a good point in the sky, high enough that it would have enough cloud matter to work with, but not so high that the humans couldn't see it. Then it got to work.

It laboured at night, using its head to push together masses of cloud and its tail to work the fine detail. Byam didn't just want the design to look like a dragon. Byam wanted it to be beautiful – as beautiful as the dragon it was going to be.

Making the sculpture was harder than Byam had expected. Cloud was an intransigent medium. Wisps kept drifting off when Byam wasn't looking. It couldn't get the horns straight and the whiskers were wonky.

Sometimes Byam felt like giving up. How could it make a dragon when it didn't even know how to be one?

To conquer self-doubt, it chanted the aphorisms of the wise:

Nobody becomes a dragon overnight.
Real dragons keep going.
A dragon is only an imugi that didn't give up.

It took one hundred years more than Byam had planned for before the cloud was finished.

It looked just like a dragon, caught as it was speeding across the sky to its rightful place in the heavens. In moonlight it shone like mother of pearl. Under the sun it would glitter with all the colours of the rainbow.

As it put its final touches on the cloud, Byam felt both pride and a sense of anti-climax. Even loss. Soon Byam would ascend – and then what would happen to its creation? It would dissipate, or dissolve into rain, like any other cloud.

Byam managed to find a monk who knew about shipping routes and was willing to dish in exchange for not being eaten. And then it was ready.

As dawn unfolded across the sky on an auspicious day, Byam took its position behind its dragon-cloud.

All it needed was a single human to look up and say what they saw. A fleet of merchant vessels was due to come this way. Among all those humans, there had to be one sailor with his eyes on the sky – a witness open to wonder, prepared to see a dragon rising to glory.

• • •

'Hey, captain,' said the lookout. 'You see that?'

'What is it? A sail?'

'No.' The lookout squinted at the sky. 'That cloud up there, look. The one with all the colours.'

'Oh wow!' said the captain. 'Good spot! That's something special, for sure. It's a good omen!'

He slapped the lookout on the back, turning to the rest of the crew. 'Great news, men! Heaven smiles upon us. Today is our day!'

Everyone was busy with preparations, but a dutiful cheer rose from the ship.

The lookout was still staring upwards.

'It's an interesting shape,' he said thoughtfully. 'Don't you think it looks like a…'

'Like what?' said the captain.

'Like, um…' The lookout frowned, snapping his fingers. 'What do you call them? Forget my own head next! It looks like a – it's on the tip of my tongue. I've been at sea for too long. Like a, you know—'

•

Byam couldn't take it anymore.

'*Dragon!*' it wailed in agony.

An imugi has enormous lungs. Byam's voice rolled across the

sky like thunder, its breath scattering the clouds – and blowing its creation to shreds.

'Horse!' said the lookout triumphantly. 'It looks like a horse!'

'No no no,' said Byam. It scrambled to reassemble its sculpture, but the cloud matter was already melting away upon the winds.

'Thunder from a clear sky!' said the captain. 'Is that a good sign or a bad sign?'

The lookout frowned. 'You're too superstitious, captain – hey!' He perked up, snatching up a telescope. 'Captain, there they are!'

Byam had been so focused on the first ship that it hadn't seen the merchant fleet coming. Then it was too busy trying to salvage its dragon-cloud to pay attention to what was going on below.

It was distantly aware of the fighting between the ships, the arrows flying, the screams of sailors as they were struck down. But it was preoccupied by the enormity of what had happened to it – the loss of hundreds of years of steady, hopeful work.

It wasn't too late. Byam could fix the cloud and then tomorrow it would try again—

'Ah,' said the pirate captain, looking up from the business of slaughter. 'An imugi! It's good luck after all. One last push, men! They can't hold out for long!'

It would have been easier if Byam could tell itself the humans had sabotaged it out of spite. But it knew they hadn't. As Byam tumbled out of the sky, it was the impartiality of their judgement that stung the most.

THE THIRD THOUSAND YEARS

Dragons enjoyed sharing advice about how they had got to where they were. They said it helped to visualize the success you desired.

'Envision yourself with those horns, those whiskers, three claws and a thumb, basking in the glow of your own cinta-mani,' urged the Dragon King of the East Sea in his popular memoir *Sixty Thousand Records of a Floating Life*. 'Close your eyes. You are the master of the elements! A twitch of your whisker and the skies open. At your command, blessings – or vengeance – pour forth upon all creatures under heaven! Just imagine!'

When Byam was low at heart, it imagined it.

It got fed up of the sea: turtles kept chasing it around and whale song disrupted its sleep. So it moved inland and found a quiet cave where it could study the Way undisturbed. The cave didn't smell great, but it meant Byam never had to go far for food, so long as it didn't mind bat.

Byam came to mind bat. But it focused on the future.

This time there would be no messing around with dragon-clouds. Byam had learnt from its mistakes. There was no tricking heaven. This time it would present itself at the gates with its record of honest toil, and hope to be deemed worthy of admission.

It should have been nervous, but in fact it was calm as it pre-pared for what it hoped would be its final attempt. Certainty glowed in its stomach like a swallowed ember.

It had been a long time since Byam had left its cave. It had chosen the cave because it was up among the mountains, far from any human settlement. Still, Byam intended to minimize any chance of disaster. It was going to shoot straight for the skies, making sure it was exposed to the judgement of the world for as brief a time as possible.

But the brightness outside took it aback. Its eyes weren't used to the sun's glare anymore. When Byam raised its head, it got caught in a sort of horrible basket, full of whispering voices. A storm of ticklish green scraps whirled around it.

It reared back, hissing, before it recognized what had attacked it. Byam had forgotten about trees.

It leapt into the air, shaken. To have forgotten *trees*... Byam had not realized it had been so long.

Its unease faded as it rose ever higher. The crisp airs of heaven blew away disquiet. Ahead the clouds glowed as though they reflected the light of the Way.

• • •

Leslie almost missed it.

She never usually did this kind of thing. She was indoorsy the way some people were outdoorsy, as attached to her sofa as others were to endorphins and bragging about their marathon times. She'd never thought of herself as someone who hiked.

But she hadn't thought of herself as someone who'd fail her PhD, or get dumped by her boyfriend for her best friend. The past year had blown the bottom out of her ideas about herself.

She paused to drink some water and heave for breath. The view was spectacular. It seemed meaningless.

She was higher up than she'd thought. What if she took the wrong step? Would it hurt much to fall? Everyone would think it was an accident...

She shook herself. She wouldn't do anything stupid, Leslie told herself. To get her mind off it, she took out her phone, but that proved a bad idea. This was the point at which she would have texted Jung-wook before.

She could take a selfie. That's what people did when they went hiking, right? Posted proof they'd done it. She raised her phone, switching the camera to front-facing mode.

She saw a flash in the corner of the screen. It was sunlight glinting off scales.

Leslie's mouth fell open. It wasn't – it couldn't be – she hadn't even known they were found in America—

The camera went off. Leslie whirled around, but the sky was empty. It was nowhere to be seen.

But someone up there was looking out for Leslie, after all, because when she looked back at her phone she saw that she'd caught it, it was there, it had happened. There was Leslie, looking dopey with her red face and her hair a mess and her mouth half-open – and in the background, arced across the sky like a rainbow, was her miracle. Her own personal sign from heaven that things were going to be OK.

leshangry Nature is amazing! #imugi #이무기 #sighting #blessed #여행스타그램 #자연 #등산 #nature #hiking #wanderlust #gooutside #snakesofinstagram

THE TURNING OF THE WORM

'Dr Han?' said the novice. 'Yeah, her office is just through there.'

Sure enough, the name was inscribed on the door in the new script the humans used now: *Dr Leslie Han*. Byam's nemesis.

Its most *recent* nemesis. If it had been only one offence, Byam wouldn't even be here. It was the whole of Byam's long miserable history with humans that had brought it to this point.

It made itself invisible and passed through the door.

The monk was sitting at a desk, frowning over a text. Byam was not good at distinguishing one human from another, but this particular human's face was branded into its memory.

It felt a surge of relief.

Even with the supernatural powers accumulated in the course of three millennia of studying the Way, it had taken Byam a while to figure out how to shapeshift. The legs had been the most difficult part. Byam had kept giving itself tiger feet, the kind dragons had.

It could have concealed the feet under its skirts, since no celestial fairy ever appeared in anything less than three layers of silk. But Byam wouldn't have it. It was pathetic, this harking back to its stupid dreams. It had worked at the spell until the feet came right. If Byam wasn't becoming a dragon, it would not lower itself to imitation. No part of it would bear any of the nine resemblances.

But there were consolations available to imugi who reconciled themselves to their fate. Like revenge.

The human was perhaps a little older than when Byam had last seen her. But she was still alive – alive enough to suffer when Byam devoured her.

Byam let its invisibility fall away. It spread its hands, the better to show off its magnificent sleeves.

It was the human's job that had given Byam the idea. Leslie Han was an academic, which appeared to be a type of monk. Monks were the most relatable kind of human, for like imugi, they desired one thing most in life: to ascend to a higher plane of existence.

'Leslie,' crooned Byam in the dulcet tones of a celestial fairy. 'How would you like to go to heaven?'

The monk screamed and fell out of her chair.

When nothing else happened, Byam floated over to the desk, peering down at the monk. She had ended up on the floor.

'What are you doing down there?' began Byam, but the text the monk had been studying caught its eye.

'Oh my God, you're—' The monk rubbed her eyes. 'I didn't

think celestial fairies descended anymore! Did you – were you offering to take me to heaven?'

Byam wasn't listening. The monk had to repeat herself before it looked up from the book.

'This is a text on the Way,' said Byam. It looked around the monk's office. There were rows and rows of books. Byam said slowly, 'These are *all* about the Way.'

The monk looked puzzled. 'No, they're about astrophysics. I'm a researcher. I study the evolution of galaxies.'

Maybe Byam had been dumb enough to believe it might some day become a dragon, but it knew an exegesis of the Way when it saw one. There were hundreds of such books here – more commentaries than Byam had seen in one place in its entire lifetime.

It wasn't going to repeat its mistakes. Ascension, transcendence, turning into a dragon – that wasn't happening for Byam. Heaven had made that clear.

But you couldn't study something for three thousand years without becoming interested in it for its own sake.

'Tell me about your research,' said Byam.

'What you said just now,' said the monk. 'Did you not—'

Byam showed its teeth.

'My research!' said the monk. 'Let me tell you about it.'

Byam had planned to eat the monk when she was done. But it turned out the evolution of galaxies was an extremely complicated matter. When the moon rose, the monk had not explained even half of what Byam wanted to know.

She took out a glowing box and looked at it. 'It's so late!'

'Why did you stop?' said Byam.

'I need to sleep,' said the monk. She bent over the desk. Byam wondered if this was a good moment to eat her, but then the monk turned and held out a sheaf of paper.

'What is this?'

'Extra reading,' said the monk. 'You can come back tomorrow if you've got questions. My office hours are 3 to 4 p.m. on Wednesdays and Thursdays.'

She paused, her eyes full of wonder. She was looking at Byam as though it was special.

'But you can come any time,' said the monk.

•

Byam did the reading. It went back again the next day. Then the next.

It was easier to make sense of the texts with the monk's help. And Byam had never had anyone to talk to about the Way before.

It didn't count its past visits with monks. Leslie screamed much less than the others. She answered Byam's questions as though she enjoyed them, whereas the others had always made it clear they couldn't wait for Byam to leave.

'I like teaching,' she said when Byam remarked upon this. 'I'm surprised I've got anything to teach you, though. I'd've thought you'd know all this stuff already.'

'No,' said Byam. It looked down at the diagram Leslie was explaining for the third time.

Byam still didn't get it. But if there was one thing Byam was good at, it was trying again and again.

Well. That had been its greatest strength. Now, who knew?

'It's OK,' said Leslie. 'You know things I don't.'

'Hm.' Byam wasn't so sure.

Leslie touched its shoulder.

'It's impressive,' she said, 'that you're so open to learning new things. If I were a celestial fairy there's no way I'd work so hard. I'd just lie around getting drunk and eating peaches all day.'

'You have a skewed image of the life of a celestial fairy,' said Byam, but it did feel better.

No one had ever called it hardworking before. It was a new experience, feeling validated. Byam found it liked it.

Studying with Leslie involved many new experiences. Leslie was a great proponent of what she called fresh air. She dragged Byam out of the office regularly so they could inhale as much of this as possible.

'But there's air inside,' objected Byam.

'It's not the same,' said Leslie. 'Don't you get a little stir-crazy when you haven't seen the sun in a while?'

Byam remembered the shock of emerging from its cave for the first time in eight hundred years.

'Yes,' it admitted.

Leslie was particularly fond of hiking, which was like walking, only you did it up a hill. Byam enjoyed this. In the past three thousand years it had seen more of the insides of mountains than their outsides, and it turned out the outsides were attractive at human eye-level.

The mountains were polite to Byam, as though there were still a chance it might ever become a dragon. This hurt, but Byam squashed the feeling down. It had made its decision.

It was on one of their hikes that Leslie brought up the first time they met. They weren't far off the peak when she stopped to look into the distance.

Byam hadn't realized at first – things looked so different from human height. But it recognized the place before she spoke. Leslie was staring at the very mountain that had been Byam's home for eight hundred years.

'It's funny,' she said. 'The last time I was here…'

Byam braced itself. *I saw an imugi trying to ascend,* she was going to say. *It faceplanted on the side of a mountain – it was hilarious!*

'I was standing here wishing I was dead,' said Leslie.

'What?'

'Not seriously,' said Leslie hastily. 'I mean, I wouldn't have done anything. I just wanted it to stop.'

'What did you want to stop?'

'Everything,' said Leslie. 'I don't know, I was young. I was having a hard time. It all felt too much to cope with.'

Humans lived for such a short time anyway, it had never occurred to Byam that they might want to hasten the end. 'You don't still…'

'Oh no. It was a while ago.' Leslie was still looking at Byam's mountain. She smiled. 'You know, I got a sign while I was up here.'

'A sign,' echoed Byam.

'It probably sounds stupid,' said Leslie. 'But I saw an imugi. It made me think there might be hope… I started going to therapy. Finished my PhD. Things got better.'

'Good,' said Byam. It met Leslie's eyes. She had never stopped looking at Byam as though it was special.

Leslie leant over and pressed her lips to Byam's mouth.

Byam stayed still. It wasn't sure what to do.

'Sorry. I'm sorry!' Leslie stepped back, looking panicked. 'I don't know what I was thinking. I thought maybe – of course we're both women, but I thought maybe that didn't matter to you guys. Or maybe you were even into… I was imagining things. This is so embarrassing. Oh God.'

Byam had questions. It picked just one to start with. 'What were you doing? With the mouths, I mean.'

Leslie took a deep breath and blew it out. 'Oh boy.' But the explanation proved to be straightforward.

'Oh, it was a mating overture,' said Byam.

'I... Yeah, I guess you could put it that way,' said Leslie. 'Listen, I'm sorry I even... I don't want to have ruined everything. I care about you a lot, as a friend. Can we move on?'

'Yes,' Byam agreed. 'Let's try again.'

'Phew, I'm really glad you're not... What?'

'I didn't know what you were doing earlier,' explained Byam. 'You should've said. But I'll be better now I understand it.'

Leslie stared. Byam started to feel nervous.

'Do you not want to kiss?' it said.

'No,' said Leslie. 'I mean, yes?'

She reached out tentatively. Byam squeezed her hand. It seemed to be the right thing to do, because Leslie smiled.

'OK,' she said.

• • •

After a while Byam moved into Leslie's apartment. It had been spending the nights off the coast, but the waters by the city smelt of diesel and the noise from the ships made its sleep fitful. Leslie's bed was a lot more comfortable than the watery deeps.

Living with her meant Byam had to be in celestial fairy form all the time, but it was used to this now. At Leslie's request it turned down the heavenly glow.

'You don't mind?' said Leslie. 'Humans aren't used to the halo.'

'Nah,' said Byam. 'It's not like I had the glow before.' It froze. 'I mean... in heaven, everyone is illuminated, so you stop... noticing it?'

Fortunately Leslie wasn't listening. She had opened an envelope and was staring at the letter in dismay.

'He's raising the rent again! Oh, you're fucking kidding me.'

She took off her glasses and rubbed her eyes. 'I need to get out of this city.'

'What is rent?' said Byam.

Which was how Byam ended up getting a job. Leslie tried to discourage it at first. Even once Byam wore her down and she admitted it would be helpful if Byam also paid 'rent', she seemed to think it was a problem that it was undocumented.

That was an explanation that took an extra-long time. The magic to invent the necessary records was simple in comparison.

'"Byam",' said Leslie, studying its brand new driver's licence. 'That's an interesting choice.'

'It's my name,' said Byam absently. It was busy magicking up an immunization history.

'That's your name?' said Leslie. She touched the driver's licence with reverent fingers. 'Byam.'

She seemed unaccountably pleased. After a moment she said, 'You never told me your name before.'

'*Oh,*' said Byam. Leslie was blushing. 'You could have asked!'

Leslie shrugged. 'I didn't want to force it. I figured you'd tell me when you were ready.'

'It's not because… I would've told you,' said Byam. 'I just didn't think of it. It's not my real name.'

The light in Leslie's face dimmed. 'It's not?'

'I mean, it's the name I have,' said Byam. It should never have set off down this path. How was it going to explain about dragon-names – the noble, elegant styles, full of meaning and wit, conferred on dragons upon their ascension? Leslie didn't even know Byam was an imugi. She thought Byam had already been admitted to the gates of heaven.

'I'm only a low-level attendant,' it said finally. 'When I get promoted, I'll be given a real name. One with a good meaning. Like Establish Virtue, or Jade Peak, or Sunlit Cloud.'

'Oh,' said Leslie. 'I didn't know you were working towards a promotion.' She hesitated. 'When do you think you'll get promoted?'

'In ten thousand years' time,' said Byam. 'Maybe.'

This was a personal joke. Leslie wasn't meant to get it and she did not. She only gave Byam a thoughtful look. She dropped a kiss on its forehead, just above its left eyebrow.

'I like "Byam",' she said. 'It suits you.'

• • •

They moved out of the city to the outskirts, where the rent was cheaper and they could get more space. Leslie got a cat, which avoided Byam but eventually stopped hissing at its approach. She went running on the beach in the mornings while Byam swam.

She introduced Byam to those of her family who didn't object to the fact that Byam appeared to be a woman. These did not include Leslie's parents, but there was a sister named Jean, and a niece, Eun-hye, whom Byam taught physics.

Tutoring young humans in physics was Byam's first job, but sometimes it forgot itself and taught students the Way, which was not helpful for exams. After a narrowly averted disaster with the toilet in their new apartment, it took a plumbing course.

It turned out Byam was good at working with pipes – better, perhaps, than it had ever been at understanding the Way.

At night Byam still dreamt of the past. Or rather, it dreamt of the future – the future as Byam had envisioned it, once upon a time. They were impossible, ecstatic dreams – dreams of scything through the clouds, raindrops clinging to its beard – dreams of chasing the cintamani through the sea, its whiskers floating on a warm current.

But when Byam woke up, its face wet with salt water, Leslie was always there.

Byam got home one night and something was wrong. It could tell from the shape of Leslie's back. When she realized it was there, she raised her head, wiping her face and trying to smile.

'What happened?' said Byam.

'I've been—' The words got stuck. Leslie cleared her throat. 'I didn't get tenure.'

Byam had learnt enough about Leslie's job by now to understand what this meant. It was worse than falling when you were almost at the gates of heaven. It sat down, appalled.

'Would you like me to eat the committee for you?' it suggested.

Leslie laughed. 'No.' The syllable came out on a sob. She rubbed her eyes. 'Thanks, baby, but that wouldn't help.'

'What would help?'

'Nothing,' said Leslie. Then, in a wobbly voice, 'A hug.'

Byam put its arms around Leslie, but it seemed poor comfort for the ruin of all her hopes. It felt Leslie underestimated the consolation she was likely to derive from the wholesale destruction of her enemies. But this was not the time to argue.

Byam remembered the roaring in its ears as it fell, the shock of meeting the ground.

'Sometimes,' it said, 'you try really hard and it's not enough. You put in all you've got and you still never get where you thought you were meant to be. But at least you tried. Some people never try. They resign themselves to bamboozling monks and devouring maidens for all eternity.'

'Doesn't sound like a bad life,' said Leslie, with another of those ragged laughs. But she kissed Byam's shoulder, to show that she didn't think the life of a wicked imugi had any real appeal.

After she cried some more, she said, 'Is it worth it? The trying, I mean.'

Byam had to be honest. The only thing that could have made falling worse was if someone had tried to convince Byam it hadn't sucked.

'I don't know,' it said.

It could see the night sky through the windows. Usually the lights and pollution of the city blanked out the sky, but tonight there was a single star shining, like the cintamani did sometimes in Byam's dreams.

'Maybe,' said Byam.

Leslie said, 'Why aren't you trying to become a dragon?'

Byam froze. 'What?'

Leslie wriggled out of its arms and turned to face it. 'Tell me you're still working towards it and I'll shut up.'

'I don't know what you're talking about,' said Byam, terrified. 'I'm a celestial fairy. What do dragons have to do with anything? They are far too noble and important to have anything to say to a lowly spirit like me.'

'Byam, I know you're not a celestial fairy.'

'No, I am, I—' But Byam swallowed its denials at the look on Leslie's face. 'What gave it away?'

'I don't know much about celestial fairies,' said Leslie. 'But I'm pretty sure they don't talk about eating senior professors.'

Byam gave her a look of reproach. 'I was trying to be helpful!'

'It wasn't just that—'

'Have you told Jean and Eun-hye?' Byam bethought itself of the other important person in their lives. 'Did you tell the cat, is that why it doesn't like me?'

'I've told you, I can't actually talk to the cat,' said Leslie, which was a blatant lie because she did it all the time, though it was true they had strange conversations, invariably at cross-purposes. 'I haven't told anyone. But I couldn't live with you for years and not know, Byam, I'm not *completely* stupid. I was hoping you'd become comfortable enough to tell me yourself.'

Byam's palms were damp. 'Tell you what? "Oh yeah, Les, I should've mentioned, I'm not an exquisite fairy descended from heaven like you always thought. Actually I'm one of the eternal losers of the unseen world. Hope that's OK!"'

'Hey, forgive me for trying to be sensitive!' snapped Leslie. 'I don't care what you are, Byam. I know who you are. That's all that matters to me.'

'Who I am?' said Byam. It was like a rock had lodged inside its throat. It was hard to speak past it. 'An imugi, you mean. An earthworm with a dream.'

'An imugi changed my life,' said Leslie. 'Don't talk them down.'

Though it was incredible, it seemed it was true that she didn't mind, wasn't about to dump Byam for being the embodiment of pathetic failure.

'I just wish you'd trusted me,' she said.

Her eyes were tender and worried and red. They reminded Byam that it was Leslie who had just come crashing down to earth.

Byam clasped its hands to keep them from shaking. It took a deep breath. 'I'm not a very good girlfriend.'

Leslie understood what it was trying to say. She put her arm around Byam.

'Sometimes,' she said. 'Mostly you do OK.'

'I didn't make a good imugi either,' said Byam. 'I'm sorry I didn't tell you. It wasn't like the name. This, I didn't want you to know.'

'Why not?'

'If you're an imugi, everyone knows you've failed,' explained Byam. 'It's like wearing a sign all the time saying "I've been denied tenure".'

This was a bad comparison to make. Leslie flinched.

'Sorry,' said Byam. It paused. 'It hurts. Knowing it wasn't enough, even when you gave it the best of yourself. But you get over it.'

You get used to being a failure. It was too early to tell her that. Maybe Leslie would be lucky. Maybe she'd never have the chance to get used to it.

Leslie looked like she was thinking of saying something, but she changed her mind. She squeezed Byam's knee.

'I'm thinking of going into industry,' said Leslie.

Byam had no idea what this meant.

'You would be great at that,' it said, meaning it.

• • •

It turned out Byam was right. Leslie was great at working in industry, and it meant they could move into a bigger place, near Leslie's sister. This worked out well – after Jean's divorce they helped out with Eun-hye, who perplexed Byam by declaring it her favourite aunt.

A mere ten years after Leslie had been denied tenure, she was saying it had been a blessing in disguise. 'I would never have known there was a world outside academia.'

They had stopped talking about dragons by then. At first Leslie had had a fixation on them.

'*I'm* fixated?' she said. 'You're the one who worked for thousands of years—'

'I don't want to talk about it,' Byam said. When this didn't work it simply started vanishing whenever Leslie brought it up. Eventually she stopped.

Over time she seemed to forget what Byam really was. Even Byam started to forget. When Leslie found her first white hair, it grew a few too, to make her feel better. Wrinkles were more challenging: it could never seem to get quite the right number. ('You look like a sage,' said Leslie when she was done laughing at its first attempt. 'I'm only forty-eight!')

Byam's former life receded into insignificance, the thwarted yearning of its earlier days nearly effaced.

The years went by quickly.

• • •

Leslie didn't talk much these days. It tired her, as everything tired her. She spent most of her time asleep, the rest looking out of the window. She didn't often tell Byam what was going through her head.

It was a surprise when she said, without precursor:

'Why does the yeouiju matter so much?'

It took a moment before Byam understood what she was talking about. It hadn't thought of the cintamani in years. But then the surge of bitterness and longing was as fresh as ever, even in the midst of Byam's grief.

'It's in the name, isn't it?' said Byam. 'The jewel that grants all wishes.'

'Do you have a lot of wishes that need granting?'

Byam could think of some, but to tell Leslie about them would only distress her. It wasn't like Leslie wanted to die. At sixty-three she still had so much left she wanted to see and do in this life.

Byam had always thought before that humans must be used to dying, since they did it all the time. But now it had got to know them better, it saw they had no idea how to deal with it.

This was unfortunate, because Byam didn't know either.

'I guess I just always imagined I'd have one some day,' it said. It tried to remember what it had felt like before it had given up on becoming a dragon and acquiring its own cintamani.

'It was like… if I didn't have that hope, life would have no meaning.'

Leslie nodded. She was still gazing out of the window. 'You should try again.'

'Let's not worry about it now…'

'You have thousands of years,' said Leslie. 'You shouldn't just give up.' She looked Byam in the eye. 'Don't you still want to be a dragon?'

Byam would have liked to say 'no'. It was unfair of Leslie to awaken all these dormant feelings in Byam at a time when it already had too many feelings to deal with.

'Eun-hye should be here soon,' it said. Leslie's niece was almost the same age Leslie had been when Byam had first come to her office with murder in its heart. Eun-hye had a child herself now, which still seemed implausible to Byam. 'She's bringing Sam, won't that be nice?'

'Don't talk to me like I'm an old person,' said Leslie, annoyed. 'I'm dying, not decrepit. Come on, Byam. I thought repression was a human thing.'

'That shows how much you know,' said Byam. 'When you've been a failure for three thousand years, you get good at repressing things.'

'I'm just saying—'

'I don't know why you're…' Byam scrubbed its face. 'Am I not good enough as I am?'

'Of course you're good enough,' said Leslie. 'If you're happy, then that's fine. But you should know you can be anything you want to be. That's all. I don't want you to let fear hold you back.'

Byam was silent.

Leslie said, 'I only want to know you'll be OK after I'm dead.'

'I wish you'd stop saying that,' said Byam.

'I know.'

'I don't want you to die.'

'I know.'

Byam laid its head on the bed. If it closed its eyes it could almost pretend they were home, with the cat snoozing on Leslie's feet.

After a while it said, without opening its eyes, 'What's your next form going to be?'

'I don't know,' said Leslie. 'We don't get told in advance.' She brightened. 'Maybe I'll be an imugi.'

'Don't say such things,' said Byam, aghast. 'You haven't been that bad!'

This made Leslie laugh, which made her cough, so Byam called the nurse, and then Eun-hye came with her little boy, so there was no more talk of dragons or cintamani or reversing a pragmatic surrender to the inevitable.

That night the old dreams started again – the ones where Byam was a dragon. But they were a relief compared to the dreams it had been having lately.

It didn't mention them to Leslie. She would only say, 'I told you so.'

•

For a long moment after Byam woke, it was confused. The cintamani still hung in the air before it. Then it blinked and the orb revealed itself to be a lamp by the hospital bed.

Leslie was awake, her eyes on Byam. 'Hey.'

Byam wiped the drool from its cheek, sitting up. 'Do you want anything? Water, or—'

'No,' said Leslie. Her voice was thin, a mere thread of sound. 'I was just watching you sleep like a creeper.'

But then she paused. 'There is something, actually.'

'Yeah?'

'You don't have to.'

'If there's anything I can give you,' said Byam, 'you'll get it.'

Still Leslie hesitated.

'Could I see you?' she said finally. 'In your true form, I mean.'

There was a brief silence.

Leslie said, 'If you don't want to…'

'No, it's fine,' said Byam. 'Are you sure you won't be scared?'

Leslie nodded. 'It'll still be you.'

Byam looked around the room. There wasn't enough space, so it would have to make itself smaller. But that was a simple magic.

It hadn't expected the sense of relief as it expanded into itself. It was as though for several decades it had been wearing shoes a size too small and now it had been allowed to take them off.

Leslie's eyes were wide.

'Are you OK?' said Byam.

'Yes,' said Leslie, but she raised her hands to her face. Byam panicked, but before it could transform again, Leslie rubbed her eyes and said, 'Don't change back! I haven't looked properly yet.'

Her eyes were wet. She studied Byam as though she was trying to imprint the sight onto her memory.

'I'd look better with legs,' said Byam shyly. 'And antlers. And a bumpy forehead…'

'You're beautiful.' Leslie touched Byam's side. Her hand was warm. 'It was you, wasn't it? That day in the mountains.'

Byam shrank back. It said, its heart in its mouth, 'You knew?'

'I've known for a while.'

'Why didn't you say anything?'

'Guess I was waiting for you to tell me.' Leslie gave Byam a half-smile. 'You know me, I hate confrontation. Anything to avoid a fight.'

'I should have told you,' said Byam. 'I wanted to, I just…' It had never been able to work out how to tell Leslie its original plan had been to devour her in an act of misdirected revenge.

Dumb, dumb, dumb. Byam could only blame itself for its failures.

'You should've done.' But Leslie didn't seem mad. Maybe she just didn't have the energy for it anymore.

'I'm sorry,' said Byam. Leslie held out her hand and it slid closer, letting her run her hand over its scales. 'How did you figure it out?'

Leslie shrugged. 'It made sense. You've always been there when I needed you.' She patted Byam gently. 'Can I ask for one more thing?'

'Anything,' said Byam. It felt soft and sad, bursting at the seams with melancholy love.

'Promise me you won't give up,' said Leslie. 'Promise me you'll keep trying.'

It was like going in for a kiss and getting slapped in the face. Byam went stiff, staring at Leslie in outrage. 'That's – that's fighting dirty!'

'You said "anything".'

Byam ducked its head, but it couldn't see any way out.

'I couldn't take it,' it said miserably, 'not now, not after… I'm not brave enough to fail again.'

Leslie's eyes were pitiless.

'I know you are,' she said.

ONE LAST TIME

They scattered Leslie's ashes on the mountain where she had first seen Byam, which would have felt narcissistic if it hadn't been Leslie's own idea. When they were done, Byam said it wanted a moment alone.

No, it was all right, Eun-hye should stay with her mother. Byam was just going round the corner. It wanted to look at the landscape Leslie had loved.

Alone, it took off its clothes, folding them neatly and putting them on a stone. It shrugged off the constriction of the spell that had bound it for years.

It was like taking a deep breath of fresh air after coming up from the subway. For the first time Byam felt a rush of affection for its incomplete self – legless, hornless, orbless as it was. This imugi body had done the best it could for the yearning heart inside it.

Ascending was familiar, yet strange, too. Before, Byam had always striven to break free from the bonds of earth. This time it was different. Byam seemed to be bringing the earth with it as it rose to meet the sky. Its grief did not fall away – it was closer than ever, its cheek laid against Byam's.

It was all much simpler than Byam had thought. Heaven and earth were not so far apart, after all…

'Look, Sam,' said Eun-hye. She held her son up, pointing. 'There's an imugi going to heaven! Wow!'

The child's small frowning face turned to the sky. Gravity dug its claws into Byam.

It was fruitless to resist. Still, Byam thrashed wildly, hurling itself upwards. Fighting the battle of its life, as though it had any chance of winning.

Leslie had believed in Byam. It had promised to be brave.

'Wow, it's so pretty!' continued Eun-hye's voice, much loved and incredibly unwelcome. 'Your imo halmeoni loved imugi.'

Sam was young, but he already had very definite opinions.

'No,' he said distinctly.

'It's good luck to see an imugi,' said Eun-hye. 'Look, the imugi's dancing!'

'No!' said Sam, in the weary tone he adopted when adults were being especially dense. 'Not imugi. It's a *dragon*.'

For the first time in Byam's inglorious career, gravity surrendered. The resistance vanished abruptly. Byam bounced into the clouds like an arrow loosed from the bow.

'No, ippeuni,' Eun-hye was explaining. 'Dragons are different. Dragons have horns like a cow, and legs and claws, and long beards like Santa—'

'Got horns,' said Sam.

Byam barely noticed the antlers branching from its temples, or the whiskers unfurling from its face, or the legs popping out along its body, each foot adorned with four gold-tipped claws.

Because there it was, the cintamani of its dreams – a matchless pearl falling through five-coloured clouds. It was like meeting a beloved friend in a crowd of strangers.

Byam rushed towards it, its legs (it had legs!) extended to catch the orb. It still half-believed it was going to miss, and the whole thing would come crashing down around its ears, a ridiculous daydream after all.

But the cintamani dropped right in its paw. It was lit from the inside, slightly warm to the touch. It was perfect.

Byam only realized it was shedding tears when the clouds started weeping too. It must have looked strange from the ground, the storm descending suddenly out of a clear blue sky.

Eun-hye shrieked, covering Sam's head. 'We've got to find Byam imo!'

'It's getting heavy,' said Jean. 'The baby'll get wet. Get Nathan to bring the car round. I'll look for her.'

'No, I will.'

'I've got an umbrella!'

They were still fighting, far beneath Byam, as the clouds parted, revealing the palaces of heaven. Ranks of celestial fairies stood by the gate, waiting to welcome Byam.

They had waited thousands of years. They could wait a little longer. Byam turned back, thinking to stop the storm. Anything to avoid a fight.

But the rain was thinning already. Down below, Byam could see the child leaning out of Eun-hye's arms, thwarting her attempts to keep him dry. He held his hands out to the rain, laughing.

Extended Copyright